WRONG PLACE
Right Time

ALSO BY ELLE CASEY

Ten Things You Should Know About Dragons
(short story, The Dragon Chronicles)

My Vampire Summer

Aces High

DYSTOPIAN

Apocalypsis (4-book series)

To keep up to date with Elle's latest releases, please visit www.ElleCasey.com

To get an email when Elle's next book is released, sign up here:

http://bit.ly/ellecaseynews

WRONG PLACE
Right Time

ELLE CASEY

Montlake
Romance

Text copyright © 2016 Elle Casey

Published by Montlake Romance Publishing, Seattle
www.apub.com

Amazon, the Amazon logo, and Montlake Romance Publishing are trademarks of Amazon.com, Inc., or its affiliates.

ISBN-13: 9781503936546
ISBN-10: 1503936546

Cover design by Lisa Horton

Printed in the United States of America

For Emilie, who brought me into the fold.
Thanks for sharing this adventure with me!

CHAPTER ONE

I close my eyes and inhale deeply after shutting the front door to my house. The sounds of my two girls talking a mile a minute and my son shouting in happiness come through the oak that separates the inside of the house from the front porch, as they go down the steps and head out to their father's waiting vehicle.

Hallelujah . . . Miles, my ex, finally followed through on his promise to pick up our children and have them for the weekend, and I plan on taking full advantage of this little mini-vacation. Just one more deep breath in and out, and I'll finally be able to relax; I will be able to temporarily forget the fact that his parting comment—whispered to me so the kids wouldn't hear—was that he'd be bringing them back early Sunday, because he has a baseball game to go to.

God forbid he bring his children to one of these events he likes to treat himself to. *Bastard.* He gets baseball games and night-clubs, dinners out with grown-ups and sex. I get hours and hours of Animal Planet—the one television channel all three of my children can agree is awesome—and the occasional superhero comic. I try not to be bitter about the fact that he has a life and I don't, but I'm not very successful.

My phone buzzes in my pocket. I ignore it, taking another deep breath in and letting it out slowly. I will not let the world intrude on my solitude, on my hard-won peace and quiet. I will finally get some of that me-time I keep reading about on all those mommy blogs.

My phone buzzes again.

Me-time! Me-time! Me-time! I want some of that me-time, dammit! I think I know how the Incredible Hulk feels in the moments before he busts out of his pants. A person can only take so much. My jeans are already feeling a little tighter.

I'm afraid that one of these days, I'm going to Hulk-out. I'm going to puff up with rage, turn green, and rip all my clothes off . . . and then I'm going to run around the house raging like a rabid beast, breaking glasses and plates, ripping down curtains, and punching holes in the walls. I smile at the carnage I'm picturing in my mind. *God, that would be so, so satisfying.* The only reason I don't indulge in the fantasy is because I'd be the only one around to clean everything up when I was done going all beast-mode on my house, and I already have enough on my plate.

Someone is texting me, and I can guess who it probably is without even looking at the screen. There are two likely candidates: my boss and my sister. If it's my boss, he can forget whatever it is he's bothering me about; I've already worked enough overtime this week to last me a month. And if it's my sister, well, she can wait too. I need some wine before I talk to her. Lately most of her conversations involve stories that make my hair turn gray, and I'm only thirty-two. I really don't need any more gray hair than I already have.

My sister started this new job a couple of months ago, and while it makes her really happy, it makes me kind of crazy. I thought she had a pretty good life before, so I didn't see the need for the big change. I still don't, actually. After she graduated from college, she moved back down south to be near me and the kids, and started up a business right away as a wedding photographer. She was single and childless, and had the perfect life, or so it seemed to me.

She's super talented, and even though the economy took a dive and she said it really affected her business, she was still making it. Still living the single life in her own place, making schedules that weren't dictated by anyone else, taking baths without worrying about what might be happening downstairs.

When I take a bath while my kids are home, it's more panic-inducing than relaxing. All I can think about is what might be happening on the other side of the door, like my kids accidentally drinking poison, my son ripping doll heads off, my daughters terrorizing their pet gerbil by dressing it in Barbie clothes. *Oy.*

Yep, my sister May had it all; and then, for some crazy reason she has yet to explain to my satisfaction, she decided it wasn't enough. She went off the range. She met this guy, Ozzie, some former military grunt, shut her business down, joined his security firm, and started acting all commando. She actually has biceps now and says things like "eyes-on" and "charlie foxtrot" and God knows what else. Whenever she starts with that nonsense, I just tune it out.

Anyway, I don't know why she needed such a drastic change, but apparently, according to her, she did. Under the surface, she's the same May I grew up with, but that's where the girl I knew ends. Outwardly, she's more confident. She seems more . . . grown-up. But at the same time, she's younger too. She walks with a spring in her step. She's *always* smiling. She's sillier than ever, and she claims to be in love with a guy she hardly knows.

Ugh. Sometimes I want to slap her and wake her up to what's really going on. Chemicals. Lust. It's powerful stuff, I get it, but I mean, come on . . . I live in the real world, where you can fall in love with a guy over a period of *years*, build a *life* with him, and *still* have him walk out on you. Love at first sight? Nope. Doesn't happen. It's not real. It's an illusion cooked up by too many misguided chick flicks and not enough real-world pain.

It's not that I'm jealous or don't want my sister to be happy; I'm just worried about the day she'll come crashing down to reality and realize she's been living in a fantasy world of her own creation, because I'm not sure either of us is prepared for that kind of devastation.

She is happy, though—for now, anyway. So I'm not saying anything negative to her about this love affair of hers. I'm not going to be the big jerk who's trying to ruin everything. Of course, that doesn't stop me from worrying. Not only is she risking her heart in this whole deal, she's also risking her life with this new job. And guess who'll be the one picking up the pieces when it all falls apart? Yeah. That'll be me.

She's working with the security company her boyfriend owns as their surveillance expert—not that she had any kind of experience whatsoever prior to being hired—and now she photographs bad guys for a living. My sweet little sister, a former straight-A student who still wears her hair in a headband and espadrilles on her feet, is hanging out in the very worst neighborhoods of New Orleans, dodging bullets. As if I needed that kind of stress in my life.

I take another deep breath in and out, trying to calm my blood pressure. *Relax, Jenny. This is just another day to get through without Hulking-out on someone. You can do this.*

I turn around and shuffle in my ratty slippers down the hall and around the corner to the kitchen. From the fridge I pull a half bottle of Chardonnay and pour myself a generous glass. It's only four o'clock, but one time zone away it's five, so I'm getting started. Who cares that these are calories I most definitely do not need? It's not like I'm going to be out dating anytime soon. Dating requires free time, and I have precious little of that.

My phone buzzes again. I swig my wine like it's an ice-cold beer and remove my phone from my pocket as I wince. *Damn, that wine is going down hard. Probably shouldn't have Big-Gulped it.* I let out a little burp as I take a look at my screen. There are four texts waiting for me.

May: *I need to talk to u. Call me.*
May: *Are u there? Are the kids gone yet? Are u drinking wine yet?*
May: *Don't get tipsy! I need to talk to u.*
May: *Are u avoiding me? I know u can hear my texts. Ur phone's either beeping or buzzing, bitch. Don't play.*

I shake my head and take another sip of my wine, this portion a little smaller than the one before. I'm totally Zen all of sudden.

It's this weird thing that happens between my sister and me; when she's in panic mode, it instantly chills me out. Because I'm her big sister, my automatic response to her being in crisis is to woman-up, to be protective, to take care of things, and to make sure the entire world isn't going to fall apart right along with her. I crumble to pieces after, when the danger has passed, where no one can see me.

It's the role I've played for her all our lives. When we were younger and the crap hit the fan at home with our parents, I was always there, stroking her hair and telling her it was going to be fine while she cried and moaned about how terrible our lives were. I had my own breakdowns later, when no one was around to witness them. I never wanted my sister to suffer on my account. It's like Big Sister Code or something to take the hits.

It's when she's being completely calm and delivering horrible news that I lose my shit. Case in point: when she first met Ozzie, she called me to tell me the story. She kept trying to casually slip in details about how somebody was shooting at her in a biker bar, and how bits of splintered wood flew up into her face and cut her. I can't be cool when I'm hearing stories like that, especially when I think my little sister is not reacting appropriately. She hasn't told me any more nutty tales lately, but I don't believe she's not getting into trouble. It's just that now she has a boyfriend she can confide in, so she hides stuff from me that she knows I'll disapprove of. That's my theory, anyway.

I like Ozzie well enough, but the minute he stepped into her life, her entire world was turned upside down and inside out, so I don't exactly trust him. Maybe her life was a little boring before. Fine. I get it. But there's a difference between being bored and having a death wish. Her days are a little *too* exciting for my taste with this new job. I feel like I always have to worry about her now, because she's not worrying about herself enough. She's too gaga over Ozzie and his whole team—the Bourbon Street Boys private security firm—to think clearly. I get that her man is hot and he's one of the good guys, but come on . . . Bullets?

I sigh, realizing that for at least the next thirty minutes I'm probably not going to be able to enjoy my peaceful weekend as I'd hoped; no meaningful phone conversation between my sister and me ever lasts less than a half hour. I put the wineglass down, lift the phone up closer to my face, and type out a text with my thumbs.

Me: *Please tell me there are no bullets involved.*
May: *No bullets, but I need ur help.*
Me: *Romance advice?*

The mean-sister in me is hoping her relationship is on the rocks. Maybe if she weren't under Ozzie's thrall, I'd be able to talk some sense into her, convince her that wedding photography is a much safer and more practical career than security surveillance.

May: *No. Computer expertise.*

Ugh. So disappointed. That's the last thing I want to talk about right now. I just ended a fifty-hour week of straight-up coding. No, thank you.

Me: *Forget it. I'm off the clock.*

My phone rings, and my sister's name comes up on the screen.

I battle with myself; do I want to come to her rescue again, or do I want to get into the bathtub and forget all this nonsense for a little while?

A text beeps and a tiny message pops up.

May: *Answer ur phone.*

Mutiny rises up in me. I put my cell down on the counter, grab the bottle of wine and my glass, and walk down the hall. I *will* have my bath, I *will* have my relaxing weekend, and I *will not* be doing any computer work for anyone, because if I have to look at another string of code in the next forty-eight hours, I am going to run away, join a cult, change my name to Feather, and marry a man three times my age with a beard down to his belly button who wears only hemp. His name will be Free. Short for Freedom, of course.

At the bottom of the staircase, as my foot is lifting into the air to begin the climb toward my bliss—otherwise known as a bathtub *with* bubbles *and* wine—my phone beeps again in the kitchen. I stand on one leg like a damn flamingo, battling my conscience once again. *Bath or sister? Bath or sister?*

The mutinous mean-girl in me wants to ignore her, but the single mom who's been rescued by May more times than she can count pauses. May did, after all, move into my house a year ago, while I escaped to our family cabin and got my shit together after Miles left me. And she'd do it again in a heartbeat if I needed her to, because that's the kind of sister she is. *Maybe I can just answer her questions over the phone.*

I walk quickly back to the kitchen and grab my cell off the counter. Another text is waiting for me along with a photo of my sister. Her eyes are crossed and she's looking as pitiful as she knows how.

May: *Pretty please?*

Knife through the heart. She totally knows how to play me. I push the buttons that will connect me to my sister's phone and put the cell to my ear.

She picks up on the second ring. "Thank you *so* much, Jenny. I really appreciate it. I need your help."

"Yeah," I say dryly, "I got that."

"You know I wouldn't bother you on your me-time weekend if it weren't really important."

I roll my eyes. "Fine. What is it? Make it quick and make it snappy, sister. I have a date with something hot and slippery upstairs."

"Uh . . . ew. What is it? A dildo? That's kind of gross that you're sharing that with me."

"No! Gah! Not a dildo! It's my bubble bath, fool!" My face is flaming hot. As if I'd tell her that. Now I know she's mental. "What do you need? Come on, I'm on the clock here. I have only forty-two hours left." I look at my watch and hate the fact that I'm wishing my kids could be gone longer. *Worst. Mother. Ever.* I will not be winning any Mom of the Year awards anytime soon.

"Ummm . . . errr—"

I cut May off. "No, ma'am. Huh-uh. There is no *ummm* and there is no *errr;* there's just you telling me what you need really quickly, me giving you my answer, and then me hanging up and getting into the bathtub."

"Wow. What did Miles do?"

I want to strangle the phone just thinking about it. I'm not mad at May; I'm just hating myself all over again for marrying that man in the first place. The only thing that keeps me from indulging in complete self-flagellation is the fact that he gave me three adorable babies. Miles wasn't a complete mistake, but he was close.

"Oh, nothing much," I say, not keeping the hatred out of my voice nearly as much as I should. "He just *informed* me as he was picking the kids up that he needs to drop them off early on Sunday."

She snorts her disgust. "Of course he did. Did you expect anything different?"

She's right. I know she's right. Why do I always do this? I convince myself he's going to be a good guy and a good father for a change, getting my hopes up. For what? To have them come crashing down, that's what. It's like I want to punish myself or something.

Good guys don't do what he did and what he continues to do at every opportunity. Leopards don't change their spots. Our own mother said that enough times that I should have internalized the wisdom, but alas . . . I have repeated her mistakes in my own life, marrying a philandering turdbasket. I think this makes me certifiably stupid. Dumb as a box of rocks, as my father used to say about the woman who gave birth to us. At least that man is gone from my life for good. He caused our family enough pain for two lifetimes with his drinking and aggressive behavior toward women, his lies, and the cheating on our mother. Now if only Miles would take a long walk off a short pier . . .

I jerk myself back to the present and away from my murderous thoughts. "I have no idea why I expected him to man-up or father-up. I should know better by now."

"Well, don't worry, because I have good news for you. *Great* news. Because I am such an amazing sister, and because I am pretty much clairvoyant, I already have a solution in place for you."

This does not bring me comfort. Normally May is pretty good in the solutions department, but I can't trust her to be totally responsible anymore, since obviously she thinks quitting a perfectly good job and joining a commando security firm where she gets stalked by killers is a good career move, and when you have three kids to take care of, you need at least one responsible adult around.

"I'm afraid to ask."

She continues, ignoring my doubt. "Ozzie and I have made plans to come over one day next week and hang out at your place. *And* I have already purchased a gift certificate in your name that will allow you to go to the mall after work that day and treat yourself to a little something special while we watch the kids."

I don't know what to say to that. I'm not even sure I completely understand.

"You're stunned, right? I knew you would be." May sounds very pleased with herself, and I have to admit, I'm feeling pretty happy with her too.

"What did I do to deserve this?"

"It's not what you've done . . . it's what you *will* do."

I close my eyes and take another deep breath. "I'm not sure I want to hear what you have to say next."

"Trust me. You're gonna love this."

"Love what?"

"Just come to my work. In an hour."

"Your work? No, I'm not doing that." I've been there once before, and that one time was enough. I was not impressed with the downtown fight-club vibe it had going on. All those lockers and weightlifting equipment, with cars parked inside? No. It's definitely no high-class photography studio like she used to have as her workplace. Not by a long shot.

"Why not? Come on, it'll just take you like an hour, max. I promise you won't be sorry. Ozzie is going to pay you."

"*Pay* me? Dammit, May! I knew this was going to piss me off!" He's trying to buy my approval; I know he is. *Bastard.*

She shifts into begging mode. "Pleeeasse, Jenny. Don't say no! I really need you!"

"You don't need me! Do I look like a Bourbon Street Boy to you? You need some kind of commando person."

She laughs. "Commando person? What's that?"

I can see the men she works with very clearly in my memory. "You know what I mean. People with muscles and tight shirts who punch people in the face for a living."

"Don't be silly. If I needed that, why would I call you?"

"An excellent question." It's silly that her response hurts my feelings. I know I put on some weight with my pregnancies that I haven't lost yet, but I do plan to join a workout program one of these days . . .

"Just come. It pays five hundred bucks for less than an hour of consulting. You said you wanted to start doing some freelance stuff, so now's your chance."

I have a hard time breathing over that. "Did you say . . . ?"

"Yeah, I said that." I can hear the smile in her voice. "Five hundred smackeroos *and* a gift certificate. Be there by five-thirty. And bring your laptop." She hangs up before I can argue, smart girl that she is.

I turn around and catch my reflection in the mirror that hangs in the hallway, getting a very clear view of the blue baggage I'm sporting under my eyes. *Nice.* I look like one of those Bourbon Street commandos punched *me* in the face.

11

I really, *really* need that bath and at least a few hours to relax, but five hundred bucks is five hundred bucks; and when child support checks bounce more often than not, having a little padding in the bank account is a good thing. *No . . . it's a great thing. Thank you, May.*

I resist the urge to take another gulp of my wine, and turn to go up to my room so I can slather on some makeup and hide the bags under my eyes. I'll take my bath later. And hey . . . I might even spring for some champagne to drink while I'm in it, since I'll soon be flush with some cash I wasn't expecting.

I'm finally able to muster a smile as I head up the stairs.

CHAPTER TWO

I can't believe I'm doing this. I don't even know what *this* is. Am I dressed appropriately for freelance computer work at the Bourbon Street Boys security company? As I wait at the stoplight just in front of the port's entrance, I look down at myself. I'm wearing jeans, sneakers with flowers embroidered on them, a white button-down blouse, and my light brown hair in a ponytail. Except for silver ball stud earrings, I left all my jewelry behind; it didn't seem right to be getting all fancy when I'd be working at the port. The vehicle of choice out here is a forklift. I don't want to embarrass myself or my sister by walking into this place looking like a goof who doesn't know how to dress for the occasion.

Checking the mirror, I note bangs that should have been trimmed a month ago hanging in my eyes. I swipe them over to the side and make sure my mascara hasn't smeared. *Good to go.* My fatigue is not doing a good job of hiding behind that foundation I used. Lucky for me, my blue eyes are picking up the slack, looking pretty dang bright and fresh if I do say so myself. The idea of five hundred extra bucks and a shopping mall gift certificate tend to have that effect on me.

The light turns green, forcing me out of my self-evaluation and into the port. Working from memory, I drive in and weave around various buildings until I see the one I want. I pull up to the warehouse and stop the car outside, letting it idle for a little while as I examine the exterior of the place.

There's no obvious pedestrian entrance, but I've been here before, so I know that I have to go over to the keypad and press the call button so that someone will let me in through the rolling door in front of my car.

I'm tempted to remain out here in the air-conditioning and try to guess what's going on behind the scenes in there, but that's just going to delay my bath event that much longer. *Might as well just admit I'm nervous and get this over with.*

I hate that I'm such a creature of habit, that working at a place other than my normal job site makes me so uncomfortable. How will I ever leave that hellhole and work as a freelancer if I can't do something as simple as one hour of work with my own sister? *Ugh.* I'm hopeless. Fear has me so strapped to my job, I'll never leave it. I'll grow old and gray there, and they'll have to force me out in the end. *I'm doomed. Doomed!*

Disgusted with myself, I turn off the ignition, grab my laptop and my purse from the seat next to me, and leave the car, slamming the door behind me. My sneakers squeak with each step as I draw closer to the door. My ponytail swings in rhythm behind me, right along with my butt. *Yo, can I get some fries wit dat shake?* I seriously need to get to the gym.

At the keypad, I lean in and press the call button as I speak. I'm sweating and my hand is trembling with nerves. "Hello?"

When all I get is static in response, I start to panic. A forklift flies past behind me, going way too fast, or so it seems. I twist around to watch it zoom away. The guy driving it turns and whistles at me, smiles, and gives me a wave. He has two teeth missing.

Oh, God. I'm a mother with three children! Ack! What am I doing here?

I take a deep breath, face the keypad, and slowly breathe out, trying like hell to calm myself. *You can do this, Jenny. Woman up. Remember: you are a beast. No, you are a honey badger. No one messes with the honey badger.*

"Come on, answer your door, Bourbon Street Baboons." I press the button again and raise my voice. "Helloooo!" The sweat is now making my shirt stick to me. *Aaaand the hits just keep on coming!* Maybe I'll get lucky and Forklift Driver Guy will swing by again and offer to take me out for drinks at the local strip club.

Nothing happens for the longest time. I'm tempted to just turn around, leave, and tell May no one was home when I came. But I know better than to think that this technique will work with her. She can be very determined when she puts her mind to something. She'll harass me and force me to explain myself, and I don't want to admit to my baby sister, who I need to protect from all things that go bump in the night, that I was scared. Scared of a toothless forklift driver and a little sweat. *Dammit.* I'm the meat in another rock-and-hard-place sandwich.

I lean in once more, picturing a video I saw of a honey badger attacking a cobra. *The honey badger don't take no shit from nobody, not even the Bourbon Street Boys.* "Hellooo? Is anyone in there or not? I'm leaving if someone doesn't open up right now."

The sound of the giant door suddenly starting to open makes me jump in fright. *Honey badger, my ass.* I quickly recover and smooth the sides of my hair back so no one will think I'm a big weenie, afraid of every little thing. *It's just a door. Relax, idiot.*

Being out here at the port always makes me a little nervous. I'm completely out of my element right now, I can admit that. I have no idea how my sister could possibly feel so comfortable around here. Maybe it's her boyfriend's muscles that give her a weird sense of security. Unfortunately, I don't have that going for me. All I have is my laptop and some pepper spray. I clamp my arm around my purse a little harder, imagining I can feel the canister pressing into my hip.

"May's sister, Jenny, I presume?" says a male voice from within. It's not Ozzie's. I don't think I've heard it before.

It takes a couple seconds for my eyes to adjust to the dimmer light inside, but when they do, I have to work really hard to keep my jaw from dropping to the floor. There's a guy more handsome than he has a right to be, standing just inside the warehouse, smiling at me.

Be cool, Jenny, be cool. "Yes, that's me," I say way too brightly, trying to cover up the fact that I'm having a total brain meltdown. He's not my type, but still . . . handsome is handsome, and there's no denying he's a looker. I take a little breath to calm myself down. "That's my name. I'm Jenny. Jenny Wexler. May's sister, yep, that's me. Computer person. With my laptop."

Aaaand cue the word-vomit. Excellent! You're on a roll, Jenny!

When he stands there looking at me, kind of stunned, I hold my laptop up off my hip a little as my face burns red. "She called me. To come here. With my computer?"

Handsome Guy holds out a hand that I'm expected to shake. "Nice to meet you. I'm lucky."

Why is he lucky? Because he gets to meet me? Should I be flattered? I step forward with my hand extended, more confused than anything and hoping he won't notice how sweaty my palms are. "Lucky . . . ?"

He shrugs, almost like he's embarrassed. "It's a nickname I got when I was ten."

Understanding finally dawns, along with the realization that I obviously need more sleep. "Nice to meet you, Lucky." His hand is warm and soft, which kind of surprises me, since I figured all the guys who work here have calluses from all the head cracking they must do.

I look around him as our hands fall away from each other, trying to locate my sister. I would've thought she'd come out and welcome me herself, but I don't see her anywhere.

"May had to step out for a little while, so she asked me to bring you in and get you started."

I try really hard not to roll my eyes, but it's impossible. She acts like she's so desperate to get me here, and then she disappears? *What's up with that?* This had better not be a trick. She will so get a knuckle sandwich if it is.

"Don't worry. I don't bite." He smiles and winks at me.

"Well, I do, so be careful." I'm back to being cranky. I could be in a hot bath right now almost done with that bottle of wine, but instead I'm in here with a guy who just winked at me, probably to make me feel better about my sister abandoning me, or because he can see I'm sweating like a pig in heat. She'd better not be out to dinner with her boyfriend, blowing me off.

His smile drops away just a little. "Well . . . okay, then."

An awkward silence ensues. I tap my finger on my laptop, and he rubs his hands together. I wait for him to make the next move, because I have no idea what I'm really doing here, but all he does is shrug his shoulders.

A noise behind him distracts me from the sweat that's starting to drip down my lower back and into my bum crack. And I thought this day couldn't get any crappier.

"You going to leave that door open all day?" a guy asks.

Lucky answers by turning his head slightly to the side and raising his voice. "Keep your pants on! We have a visitor!"

"Who is it?"

"See for yourself!" Lucky gestures for me to step toward him. "Come on in. Don't worry, I'll keep my distance."

"Keep your distance?"

"I wouldn't want to get bitten." He winks again.

My face goes redder. It's on the tip of my tongue to apologize for being such a b-word, but I figure that'll just start another one of those awkward silences again, so I say nothing. Instead, I step into the warehouse and try not to jump as the door starts sliding closed behind me. *Damn, that thing is loud.*

As the door booms shut, a movement off to the left catches my eye. A giant of a man is emerging from the darkness, and he's completely wet, his shirt and shorts sticking to every inch of him. *Holy smokes. I didn't know they grew them that big.*

This must be the guy my sister has talked about several times. If I recall, he has actually attacked her on more than one occasion, apparently as some sort of test. I think he's the guy in charge of workouts or something. That would explain the copious amounts of sweat I see pouring off every part of his body.

I narrow my eyes at him as I realize he might be crazy enough to imagine I'm game for those kinds of shenanigans. If he even thinks about attacking me, I'm going to smash him over the head with my laptop and then make him buy me a new one. *What's his name again?*

"Dev," says the guy, as if he's read my mind. Giant strides that would take a normal guy twice as much effort put him in front of me in seconds. "You must be Jenny. You look just like your sister."

His smile is disarming, especially with that dimple he has on the right side and those sparkling blue eyes to back it up. And that body . . . damn. Now this guy . . . he's my type. I can feel my face flush all over again as I realize just how cute he actually is. And big. His hands are huge. They look to be about the size of my dinner plates. The lonely single woman part of my brain takes over and wonders if certain other parts of his body are also proportional to his height, and I strain to keep my eyes above hip-level.

I have to tip my head back to see his face as he stops in front of me, which is way better than staring at his crotch. *Holy sexy time.* I hold my hand out automatically to shake his, and he responds by rubbing his palm up and down on his leg.

"I'm really sweaty."

I take my hand back and rest it on my chest. *So much for sexy time.* "That's okay. It's nice to meet you." Sweaty hands the size of dinner plates? No thank you, not unless I'm also hot and naked.

Crap, did I just really think that? How embarrassing. He's introducing himself in his place of business, and I'm undressing him with my eyes. Talk about unprofessional. May will never ask me to freelance for her boyfriend's company again if I don't get control of myself. *Maybe I should buy a dildo.*

There are droplets of sweat all over his head, slowly dripping down the side of his face. He's completely bald, so the effect is pretty impressive; it's both gross and sexy at the same time. He has sweatbands on his wrists, and he uses one of them to wipe the salty water out of his eyes. It's then that I notice he doesn't have eyebrows either. Why I find that even sexier is a mystery to me. *Dammit. Dildo it is.*

"You here to help us out with the Blue Marine case?" he asks.

I shrug, glad to have someone here thinking about the business at hand and not sex toys. "I have no idea, actually."

Lucky speaks up. "I haven't had a chance to give her a briefing yet. She just got here."

Dev nods. "Gotcha."

Lucky turns around to look at a staircase at the far end of the warehouse. "Actually, I need to grab the file from upstairs. Do you mind showing her over to the cubicles and getting her hooked up for me?"

Dev smiles again, making my heart go pitter-patter. "No problem." He starts walking across the warehouse. "Follow me, Jenny. Let's get you plugged in."

I hesitate, wondering where I'm going, what I'm doing, and what this is all about. "What's Blue Marine?" I ask Lucky's back as he walks away.

His voice echoes around the warehouse as he answers me while running up the metal stairs, taking two at a time. "It's a case we're working on. I'm going to grab a non-disclosure for you to sign and a record of the work I've done so far. I'm just stuck in this one spot, and May said you could help."

I nod, accepting his perfectly reasonable explanation and turning to follow the bald man, who is now almost all the way across the warehouse. Finally, things are starting to make sense. My nerves calm just the slightest bit.

Dev pauses, looking over his shoulder at me, smiling with that dimple again. "You coming?"

Coming? Gah! That word! My face gets hot again. "Yes. I'm . . . on my way." My heart is speeding way too fast, and my feet feel like they have lead in them. This should be such a simple thing, walking into my sister's workplace and doing a little job for her. Why does it feel so momentous? She trusts these people, so they have to be good guys, right? I have nothing to be afraid of. Not even the fact that it's been so long since I've had sex that I can't even have a normal conversation with a guy without imagining all the wrong things and reading sexual innuendo into simple sentences.

A huge boom coming from behind me has me skittering toward Dev faster than I thought possible. And I'm so focused on getting away from the scary sound that I don't see him running toward me, and we smash right into each other. All the air is knocked out of me and I feel myself falling.

His huge arms reach out and catch me when I'm about halfway down to busting my ass. We look like partners in a really random swing dancing class. Thank goodness he rescued both me and my laptop, because the floor in here is solid concrete, and I don't think either one of us would have escaped unscathed.

It's a moment later that I realize he has now transferred a good portion of his sweat to my body. *Ew.* I try not to grimace, but it's impossible. I smell like sweaty bald guy now.

"Sorry," he says, righting me and then stepping away. "Got some sweat on you."

When I'm back on my feet again, Dev and I turn simultaneously to look at the big warehouse door. It's still vibrating on its tracks and it looks like there's a giant dent in it, bulging inward. The sweat transfer incident moves to the back of my mind, supplanted by the more immediate weirdness.

"What the heck was that?" My voice is unnaturally high.

"I have no idea, but it can't be good." He steps around me and pushes me a little so I'm fully behind him.

I try to move around to be next to him, but he blocks me, stepping in my path.

"What're you doing?" I'm hugging my laptop to my body, partially to protect it and partially using it as a shield. I've got enough Dev-sweat on me for one lifetime.

He twists his head around and looks down at me. "What does it look like I'm doing? I'm protecting you."

"Protecting me?" I lean out sideways to look around him at the entrance to the warehouse. "From what?" I pause to consider what he's actually saying and then look at the dent in the big door. I'm pretty sure it wasn't there before. "Please tell me that was the sound of the door locking."

Another boom rattles the door on its hinges, and then there's shouting coming from outside. I can't make out a word that's being said, but whoever it is sounds really angry. A random thought about the forklift guy being jealous over me being in here floats through my head before my fear takes over. I feel like I'm about to pee my pants. "Seriously, what was that?"

Dev grabs me by the upper arm and starts dragging me toward the darker area of the warehouse. "Come on. Let's go."

"Go? Where? Where are we going?" My panic level is high, like level ten right now. If I were a possum, I'd be stiff on my back, legs straight up in the air. *Nothing to see here! Just a dead possum. Move along, people . . .*

"Somewhere safe." He's all business now, no longer smiling or flashing that cute dimple at me.

I can feel his hot hand through the material of my shirt, and I don't like any part of this manhandling that's going on. I dig my heels in and jerk my elbow out of his grasp.

"What are you doing?" he asks, his voice rising. "We need to go!"

"Go *where*?" I stomp my foot, reminding myself of my three-year-old son, Sammy. "I'm not going anywhere with you until I know what's happening." I take a few steps away from him. "Is this some kind of joke? Is this some sort of weird initiation?" I point at him. "I've heard about you guys. I know you like to play practical jokes on people who work with you." My sister is so going to get a nipple twist for this. One for each boob.

He takes a step toward me with his hands held out. His voice is much calmer than before. There's no dimple going on though, so he's not fooling me. "I promise you, this is not a joke nor any kind of weird initiation. There's something going on outside, and I need to make sure you're safe before I investigate what it is."

"But what about my sister?"

"Your sister is with Ozzie, so she's fine. Come on." He takes me by the arm, more gently this time. "Please, follow me."

Even though this is the most ridiculous start to a new job I've ever experienced, I can tell Dev is serious. And it seems like he wants to do the right thing by making sure I'm okay before he moves on to the next step, so I decide to play along. But if this turns out to be some sort of weird initiation or hazing ritual, heads are gonna roll.

CHAPTER THREE

Dev's hand slides from my arm down to my hand as he drags me through the warehouse to our destination—a destination I do not yet know. I'm trying not to have all these silly, girly reactions to holding hands with this strange man, but it's impossible. I can't remember the last time I felt a man's fingers wrapped around mine. I *can* say I've never felt anything quite like *this* before; his hands are huuuuge. This must be what Sammy feels like when he holds his father's hand. Of course, Sammy is three and I'm thirty-two, and I should be over stupid things like this. Ridiculous, the things that will flow through a person's head when she feels like she's running for her life.

"Am I in danger?" Dev doesn't answer me, so I continue, my sneakers squeaking in fast rhythm as I nearly run to keep up with him. It's a good thing I'm not wearing corduroy right now or I'd be setting my thighs on fire with all the friction I'm kicking up. "Because I didn't sign up for any danger when I told my sister I would come here and help. I'm not into danger like you guys are. I'm into warm baths and wine and quiet. Quietude. I like quietude. I'm no commando. I always wear underpants." Apparently, when I panic, I overshare. It's weird, learning new things about yourself when you're over thirty.

My pleas are falling on deaf ears. Dev says nothing as we rush past a set of cubicles.

"Is this where I'm supposed to work?" I look over my shoulder, the comfortable-looking chairs and cubicles disappearing in the distance. I complained before about coding, but I won't complain anymore. *Just let me code! I don't want to run from strange sounds!*

"Later," he says.

Another boom echoes out behind us, this time fainter because we're farther away. I pick up the pace, no longer interested in those damn cubicles. *Screw coding . . . get me outta here. He better be bringing me to a back door.*

"Is somebody trying to get into the warehouse?" I ask, fearing the obvious.

"Could be." We reach a hallway and he turns right and then takes another quick left.

"Where are we going?" I'm whining now. I can't help it. I'm so going to kill my sister when I see her again. Forget nipple twists. Those are for minor transgressions; I'm going to put her in a figure-four and make her beg for mercy.

"You'll see."

He stops at a door that has a keypad on the outside of it. He jabs in a code, and the click of a lock releasing follows.

Pushing the door open with his shoulder, he takes me by the elbow and drags me in behind him. A dim overhead light illuminates the small closet-sized space we're now standing in. I am *so* not impressed with this rescue plan. There are mops hanging on the wall, for God's sake.

I crane my neck back to look up at him. "You're seriously hiding me in a broom closet?"

Dev doesn't answer me. Instead, he reaches over and starts pressing buttons on a keypad hidden behind one of the mops on the wall. As he enters another code, the keypad lights up, displaying both the numbers and a black screen below it. This device looks a lot more sophisticated than the one on the outside of this closet, which should make me feel more secure, but instead it makes me more worried. *Exactly how much trouble am I in right now?*

Dev finishes with the code and puts his first three fingers on the screen below. The click that I hear when he's done is much more substantial this time, leading me to believe it's a more secure place that we'll be entering; which is awesome, because this closet we're in now is only good for protecting janitorial supplies. A portion of the wall housing a shelving unit separates from the back side of the space and swings inward.

Whoa. Super-secret hideaway bat cave. I'm not sure if I should be impressed or worried that I'm about to enter it.

Dev steps inside and turns on a light. I can't see all of what's behind him, but what I can see is enough to make me scared all over again.

"What the hell is that?" I'm pointing to a space that has not just chairs and tables, but a bank of computers and a row of bunk beds. There's enough room for at least ten people in there.

He reaches down and takes my hand again, pulling me through the door. "This is a panic room. But you're not supposed to panic when you're in here, because you're safe. Stay calm."

When I'm clear of the threshold, he shuts the door behind us. There's a long *beeeeeep* and then the sound of locks clicking into place. The place is as silent as a tomb, and I can now smell the strong scent of iron coming off of him, probably from his workout or whatever he was doing before I came in through the door of this crazy place that I am now going to call the Hotel California. If he tells me I can check out any time I like, but I can never leave, I'm going to do something he seriously won't like. I'm not sure what that thing would be exactly, but I'm sure I can come up with something.

"You have got to be kidding me," I say, snorting my disbelief. "Not panic? Stay calm? Dude, you *must* be high."

He lets go of my hand and walks over to a telephone that's hanging on the wall. Without responding, he picks up the handset and presses a single button. He waits in silence, and I pass the time by listening to my heart beating in my ears. It's going way too fast. I look around to see if they have any of those electric heart attack paddle units attached to the wall. I might need one of them soon.

This cannot be happening. This has to be some kind of joke, but I have no idea why my sister would work with a bunch of jerks who play pranks like this on people when they show up for their first day of work. That guy Ozzie must be seriously good in bed for her to put up with it. I knew I shouldn't have backed out of my bathe-and-drink-wine plan. *Stupid, stupid, stupid . . .*

Dev puts the phone back on the hook and shakes his head, hissing out a sigh of frustration.

"What's wrong?" I'm not even sure I want to hear his answer.

"I can't get through upstairs. Maybe Lucky isn't up there anymore."

I reach into my back pocket and pull out my cell phone. "That's it. I'm calling my sister. I'm not playing this game anymore. You guys can find yourself another freelancer to help you with your marine case or whatever it's called."

He sighs. "Your cell won't work in here."

I look up at him, suspicious. "Why not?"

"Because this is a panic room. The walls are three feet thick. No signals get in or out." He tilts his head very slightly toward the phone on the wall, letting me know that this ancient piece of junk is our only mode of communication with the outside world.

Unfortunately, I've seen just about every bad-guy action movie there is, and I know for a fact that all you need to take down that piece-of-crap wall phone is a damn pair of scissors to cut the outside line. *We're doomed. Doomed!*

I throw my hands up in frustration. "Well, that's just dandy, isn't it? What am I supposed to do now? Just sit here and wait for someone to come kill me?"

He doesn't answer me. He just stares.

I look around the place to avoid catching his eye. It's making my blood pressure go nutty to have him focusing on me like that. "You must be crazy if you think that I'm going to sit here in your little Hotel California panic room and relax while you guys play cops and robbers outside."

"This isn't a game, Jenny. This is serious. And until I know what's going on out there, you're not going anywhere." His voice is softer. Mesmerizing, almost.

I put my hands on my hips, turning my attention back to him, giving him my full-on angry mom stare.

"I'll have you know that I am *very* familiar with the laws of this state, and I know for a *fact* that you can't keep me in here if I don't want to be in here. That's called false imprisonment, buddy, and I'm not going to stand for it."

He raises what would be an eyebrow at me, except that he has no eyebrow there. It still works to express the challenge he's throwing out at me, though. "Is that so?"

I stick my chin out. "Yes, that is so."

He gestures at the door. "Go ahead, then. See yourself out."

"Fine. I will." Yes, I'm scared that I'm walking out into a bad situation, but not scared enough that I'm going to back down. *I'll show him who's the boss of me.* I can hide in a cubicle. No problem. My cell will work out there, and I'll dial 911 and get the *real* cops over here, not these Bourbon Street Butthead wannabe cops.

I walk over to put my hand on the door, but there's no knob there, just a keypad. I chew on my lip and stare at it. *Do I remember the code he entered? No. I do not. Dammit.*

I turn around. "You need to unlock the door for me."

"Sorry, but I can't do that."

"What do you mean, you can't do that?"

He shrugs. "We have protocols in place for these types of scenarios, and the protocol for alien entry with a civilian inside the warehouse requires that one of us secure the civilian and wait for contact from the outside before we open the door. And I was the lucky guy who happened to be standing with the civilian when the threat presented itself." He smiles at me with that damn dimple.

"Protocols? Aliens?" I turn back around to face the door and smack it. Then I start pressing random buttons on the keypad. "Protocols, my big, fat butt. I have things to do and places to go, so your protocols need to step aside, Buckrod."

"Your butt isn't that fat."

My hand freezes in mid-button-pressing. I slowly turn. "Are you kidding me?" He's seriously going to talk about my *butt* now? He must want to die.

He shrugs. "A couple months with me, and I'll have you sporting a six-pack under that blouse."

My jaw drops open and just hangs there. I'm speechless. And it takes a lot to render me speechless, trust me.

"Why don't you just take a seat for a little while, and we'll wait and see if we receive contact?"

I stare at him like he's crazy, because he obviously is. Finally, my throat unlocks to let my voice free. "First of all, don't talk about my butt! You don't even know me! And second of all, you expect me to just *sit* here for hours on end while we wait for someone to *maybe* call us? How do you know that they even know we're in here? They're probably out there wondering what the heck we're doing! They probably think we just went for a stroll somewhere. They're probably all sitting around waiting for us to come back."

He crosses his arms over his chest. "Do you really believe that?"

I shrug angrily and glare at my feet. He's making me feel stupid, but I can't seem to stop this train from running down that track. I open my mouth to argue some more, but he cuts me off.

"You heard that big noise—I know you did. Somebody who didn't have the access code was trying to gain entry into the warehouse. That tells me it's got to be trouble. Standard protocol requires that all personnel secure themselves and secure the building when something like that happens. Then we confront the threat if necessary. My team is doing that right now while I keep you secure in here. We have communication lines set up all over the place, so it's only a matter of time before someone reaches out to us. All we have to do is wait."

I snort in disbelief. "Please tell me you have a better plan than this." I'm no security expert or Bourbon Street *Boy*, but even I can see the holes in this stupid so-called protocol.

He frowns. "Why? What's wrong with our plan?"

I look around the room with my eyes bugging out. "You do realize that all a bad guy would have to do is start a damn fire in this place and we'd be burnt into two crispy critters before anybody *reached out* to us."

He shakes his head, like I'm the pitiful one with no brain juice on tap. "First of all, we have a state-of-the-art fire suppression system in place all over the warehouse. Second of all, this panic room was specifically designed to withstand a fire that lasts up to six hours. Believe me, if somebody wants us bad enough that they're going to try to set our warehouse on fire, they'll have to bring a whole army to be successful."

"I guess I'd better hope they don't bring an army then, huh?"

"Maybe."

We glare at each other as the seconds tick by. I feel an epic stare-down competition starting, and I smile with sinister, wicked glee because I'm totally going to win it. I do this with my kids daily, so I have a lot of practice, and I crush their sorry butts at it every time. *Boo yah, tall man, you can suck it because you are so going down right now. Feeeel the dry eyeball burn . . .*

More seconds tick by. My eyes are starting to get a little tacky. Is there an advantage to staring someone down from seven feet up? I think there must be, because he's not flinching. His eyeballs are still glistening, whereas mine probably look like hundred-year-old marbles. Dull. Frosty. *Damn. I think my eyelids are stuck to them now.*

"You're not gonna win," he says. "You should just give up."

"Oh, yes, I am going to win." I shift my weight to my other foot. "I can do this all day. I have three kids."

"Oh yeah? Well, I have one kid who's more like four kids, and I don't go down easy."

I blink, so surprised to hear that he's a father that I lose my focus. *Dammit!*

He points at me. "You lose."

I roll my eyes, turning around so he won't see me blinking over and over trying to rehydrate my poor raisin-like eyeballs. "What are you?" I ask. "Ten years old?"

"No, actually, I'm thirty-five, but I'm also the winner." He reaches over and picks up the telephone handset again.

"Someone had better answer that damn phone," I mutter as I walk over to one of the comfortable-looking armchairs. I place my laptop on the side table next to it and my purse on the floor, and then drop down into my seat as I wait in silence for someone to answer our call.

I'm tired of fighting this man. I just want to get out of here and back to my boring old life where I act like an adult and don't enter into staring contests with near strangers who shouldn't look that good when they're sweaty.

CHAPTER FOUR

I know the moment someone picks up on the other end of the line because Dev's face lights up and his mouth opens as he prepares to speak. Then he doesn't say a word. He just stands there like an empty-headed, bald-ass mannequin.

"What's going on?" I stand, getting this crazy idea that I'm going to go over and huddle up next to him, press my face to the receiver, and listen in on the conversation.

He holds a hand up at me like a stop sign, freezing me in my tracks.

I frown. I do the same thing to my kids when they're bugging me and I'm on the phone. I'm a grown woman, but for some reason, in the last half hour, I've been reduced to a young teen in this man's presence. Possibly a pre-teen.

On another day I might actually enjoy this, because I always feel way older than my actual age, but not today. Today I want to be a part of the real world where I'm a grown-up and I get to decide where I'm going, when I'm going there, and how I'm going to get there. This whole being-locked-up-with-a-crazy-sweaty-commando thing is making me stir-crazy. That movie *The Shining* comes to mind.

My captor is all serious now, his non-eyebrows drawn together as he stares at the wall. "I acknowledge with code Harbinger." He pauses after this mysterious transmission, nods, and then continues. "Yes. Okay. Got it."

Dev hangs up the phone and walks over to drop down into the chair opposite me. His legs spread open and he rests his elbows on the arms of the seat. The fingers of one hand come up to rest on his lips. The other hand dangles in the air at his waist, hanging casually as if he doesn't have a care in the world . . . as if he didn't just act like some army sergeant in an action movie where someone's trying to assassinate the president, the White House is full of terrorists from Uzbekistan, and he's the only G-man on the inside. He's staring at me like he's considering buying me at an auction or something.

Gulp. Holy hotness. I feel like a piece of meat, and I like it. What's wrong with me?

"Well?" I sit back down in my seat and attempt to smooth out the wrinkles in my pants, trying to distract myself from my nutty thoughts as I wait to hear the news about our hopefully imminent rescue. I'm happy to know that the bad guys have not cut the telephone lines here like they always manage to do in the movies. At least something is going right today.

Dev's hand moves away from his face and he sits up a little. "Someone did try to breach the warehouse entrance, but it's been handled. Now we just need to wait until one of the team or a member of the police department can come and let us out."

This makes no sense to me. I ignore the first part of his statement—something too distressing to acknowledge without some more internal processing first—and focus on the second point. "What do you mean, someone has to come and let us out?" I look over at the keypad. "Don't you just have to go over there and type in some numbers and put your fingerprints on the screen?"

He gives me a sheepish look. "Normally, yes, but . . . uh . . . I might have been a little overeager about getting us to safety when we came in."

I back my chin up into my neck. "What's that supposed to mean?"

He dips his head, and when he answers, I notice that his face is a little pinker now than it was before. "There are two ways to enter this room. One way, you can just tap the keys to get in and out, and the other way, you go in, and you're kind of stuck inside until someone comes from the outside to let you out."

This doesn't compute. *What kind of messed-up system do they have here, anyway?* My words come out measured and slow. "Why would you have a door to a panic room that doesn't open from the inside?" You'd think people whose whole business involves dealing with criminals and security would be smarter about how they set up their locking systems. *Duh. I'm trapped in the lair of the Bourbon Street Boneheads. Awesome.*

He doesn't sound as embarrassed as I think he should when he explains. "Well, it's the same concept as a home alarm, in a way. There are two different codes you can enter when you want to go in; one code just shuts everything off, but the other code is used when somebody's holding you at gunpoint. It shuts everything off, but at the same time, silently alerts the monitoring team to the fact that there's something fishy going on, so they can send law enforcement to intervene. Certain members of the New Orleans Police Department have the access code too."

I only have to think about that for a few seconds before the obvious problems jump right to the front of my mind. "So, then, what you end up with when you use the second kind of code is a bad guy with a gun locked inside this room with you." I nod my head sarcastically, thinking how ridiculous these people are. "I see. That makes complete sense."

33

He shrugs. "It does if you have the kind of training we do."

My eyebrow goes up. "And what kind of training would that be? The ability to hypnotize people into putting their weapons down, lying on the couch, and giving up?"

"No. We're all trained to relieve people of their weapons in a very short space of time. Let's just say that anybody who came in here with one of my team and a weapon would not be leaving here with that weapon."

He's pretty full of himself, but to be fair, I have seen his and Ozzie's physiques, and my sister does have some biceps now, something she's never had before. Who knows . . . maybe he is a ninja disguised as an NBA basketball player. I move on to my next most logical argument.

"Why not just use one code that will open the door and let people go in and out? I don't get how having it locked from the outside is any kind of benefit to somebody inside here."

He sighs like I should be the one riding the short bus. "Then it's just a door. But if it's locked from the outside, no matter what a bad guy does to the person he's in here with, he's not going anywhere until one of my team comes to get him. There's no way he can escape. It's not just a door; this way, it's a prison."

"But why do you think anyone breaking in to the warehouse would want to hang out in your panic room in the first place? Why would someone force himself in here of all places?"

"This is where someone choosing not to fight would come. If someone came into the warehouse searching for that someone, he'd follow." He shrugs, as if this makes complete sense.

I take a quiet, deep breath in and out to calm myself down. Today will not be the day that I die hard. No, it's time for me to get the hell out of here and back to a life that doesn't include any of these Bourbon Street Buffoons. "How long is it going to take before our rescue party arrives?"

"The team has a few things to wrap up outside first. Maybe ten minutes?"

After I think about that for a little while, I decide that I can live with ten minutes. And now that I know everything is mostly okay, my natural curiosity takes over. "So, you have a son, you said?"

He nods. "Yep. He's five years old and a terror on wheels."

"Is he as tall as you are?"

Dev gives me a slight grin. "Now that would be something, seeing as how he's only in preschool right now." He goes from stern to teasing so quickly it makes my head spin. In a good way, though, like I just took a ride on a smallish roller coaster.

I roll my eyes. "You know what I meant."

Dev's smile comes out in full force, and it's nearly blinding, it's so big. It makes me go all warm inside. "He is big for his age, but his mother was pretty small, or I should say she *is* pretty small, so he may end up in the middle somewhere." Dev's smile fades a little at the end of his explanation, which only makes me want to know more about what makes him suddenly sad when he's obviously talking about the apple of his eye.

"Is his mom around?"

He stares at me for a long time, so I start to worry that I've stepped over that polite boundary that's always a little blurry for me. It is maybe a little pushy to ask that question, but we're stuck in a freaking panic room together, so it seems like normal societal rules should be a little more relaxed. Or maybe it's the fact that he's been sweating so much in my presence that makes me think we can ask each other about loves lost. There's only one place in my life I've seen a man that sweaty, and it was in my bedroom.

A few seconds later, I can't take the silence anymore. "Was that too personal? Sorry, I get a little nosy when I'm nervous."

He's back to smiling, so my anxiety lessens just a tiny bit. Maybe I wasn't being rude after all.

"You don't have to be nervous," he says. "I'm here."

"And that's supposed to make me feel better?"

He tilts his head to the side. "I make you nervous?"

I snort. "Yeah. Duh." *Dammit. I'm back to being a teenager again.*

He's smiling. "Why would I make you nervous? I'm one of the good guys."

I shrug. "So you say. But I'm on my first day of a freelance job here, my sister is nowhere to be seen, and I'm sitting in a panic room with a guy I just met, who talks about being some sort of commando karate chop person who takes bad dudes out and relieves them of their weapons and locks them up in this prison. I don't know how that's supposed to calm my nerves. It's kind of doing the opposite, if you want me to be honest."

"I always want you to be honest," he says, losing his smile.

The weight of a double meaning is there, but I don't really know where it's coming from or what it's all about, so I don't play along. I'm tired of looking like a dingbat in front of this guy.

My gaze roams the room again. I'm afraid to continue with the conversation, knowing that my natural curiosity has already gotten away from me once. The way my heart is racing, I'm bound to start asking questions even more personal than the ones I already have; it's kind of a defense mechanism I have: stun them with disbelief and distract them from my flustered demeanor with a barrage of socially unacceptable interrogations. Not very elegant, but it usually works. Not so much with Dev, though . . .

He surprises me by speaking as if he hadn't hesitated before. "My son's name is Jacob. His mother hasn't been around since the day he was born. She pretty much took off." He looks down at his hands. "Yeah, so that's pretty much it. My life in a nutshell. Not much more to say." He picks at his fingernails, frowning.

My mind is racing with questions now. *Who cares about society's rules? I want to know what makes this guy tick!* I smile to put him at ease. "If you thought that sharing that little bit of information was going to stop me from asking more questions, you obviously don't know me or any woman very well."

He gives me a slight nod. "I would say you are correct in that assessment. I'm terrible at reading women. I always get it wrong."

"Did you have any sisters growing up? Or girl cousins?"

"The only girl that I had around me when I was growing up was Toni, and she didn't come into the picture until I was well into my teens. Around sixteen or so."

"Who's Toni? Is that your ex-wife? Girlfriend? Is that Jacob's mom?"

"No. Toni works here with me, and we grew up in the same neighborhood together. She's lived in New Orleans all her life. Toni and her brother Thibault were kind of like another family to me. Along with Ozzie and Lucky, too."

I lean in a little. "I think I heard May say a few things about her. She's, like, really badass and gorgeous and somebody you don't want to mess around with, right?"

Dev laughs and nods, his body relaxing a little deeper into his seat. "Yeah, that's her. There's nobody tougher."

My vision fades into a haze as I stare off into the distance. I'm picturing myself as a little Rambo chick, kicking ass and taking names, earning the respect I hear in Dev's voice.

"What are you thinking right now?" Dev asks.

I answer without hesitation. "I'm thinking how awesome it would be to be described that way by a guy like you." My ears go a little pink when I realize I've revealed a bit too much of my hand.

"A guy like me? What do you mean by that?"

I shrug, trying to play it cool. "I don't know . . . a guy like you. A guy who . . ."—I gesture in his general direction—". . . likes to train and get all sweaty all over the place." The perspiration has stopped pouring down his body, but his clothing is still wet and sticking to him.

He looks down at himself. "Oh. I gotcha."

My eyes follow his lead and land on his crotch. I quickly look away, but not before he catches me ogling him. I start waving my hand in front of my face. They seriously need a fan in here. *Is this early-onset menopause?*

Silence ensues. Both of us are trying not to look directly at each other, but it's like our eyes are refusing to obey. It's silly; I'm totally blushing. It reminds me of high school.

"You know, you could become like Toni if you wanted to."

I frown at that. "What?"

"I said, you could look like Toni if you wanted to. You have a great frame; you just need to do a little weight training to build up some muscle."

I don't know why this is making my face get even hotter and my body all tingly. *He's looking at my frame? He thinks I have a great one? Didn't he see my big butt?*

"It wouldn't take you very long, either," he continues, oblivious to my freak-out. "If you're anything like your sister, you could get it done in less than six months." He shrugs. "Not that you *need* to do anything. I'm just talking about strength training here, not changing your body. Your body is fine the way it is." He almost says something else, but then he stops himself and looks away for a second.

I flap my hand around the front of my face, trying to wave away his comments and the waves of heat coming off my skin. Talk about embarrassing. I eat way too many Fudgsicles to look like I imagine Toni does, not even in six years, let alone six months.

He's just being nice when he says my body is fine the way it is. He must have gotten too much sweat in his eyes or something. "I don't have time for that stuff. I have three kids and a job . . ."

He shrugs. "You could find the time. If you did more freelance work, you'd probably have more free time right away. You could make your own schedule, work out when the kids are in school or daycare."

I snort, no longer embarrassed by the conversation or my weird reactions to being in an enclosed space with him. "Oh, believe me, I will not be doing any more freelance work. Not that I did any to begin with."

"Why not?"

My hands drop to the seat on either side of my legs. I stare at him intently, waiting for him to figure the answer out on his own.

"Why are you looking at me like that?" He's grinning, the fool.

"You really don't know, do you?"

"No, I really don't."

I open my mouth to give him a piece of my mind, to tell him that you don't invite a prospective freelancer to your warehouse, lock her in a panic room for an hour, tell her that some crazy person is trying to break in to the job site, and then suggest she work more hours for you. Calling them Bourbon Street Boneheads is giving them too much credit. It's more like I've entered the lair of the Bourbon Street Bimbos.

Before any of these choice words can make it out of my mouth, though, I hear a beep and a click, and the door to the panic room opens.

CHAPTER FIVE

May's head appears around the side of the door. "Jenny? Are you in here?"

I stand up and grab my purse off the floor by my foot and throw the strap over my shoulder. "Yes, I'm here. But I'm not staying, you can be damn sure of that."

I walk quickly to the door as it swings open more fully. Behind my sister is the hulking form of her boyfriend, Ozzie. He takes up almost the entire doorframe.

Ozzie looks over our heads and fixes his gaze on something behind me. "You good in here?"

Dev answers. "Yeah, we're fine. Just a little antsy, maybe."

I look over my shoulder and narrow my eyes at him. "*Antsy?*"

He's grinning as he shrugs. "What would you call it?"

Honestly, I could call my attitude a lot of things. Antsy might even work. But right now, I'm too mad to debate the issue. I turn my attention back to my sister. "Sorry, May, but I have to get out of here."

She holds her hands out at me. "No! Don't go! Please stay."

I shake my head. "Nope. Sorry, but I've had enough." I step around her and her boyfriend and out the door. I've got to get out of this warehouse before they lock me up in another windowless room.

I'm moving fast, but my sister is having no problem keeping up. "Jenny, you don't understand. None of this was planned. It's totally random! Everything's fine now. You can get the work done in an hour, and then you can go back home, and it'll all be over. And you can have the money and the gift certificate."

"You can keep your money *and* your stupid gift certificate. I'm done."

"Why are you so mad?"

I stop so fast, she runs into my back and scrapes my heels with her shoes. I twist my head around to glare at her. "Are you *serious*? You can't possibly be that dense, May."

She frowns at me. "Dense? That's kind of harsh, don't you think?"

I shake my head at her, thoroughly disappointed. "I have no idea what's happened to your attitude in this place, but I don't like it. Unfortunately, I don't have time to debate it with you right now because I have less than forty hours before my kids are back, and I'll be damned if I'm going to let you ruin it for me."

May's face falls. "You really think I'm ruining your weekend?"

I throw up my free hand and let it fall down to slap my thigh. "Are you kidding me, May? I've been locked in a panic room for almost an hour with a giant, sweaty ninja guy!"

"How do you know he's a ninja guy? Did he show you his swords?"

My eyes bug out of my head. I don't even know what to make of this statement. She can't be serious.

May continues. "Listen, Jenny, I know you're upset, but it's only because you don't really know what happened. And getting locked in the panic room was a mistake. It's all just a bunch of little misunderstandings. I promise, it's going to be fine. And the job hasn't changed. We still need you, and I think this is going to be something really easy for you, because you're so smart with computers and everything."

"Do *not* try to flatter me, May. You know that doesn't work with me."

"Since when? I flatter you all the time to get my way."

I sigh. "You're not going to wear me down with your silliness, either. Not this time. I have to go. Call me later."

I turn around and start walking in the direction that I think will take me to the front door. After a couple turns down some hallways, the cubicles come into view, telling me I'm on the right track. As I pass the last one, someone approaches from the opposite direction. I slow, but don't feel nervous about who this stranger might be, because I sense May coming up behind me and she's not yelling at me to run.

"May, is that you?" the man asks.

"Yes, Thibault, it's me and my sister, Jenny. Have you guys met yet?"

As the man draws nearer, I get a better view of his face. He's just a little bit taller than I am, with very dark hair, and he's wearing black cowboy boots, jeans, and a tight black T-shirt with the sleeves rolled up a little. I'm pretty sure there's not an ounce of body fat anywhere on him. He's more compact than Ozzie, but no less intimidating. It's a good thing he's smiling so much, or I might worry that he's the guy planning to steal things from the mysterious lockers in the panic room.

"No, I haven't had the pleasure yet." He stops in front of me and holds out a hand. "Nice to meet you, Jenny."

I take his hand because I don't want to be rude, even though he's slowing down my exit. "Nice to meet you too."

Thibault looks over my shoulder at my sister. "She's angry, huh?"

"Yes, just a little. I was trying to explain to her that it's really no big deal, and that she can still do the work for us and then go home to enjoy her weekend, but she doesn't want to listen."

Thibault's smile fades and his expression turns serious. "I'm not so sure that's such a good idea."

I look over my shoulder at my sister. "See? I told you. I'm going home." I move to go around Thibault, but he sidesteps to block my progress.

His smile is apologetic now. "If you could just hold off on leaving for a minute, I think Ozzie would like to talk to you." He nods at something behind me.

"Well, if Ozzie wants to talk to me, he can call me on my cell. I have somewhere I need to be."

As I take another step forward, Thibault holds out an arm. I stop in my tracks and look down at the offending limb. *What in the heck does he think he's doing?*

"Hey, Ozzie! You want to come over here and discuss the situation with May's sister?"

I turn around, and the sight of Ozzie and Dev striding through the darker cubicle area toward us has me hesitating. They look like storm troopers or something, the way they walk in tandem with their shoulders swaying forward and back, forward and back.

Be still, my heart. I know these guys are crazy, but I can kind of see in this moment why my sister is so gaga over them. They make stupid shit like being locked in a panic room seem not nearly as awful as it is.

I want to slap myself when I realize I've been distracted by my own hormones. *Illusions. Hotel California alert! It's all just illusions, Jenny! Get your head together!*

"Let's take this upstairs," Ozzie says.

"Good idea," my sister agrees.

43

"No! Bad idea! I'm not going upstairs or anywhere else with you people. I'm going outside to my car, and I'm going *home*."

I turn around in a rush and shove Thibault's arm out of my way, spinning him sideways. I refuse to listen to whatever nonsense they're going to say to me, and I am done with this failed big-sister rescue. May will get an earful from me later.

The squeaking of my sneakers echoes around the warehouse as I make my way across the large open space, to the keypad that will open the main door. *Freedom. I'm almost there.*

Behind me comes the sound of someone else's footsteps, but I don't turn around to see who they belong to. I know it's not my sister, because the footfall sounds heavy.

I am done playing around. I'm done pretending to be someone I'm not. I'm a mom and an employee of a second-rate software development firm, and I just need to keep my head down and my nose clean for the next forty years until I can retire and travel. I'll wait until then to have a fun life. *A freelancer . . . ha! What in the hell was I thinking?*

"Hey," says a voice from behind me.

I say nothing. I'm almost to the keypad.

"Where are you going in such a hurry?"

I abandon my escape temporarily and spin around.

Dev stops short just behind me, his arms still in jogging position. He smiles innocently at me, making me want to scream.

"Where am I going? I'll tell you where I'm going—I'm getting the hell away from you people. Someone just tried to break in here in the middle of the afternoon and you're all acting like it's no big deal."

"It's evening, actually."

"Whatever!" I feel like tearing my hair out. *Is he crazy? Is that what his Kryptonite is?* Lunacy might explain his lack of a wife, despite how good-looking he is.

He presses his palms together in front of his waist. "We deal with random criminal activity all the time. It's really no big deal."

"Dude . . . I don't know what you all have been smoking in here, but I'm not interested in those kinds of hallucinations. I live in the real world."

Dev reaches up with one hand and rubs at his bare scalp. Then he pulls it away, looks at his palm, and frowns. Rubbing his hand on the front of his shirt, he gives me an awkward grin. "I hate to tell you this, but you actually *can't* leave right now."

I stare him down, silently daring him to say that again.

He doesn't even blink.

"Oh. So we're playing this game again?" I won't lose a stare-down contest a second time.

He shakes his head, looking almost sad. "It's not a game, I promise. We've got a call in to the police, and we're waiting for one of their officers to stop by and have a little conversation with us about what happened, and we'd really like for you to wait until we finish that before you go."

"Why?" If he doesn't give me a really, really good reason, I'm outta here. I will totally leave here and never glance in my rearview mirror, not even once. *Goodbye, Bourbon Street Boys, and hello, reality.* The thought makes me a little sad, which is totally and completely irrational, of course. I don't need to see this Dev guy again. He's nothing to me. A practical stranger. *A sexy one.*

"Because we want to assess the threat, and we want to figure out exactly what's going on before we put you out there where you might be in danger."

My heart skips a beat. "Danger?" I gulp, having a hard time swallowing past the lump that's materialized in my throat. "Why would I be in danger?"

He shrugs. "Because you were here when everything happened."

45

I feel a little better after his brief and completely unconvincing explanation. "Yeah, but I was *inside*. Whoever caused the problem was *outside*. And I don't know if they got into the warehouse, but I know for a fact they didn't get into the panic room, so why would I be in any trouble?"

"We won't know until we know."

"That makes absolutely no sense." I really feel like I could poke one of his eyes out right now, I'm so frustrated.

"Would you like some jambalaya?"

His question comes from so far out in left field, I don't know how to respond. My mouth opens but no words appear to save me from looking like a fish out of water.

May, Ozzie, and Thibault come walking over from the cubicle area, talking among themselves. May comes right for me, no doubt with plans to convince me to stay.

Dev continues. "Ozzie is an amazing cook, and he made one of his best dishes earlier today. We have some leftovers, and I'm starving. Would you like to share some with me?"

I know it's completely crazy, and I know I should probably just get the hell out of here, but when he says the words, my stomach growls really loudly, and I realize that I haven't eaten anything all day. And that glass of wine I drank earlier feels like it's eating a hole in my stomach.

"Good. You didn't leave," May says as she stops at my side.

"I'm trying to convince her to have some jambalaya with me."

"Great idea!" says May in an overdone, cheerleader-type voice.

I chew my lip as I decide what my next move should be.

"I promise . . . I'm not messing around," Dev says, his voice warm and assuring. *Liam Neeson ain't got nothin' on this guy, damn him.*

May is giving me her puppy-dog eyes again.

I'm starting to fold and feel powerless to stop it. "How long will it take? For the police to get here and for you to make your statement or whatever?"

"No more than an hour." Dev gestures toward the stairs. "Come on up. This will be the best jambalaya you'll ever have. If it isn't, I'll let you use your sister's Taser on me."

"I have it locked and loaded," she says, nodding like a bobblehead doll.

So, so tempting. I take a deep breath in and out before answering, trying not to laugh at his promise.

"Fine." The teenager in me is giggling over the fact that this feels a tiny bit like a date. Like an invitation to meet in the school cafeteria and sit at the same table during lunch hour.

With my mind made up and a plan in place, I feel better. I sigh and shake my head as I walk beside him to the bottom of the stairs. May stays behind to chat with her boyfriend and Thibault.

I must be high to have let him talk me into eating dinner here. Maybe I *should* work as a freelancer for these ridiculous people, because apparently I could fit right in, given the complete lack of decision-making skills I'm showing right now.

Thank goodness Miles has the kids, is all I can think. And then I realize how awful that thought is. It's at that point that I realize how far I've already fallen. Into what? I have no idea, but it can't be good.

CHAPTER SIX

"Oh my god, this is *so* good." I'm talking with my mouth full of food, and I'm pretty sure I have a couple grains of rice clinging to my lip, but I can't stop myself. Hell, I can't even slow down. I've eaten an entire bowl of jambalaya in less than five minutes. Dev was right; Ozzie is an amazing cook.

Everyone is still downstairs except for Dev and me, but as soon as the big man comes up I'm going to tell him I'm a fan. Even if I am still mad at him and his team, a talent this strong should be rewarded. Besides, maybe I could convince my sister to invite me over for dinner more often. At her place, of course. I'm not coming here again. This will be my last meal at the Bourbon Street Boys Café.

"I know, right?" Dev nods. "I've probably eaten this meal fifty times now, but it never gets old."

"Fifty times? Wow. Does he make it every day?" I dip a hunk of French bread into the sauce and take a hearty bite of it, not caring that this marks me as a piglet. Thank goodness Dev is just as hungry as I am. His nose is so close to his bowl, I'm surprised he hasn't splashed the spicy sauce up into his nostrils yet. He's already on his second helping.

"No. Maybe once or twice a month. He has a pretty big repertoire, and he likes to cook, lucky for us."

"You don't know how to cook?"

"Not really. My mom always tried to teach me, but I'm not a very good student." He gives me a half smile, and I can almost picture him as a small boy. The vision reminds me of my son, Sammy, and makes me go warm with happiness.

I smile. "Oh, I don't know if I believe that." I realize after I say it that it sounds like I'm flirting. My face feels a little warm, but I'm pretty sure it's the spice in the jambalaya and not the little wink he gives me.

"Believe it." He holds up a hand that I'm absolutely sure could palm a basketball with no effort. "It's hard to use regular-sized knives with paws like these." He uses that paw to pick up another piece of bread and dip it into his sauce. A big slice from the thick baguette looks like a crouton in his giant fingers.

"You do have pretty big hands." *Is he thinking the same thing I am?* I squirm in my seat a little bit. *Damn, this jambalaya is spicy.* I reach up surreptitiously and pull the collar of my shirt out a little.

He shrugs. "It comes with the territory."

I'm confused. "Being a trainer?"

He shakes his head. "No. Massive growth spurts."

I put my spoon down, intrigued about his history. I've never met anyone taller than six-two. "You had more than one?"

He's chewing more slowly and looks as if he's considering my question, not sure he wants to answer it. Once again, I'm worried that I've gone too far with my interrogation, but then he responds as he stares into his bowl.

"I guess I had my first one around twelve years old. I grew an entire foot over the summer. Then I had another one when I was around fifteen. The third one when I was around eighteen." He looks up at me with a wry grin. "Let's just say it left a lot of stretch marks on my back."

"Wow. So, how tall are you?"

"Seven feet even."

I don't know why, but that makes my heart flip. "Holy crap." I grab my spoon and act like I'm going to take another bite of my meal, even though every last bit is gone. I'm afraid that I've insulted him with my reaction, so I scramble to pick up the pieces of the conversation as I scrape up speckles of sauce and collect them over on the edge of the bowl.

"That's really cool. I'll bet you can reach everything on the top shelf." I feel like thumping myself in the forehead with my spoon. *Good one, Jenny.* It's as if I've never talked to a man before.

He laughs. "I haven't met a shelf I can't reach yet, unless you count the ones at Costco. But I'm pretty good at climbing, so I think I could handle those too."

I sigh with jealousy. "You have no idea the struggles that I have being only five-three."

"Oh really?" He puts the spoon down. "Tell me about it."

I know he's mocking me, but I play along like he's not. "Well . . . I have a step stool that I have to carry around the house with me so that I can access my pantry, my linen closet, *and* my clothes closet." I pretend-frown to make sure that he'll be suitably impressed by my very sad story.

"You poor thing. I never realized how challenging it could be to be so petite." His smile has turned upside down into a very overdone frown.

I know he didn't mean it as a compliment, but being called petite makes me very happy. "Yep. That's my personal struggle. I don't like to complain, though. I just suffer in silence . . . try to be strong for all the other height-challenged people out there who look up to me . . ."

He laughs and leans back in his chair, wiping his mouth off with a napkin that he then throws on the table. He laces his hands and puts them behind his head, leaning back so he can stare at the ceiling. "Ahhhhh . . . ," is all he says.

"So, you said your son might be tall for his age, huh?"

Dev swivels his head to the left and right, using his stationary hands to rub his scalp. Then, without warning, he lurches forward in his chair, stands up, and grabs both of our empty bowls to walk them over to the sink.

I'm stunned by his out-of-the-blue reaction, wondering if I missed something. I feel like I should apologize, but I'm not sure what I'm sorry for. *Is that rude? To ask about your kid's height?* I guess I'm not used to talking to men about their children. Usually, it's just the other moms hanging around waiting for their kids to come out of school that I interact with, and they all seem very happy to compare the heights and weights of their children. It's almost like a competition, in fact.

Dev rinses the dishes at the sink, but just as I'm about to apologize, he speaks. "I'm not really sure where my son falls on the height chart."

I have about ten questions on the tip of my tongue, but I'm not completely deaf, dumb, and blind to body language. This is a subject he doesn't want to discuss for whatever reason. Maybe he thinks it's a mother's job to worry about those things. Maybe he feels bad about the fact that Jacob's mom isn't around to participate.

My mouth switches over to autopilot while he cleans up the kitchen. "My son is actually small for his age. I guess he takes after both of us. His dad and me. But both of my daughters are at the higher end of the height chart at the doctor's office. I don't know if they're going to hang on to that height into adolescence, but I'm keeping my fingers crossed."

"You don't want them to have to struggle with that whole height-challenged thing you have going on." I can't see his face, but I can hear the smile in his voice.

"Exactly." *Phew.* I'm relieved he doesn't sound stressed. Hopefully that means I haven't totally offended him.

"What are their names?" he asks me.

"My oldest daughter is Sophie; she's ten. My middle daughter is Melody, and she's seven. And my son Sammy is not quite four. He's got a birthday coming up next month. The older two are pretty easy, but he's a real handful."

Dev turns around after finishing up his cleaning and comes back over to the table, turning his chair around backward and straddling it. He folds his arms over the top of the seat, giving me his full attention. "I think it's a boy thing. My son is always going a hundred miles an hour. I hate to say this, but I actually look forward to coming to work sometimes."

I have to laugh at that. "I know *exactly* what you mean." I look at my watch and then hold it up. "I keep checking to see how much time I have left on my weekend."

"Oh. They're gone? I thought they were with a sitter."

"No, they are at my ex's house until Sunday afternoon." I pause for a moment. "Why did you think they were with a sitter?"

He shrugs. "I don't know. I guess you were in such a hurry to get out of here, I thought it had something to do with your kids."

"I don't get it," I say, my voice probably more sharp than it should be.

"You don't get what?"

"Are you guys completely and totally desensitized to the real world?"

"I don't think so."

I gesture toward the door we entered to get into this room. "A half hour ago, you and I were locked in a panic room together because somebody was trying to break in to your warehouse in the middle of the afternoon." I hold up a finger to stop him, knowing he's about to correct me on the time of day. "Afternoon, evening, whatever. It's still light outside. People don't break in to other people's places of business when it's still light outside."

"I agree."

I don't know what to say to that. He's supposed to be arguing with me.

He takes over the conversation. "It's not something you see every day, for sure. We're not even certain at this point that it *was* a break-in attempt. And I'm sorry about the whole panic room mess. It's just that . . . you're not one of the team and I know you're not trained for that kind of thing, so I went a little overboard in trying to keep you safe."

Now I feel bad about being rude to him. And for thinking he's as dumb as a post. Maybe he's just . . . protective. Like a wolf. The wolf shows on Animal Planet are some of my favorites.

My voice comes out strained. "I appreciate you wanting to take care of me and doing what you thought was best at the time."

I feel like crying. I've always wanted to have a man in my life who I could count on, who would protect me and my children when the poo hits the fan. It just didn't work out that way for me, but that doesn't necessarily mean it has to be that way for everyone. Maybe Dev is the whole package. Maybe he's a good dad *and* a good man, too. He's going to make a great husband someday if that's the case.

I realize as I have this thought that I'm really happy for my sister. Even though she has to work with these nutballs, she has a man by her side who I know would take a bullet for her. And he's great with his dog, Sahara, and May's dog, Felix, so maybe he'll be a good dad, too. I could almost imagine that whatever bullet hit him wouldn't penetrate. He looks like a superhero. And now, when I look at Dev, I see those same qualities in him.

He nods, accepting my unspoken apology.

"You have to understand—this kind of stuff is just not normal for me. And it's not normal for my sister, either. I honestly don't understand why she's working here." It feels really good to say that out loud.

Dev just kind of stares at me, and I'm having a hard time reading his expression and his body language. "Why are you looking at me like that?"

"I'm just wondering if you're telling me the truth, or if you're telling me what you want the truth to be."

"I'm telling you the truth, of course." *How rude. What's he even saying?* I'm back to being miffed at him again. It's like riding a roller coaster just sitting across from him and chatting about what should be nothing.

He goes into silent mode once more.

My good humor levels are quickly draining down to zero. "Do you want to explain yourself?" I resist the urge to start tapping my toe.

He shrugs. "The question is, do *you* want me to explain myself?"

I cross my arms over my chest and sit back deeper into my chair. "Yes, I do, Dev. I would *love* for you to explain to me what you think it is I'm thinking or saying." *Shuh, right. He doesn't know me.*

"You're the big sister, right?" He doesn't seem intimidated at all by my challenge.

"Yes." I don't know why I'm feeling defensive about the fact that I fall first in the birth order, but it seems like a demerit in this evaluation or whatever it is he's conducting.

He tilts his head. "My guess is that when you guys were growing up, you were the protector. Am I right?"

54

I look around the room a little bit before answering. It's really pissing me off that he's already guessing correctly about my life. He's only known me for an hour, and I never got the impression from May that she and Dev have ever sat down and had any meaningful conversations before. I hate to think I'm such an open book. Open books are boring; being mysterious is way sexier.

I almost laugh out loud. *Me. Sexy? Ha!* Maybe ten years ago, but not now, and not in my near future, either.

Dev is waiting for my answer. I hate to admit he's right, but what's true is true. "I might have been her protector. From time to time."

"No, I'd say it was probably more often than that."

I roll my eyes. *Busted.* "Whatever."

"There was something going on in your family that was really difficult for both of you. Maybe you had a parent who was hard to live with?"

I unfold my arms and rest my hands on the edges of the chair, pushing myself upright. I think I'm experiencing that sensation that's described as being on the hot seat. And these dining room lights feel just a little bit too bright. Dark memories involving my father's drinking and the aggression that always followed are pounding on that locked door in my brain. *Bail out! Bail out! You're going down!*

"That's a pretty personal question, don't you think?"

"You asked me what I thought, and I'm telling you. When you look at your sister, I'm guessing you see a flighty, irresponsible yet intelligent girl who still needs your protection . . . *from time to time.*" He winks at me to take the sting out of his mockery.

I really, really want to argue with this man, but he's making it very difficult. He just described my sister and our relationship to a T. *Am I really that easy to read? Damn.* I'm never going to Vegas. I'll lose everything I have.

"So?" I shrug, like it's no big deal that he just got into my head and almost woke up some ghosts from my past after knowing me for only an hour. "What if I do see her this way? It's no insult to her. She knows she can occasionally be flighty and irresponsible. And she knows I love her no matter what."

"There's nothing wrong with you having this vision of your sister, except for the fact that I would say it's inaccurate."

I lift a brow at him. "Oh, right. So, you know my sister better than I do. Is that what you're saying?"

"Not exactly. But I'll tell you this: unlike you, I have no pre-conceived notions of your sister based on things that she might have gone through earlier in her life. I knew nothing about her background before she started here. So, when I saw her for the first time and then interacted with her afterward, I formed an opinion of her based on who she is as a grown woman, today."

He leans in closer to me, but I'm not backing away, even though it's giving me a mini-stroke to have him this close. "And what I see, first of all, is a really big heart. I also see that she's highly intelligent and good at thinking on her feet. She's very trainable and very coachable because she has an eager, open mind, which is a huge asset in this business. She's incredibly artistic and talented behind the camera. And she has a sense of adventure that I don't think she even realized was there until she walked through our doors."

I have to admit, I'm a little blown away. It makes my heart go mushy to hear this man describe my sister in such a compli-mentary way. Who wouldn't want to be all those things? I don't know that I agree with the entirety of his assessment—that she's this big adventurous person—because all of our lives I've pretty much seen the opposite, but that doesn't lessen the impact of what he's said.

"Well. Those are all very nice things for sure."

"And it's all the truth. No embellishment." He smiles.

I'm about to tell him the one problem with what he's said, that how, like me, my sister has refused to take risks all her life—up until just recently, anyway—when the door opens and three people enter the kitchen area, stopping our conversation cold.

CHAPTER SEVEN

May is the first person through the door. Behind her is Thibault, and the last person in is Ozzie. May is trying to appear cheerful, but she has that crazy look in her eye, so I know she's covering up her real emotions. The other two look like they're going to a funeral.

I stand. "What's going on?"

Dev speaks before anyone can answer. "Did you guys figure everything out?"

Thibault responds. "Not really."

"Why don't we all have a seat at the table here so we can discuss it?" Ozzie suggests.

It's on the tip of my tongue to argue and tell them that I'm leaving and I really don't care what's going on, but the look on my sister's face stops me. She's giving me those puppy-dog eyes. *Dammit. Foiled again.*

"Fine." I sit down in my seat with a long-suffering sigh. May is so going to pay for getting me into this mess and forcing me to stay in it. Very soon, too. Forget that revenge-is-a-dish-best-served-cold nonsense. I like my revenge served up hot and fresh, baby. Piping hot, so it burns like a mofo.

Once everyone is seated, Ozzie leans forward and puts his forearms on the table, folding his hands together. His eyes sweep the space, looking at each person around the table individually for a moment before he speaks. It's very effective at getting total silence.

"We've filed a report and had a conversation with a detective from the New Orleans Police Department. There's a couple hundred dollars' worth of damage to the front door, but that's not really an issue. The door still functions." He turns to look at me. "However, your car is parked outside."

I wait for him to say something else, but he seems to be waiting for me to respond. I shrug. "Yes, it is." Then it hits me, and anger rushes in. "Did they do something to my car too?" My insurance deductible is huge. *This is going to suck.*

He shakes his head. "No. Your car is fine."

Relief floods through me.

"However, I have a concern that whoever's responsible for the damage to our door has taken note of the fact that your car was parked outside."

My mouth kind of falls open, because I feel like I should say something, but I have no idea what the appropriate response is. I just don't get what the big deal is. It's a frigging parking lot. Where else would I put my car? I look around at the others for signs that they get me. *He's not making sense, right? Or is it just me?*

When my sister starts speaking, her voice comes out very soft and slow. This is how she talks to my children when she's trying to convince them to go to bed on time and she anticipates that they're going to argue and whine. My hackles go right up and stay there.

"Jenny, we're not exactly sure who is responsible for causing that damage. Now, of course we hope that it's just some random thing, that some drunk guy went a little crazy doing doughnuts out in the parking lot or something, and accidentally hit the door.

But we can't ignore the fact that there are bad people out there who would like to get in our way."

I look at her like she's nuts. "What in the hell are you talking about?"

Thibault gives me a tight smile. "We're in the security business. We also work with local law enforcement to help build cases or find probable cause evidence to obtain warrants and the arrests of certain criminals who are at large. Most of our work is done confidentially and behind the scenes, but every once in a while, someone is made aware of our involvement, and occasionally we have to deal with threats."

"Threats?" I hate how weak my voice sounds.

May speaks before anyone else has a chance. "It's probably nothing. We're just being overcautious, like Dev was today when he locked you in the panic room." She flashes him a sideways glare.

Dev rolls his eyes. "I already apologized to her. She understands." He looks over at me. "Right, Jenny? You understand it wasn't intentional."

I'm still stuck on the whole threat part. "Yeah, whatever." I shift my attention over to Ozzie. "So, you're telling me that because I had my car parked outside and some dickcheese—pardon my French—decided to come over here and . . . I don't know what . . . storm the castle? That now I'm somehow involved in your problems?" I shake my head. "No. I do not accept that." I stand, tired of the games, tired of these conspiracy nuts, and tired of being checked in against my will to the Hotel California.

Dev looks up at me. "Where're you going?"

My voice comes out so loud, it bounces off the walls. "I'm going home!" I look at my sister, pausing a moment to bring my volume down a few notches. "I'm sorry, May, but this is ridiculous. This may be the life that you've chosen for yourself—and God help me, I have no idea why—but this is not anything that I want to be involved in." I look at Ozzie. "Thanks for the offer of the freelance work, but I'm afraid I'm going to have to decline." My gaze moves to the other people at the table. "It was nice meeting all of you. And no offense, but I hope I never see any of you again."

I lift my purse from the floor next to my chair and walk to the exit. Grabbing the handle, I try to push it down and pull the door open, but nothing happens. I don't turn around when I speak because if I look at any of their faces, I'm going to start yelling again. They knew I was going to be locked in, and yet they just let me walk on over here alone to make a fool of myself. *Bastards.*

"If somebody doesn't come over here right now and put the secret code into this keypad thingy, I am seriously going to break something."

I hear chairs moving and then footsteps. A familiar voice comes from behind me. "Let me get that for you." A giant hand appears over my shoulder and presses a four-digit code into the keypad. There's a click telling me that the tumblers inside the lock have moved and I'm now free to go.

I grab the door and yank it open, stepping through to a room full of swords and other ridiculous-looking weapons. *Who needs nunchucks with spiked balls attached?* A light goes on automatically, illuminating the space that I mostly ignored on our way in. There's another door at the far end with another keypad. "Jesus Christ. This place is like a prison." I'm not even going to comment on all the kooky weapons around me.

"Don't worry, I'm right behind you." It's Dev again. I'm really angry at myself, because I want to be pissed at him, and I want to blame him for everything that's happening right now, but he's being so nice it's impossible for me to follow through on that emotion. I decide Ozzie's a better target. He's the one who took my sister into this place and somehow convinced her to stay. He's the one saying I should be worried about where I parked.

We get to the next door, and I wait very impatiently for Dev to open it. He steps up next to me and puts his hand on the keypad, but he doesn't do anything. I don't look at him, because seeing those eyes and that dimple will weaken my resolve.

"Just put in the code and let me go."

He clears his throat. "Can I call you sometime?"

My heart pretty much stops beating altogether at this point. It's actually quite painful in my chest cavity right now. He's making a joke when I'm this vulnerable. *Ugh*, he's worse than the lion *and* the seahorse. He's the anglerfish, who latches on to his mate and eventually absorbs himself into her skin until he's just a disgusting lump on her back.

I put my hand over my heart and turn to look up at him. "Is this some kind of joke? Is this *funny* to you?"

He shakes his head. "No. Maybe bad timing, but . . ."

I laugh angrily. "Yeah. Pretty much the worst timing you could possibly come up with." I gesture at the keypad with my chin. "I need to get home. Please, Dev." I feel like crying. I think maybe he was asking me out, but he couldn't have been. Why would he? I'm a mom who looks like an ice-cream addict, and I was really rude to the people he calls family. And even if he was serious, I couldn't do it. This isn't my world. He's gorgeous and sweet and a dad and all that, but he's also a Bourbon Street Bonehead.

He touches the code into the keypad without saying anything else, and I don't hesitate a moment before grabbing the handle and opening it so that I can go out to the staircase below. I want to scream and tear my hair out when I see another keypad at the big, main door, but then I notice Lucky is there and he's waving up at me.

"Could you get the door for Jenny?" Dev yells out to his coworker below.

Lucky looks a little confused. "She's leaving?"

I don't wait for Dev to confirm. "Yes! I'm leaving." I bang down the stairs, hanging on to the railing tightly, because if I trip now I'll end up in the hospital, and I don't have time for that nonsense. I need to get home. *Bath. Sleep. Kids.*

Lucky shrugs and then turns to enter the code. I'm at the bottom of the stairs when the big door begins to slide open. I'll admit, there's a little piece of me fearing that there's going to be some bad guy with a machine gun standing outside, but when the only thing that greets me is the sultry night smelling of the Mississippi River, I relax. I think I've had more adrenaline pumping through my veins today than I have in the past year. I feel like I'm high. No wonder I'm having these ridiculous thoughts about men and animals and seahorses.

"Be safe," Dev says from somewhere behind me.

"Yeah, okay." He doesn't see me rolling my eyes. These people are crazy. Of course I'm going to be safe. All I'm doing is getting into my car, driving home, and taking a bath. That's it. Oh, and I'm also going to drink an entire bottle of wine by myself. And then if I'm lucky, I'll find a nice chick flick to watch on television, pop some popcorn, eat a couple scoops of ice cream, and fall asleep on the couch. I never get to do that stuff when my kids are around. Embracing the couch potato lifestyle, that's what I'm all about. *Ice cream addicts, unite!*

This is my chance to live like I'm single again. Like I have no responsibilities and calories don't matter. I can't believe I almost blew it by working on my day off. Ha! What nuttery is this? I can go home right now and pretend that I'm fresh out of college again and I have the entire world as my oyster in front of me, and that there's a man out there who's both a great husband and a great father just waiting to sweep me off my feet, look me in the eyes, and say: "Jenny, do you know how amazing you are? You're funny, you're intelligent, you're adventurous . . ."

Shit. It's Dev's voice that I hear echoing in my head, and I almost start crying when I realize that it's not me who's being described; it's my sister. Some girls have all the luck.

I use my key fob to open my car door and get inside. My car starts up immediately, and the climate control blasts me in the face, hot humid air that makes my future warm bath start to feel like a really bad idea. Sweating in the bathtub suuuucks. The bath is now officially out, which makes me want to punch something. *What more could possibly go wrong today?*

I drive away, refusing to look in my rearview at the warehouse— the evil place that stole my sister and my bath away from me. The more I think about those people in there and what they do, and what my sister is wrapped up in, the sadder I get. Two miles away from the port, I burst into tears.

I cry almost all the way home, and I don't even know what the damn tears are for. Are they for May? Are they for me? Are they for my past mistakes, or the future I'll never have? Maybe they're for all of the above. I obviously need to get my head examined, because shit is seriously messed up in there. There's not enough ice cream in all of New Orleans to fix this.

I'm not sure how I got home. My brain took over and put the driver-me on autopilot. I remember leaving the warehouse and then pulling into my neighborhood. I hope I didn't run anyone over in my daze.

After parking my car in the driveway, I walk into my house. I'm so exhausted, I go straight upstairs to my room and flop down onto my stomach on my bed. Not a single thought passes through my mind before I'm sound asleep.

CHAPTER EIGHT

A vague dinging sound coming from somewhere in my house penetrates the sleep-fog filling my brain. In my half-dream state, I imagine that I have something cooking in the microwave, and it's time for me to take the food out. Another ding comes, louder this time, or so it seems. Apparently, my microwave has a mind of its own. It's nagging me: *Come get your food, woman!*

As I become more fully awake, I realize it's not my microwave talking to me; it's my telephone. Someone is texting me. I groan, knowing who woke me up, regretting that I have the hearing of a mother with small children. My shit is bionic.

"Go away, May!"

I grab one of my pillows and push it over my face. I could happily fall back to sleep under here, except for the fact that my breath is totally rank. *Damn . . . roadkill breath? How did that happen?* Then I remember the jambalaya. "Ew." I throw my pillow off the bed, telling myself I'll wash the pillowcase later. I'm pretty sure I drooled on it with my jambalaya stink-breath. *Double ew.*

I'm not going to answer that text, but now I'm too wide awake to go back to sleep. I roll out of bed and shuffle into my bathroom, too exhausted mentally to actually lift my feet more than a few millimeters off the carpet. Once there, I stare into the mirror at the horror show that is my face.

My makeup has smeared from my eyes down to my jaw. I'm surprised I didn't cause any car accidents on my way home looking like this. Anyone seeing this face would have thought I was a zombie after their brains. My hair has a big knot in the back of it, and the left side of my 'do is pressed in like it's been glued in place.

"Beaauuuutiful. Gorgeous!" I put my hands on my cheeks and push them in, puckering the whole front of my face up for a few seconds. It's not an improvement.

When Miles announced that he no longer loved me, and that he was leaving me with three little kids to start his new life alone, I did plenty of crying, and I smeared lots and lots of makeup down my face in the process. It's been a year now, so I was kind of thinking I was over having random breakdowns in the middle of the day, vomiting for no reason at inopportune times, and binge-eating massive amounts of Ben & Jerry's ice cream. But apparently not. Apparently I still have some unresolved issues to work through. Imagine that.

My phone dings again. I remember where I left it now; it's at the bottom of the stairs in my purse.

I should probably brush my teeth, remove my makeup, and do something with my hair, but what's the point? The kids are gone, I have no life outside of being their mother, and my sister's going to hang out with the Bourbon Street Buttheads all weekend, so I don't have to worry about her dropping by. She doesn't have time for me anymore. She's too busy with her new, stupid job.

I scowl just thinking about it. Now I look like an angry zombie. I hiss at my reflection.

I could go shopping, even though it's getting pretty late, but I really don't have a whole lot of discretionary income to splurge on myself. I hate that I got teased today, that I almost had a gift certificate from the mall in my hot little hands and five hundred extra bucks to spend. That's not something that happens to me very often. I'm lucky if I get child support checks on time, and my boss doesn't believe in bonuses.

A fleeting thought dances across my mind. I *could* do freelance work. It doesn't have to be at the warehouse; it could be anywhere. I could go online to one of those freelancer sites and sign up. And I wouldn't have to actually *take* any jobs; I could just use it to see what's out there. I've been saying for years I want to do it, but I've always been too busy with the kids. Too worried about the risk. A single mom can't afford to go without a paycheck, something a freelancer has to do sometimes. And freelancing while also working another job means missing out on time with my kids, which is definitely not an option, especially with an ex like Miles who never picks up the slack. My watch says I have over thirty hours left before they're back. That's enough time to start the process . . .

My heart goes nuts at the very idea. *Too much risk. Forget about it. Just keep your nose to the grindstone, Jenny.*

Knowing I'm not in a position to flip my world upside down by starting a new job, I try to imagine how I could jazz things up a bit. I chew my lip as I think about it. I don't have to change my work life. I could just . . . try to get out more. I could even join one of those online dating sites. Find a mate. Or just go out for coffee with a guy. Start slow. Get dressed up and feel pretty for a change.

I look at myself in the mirror again and laugh. "Yeah, right. Go ahead, Jenny, take a selfie. Put that zombie look up on your website profile and see how many date requests you get." *Damn.* The way I look right now, there's not a single man in all of Louisiana who'd want to have coffee with me. Not even the guys out in the bayou missing half their teeth who catch catfish by letting them swallow their arms whole. Noodling, they call it. I couldn't even get a date with a *noodler*, that's how bad off I am right now.

I stick my tongue out at myself and then turn around to leave the bathroom, flicking the light off as I go. I walk down the stairs and ignore my purse and the phone inside it, making a beeline for my tiny home office to the left of the front door. I'm just going to check and see what's on the freelancer sites. No big deal. *No risk in looking, right?* I'm not two steps into the room when I realize my problem. My big, fat mistake.

"God*dammit!*" I turn and rush back to my purse, throwing it open, all the while knowing what I'm going to find inside: nothing.

I close my eyes and try to retrace in my mind the steps I took after I left the panic room. *Did I take my laptop with me?* I remember grabbing my purse, but I don't remember taking the computer. And I don't remember putting it in my car, and I don't remember setting it down here inside the house anywhere. *Dammit, dammit, double dammit!*

Just in case my rearview memory is wrong, I grab my keys and run outside. The neighbors have seen me looking pretty rough over the past year, so I'm not worried about any of them viewing my latest zombie chic look. *Let 'em judge.*

I press my face against the driver's window and scan the inside of my car. All I see is the random garbage that always floats around the vehicle that acts as a taxi for three little kids.

I open the rear door anyway, trying not to let the dread overtake me, and climb into the backseat. Looking around, I mumble angrily to myself. "Come on, you bastard. Be in here. Be in here!" Crap is flying everywhere as I toss the entire backseat area. I've almost managed to convince myself that my laptop is here, buried under something. It has to be.

I find three random shoes that don't match, two fast-food meal boxes with empty wrappers inside, about a hundred petrified French fries scattered all over, and a rotten apple core shoved in the crack between two seats. I'm so disgusted with my life, I can't even comprehend it right now. How did I get to this place? Fall so far? I'm a crazy zombie wading through the remnants of at least five horrible meal choices for children who deserve much better than the mess I've become.

I leave the car, slamming the door in my anger, and march back up the front steps. I cannot believe that I forgot my computer at the warehouse. My computer is my life! I left there in such a huff—how am I going to go back and be cool about retrieving it? They're going to think I left it there on purpose. They're going to think I'm coming back to beg for that freelance job. Just the very idea makes me so angry I could spit. So I do, right there on my bushes. Twice.

Once inside the house, I take several long, deep breaths in an effort to calm myself. I'm obviously overreacting as a result of being in not-really danger today. Being trapped in a panic room has to leave scars, even though there was nothing technically wrong, right? But I can move past it. Nothing happened. I'm safe. Hell, it was probably that idiot driving the forklift who banged into their door, and they're all so paranoid over there, they think it was some gangster coming to mow them down with an AK-47.

Whatever. I'm not going back there. May has to bring me my computer. And she's going to have to bring it right *now*, because I need it. Maybe I'm going to join a dating site. Maybe I'm going to find some freelance work. Whatever. I can't do any of it without the computer. And it's her fault I left it there, so she has to fix this.

I dig around in my purse until I find my phone. There are three messages from May, all of them showing concern and asking me how I'm doing.

My fingers blaze out a response.

Me: *I'm fine. Forgot my computer at the warehouse. Please bring it to me right away. It's in the panic room.*

I grind my teeth as I stare at the phone and wait for a response. The seconds tick by. I start tapping my toe with impatience. She was in an all-fired hurry to reach me just five minutes ago, waking me up out of a sound sleep on my weekend off, and now she's disappeared. *Perfect. So, so perfect for my life right now.*

May: *Okay. No prob. B there soon.*

My jaw goes off-kilter as I read the message several times. I'm suspicious. My sister is never this short and sweet about anything. I can't decide if I'm just being paranoid, if this is some kind of trick, or if Dev was completely right about my sister and he actually does know her better than I do.

Just the thought of that makes me want to throw my phone across the room, but I don't have any extra cash, and I don't have the best luck with these stupid devices, so I don't. Instead, I toss it back into my purse and wander down the hallway to the kitchen. I'm on a mission.

I have a new plan now. I'm going to force May to stay here in this house, have two or three glasses of wine with me, and explain exactly what the hell she's doing working for those bozos and hooking up with that guy Ozzie. I mean, come on . . . Apparently they're magnets for criminal activity. It's dangerous over there, and she's a wedding photographer, for chrissake. She doesn't need to run around with a pack of police wannabes just because it pays well and has good benefits. She was doing just fine before. And she might not have any children of her own, but she's an aunt to my three babies, and that bears some responsibility. She needs to take better care of her own personal safety. How would I be able to tell Sophie that her favorite aunt, the one she plans to run away to when she turns sixteen, is dead? *No. No, no, no, no, no. This is not happening. I have to fix this.*

Satisfied that I have a sound plan and excellent reasons for executing it, I pull out two glasses and make sure that I have a nice fat bottle of wine chilling in the fridge for when she arrives. The thought passes through my mind that I should go over to the mirror and try to fix my face, but then I decide it's probably better if she sees me totally messed up like this. I need to twang those heartstrings of hers, and Dev was right about one thing: May does have a really big heart.

As soon as she sees how much this is upsetting me and how worried I am, she'll be in the right frame of mind to listen to reason. I'm going to pull out all the stops for this one. I feel like I'm actually saving her life by doing it.

The righteousness of my awesome plan puffs my heart up and makes me feel as though for the first time in a long time I'm actually doing something that matters. That's me. Big Sister Jenny. Watch out, bad guys, because nobody's going to hurt my little sister; not if I have anything to say about it.

CHAPTER NINE

I hear May's car pull up in the driveway, so I hustle into the kitchen and take the bottle of wine out of the refrigerator. I'm not going to ask her if she wants any; I'm just going to give it to her and guilt her into drinking it. The doorbell rings as I'm pulling the cork. I pause and frown as I look toward the hallway. *We're using doorbells now?*

"It's open!" I yell, annoyed. She knows I don't lock my front door when I'm home during the day, and she has a key besides. I pour two glasses of wine almost to the brim. I need to get my sister buzzing so I can talk some sense into her.

Yes . . . it's true. I am willing to drug my sister to get her to see reason. Big Sister Code allows this in emergencies, and this is definitely an emergency.

The door creaks open.

"I'm in the kitchen!" I trill. I need to throw her off the scent of my anger by acting like everything's hunky-dory, like I just want some bonding time with her. She'll never see my sneak attack, big-sister advice coming until it's all over but the crying.

The wood floors groan as May makes her way down the hallway. I put the bottle of wine down slowly, a trickle of confusion and then fear floating through my brain. My sister doesn't weigh enough to make my floors sag.

"May?"

She doesn't answer. *Oh, God. Someone who's not my sister is about to enter my kitchen!* My knife block is on the other side of the room; I'll never make it there in time to grab one.

I snatch the corkscrew in my right fist and hold it up at my shoulder with my arm cocked back. If it's a bad guy with a gun, I'm probably doomed, but I'm at least going to try to poke a hole in him on my way down, get me some DNA. I watch CSI. I know all they need is a speck of it.

A giant of a man comes around the corner, stooping over to avoid hitting his head on my doorframe as he walks into the kitchen. I just stand there, my weapon and DNA-collection strategy forgotten.

"Hey, Jenny." His eyes travel from my face to my hand, and then to my weapon. "Not expecting me, I take it."

I slowly lower the corkscrew to the counter and place it down gently. I'm trying to rein in the emotions that want to run wild all over this guy. He is so lucky I didn't have a knife in my hand; I might very well have thrown it at him, given how mad I am right now. I cannot believe my sister sent Dev in her place. My heart is breaking.

He holds up my laptop in front of him as a shield. "I come in peace."

I shake my head slowly. My sister has violated so many sections of the Sister Code today, I don't even know where to begin as I try to list all of her transgressions in my head.

"Is that wine for me?" he asks, glancing at the counter.

I look at the two glasses. "No, actually, the wine was for me and my sister. But I guess she was too busy to bring me my laptop or to sit down and chat with me." I don't know whether to cry or throw the wine glasses across the room. I'm considering doing both.

Dev takes a couple more steps into the kitchen and puts the laptop down on the counter. "She was going to bring it over to you herself, but I asked her if I could do it instead."

I stare at him and blink a few times.

"Are you mad?" he asks cautiously.

I huff out a breath. "Not at you."

"Don't be mad at your sister. She thought she was doing a good thing."

"A good thing? By avoiding me?"

"No. By sending me over."

"Why would you coming over here be better than her coming over?"

His face goes a little red and he shrugs. "I don't know . . . maybe she . . ." He stops there and stares at the wine.

Oh, God. She didn't! She's not! She's not playing matchmaker is she?! Ack!

I can't look at him anymore; it's too embarrassing. "Never mind. Here, have some wine." I hand him a glass, sloshing a little wine out of it in the process. I grab my drink and mumble under my breath, "I know I'm going to," before taking a big swig of it.

Dev takes his glass and holds it up in front of him. "Cheers."

I've already taken a huge sip, but I hold my drink up too and nod as the two glasses touch. "Cheers." My voice comes out strained because my wine has shrunk my vocal cords or something.

He takes a sip and winces. He tries to smile but it comes out more like a grimace.

"What?" I ask. "You don't like wine?"

"No, I do. Just not . . . white wine."

I snort at his obvious lie. "No, you mean crap wine. I get it. I'm not one for splurging on alcohol, I guess." I shrug as I stare down into the glass I'm taking another sip from. *Sip, gulp . . . who's counting?*

He takes another very small drink from his glass. "No, don't worry about it. This is great." He holds the glass up at me again and grins really hard.

I shake my head and speak softly, trying not to be charmed by the fact that I can read every last emotion he's experiencing on his face. "You are such a terrible liar."

His grin is sheepish. "Yeah, you're probably right."

I'm sure he thinks I was insulting him, but I wasn't. I have this thing against men who are good at lying. It's refreshing to be standing in front of one who's only good at telling the truth.

I lean on the edge of the counter. A glance at the clock tells me it's almost ten. "Don't you have to get back home to your son?" Another sip has my glass almost empty, and it's a big glass, too. Normally, I'd care about coming off as a lush, but not tonight. Tonight I'm kid-free and pissed off . . . a powerful combination. *Bring on the alcohol!*

"He's with my mother right now. She helps me out a lot."

Kid talk. I can hang with that, even when I'm buzzing. "Does she come to your house, or do you take your son to her?"

"She comes to my place. My son is . . . more comfortable there."

I nod. "I get it." I throw my arm out for illustrative purposes, calling his attention to the fact that it looks like my kitchen was vomited on by a unicorn; every color of the rainbow is here, represented by various dolls, action figures, trucks, and games. "My kids have all their toys here. It's usually easier for May to come and watch them at our place when I need her."

"So, May helps you out a lot?"

I shrug. "She used to." I hate that my heart feels like someone is pinching it. I massage the rib space over it with my first two fingers and take another sip of my wine.

"Why did she stop?"

Guilt hits me when I realize that I've led him to believe May has dropped the ball on me and the kids. "I guess I shouldn't have said it that way. She hasn't stopped, she's just . . ."

Dev nods slowly. "I get it. You think now that she's working with Ozzie, you won't be seeing her so much anymore."

He's way too perceptive. My chin goes out a little. "You think I'm wrong about that?"

"Maybe you'll be right for a little while, but I think May will come around. This whole thing with the company and with Ozzie is all new stuff, but once she gets the hang of it, she'll refocus and remember what the more important stuff is."

"How do you know?" I hate that I'm holding my breath, waiting for his next words, but I am; there's no point in denying it. I want to believe that he's right. I want to believe that he's as perceptive as he seems and that I haven't lost my sister to his muscled colleague.

"It's pretty much how it happened for all of us."

Dev puts his glass on the counter, and I put mine down next to his. I want to be sober for this part, and I can't trust myself to stay on plan if I have that glass in my hand and the bottle nearby for a refill. I fold my arms across my chest. "Really? To you too?"

"Yep." He taps his finger on the counter, seeming distracted as he answers me more fully. "I was the fourth person to join the team. First it was Ozzie, of course; then there was Thibault. Lucky came next, then me. And last there was Toni."

"Is there any particular reason why you all came in at different times?"

"Well, there were reasons, but they're not important. My point is that when you first join the team, it can be really overwhelming." He looks up at me, the joy he has for his work shining out from his eyes. "It's totally different from any other kind of job; we're like a family more than just work colleagues. I mean Ozzie, Thibault, and

Toni grew up together, since they were practically babies, so they know each other inside and out. Lucky met them when they were just in grade school. When a group like that asks you to come be a part of what they're doing, and they're doing this thing that's really different and exciting, and sometimes a little dangerous, it kind of takes up all your head space for a while. But then your duties get mostly evened out, and you all figure out what you're going to be doing each day, and then it becomes pretty much like a regular job."

"Except for the fact that you have to worry about people shooting at you."

He smiles. "That's a bit of an exaggeration. We're not police officers out on the streets dealing with criminals. We're mostly working behind the scenes."

"Then why is someone trying to break into your warehouse?"

He shrugs. "We're not even sure somebody *was* trying to do that. It could have been someone trying to break into a random warehouse because they thought something valuable might be inside, and not necessarily something aimed at us. Crime at the port is kind of a given. And like I said before, I was just being extra careful with you because you're not part of the team; you're a civilian, and you're May's sister. She'd kill me if anything happened to you while I was supposed to be watching out for you."

I laugh. "And you're afraid of my sister?"

He holds up a hand. "Hey. Don't laugh. And do me a favor . . . don't underestimate your sister like I did."

He's serious, and I'm definitely intrigued. "I sense there's a really good story here."

He lifts an eyebrow. "You got a couple hours? Because I have some stories for you. Things you won't believe."

I shrug, feeling more awake and less interested in getting tipsy than I was before, but not wanting to seem overeager. He did lock me in a panic room today, after all. "Well . . . I was going to take a bath, but I decided that it was a bad idea and took a nap instead. So now I'm never going to get to sleep on time. I guess you might as well stay for a little while and share some of those stories with me."

Dev's eyes go to my refrigerator. "You got anything to eat in there?"

I look at the fridge and then at him. "We just ate, like, two giant bowls of jambalaya each a few hours ago. How can you possibly be hungry again?"

"Have you seen this?" He gestures from his toes to the top of his head. "It takes a lot of calories to keep this machine running in top condition."

I laugh, feeling my cheeks go a little pink in embarrassment. I have noticed that his body is in top condition; that's what's making it so difficult being in the kitchen with him and feeling comfortable about it. I need to move this party into the family room, where we can have more space between us.

I nod. "Okay, yeah, I get it. Unfortunately, I cleaned out my fridge last weekend, so there really isn't much in there." I won't mention that my pay and Miles's sporadic child support doesn't leave a lot left over for extra snacks. My mortgage is ridiculously expensive.

He pulls out a cell phone. "Do you mind if I order a couple pizzas?"

I'm a little surprised that he seems to think he's going to camp out here long enough to have a meal, but then I figure, *What the hell; it's not like I'm going anywhere.* I wave at his phone. "Go ahead. Knock yourself out."

I grab our wineglasses and secure the bottle under my arm. "Come on. Let's go in the family room, where we'll be more comfortable."

"Good idea. I'm right behind you."

Leaving the kitchen, I head out into the hallway. An image flashes out of the corner of my eye, and I hesitate. My head swivels to the right to see what it is, and I catch my reflection in the hallway mirror. *Holy shit.* I look like Death warmed over.

"Oh, my freaking *god*." I whisper. *I'm still sporting the zombie look! Holy crap! My hair! My face! How embarrassing!*

I turn to look at Dev over my shoulder, trying to figure out from his facial expression if he noticed. He gave me no signs at all in the kitchen that he did, which is completely and totally weird. *Does he think this is my normal look? That I did this to myself on purpose?* He's still on his cell, probably trying to find the phone number of the pizza place.

I rush down the hall and into the family room. I slam the bottle down on the coffee table, almost dropping it on the floor in my hurry to release it. The glasses go down next, and then I'm standing straight, but turned away from him as he enters the room. I pretend my curtains need a serious looking-over.

"I'm just going to run upstairs for a minute," I say, sidestepping toward the hallway with my back to him. "And put on some clean clothes."

"You don't have to change on my account."

I try to laugh, but it comes out too shrill to sound natural. "Ha, ha! No! That's okay! It's no big deal. I get smelly when I sleep, and I had that nap . . ." *Oh, Jesus Christ, did I just say that out loud? What is wrong with me?*

He laughs. "Did you say 'smelly'?"

"Oh, shut up." I run out of the room and up the stairs, pounding every last one of them on the way. It sounds like a herd of elephants has been let loose in the house.

"You like pepperoni?" he shouts out behind me.

"Yeah! Whatever!"

I rush into my room and go about fixing the horror show that is my face and hair, throwing on a fresh pair of jeans and a newish top too. As I stand in front of my bathroom mirror and use two tablespoons of toothpaste to try and vanquish my horrible jamba-laya breath, I make my plan.

Don't worry, Jenny, you can do this. You can make him forget what he witnessed before. Just distract him with witty repartee and amazing facts you've learned from watching a hundred hours of Animal Planet with the kids, and he'll forget that you looked like the bride of Franken-stein when he first got here.

Yeah. Nothing will go wrong with this plan. It's totally solid.

CHAPTER TEN

After taking and releasing a few deep breaths at the top of the stairs, I walk down very calmly. My hair looks decent, I've got enough makeup on to cover the worst of my flaws, and I've used half a tube of toothpaste. My tooth enamel may be in trouble now, but I'm determined to erase Dev's most recent memory of me looking and smelling like a zombie who had just finished eating someone's brain. Now that I've had my super-speedy makeover, I'm ready to face the man who makes my heart go pitter-patter, and I will not freak myself out by imagining that this is a date.

The smell of pepperoni hits me as I reach the last stair. "You already got the pizzas?"

Dev is sitting on the couch with three pizza boxes stacked up in front of him. He grins at me as I enter the room. "Yep."

"You'll have to give me the name of the place where you ordered from. I can never get anyone here in less than thirty minutes."

Dev looks at his watch. "You've been gone for forty-five."

I look at my wrist and frown. "Nooo . . . All I did was change my clothes."

He lifts up the lid on one of the boxes of pizza. "Whatever you say."

I stand there in the middle of my family room, trying to decide if I should keep fighting this losing battle, or just admit defeat. He doesn't seem bothered by the fact that I put in a little effort. He's lifting out a slice of pizza, his mouth already partly open in expectation of shoving it in.

"What would you like to drink?" I ask, giving up on the charade. *It's just common courtesy not to have someone over for pizza looking like a Yoda bat, right?*

He pauses with the tip of his pizza triangle at the edge of his mouth, tilting his head toward the kitchen. "I also bought a couple liters of soda that I put in the other room. Help yourself."

"Would you like some?"

"Sure. I'll have some wine, too." He winks at me. "Going to get my drink on."

I try not to smile. "Don't you have to drive?"

He folds the pizza long-ways, eating half of it in one bite as he shrugs. Now his mouth is too full to respond.

I shrug as I turn toward the kitchen. He doesn't seem worried about it, so I'm not going to fret. If I think he's had too much to drink, I'll call him a cab. But the fact that he's seven feet tall and he's about to eat three pizzas tells me I probably don't have to be concerned about his blood-alcohol level. He'd probably have to drink that entire bottle of wine for it to affect his ability to drive.

I make quick work of getting two icy glasses of soda and a second bottle of wine, bringing them out to the family room so that I can sit down and watch him ingest more food than I previously thought humanly possible. Putting the glasses down on the table next to the pizza boxes, I choose a spot two cushions away from my guest. Any closer and I'd be making a move on him.

He flips up a box top for me. Two other pieces are already missing. The man has eaten three pieces of pizza in less than five minutes. *Impressive.* I love cooking for people who like to eat. The idea of inviting him for dinner sometime jumps into my head, but I quash it immediately. No need to get ahead of myself. Besides, he's a Bourbon Street Boob.

"Help yourself," he says. "It's pretty good, actually."

I was thinking I was going to say no when he offered, but when the scents of the melted mozzarella and the delicious, greasy pepperoni hit me, I can't do it. "Okay. But just one."

"It's been hours since we ate last. You should be hungry again. Have two or three." He pauses and turns to look at me, waiting for my answer.

I reach into the box and gingerly pull a slice out. "I think I'd better stick with one. I have a bit of a love affair with carbs, but carbs don't particularly love me, so I try to avoid them when I can."

"I think I'd fall into the deepest depression known to man if I couldn't enjoy my carbs," Dev says. He folds his crust and puts the entire thing in his mouth. His cheeks bulge out as he chews.

After seeing that, I'm not nearly as worried about being lady-like as I was two seconds ago. I don't think he's one to appreciate or expect someone to eat like they're at a tea party with the president's wife. I shrug, feeling more comfortable in his presence. "I'm sure with the workout schedule you have, you could eat as many carbs as you wanted and they'd all just burn off the minute they hit your stomach."

He nods. "Probably."

"Have you always been in shape?" I take a bite of my pizza to stop myself from saying anything else. What I've already said is bad enough. I might as well have just come right out and told him he has a great body.

"I've always played sports. That makes it easier to stay fit. But I didn't actually start working out with weights and doing other kinds of training until I suffered a really bad injury and had to go through rehab. That kind of got me interested in the whole aspect

ELLE CASEY

of building up my body to make it a more efficient machine for what it needs to do."

I chew slowly, trying to figure out if I've noticed any signs of a former injury in anything that he's done. I haven't seen a limp or any stiffness in his movements that I can recall. "How long ago was your injury?"

"It happened when I was eighteen. Motorcycle accident."

I take another bite of my pizza and a sip of soda, hoping he'll elaborate and not force me to start another interrogation.

"Ever since the accident, I've focused on keeping myself strong, so if I'm ever in a bad situation again, I can handle myself and have a shorter recovery."

"I guess that comes in handy in your line of work."

"For me, it doesn't matter so much. But for the others, sure. It helps a lot."

"What do you mean, it doesn't really matter for you? Why are you different from anyone else?"

He doesn't look very happy with his answer. "Well, first of all, I'm not really good for use out in the field, and second of all, I have other things going on that make it difficult for me to participate like everyone else does."

"Is it because of your injury? Is that why you can't participate?"

He shakes his head as he reaches into a pizza box, separating crusts so that he can grab another piece. This time he pulls out two pieces and flips one on top of the other, making a pizza sandwich. He takes a large bite and chews it for a while before answering.

"No, actually, that has nothing to do with it. My height is the problem. Once people get a bead on me, their eyes don't pass over; they just stare. And then they don't forget me after. Even if they never talk to me or find out what my name is, they always remember that guy who they were absolutely sure must be some sort of famous basketball player who they saw at the store or the mall or the gas station or whatever. I just can't move through life without being noticed, and that's not a real asset when it comes to security work."

"I would think that *would* be a real asset with security work. It's very intimidating. What could make a person feel more secure than having a big giant of a man standing there?"

He pauses. "Do I intimidate you?" He sounds sad about that.

I immediately feel bad. "No, no, no. That's not what I meant. I mean, before I got to know you, you might have been a little bit intimidating, but now that I know you, you're not intimidating at all."

He smiles. "I'm pretty sure that was supposed to make me feel better."

I lean over and shove his shoulder. "Stop. You're making me feel bad. You know what I meant."

He's a good sport and tips over, making it look like my shove actually had an effect on him. He's smiling. "Yeah, yeah. Whatever you say."

My face is getting warm again. I could keep messing around with him and turn this into a serious flirting session, but I don't want to make him uncomfortable. I know he's just being a nice guy like he is with everyone. My sister May really likes him, and now I can see why. He's more than just a little bit adorable.

I search for a way to get back on track and away from this schoolgirl silliness that wants to overtake me. "You said that there were two reasons why you couldn't really participate. What's the second reason?"

He chews his food, his eyes roaming around the table, the room, and then over the boxes. He takes a moment to poke pepperonis falling from his pizza sandwich back inside. "I have responsibilities at home that are a little more involved than the other guys on the team."

"Do any of them have kids?"

He shakes his head. "None of them are married either."

"But you're not married, right?" My heart squeezes in my chest a little as I wait for his answer. I don't see a wedding ring on his finger, and he told me that his son's mother left right after he was born, but that doesn't necessarily mean he isn't with someone. I guess I just assumed he wasn't. I hope I'm not wrong about that. *Not that this is a date.*

"No, I'm not married. But having a young son is a lot of work." He shrugs his shoulders, and there's a hint of melancholy there.

I nod deeply, because I feel his pain. I feel it, I live it, and I breathe it. "I hear you. It's like your work is never done. You work all day, and then you come home and there's more work waiting for you. Even when the kids are sleeping, it still feels like it's never going to end. I work until I collapse, every single night."

He looks up at me. "I know, right?" He puts his pizza down and brushes his hands off over the box, then reaches over and grabs his soda and leans back on the couch, throwing his free arm over the cushions. He lifts his leg and rests his ankle on his opposite knee. "My son can be sound asleep, and I'll be in my bed down the hall, and I swear, I hear when his breathing changes just the tiniest bit."

I bounce up and down on the couch a little, excited to be talking to another parent about something I know only too well. "Same for me! It's crazy. If I hear anything that sounds out of the ordinary, I spring up out of bed because I have to go check to see what it is. I don't know what I'm expecting; it's not like some kidnapper is going to crawl into my kid's window on the second floor and snag her. Of course, I get there and find out it was just a change in her breathing pattern or whatever, or one of my son's action figures has fallen out of his bed onto the floor."

He laughs. "I check the locks on my son's window twice before I go to bed. Every night. I'm so paranoid somebody's going to try to get in there or he's going to fall out."

It feels so good to be sharing mutual parental paranoia with another person. "Ha! And here I thought I was the only one with OCD tendencies where my kids are concerned."

He shakes his head. "Nope. You're not alone. Trust me."

Neither of us says anything for a long time after that. The silence should probably be awkward, but it's not. I'm just enjoying being in the same room with somebody who hears the whack-a-doodle things that I do and doesn't think I'm whack-a-doodle for doing them.

"We should get our kids together someday." I smile at him. "Our sons would probably bring the walls down and have a ball doing it."

Dev's reaction is not at all what I expect. Instead of nodding and smiling and saying that might be a lot of fun, his face falls and he turns back around to face the pizza boxes. Both of his feet go to the floor and he leans forward, putting his forearms on his knees. After about five seconds he leans over farther, flips up the top on another pizza box, and grabs another piece of pizza. "Yeah. Maybe. Someday."

It's like a knife has been shoved into my chest. Did I totally mis-read the situation? Did I overstep my boundaries somehow? Does he hate my kids without even meeting them? I replay the moment in my head, along with the moments before, trying to find out where I slipped up, but none of it makes sense. I don't think I said anything rude. Is it just that he doesn't want to get to know me any better? If that's the case, what is he doing here having pizza and wine in my family room?

Instead of asking more questions and risking saying something even worse, I focus on finishing my crust. I keep my cup in front of my face, taking a sip after each bite in an effort to hide my expression. I'm afraid that too many of my feelings are showing.

"It's too bad that you can't do that freelance work for the team," he says.

I blink a few times, realizing that he's changing the subject and putting us back on the footing of being potential future coworkers. I don't think a cold shower could've been more effective at calming whatever ardor might have been growing in my heart for him.

I put my cup and the pizza crust down on the table and stand. Brushing my hands off on my pants I look down at him. "You know what? I just realized I have a lot of work I need to get done."

He looks up at me, his chewing slowing. He frowns a little but doesn't answer right away.

I take a step toward my home office. "I'm just going to hook up my laptop while you gather your stuff together." I gesture at the pizza boxes.

He nods. "Yeah, sure. Go ahead. Don't mind me."

I walk away toward the kitchen to retrieve my laptop, sad that something fell apart and I have no idea what the cause was, but glad to be getting back on regular footing again. Having a man in my house, sharing a meal with a cute guy . . . this is all too strange for me. I'm ready to get back to my normal, boring, lonely life, where my kids go away on rare weekends with their father and I catch up on work at home. I'm not even in the mood to pop popcorn and watch a chick flick anymore. *This sucks.*

CHAPTER ELEVEN

I take my laptop into my home office, forcing myself not to glance at Dev still sitting in the family room as I walk by. I'm hoping he'll take the hint, pack up his stuff, and leave. There've been too many awkward moments between us, and I'm worried that the longer he stays, the more I'm going to continue trying to find ulterior motives on his part for being here.

It's a simple enough task to put my laptop down on the desk and plug in the cords that are waiting. I bring up the Internet and stare at a blank page. The search engine window is calling out to me, asking me what I want to do, where I want to go, and what I want to look for.

I'm trying to ignore the rustling sounds I hear in the other room, assuming it's Dev getting the pizzas together so he can take them home. I should be happy that he's following my instructions to leave, but I'm not. He's such a nice guy, and he seems like a dedicated dad. Maybe even a good dad, a rare beast in my world. Like the amur leopard. One day I will do the dating thing again. It's not going to happen with him, obviously, but it will happen. I don't plan on dying an old maid.

The search window is staring at me. *I could go on one of those dating websites. Check it out . . .*

The minute the thought flows through my head, I can feel my face starting to burn. No, that would be silly. I'm not dating material right now. I'm too newly divorced. Too . . . mothery.

Instead, I go on one of the freelance sites I've heard about from my coworkers. Apparently I can put up a profile that lists all my skills, and anybody looking for a freelancer like me could find me.

I go to the website for a look but all it does is depress me. I already have so much stuff I have to get done at my current company, I can hardly keep up. Sammy was sick last week, and I missed an entire day of work because the daycare wouldn't take him, so now I have to do all the things that I missed in half the time. They run a very short-staffed operation there, so there's no hope of anyone helping me out.

Nope, I can't take more work onto my shoulders. My kids would never see me. Not that they'd mind, probably, because while the cat is away the mice definitely play in this house. The last time I left them to their own devices and tried to do some work at home, the girls covered Sammy in greasy diaper rash ointment and then topped it off with talcum powder. They said they wanted to make him look like a ghost to practice their Halloween costumes. He looked like a ghost for the entire two hours it took me to wash it all off of him. That stuff sticks like nobody's business, and its base is fish oil, so our bathroom and a couple of our towels still smell like anchovies.

I'm always torn when I catch the kids doing things like this. I can't decide if it's sibling love and the girls inviting Sammy to be a part of their games, or sibling torture with him as the easiest victim. I've fallen back on the theory that if it were the more vicious type of play, Sammy would let me know, and he never seems to mind, so I don't get too upset about it. Besides, they *did* do a really fantastic job of covering every square inch of his skin. If he decides he wants to go out on Halloween as a ghost, I've got the costume part covered.

That's a whole other thing I have to deal with. Halloween is just weeks away, and the kids are already harassing me about costumes. I jump on my keyboard and do a quick search on Amazon for potential ideas. There are at least fifty pages of options, so I close the window down and take a breath. Maybe I could get them to go as the Three Stooges. It would fit my life pretty perfectly. I write on a little notepad next to my computer to remind myself to ask the kids what they want to be so I can get the costumes in time.

I put the pen down and, once again, find myself staring at my search engine window. *Where do I want to go from here?*

A door opens and closes somewhere out beyond my office, interrupting my train of thought. I'm sad that Dev is gone, but I can hardly complain, since I'm the one who asked him to leave. I totally and completely suck at interacting with the opposite sex.

I bite my lip as I stare at the computer. It's nuts that a near stranger leaving my house makes me so sad. *Crazy. I seriously need to get a life.*

It's that thought that sparks my inspiration. I *could* go on a dating website. It doesn't mean that I'm actually going to look for a date. Browsing is not the same as being desperate for a man. *I could just see what's out there, right?*

I do a quick search and click on the first service that pops up. I assume if they're on the top of the search results, they're either spending a lot of money to be there or they're really popular. That means there will be a lot more candidates to choose from, and having a greater pool of candidates sounds like a good idea. I click the mouse around the site, trying to get to the meat market area. *Time for Momma to go shopping for some prime beef. Wakka wakka.*

Unfortunately, it won't let me search for anyone unless I have a profile started. Knowing what I know about marketing and getting website users to engage, I'm not surprised. They want you to stick around, and in order to do that, they ask for a little commitment.

I shrug. *What the heck? What's the big deal?* I can just put up a little profile. No harm in that. I don't have to make it public so people can see it. I'll just use it to do a little surfing.

I start the process by giving my name. They promise to only reveal the first initial of my last name. *W.* Then I get to the part where they ask for a credit card. I'm wary about putting my financial details anywhere online, because being a computer engineer puts me in the perfect position to know how easily that information can be accessed by the wrong people.

I could take the time to test the vulnerabilities of this site to hackers, but why bother? I have my own less-intrusive and less-illegal way of handling those turds. I'm using my special credit card—the one that has a minuscule credit limit, the one I use for all of my online purchases. If somebody gets the details of this card, they're not going to get very far. They might enjoy a night out on the town at the dollar movie theater with a box of popcorn and a Coke if they're lucky and I've paid it off recently.

Now that I've entered my information, I have full access. I'm being asked whether I'm looking for a man or woman, whether I'm a man or woman, the age of the person I'm interested in, and whether certain peccadilloes bother me, like smoking or being overweight.

I snort. So many choices. What the heck. I'm used to sizing a guy up with a glance and deciding whether he attracts me or not. I'm not sure there is a profile I could choose on here that would result in a list of men who'd definitely be my cup of tea. *Shouldn't personality figure in here somewhere?*

I don't know what I'm looking for other than, *yes*, a man. I scan my choices. Should I be a cougar? Should I look for somebody young, who wouldn't mind playing with my kids because he's a kid himself? That seems like a bad idea. The last thing I need is another child in my household. How about a guy my age? We could be at the same point in our lives. Maybe he'll have kids like me. That could work. Or it could be complete and utter chaos that pushes me over the edge into insanity. Maybe I should go for an older man. A guy who's already fixed financially. A guy who's been there and done that, who can teach me the ways of the world. A guy who has high blood pressure and an AARP discount.

This whole process is already frustrating. I click over to the part of the site that allows me to put in my own profile, thinking maybe I'll have more luck with that. Several boxes are presented to me, and all I have to do is click on the ones that describe me.

So far so good. I am a woman—*click*—and I am between thirty and thirty-five years old—*click*. Now the computer wants to know if I'm fit, if I'm athletic, or if I've gone a little soft around the middle.

Ack! This is horrible. Soft around the middle? I look down at my waist and then risk pinching the front of my belly. *Egads! Soft? I might as well call myself Pudding Wexler!* Why did I think this would be a good idea?

A noise in the doorway behind me makes me jump. I turn around, shocked to find Dev the giant standing there.

I speak before thinking. "I thought you'd left."

"Oh." He tilts his head in confusion. "Did you tell me to go? I must have missed that."

I have to think about that for a second. "Well . . . I guess I didn't specifically say it, but I did say that I had some work to do." Now I feel terrible that I'm having to explain that I attempted to kick him out and he didn't take the hint.

"Oh. Damn. Heh-heh. Awkward." He reaches up and rubs his bald head.

"No, no, don't worry about it." On top of feeling bad about making him feel so embarrassed, now I'm not even sure I want him to go. "Stay if you want. Just . . . I'm . . . in the middle of something."

He steps farther into the room. "What are you working on? Stuff for your regular job, or freelance work?"

I quickly minimize the dating site window. *How embarrassing!* He totally just caught me on a singles site, and I'm doing it right after having pizza with him. Will he think that he inspired this activity? I wish I were one of those turtles on Animal Planet. I'd pull my head into my shell and not come out until he was gone.

Unfortunately, I'm not a turtle and I have nowhere to go. "No. It's neither of those things." I want to roll my eyes up into my head at how stupid I am. I totally could've just lied and thrown him off the scent, and he would've left me alone. Now I see the light in his eyes that tells me he's not going to just let this go.

"Why are you so embarrassed?"

I breathe out a long sigh of defeat. He's smiling. *Does he know how powerful that dimple is?*

"Okay, fine. If you must know, I was on a dating website." I look away, tapping the shift key over and over again with my thumb to cover up my embarrassment.

"Cool. Can I read your profile?"

My jaw drops open. *Is he serious? Does he honestly think this is some kind of spectator sport? That I want him to watch me wallow in my loneliness?* "Uh, no. You can't." My face is so pink right now.

Undeterred, he grabs an extra chair and drags it over, placing it next to me. Turning it around, he straddles it and sits down, his arms resting on the top of the seat back. "Which site is it?"

I don't say anything. I just open up the window and gesture at it.

"Oh, I'm on that one," he says matter-of-factly.

"You are?"

"Yeah. Why? Does that sound so crazy to you?"

"I have no idea, actually. I guess I didn't picture you as the type."

He's smiling, apparently enjoying my discomfort. "What's the type?"

I try to smile but it comes out more like a grimace. "Desperate?"

He frowns at me, reminding me of a teacher I once had who was really good at scolding students with a mere furrowing of the brows. "If desperation is what brings people to dating sites, there are an awful lot of desperate people out there."

"There are. Look at this." I click on a few buttons to give him some statistics that are right there on the website for everyone to read. "Did you see this? They have over a million users."

"Sure. That's no surprise. There are a lot of single people out there. It's a big world we live in."

I turn to face him, even though he's really close. "So, you don't think it's a desperate move to join a dating website?"

"No. No way. I think these sites are made up mostly of single people who don't like going out to bars and who maybe have kids or jobs that keep them from going to parties and other places where they might meet single people. What else are they going to do? Go to the grocery store and scope people out in the produce department?"

I like the way he's described the people who are on the site. People like me. Now I don't feel quite as dorky as I did before. "It is really hard to meet people, especially when you have kids."

"Tell me about it . . ." It seems like he has more to say on the subject, but then he just stops and looks away.

"So you're on the site, huh?" A devious idea pops into my mind. I start clicking with the mouse.

He leans over. "No, no, no-no-no." He tries to grab the mouse out of my hand, but I put my arm up to block him.

"Stay away. Nobody touches my mouse."

"You're not going onto my profile, are you?"

"Of course I am." I can't keep the smile out of my voice. "I want to see how you've described yourself."

He's laughing and moaning at the same time. "Oh, God, why would you do that to me?"

"Because. I'm having a hard time figuring out how to do my profile. Maybe if I look at yours, it'll inspire me."

He laughs. "Other than both of us having kids, I cannot imagine that you'll find any similarities between the two of us."

I know he didn't mean to be rude, but it makes me sad to hear him say that. I thought we were more compatible than that.

I shrug. "Maybe."

"We *do* have the same sense of humor, though," he says.

"Well, I think you're funny."

"Thanks."

"Funny looking." I giggle. This is a joke I learned from my children.

He puts his hand over his heart. "Oh, man, that was cold."

I reach out and put my hand on his arm and pat it. "Just kidding." I take my hand back and click on some more areas on the site. "Sorry, but my sense of humor is at third-grade level right now."

"Okay, I've got one for you." He leans in and stares at me. "What's the worst part about eating a vegetable?"

I think about it for a few seconds, and unable to come up with something that might sound clever, I give in. "I don't know."

"The wheelchair." He winks at me.

My hand goes up to my mouth. I can't believe he just said that. "Oh my god. That was so bad."

He leans back a little, holding on to the top of the chair. "Yeah, it's handicap humor. My son is an expert."

That strikes me as both really wrong and totally not PC. But I can't imagine Dev is the kind of parent to joke about handicapped people with his young, impressionable son. "Is it some kind of stage he's going through?"

"You could say that." He doesn't elaborate, and I don't want to ask any more questions about it. I don't want him to think I'm judging his parenting, even though at this point I'm finding it a little weird.

I turn my attention back to the computer where I'm entering the search criteria to try to find Dev's profile.

"It's not like I put my real name on there as my username," he says. "Like you said, there are over a million users of the site. You're never gonna find me."

"Don't be so sure," I say. "All I have to do is describe you, and it should bring up your profile in the results."

"You think you know me that well already?" He's definitely throwing out a challenge.

"We'll see." I smile as I click away.

CHAPTER TWELVE

My fingers hover over the keyboard.

"Let's see . . . if I wanted to hook up with a guy like Dev, what characteristics would I be looking for?" It feels safe to say this, like I'm a hypothetical girl scoping him out, not myself. It's stealth flirting. I'm totally a black heron, tricking my prey into thinking it's nighttime with my wings spread open above the water, convincing the little fishies that it's safe to come out and play. *Gotcha, little minnow!*

"Be careful, girl."

I forge on, heedless of Dev's warning. I think it's actually spurring me on. "First of all, I have to select the correct age. I'm going to go ahead and select . . . between thirty-five and forty." My fingers hesitate for only a moment before clicking the box. I'm pretty sure that's what he said to me in the panic room.

"You're a man. That's easy. And I assume you are looking for a woman?" I look at Dev for confirmation. All he does is shrug, but that dimple appearing on his cheek tells me that I am right once again.

"Let's see . . . you are a non-smoker." I click another button. "And I would say that you are *very* athletic." Another click. "And you believe in a healthy lifestyle, so you're probably just a moderate drinker."

"Don't get cocky."

I laugh. "Oh, I've only just begun, believe me." I pause to peruse my options. "Aaaand moving on . . . let's see. Hobbies . . ." There are several for me to choose from, and even though we've just met, I can already see several that apply. I click in rapid succession. "Sports. Weightlifting. Exercise. Martial arts."

"Martial arts? Why did you choose that?"

I turn and look at him so he can see me roll my eyes. "It would've been really difficult for me to miss all fifty of those ninja swords in that room, don't ya think?"

"Who says they're mine? It's Ozzie's place."

"Yeah, but he doesn't strike me as the sword type. Besides, my sister said something about you being a ninja guy once, so I figured they had to be yours."

"Points for having excellent powers of observation."

I get a little giddy with pride as I turn back to the computer. "Exactly." I wiggle my mouse to wake it up. "Okay, so where was I? Yes, I'm about to narrow down my choices even further." I click a few more boxes. "Family-oriented. Prefers smaller group activities to large crowds." That one I'm not so sure about, but I don't want him to know that I'm not confident, so I just keep going.

"Not into religious activities, enjoys other people's cooking but doesn't cook, does not have one favorite type of food." *Click, click, click.* I turn my head to look at him. "How am I doing so far?"

He shrugs. "We'll see."

He doesn't sound nearly as sassy as he did before, so I must be on the right track. There are a few more choices left, and I consider them carefully. I have engineered sites with huge data sets before, so I know how search results are tallied and collected. This system doesn't look too complicated. It's just a matter of me getting close enough, and the right combination of correct inputs will bring up the results I'm looking for.

"Seeking . . ." Now's my chance to describe the woman who I think Dev is looking for. This part is a little more complicated, but I think I can do it. What I'm going to do is describe the woman who I think would best suit him. He seems like a pretty self-aware guy. My guess is he's looking for someone who would be a good match. He's not one of those guys who's searching for a woman who's completely inappropriate.

"Okay, you are seeking a woman who is between the ages of thirty and forty. I suppose you would prefer that she be athletic and fit, but I think you'd be willing to take someone who's not really there yet, because you enjoy working out so much that it would be something you'd want to share with somebody and help them discover."

"Very nice." I can see him nodding out of the corner of my eye.

Encouraged, I continue. "You are interested in someone who likes small group activities versus large group activities. You are also okay with a woman who has children. And you're looking for someone who likes the outdoors, who likes sports, and who has a good sense of humor."

There are several other criteria I could select at this point, but I don't want to go too far and accidentally exclude him. I think I'm doing pretty well with what I have. The final thing I need to do is select a geographic region.

"Where do you live?" I ask.

"Oh, no, no, no. You have to find me on there. On the site. You have to describe me to find me."

"Yeah, but where you live has nothing to do with you as a person, as a candidate for a dating site."

"On the contrary. Where a person lives says a lot about them."

I shrug. "Fine." I click on the geographical region that puts him within fifty miles of the warehouse. *Done.* "Okay, then, we're all set. You ready to go?"

"I was born ready."

I click the Search button, feeling silly that my pulse is racing a little. There's a little heart icon spinning on the screen, telling us that the results are being gathered. It's taking a lot longer than I expected it would, but this is encouraging. I think it means that the list is going to be short.

I turn to look at him. "You know you could just give up now. Admit defeat."

He laughs. "I could say the same for you. It's not too late. The results aren't in yet."

I shake my head. "Huh-uh, forget it. I am *so* going to win this."

The heart icon finally stops spinning and a new window pops up with a list of candidate profiles. Each one is a single line with a quote from the beginning of their personal statements. There are no pictures and no real names, just usernames.

"Oh, ho ho!" I say. "A new level of challenge to the game." I scan down the list, seeing if anything jumps out at me. There are two that look particularly promising, but because it's such a small snippet of what the person has put about himself, there's no way for me to be sure until I click on the links and read more.

I look at Dev again. "Care to raise the stakes?"

"What *were* the stakes exactly?"

I have to think about that for a second. *Did we have stakes?* I can't even remember what got us in front of this computer together now. "Actually, I have no idea."

"Dinner?"

I'm confused by his response. "The pizza? You already paid for it."

"No, not the pizza. Another dinner. Winner gets treated, loser pays."

I nod. Now we're playing for realsies. And this is something I can actually enjoy. I mean winning is awesome, but winning a meal with a hot guy is better, even if it's just a friend thing. "You're on. So, what're the rules?"

He shrugs. "You tell me."

I like that I get to be the one to decide how we play the game. With great power comes great responsibility; I learned that from Spider-Man. "Okay, so we have a list of candidates here, and I suspect that of the people on this list, you are one."

I wait for his response, but he's like a world-class poker player the way he has zero expression on his face. *Dammit.*

I continue. "I will keep it like this where I can't see any photographs, and using just these simple one-liners I will select my top three choices. These will be the three people who I believe could be you."

"I thought you were supposed to pick me right off the bat."

I hold up a finger. "Let me finish. Right now all I can see is a single sentence, which isn't much to go on. So I will click the Read More links on only three of the candidates, and I won't look at the photos. And after I have read the details on those three candidates, I will tell you which one is you."

"How can I keep you from looking at the photographs?"

I scan the site really quick and point at the screen. "Look. You can choose to browse without photos. That way, there'll be no cheating."

"I can deal with that." He looks very happy with himself.

We'll see who's smiling when this is all over. "Ready to go?"

His grin is so big, I'm suddenly very suspicious. "Oh, yeah, no doubt," he says. "Let's go. I'm definitely ready to have a delicious *free* meal. Did I mention I have a big appetite?"

The deal has been struck and the challenge laid down. Unfortunately for him, it will be me enjoying a delicious dinner paid for by him, not the other way around. *Ha!*

I scroll through the twenty-four choices I've been given, making sure to de-select the photo option. Most of the profiles' one-liners are too corny to have been written by Dev; at least thirty percent of them mention how they like long walks on the beach or reading poetry. *Bleck*. Dev is way more original than that.

There are actually five double-click possibilities. I chew my lip as I try to decide which three are more likely. I finally eliminate two when I see that they lack the more unique romantic vibe that I think Dev might have inside him. He could have left me in the dust at the warehouse, but his first priority was convincing me to let him play savior. That's knight-in-shining-armor material right there.

I'm now left with three candidates. The first ad's one-liner says: '*Still looking for my favorite person.*' The second ad says: '*I believe in love at first sight.*' And the third ad says: '*Take my hand, and we'll wander off somewhere together.*' I delete all but those three candidates from the screen and swivel my chair sideways to face Dev. "Okay, I'm almost there. One of these is you."

"You think so?"

A sliver of doubt slides through me when I see the look on his face. But I ignore it, because I know I can't lose in this game. Either he pays or I do, but we're going out to dinner together.

I turn so my back is to my computer. "Go ahead and click on the first one and make sure there're no profile pictures showing. I don't want to see a picture of your face and be accused of cheating."

He picks up his chair and moves it closer to the desk. "You mean you don't want to see a photograph of some dude that's not me."

"Whatever."

I put my hands over my eyes and inhale when he leans in close to me. I can smell his laundry soap, or maybe his cologne. It's very sexy, and way too tempting. I make myself stop breathing so that I don't get mesmerized and say something stupid. The sound of my mouse clicking comes, and then the smell of Dev disappears. I can breathe again, but it's not nearly as much fun.

"Okay. You're on the Read More page and there's no photograph."

I open my eyes and move my hands away so that I can turn around and read what's on the computer screen. There's a long paragraph written by a mystery man who's looking for love. He's describing the perfect date. It could be Dev, but then again, I'm not sure. I need to withhold my decision until I've read them all.

After I've absorbed everything there, I turn and cover my eyes again. Dev does his part of the deal by selecting the next profile and verifying there's no photo. He probably doesn't need to do that anymore, but I love having him move in close.

I turn around at his signal and quickly scan the page, knowing within seconds that this one is not him. "You can delete this one. This one isn't you."

"Are you sure?"

"Yes. Don't try to throw me off the scent. I'm sure."

"Okay," he says. "If you say so."

The third and final candidate is now on my screen with a big question mark where his profile photo would be if I hadn't de-selected that option. This one and the first one are so close, I almost can't tell them apart.

"This is really tough."

"Why do you say that?"

"Because. These two guys are like the same person."

"I don't see it." He leans in and squints at the screen like he's trying to glean a deeper meaning from it just by getting closer.

I point at the second paragraph. "Look. Both of them say that they are looking for a woman with an adventurous spirit and a certain *je ne sais quoi*." I snort. "Who says that?"

"We live in New Orleans," he says. "You can expect to see a little fancy French once in a while."

"Not from a guy. Not like this."

He turns to face me. "You're trying to get out of our bet, aren't you?"

"No, I'm not. I just have to figure out which one of these is you, that's all. And I'm just saying . . . it's weird that they're so similar." I look at him sideways. "Do you have a twin brother you haven't told me about?"

"Not that I'm aware of."

I shake my head slowly at him. "You're messing with me. I know I'm right."

He laughs. "You seem awfully confident that even one of them is me. I think you'd better consider surrendering before you commit any further to your failure."

I shrug and go back to the computer, feeling sad all of a sudden. "I'm not really the surrendering type." It's why I stayed with my ex for so long. I should have gotten out after Sophie was born, but I stuck with it. It's not all bad, though; I have two more angels under my wing.

His voice softens. "Well, that's something to be proud of." He's not mocking me, even though he probably should be. I have no idea why that lame statement popped out of my mouth. Am I looking to throw a pity party or something? *Gah. Talk about a cold shower.*

He clears his throat as if he's about to say something else that will embarrass me even more, but I stop him by speaking up.

"Okay, pay attention now. I'm about to make my decision."

He starts strumming his two forefingers on the desk, enhancing it with sound effects from his mouth. "Duh, duh, duh, duh, duh, duh, duuhhh . . . and the winner is . . . ?"

I click on the last one, opening the profile up completely again. "This is you, Dev." I slide the mouse over to click on the link that will reveal the photograph, but Dev's hand on my wrist stops me before I get there.

"Before you do that, tell me why you didn't pick the first one."

My wrist is getting tingles where he's touching it, and I suddenly feel very warm all over. When I turn to look at him, his face seems like it's just inches away. My breath comes out kind of whispery. "Because the other guy seemed sad or something, and I don't see you as a sad person. Besides, I have to assume your son is your favorite person, so . . ."

He pulls his hand away and backs up, his expression blank—a mystery.

I click the link on the third ad and find a stranger's face staring back at me. My face falls. "Oh, poo. I really thought I had you."

He leans over and takes control of my mouse. "You almost did." He closes down this profile and opens up the first one, which I rejected for being too sad. The first thing I see after he clicks on the link is Dev's face.

My heart sinks. "Oh. Shit." I turn to look at him. "Dev, I'm sorry." Not only did I call him sad, but I also basically just told him he's a crap father. Why didn't I think before I opened my big mouth? Of *course* he wasn't including kids in the "favorite person" question. Not on a dating website!

He stands. "No big deal. Don't feel bad. Unless you're worried about buying me dinner."

I look up at him, incredibly relieved that he's not holding my careless words against me. "Worried? Why would I be worried?"

He smiles and shrugs. "Not everybody's a good winner. I've met a lot more sore losers than good winners in my life."

Maybe my assessment wasn't that far off after all. I can see now where the sadness I sensed in that ad is coming from, and

I also know how he was able to hide it so well. He's strong. Not just with those muscles of his but with his heart. He's one of the good guys.

But I don't say any of that out loud. Instead, I try to keep the party rolling. "I'm not a sore loser, Dev. I will buy you dinner wherever you want, and go whenever you want to go."

He claps me on the back of the shoulder. "Great. It's a date." He turns around and walks out of the room.

I'm too stunned by his choice of words to respond right away, but then I realize he's making the sounds of a person leaving. "Where're you going?" I shout at the door.

"Gotta get back home! My mom is waiting for me. She doesn't like to stay up too late."

I stand and smooth down the front of my clothes, sad that he's leaving, but realizing it would be really silly of me to ask him to stay. What would we do? Play Xbox? He called our future dinner a date, but I can't just assume he meant it that way. Besides, he's got baggage. Do I really need more baggage in my life right now? I've got a whole entire truckload of my own to deal with.

I wait for him at the front door. He arrives with nothing in hand. "Don't you want to take your pizzas?"

"What pizzas?"

I lean past him and look into the family room. The three boxes are still there. I point.

He shrugs. "Just empty boxes. I could put them in the recycle bin for you, if you want."

"No, no, don't worry about it." I look from his toes to the top of his head. "I guess it does take a lot of calories to run that machine."

"You know it." He smiles. "So, I'll give you a call about that dinner?"

I nod. "Sure. You can get my number from my sister."

He winks at me. "I already did."

I can't think of what to say that won't make me look and sound like a blushing, stammering schoolgirl, so I just smile. And then I grab the front door and pull it open for him. "Have a nice night."

"You too." He leans down and kisses me on the cheek so fast, I don't even see it coming until it's over.

My hand floats up to my cheek as he walks out onto the porch and down the front stairs to his waiting vehicle. It is the dead ugliest car I've ever seen in my entire life. So ugly it shocks me out of my happy, floaty cloud.

I laugh. "What *is* that thing?"

He turns around and walks backward. "What?"

I point at the banged-up beast in my driveway.

"My car? You're kidding me. You don't know what this is?"

I'm holding my cheek where he kissed me, smiling and shaking my head.

He pulls open the door, a loud creaking noise echoing all over my front yard and into the neighbors' yards too.

"This, my young, naïve woman, is a Pontiac Phoenix. A classic. A real man's car."

I lift my brows as high as they'll go before answering. "If you say so." I slowly shut the door on his offended expression, and then I collapse in giggles in the front hallway. *Damn.* My face hurts, I'm smiling so hard. I haven't felt this good or this young in a really long time.

CHAPTER THIRTEEN

I'm in the kitchen preparing eggs and bacon for the kids' Monday morning breakfast when Sammy comes downstairs crying.

"What's wrong, little man?" I put my spatula down on the counter next to the stovetop and turn to face him, squatting down so I can be at eye level with him.

"My tummy hurtth." Big fat tears slide down his cheeks.

I rub his belly gently. "Are you sure?" I ask him this because he's had a lot of these so-called tummy aches lately, but the doctor hasn't found any medical reason for it. I'm starting to suspect there are issues at the daycare that Sammy's not sharing with me.

"Yeth, I'm thure. And I don't haffa poop tho don't tell me to go thit on the toilet."

I have to hold in my laughter. He looks so offended.

I nod. "I understand. But, you know, it doesn't hurt to sit on the potty for a little while just to be sure."

"I knew you were gonna thay that." He puts his hands on his belly, rolls his eyes, and moans. "Ohhh, it hurtth!"

I let out a long sigh. I'm not even an hour into my day yet, and I'm already screwed. My boss is going to love this one.

"Would you like some eggs and bacon before you lie down?" If this is a false alarm, he'll be tempted.

He shakes his head without hesitation. "No. My tummy really hurtths."

I pick up the spatula and wave it at the entrance to the kitchen. "Okay. Go back to your room or go lie down on the couch in the family room, and I'll bring you some of our special tea."

"Okay, Mommy," he says with the most pitiful voice I've ever heard. "Thank you for taking care of me."

Aaaand my heart melts right there on the kitchen floor . . . This kid knows how to play me like a guitar virtuoso. *Twang twang* . . . and I'm toast.

Sophie wanders into the kitchen next. "What's wrong with him?" my ten-year-old asks, gesturing at the little guy who just shuffled past her like a disinterested zombie, his pajama bottoms so long they tuck under his feet.

"He's not feeling very well this morning."

"Oh, boy, here we go again." Sophie rolls her eyes.

I point at a seat with my spatula. "Sit. And be nice. He can't help it that his stomach hurts."

She drops her voice. "Mom, you know he's totally faking it."

I shake my head. "I don't think so. Not this time, anyway." I push some eggs around, wondering if anyone is going to eat them. They're not looking so great.

She hisses out her disbelief. "Whatever."

I could engage with her, but right now I need to save my energy for the excuse I'm about to make to my boss. He has a way of making me feel desperate and sneaky, even when I'm telling the truth about why I can't come to work. It's not like I'm hungover and blaming it on a little kid's fake stomachache.

Melody comes into the kitchen next, which is completely normal; my almost-eight-year-old is always the last one down the stairs, the last one out the door, and the last one in bed. And right now, she's still half asleep, which is also status quo.

"Good morning, Merry Sunshine," I say in an especially bright voice.

"Morning, Mama," she mumbles. She gets up on the stool in front of the kitchen counter and rests her chin in her hands. A few seconds later her head drops to the side, startling her awake.

I put a big glass of orange juice in front of my very disoriented, sleepy daughter. "Drink this. It'll wake you up."

"Do we have to go to school?" she whines, taking the glass and holding it in front of her while she waits for my answer.

"Yes, you have to go to school. What did you guys do with your dad this weekend, anyway? Why are you all so tired?"

Sophie pipes up, sounding very happy about the information she's delivering. "We got to stay up until one in the morning."

I put my spatula down gently on the counter, trying like crazy to control my temper. I so want to Hulk-out right now.

"Great. Excellent," I say with exaggerated patience. "I suppose you also ingested ten pounds of candy."

Melody perks up. "More like a ton." She is also very happy about her weekend.

Bastard, Miles! I am going to kill you!

"Sammy barfed," Sophie says. "It was disgusting."

Melody's grimacing right along with her sister. "Yeah. It was disgusting. Daddy's girlfriend got really mad."

"I don't like her," Sophie says before I can interrupt. "She's totally stuck-up."

"Sophie! Don't say that!"

Sophie shrugs. "Well, she is."

This is the first I've heard of Miles having an actual girlfriend. I thought he just dated girls who are barely legal, avoiding all forms of actual commitment.

I poke at the eggs. "So, Daddy has a girlfriend, huh?"

"Yeah. But he said not to tell you and that it wasn't any of your business." Sophie seems to delight in delivering this little nugget of information. If I didn't know any better, I'd think she's enjoying getting me worked up.

My grip on the spatula goes very Hulk-like. I flex a few of the muscles in my arms and legs, just for fun. It helps keep my mind off the fact that I want to murder the father of my children right now. How dare he play games with our kids?

"He's right," I say as cheerily as I can. "It's not my business and I don't care."

Melody speaks next. "But if he has a girlfriend, he's never going to come home."

I drop the spatula in the pan, turn off the stovetop, and turn around. "Melody, honey, you need to stop thinking that way. Your daddy and I are never, ever, *ever* getting back together." *Thank you, Taylor Swift, for reminding me that I am not the only woman in the world in this position.*

"Not if he has a girlfriend," she says, pouting.

"No, not if he does and not if he doesn't. It just isn't going to happen."

"But don't you love him?" Melody asks, nearly crying. Both of the girls are staring at me now, waiting for my answer.

How do you tell your children that you've seriously considered running their father over with your car on more than one occasion? That you cannot remember what you ever saw in him? That you think he's a lying scumbag who doesn't deserve to even be their father?

I sigh. There is no way to say these things. You just have to lie or dance around the truth. I always try dancing first . . .

"Babies . . . I love that your daddy gave me the three most beautiful children on the planet. I got very lucky meeting him."

"You're avoiding the question," Sophie, the too-smart-for-her-own-good child, says.

"Who wants eggs?" I ask brightly, not ready to step knee-deep into the lies this morning.

"They stink. I'd rather have pancakes," Melody says, holding her nose closed.

I whip around and start shuffling pans around. "Pancakes it is!" I'm not normally the kind of mom who runs a restaurant with a full menu out of my kitchen, but at this point I'll do anything to avoid a conversation about Miles. "You girls go get dressed, and by the time you're done, the pancakes will be ready."

They slide from their stools and shuffle off to their rooms, grousing at each other the entire way.

Once again, I'm left to deal with the fallout that comes from Miles spending a day and a half with our kids. Sammy's sick from all the sugar, and the girls are suffering the aftereffects of crashing down from a glucose high, manifesting as extreme fatigue and crankiness. I won't be one bit surprised when the nurse calls from school today to tell me my girls need to be picked up.

I reach over as I'm pouring some Aunt Jemima pancake mix into a bowl to grab my phone so I can call my boss. Might as well get it over with.

CHAPTER FOURTEEN

I'm staring at the phone, not quite believing what I just heard.

"What do you mean, I don't need to bother coming in?"

My boss's laugh is decidedly uncomfortable. "What I meant was that we're going to be doing a little restructuring in the coming weeks, and so you being out with your sick kid is kind of good timing for us. For *you*, I mean."

"I don't even know what that means. Good timing?" My blood pressure is going through the roof and there's a weird ringing in my ears. "How can my sick child be good timing for anything or anyone?"

His tone turns cajoling. "Come on, Jenny, you know it's been real tough for us over the past six months. We had a meeting with our investors, and they recommended that we cut a few positions. We had to make some really difficult decisions. Good news is, you'll be one of the lucky ones who gets to have a little bit of a severance package. In the end, you'll have some more time with your family, which is always good, right?"

"Lucky? What? More time with my family? What the . . . Are you *punishing* me because I'm a single mother? I told you, my son is *sick*, Frank. This is not a joke. This is not me calling in because I'm hungover, like I'm sure George has already done this morning."

George is single, like most of the people I work with, and a notorious party animal; he's always the one with the lampshade on his head and his hairy butt on the photocopy machine at the Christmas party. I've seen it. It's not pretty. It could explain why he's still single. A man with that much butt hair should never advertise it so publicly.

"No, this has nothing to do with your status as a single parent or the fact that your son is sick. Jenny, I believe you. I know how it is with kids; they get sick all the time. Remember, I have two of my own."

"Yes, Frank, and you have a wife at home who doesn't work, lucky for you, so none of us have ever actually seen your children interfering in your ability to come to work at six in the morning and leave at ten at night."

He loses the nicey-nice tone to his voice. "Nobody is questioning your dedication to the job, Jenny. You're a fantastic engineer. You know your stuff. That's why I'm not worried about you. You'll find another job right away."

My chest feels really tight. It's all finally sinking in. I'm being fired. *Holy shit, I'm being fired! What am I going to do? How will I pay my bills?*

"How could you possibly know I'll find another job right away?" I ask, on the verge of hysteria. "The economy isn't that great. And you know the startups aren't paying shit right now." *Great. He made me swear.*

"So? Don't go for a startup. Why don't you get a job with the power company or something?"

"Do you want me to jump into the Mississippi, Frank? Because you know that's what I'd do if I had to go someplace like that every day. There could not be a more boring job on the entire planet."

"Okay, then, do some freelance work. I know you've been wanting to try that. The severance will give you a couple months' pay, so you can relax and give it a shot."

I snort in disbelief. "Oh, that severance package had better be more than two months' pay." *He can't be serious. Two months?* The last guy who got laid off got nine. *Nine!*

~ Frank sounds nervous. "Why do you say that?"

"Because. I'll bet if I did a little analysis on the people who are staying and the people who are going, it'll be the people with kids who are being let go. It'll be the single parents and people over thirty first out the door. And don't think I won't cause a fuss about that either. This is unfair. This isn't right. It's illegal to fire people for having kids at home. You're just using this as an excuse to get rid of us and hire young kids fresh out of school for half the pay."

"Okay, Jenny, I can hear that you're upset. And I completely understand, because you weren't expecting this to happen today. I'm sorry to be blindsiding you with it, honestly, I am; but there's nothing I can do. It's out of my hands."

"I'm not going to stand for this." I sound like a big justice-seeker, but both Frank and I know better. I'm no Green Lantern. I have all these threats I'm ready to deliver with gusto, but I know I don't have it in me to follow through. I'm so screwed right now. I'm going to have to sell the house. *Where will we go? Where will we live?* May's townhouse is way too small for all of us, and I'd rather be homeless than move to my mother's place. I can see her for the occasional holiday, but living together would never work. Being with her for too long reminds me of how she kept us in that house with our jerk of a father when a better parent would have left and spared us all a lot of pain. I'll probably never forgive her for that, especially now that I have children of my own. At least I learned one lesson from her: never stay in a relationship that will turn your children into victims.

He sighs. "Well, you could take it up with the investors if you want, but I wouldn't recommend it."

"Why not?" I can already picture myself busting into a conference room where they're no doubt plotting how to hire people and get them to work twenty-four-hour shifts for free. I actually have a cape on in this vision.

"Because. We live in a small world down here. You form a reputation for getting angry at your employers and demanding big severance packages, and word will get around. Nobody's going to want to hire you."

He's trying to scare me into shutting up. I swear I can see my skin turning green, and my pajama pants are getting tighter by the second. "I'm going to hang up the phone now before I say something I'm going to regret."

"Okay. I get it. No hard feelings, Jen. I wish you the best of luck. When do you think you can come in and get your things?"

I grind my teeth for a couple seconds before answering. "Just put my stuff in a box, and I'll come pick it up *when my son isn't sick anymore.*" I slam the phone down on the counter, grab the hair on the sides of my head, squeeze, and scream.

I hear shuffling feet, and then my son appears from around the corner. "Mommy? Are you okay?"

I let my hair go and battle to keep the tears from popping out for my baby to see. "Actually . . . I feel like turning into the Incredible Hulk right now and smashing things up a little bit. But I'll be fine in a couple minutes when I calm down."

He smiles. "I like the Incre-bull Hulk. Ith your thkin gonna turn green?"

I get on my knees and hold my arms open wide. "Come give Mama a hug."

He runs over and throws himself into my embrace. "Don't worry, Mama. Itth gonna be okay."

I pat him on the back, my heart soaring as I imagine him being a strong man someday, comforting a wife or child like he's doing for me right now. *At least I'm doing something right.*

"I know, baby. I know. Don't worry about your old mama. She won't turn into the Hulk or bust anything up. She's going to be okay."

He pulls back to look at me earnestly. "It might be fun to butht thome thingth up, though."

I laugh. "You're probably right." I hold him tighter and bury my face into his neck, inhaling for all I'm worth.

"That ticklth." When he giggles, it sounds like a whole chorus of angels are delivering a healing song to my bruised heart. I take in a deep breath and let it out, hoping some of the negativity that Frank brought into my life is escaping with it.

I have no idea what I'm going to do now. Even just holding my shit together is a tall order. But I need to do that for my kids, even if I can't do it for myself, because I'm a mom, and that's what moms do.

CHAPTER FIFTEEN

Okay, so . . . Deep breaths, in and out. My skin isn't green, my pajama pants still fit, and Sammy is installed on the couch with a cup of peppermint tea and a box of animal cracker cookies. *Cookies for breakfast! Mom of the Year! Woo hoo!* With the girls at school and Sammy happily watching *Barney*, I have a moment or two to figure out what I'm going to do with the rest of my life. *No big deal. No pressure.*

I feel like a sloth. I have no energy at all left in my body. I could lie down on the couch and slowly drop kernel after kernel of popcorn into my gaping mouth while staring off into space and be perfectly happy. Unfortunately, I don't have that luxury. I have a mortgage to pay, three kids to feed, and an ex-husband who's not really that great at making sure his support checks aren't rubber.

Obviously, I need to find another job. The severance package, whatever it turns out to be, is not going to get me far. The economy shows signs of picking up, so I don't think I'll have a problem actually finding a job; the question is whether I'll find one with a boss who will put up with the fact that sometimes one of my three kids will be sick, and that because I'm here alone, it'll mean that I have to stay home with them.

A little voice in the back of my head is chanting: *freelance, freelance, freelance.* It gives me a stress stomachache, probably very similar to the one Sammy is suffering. *It's so unpredictable! You never know whether you'll be working or struggling to pay the bills! If Miles loses his job his insurance on the kids will get canceled!* A regular paycheck is all I've ever known. I don't know if I can handle all the risk that comes with freelancing.

I pick up my cell phone and look down at the text messages that have come from my sister over the past couple days. My stomach is in knots as I consider calling her. It's probably too late. Ozzie's probably already hired someone else for that job. Why was I such a bitch earlier? Why did I have to go ballistic at the warehouse? Those people were just trying to help me out by giving me a little extra money for what was probably not a big deal.

Having a job gave me a sense of security, but I should've known better. In this industry, you never have a job for long. Companies are always selling out, going out of business, or changing mission statements. It's a dog-eat-dog world, and people like me are Purina ALPO—even easier to eat than another dog. *Nom, nom.*

I take a few more deep breaths. At this point I'm almost ready to start hyperventilating. I walk over to sit down at the kitchen table, bringing my phone with me. It's time to face the music, swallow my pride, and put on my big-girl panties.

"Pick up, May. Pick up." She'd better answer soon, before I chicken out.

"Hello?" says my sweet sister. Just hearing her voice makes tears rush to my eyes.

"Hello. It's me."

"What's wrong?" Gone is the sweet voice, and in its place the demanding one. The concerned one. And that's what does me in.

I start crying and my throat squeezes shut. When I can finally talk again, I sound like a total mess. "I got fired."

"Fired? When? Why? You're their best employee! What happened?"

"I guess I'm not so great after all." I try to laugh, but it comes out more like a choking sound. "I called in sick because Sammy's got another stomachache, and they just laid me off."

"They can't do that. They can't fire you or lay you off because your child is sick."

"I'm not sure it has anything to do with that. Or maybe it does. I've called in several times over the past year because one of the kids has been ill. Anyway, the end result is the same. I'm jobless as of today."

"Did you get some kind of severance package?"

"That's what I hear, but I also hear it's only two months' pay, so it's not going to get me very far." I stop to consider how much detail I actually want to share with my sister. She has her own problems; she doesn't need to be burdened with mine.

"How much money do you have saved up?"

I laugh bitterly. "Are you kidding me? Savings? What's that?"

"Okay, no need to panic. We can figure something out."

"There's nothing to figure out, really. I was just calling to see if you still have that freelance job available." The humiliation is strong. I'm actually almost to the point of begging my sister to get me a job from her boyfriend.

I'm on tenterhooks waiting for her response, but thankfully it comes pretty quickly. "Of course! We haven't hired anyone else. And besides, even if we had, there's still work for you to do here."

"You're just saying that to try to make me feel better."

"No, I'm not. Trust me. Now that I'm with Ozzie, I get to hear about everything that goes on with the company behind the scenes. He said just last night that in the last couple years, their jobs that involve computers have doubled."

"But you already have somebody there for computer work, right?" I try to remember the guy's name, but all I can remember is how beautiful he is and how nice and white his teeth are.

May fills in the blanks for me. "You mean Lucky. Yes, we have Lucky, but he's not that kind of computer guy. He's not an engineer like you are. He's a financial person. He can get into people's financial records and see what's going on there, but he cannot get into hidden folders or hack into things."

"Hack? You want me to hack into things?"

Suddenly May sounds very cheery. "No! Did I say 'hack'? I didn't mean hack. Don't be silly." She snorts, a sure sign she's nervous about me knowing exactly what she's talking about, but I let her continue uninterrupted. She has at least captured my interest.

"For example, in this case that we want to hire you for, we're looking into this company's financials because there's something off. One of the owners suspects some sort of embezzlement. But Lucky's not able to access everything on the computer. Or at least he *thinks* he's not able to access it. He believes there are some hidden files somewhere, but he's not the guy who can find them."

Without knowing more than this, I already feel confident that I could help them. It's the only ray of hope that has shined into my morning thus far, so I'm going to run with it. Reality can come and crash my party later if it must.

"I might be able to help. I wouldn't know until I saw the files or the hard drive itself."

"Okay. So you need to get to the actual hard drive? Is that what you're saying?"

"It's always the best way, but it might not be critical. It might depend on what kind of encryption they've used, if they've protected any work behind a firewall, if they've put things on the server or the local drives. It would be a lot easier if I could get my hands on the actual server itself and then the individual computers being used by the employees."

"Okay. Awesome. I knew you could do this. So, here's the plan . . ."

I've never heard May sound so sure of herself. It makes my crappy morning much less crappy. *My baby sister is growing up.*

"I'm going to go talk to Ozzie and share what you've told me. And you're going to go get dressed and brush those hairy teeth of yours and un-knot that 'do, so that when you come over here to the warehouse, my coworkers won't think you're some crazy person standing on the edge of a cliff ready to end it all."

"I can't, remember? I have Sammy. I can't send him to daycare like this."

"Is he really sick, or is he just faking it?"

I turn around to look at my son. He's happily munching away on animal cracker cookies. "I'm not sure. He's probably not that bad off. I think he's having a problem at daycare with another kid or something . . . maybe a teacher."

"Fine. Bring him with you."

I'm warring with myself over this plan. I'm capable of doing the work—I don't have to worry about that part anymore—but I'm still not positive I should take the job. If I mess anything up, it won't be just on me, but my sister too. I don't want to let her down.

Then again, it's not like I have a choice. I need to pay the bills, and this is the easiest avenue for me to take right now. I haven't even had to put in a CV anywhere.

"What's the matter?" May sounds annoyed.

I sigh, because I feel like I'm stuck between a rock and a hard place.

"Need I remind you that the last time I was there, you had some sort of break-in attempt and I was locked in a panic room for an hour?"

"Jenny, we already told you, that was a mistake. Yes, somebody may have tried to break in, but that kind of thing happens at the port."

"Exactly my point. Why would I bring Sammy there? And an even better question, why would you go there?"

"I've been working here for more than two months. I've been here every single day, and we haven't had even one problem." She pauses to huff out an annoyed breath. "I've talked to the guys and Toni . . . This has never happened before. It was a random, isolated event, and it probably doesn't mean anything. The police are on it, and so is the team. Together, we're going to figure out what went wrong. Even if whoever did it is stupid enough to try it again, it won't matter, because now we've got cops outside watching our place, and we've got even more cameras up than we had before."

"You have police officers out there?"

I can hear the smile in her voice. "Yes. Doing a lot of work for the police department has its perks. Bourbon Street Boys is a big asset to the city of New Orleans, so the police aren't going to let somebody come in here and mess with us."

"And the police have the money to pay salaries for that kind of surveillance?"

"Don't worry about it, Jenny. You're over-thinking things. We've helped them gain so much funding through the work we've done by increasing their case-closure rate, they're very happy to help us when we need it."

I'm both pleased and sad that my sister lumps herself in with this group and says *us* whenever she's talking about them. I might actually be kind of jealous. I've never been part of an *us* before at work. I was always working alone in my own cubicle, on my own little projects, living my own life, because the people around me didn't have the same issues or motivations that I had. In my line of work, or at least in the places where I worked, there weren't a lot of married people with kids. I always felt like the old lady in the room. And I never understood what was so fun about photocopying butts at parties.

"So, there's no chance I can do this work here at the house?"

"You want the entire team to come over and brief you in your family room?"

Now I feel silly. "The entire team? Why is the entire team involved?"

"The entire team is involved in everything we do. It's not a dictatorship, it's a democracy. Everybody gives their input, and then Ozzie makes the final decision, taking all the input into consideration. He's a really fair boss."

Hearing those words—"fair boss"—makes me start crying again. "What's wrong now?"

I shake my head. "Never mind. I'm just having a chick moment."

May's voice softens. "You're entitled. You got laid off today. And stop saying you were fired, by the way. You were *laid off*. People get fired for being assholes. People get fired for not doing their jobs. And I know that neither one of those situations applies to you. You worked, like, sixty hours a week at that place, you took work home with you that you couldn't finish there, and you might have missed some days because of your kids, but you always made up for it. I know you, Jenny. You're no slacker."

I smile through my tears. "You always were my biggest fan and cheerleader. I don't know what I'd do without you. You know that's why I worry."

"I do love you, yes, but I speak the truth. And you need to listen to me for once in your life. I know you worry about me, but I'm okay. I have Ozzie and all the others at my back. Bad guys have to get through them to get to me."

Now's not the time for me to remind her that one bad guy got to her pretty easily just a couple months ago when he finally figured out where the eyewitness to him shooting people in a bar lived; besides . . . her team did show up in time to help her out, so she'd have reason to argue with me. And I'm done arguing with my sister.

"Hey, I listen to you."

"Sometimes you do, sometimes you don't. So, what time can you get here?"

I look up at the clock. It's almost nine in the morning. "It's gonna take me about forty-five minutes to get myself and Sammy ready, and then if I leave here right away, it'll take me probably thirty minutes to get there. Should we say ten-thirty?"

"Okay, eleven it is."

"I said ten-thirty."

"Yeah, but I know how long it's going to take Sammy to get off the couch and out of those cookies, so I'm giving you an extra half hour."

Part of me wants to get pissy with my sister and part of me wants to hug her. It's scary how well she knows my family. "Okay, see you at eleven. Is there anything I should bring?"

"Whatever you think you might need to get into someone's computer, and your smile. That's it."

"Is Felix there with you? Because I'm going to need something to distract Sammy."

"Of course Felix is here. He's my right-hand chihuahua. But don't worry, I'll help with Sammy." She turns on the cheerleader mode again. "You're not alone, Jenny. I'm with you, the team is with you . . . It's like a family here. You'll see."

If she wanted to turn me into a puddle of goo, that was probably the best way to do it. I need to hang up before I turn into a blubbering idiot. "See you at eleven."

"See you then. I love you, Jenny. Don't worry, everything is going to be okay. I promise."

CHAPTER SIXTEEN

It's embarrassing how right my sister is about my ability to be any-where on time when the kids are involved. It's 11:05 as I'm pulling up in front of the warehouse. The dent in the door that I remember from before is gone, and in its place is fresh paint. *Geez, these guys don't mess around.* I guess appearances are pretty important to them.

"Where are we?" Sammy asks from the backseat.

"This is where Auntie May works. And Felix is here, and he wants to see you." My son loves May's dog. I turn off the car and turn around to look at him. He has cookie shrapnel all around his mouth. "Now, you promised that you would be a good boy for Mama, right?"

He nods. "I promith."

"Good. And Auntie May is going to play with you, and Felix is going to play with you, and you're going to be a good boy so that Mommy can do some work. And then when we're all done, we'll go to McDonald's." *Mom of the Year strikes again.*

A big grin lights up his face, and he starts banging his hands and legs on his car seat. "McDonald'th, McDonald'th, McDonald'th."

"But you have to be good. This is somebody's house, Sammy. This is somebody's work, too."

His banging stops and he nods in earnest. "And I get to go to work with you becauth I'm thick."

"Well, normally I don't like taking sick children to work. That's not nice for the other people, because you can make them sick. So you should make sure to stay away from all the people in there."

Sammy's expression changes. Now I see a tiny glimmer of fear in it, and I feel guilty for making it appear.

"Are they mean?" he asks.

I shake my head vigorously. "No, they're not mean at all. They're really nice, actually. It's just that if you have a virus that's giving you that tummy ache, we don't want these nice people to catch your virus, right?"

He thinks about it for a couple seconds, blinks a few times, and then nods. "We don't want anybody to get my viruth."

I smile at him encouragingly. "Exactly. Let's keep our cooties to ourselves."

He giggles. "And we'll keep our booteeth to ourthelves too."

"Yes. Keep your booty to yourself too." I roll my eyes and turn around. It's probably not a good idea to encourage the potty talk right now, but I need for him to stay cool and comfortable. All I need is for Sammy to unleash the beast within, and it'll all be over. He's most likely to do that when he's trying to impress people he's just met. He could get me laid off before I even start working.

I get out of the car, remove Sammy from his seat-harness, and take his hand so he can walk next to me. My laptop is in its case, slung over my shoulder with my purse. "Do you remember how to introduce yourself?"

"Yeth, Mama. I know. I lithen to you all the time when you're telling me."

"*All* the time?"

We're at the door when he answers. "Well, motht of the time. Thometimeth, I don't wanna lithen."

"Well, at least you're honest," I mumble.

I lift my hand to press the buzzer on the keypad, to let them know we're here, but before I get there, the door starts to open.

Sammy jumps back in surprise, and looks up at it with eyes full of wonder. "Whoa. Thatth a big door."

I smile down at him. "Yep. This is a warehouse. It's kind of a weird place for Mama to work, but I'm trying to look at it as interesting and different. Not everything that's different is bad. Sometimes different things are good." I hope my advice is sinking in and that maybe it'll apply to his daycare situation. I have a feeling there's a new kid on the block who's inserted himself into the pecking order in a spot that Sammy doesn't agree with. I make a mental note to call the daycare and talk to the director.

May is at the crack of the door as soon as it's big enough to reveal a person. She grins at me first and then she looks down at Sammy. "Sammers! You made it!"

"Whereth Felix?"

May laughs. "I guess I know where I stand." She gestures for us to come in. "Felix is just over there by that exercise equipment, Sammy. You can go over there and play with him, but don't touch any of the equipment, okay?"

I give my sister a hard look that says, *How long do you think he's going to listen to that rule when none of us are watching?*

She looks at me as she continues. "I'll be right over. And when I get there, I can show you some of the equipment if you don't touch it first."

Sammy goes running over to the makeshift gym, yelling as his little shoes slap the concrete floor. "I won't touch anything! I promith!"

There's nobody around but May and me. I'm a little sad that Dev isn't here to say hello.

"Where is everybody?" I ask, trying to be cool.

"They're upstairs. I figured you probably wouldn't want to be overwhelmed on your first day, especially after everything that happened . . ."

I wave my hand at her to stop her from going down that path. "I'm doing better. Better, but kind of walking a thin line between sanity and insanity, so if you could just not talk about it while we're here, that would be awesome."

"Okay, no problem. But after you're done working, we're going to talk about this. About your job, about the panic room, about Dev." She wiggles her eyebrows at me.

I ignore the innuendo I'm sure she's just delivered. I'm not ready to analyze his possible motives toward me yet. For the first time in my life, I'm ready to keep a secret from my sister. I don't know if this is a good sign or a bad one.

"Okay, whatever you say."

May squeezes me around my shoulders as we walk side by side. "So, are you excited to be here?"

We head toward Sammy. "Do you want my honest answer or my playing-nice answer?"

"Be honest. I can handle it."

"Well . . . I would say that I'm grateful to be here. I'm grateful for the job, even though it's just a one-time freelance thing. If Ozzie could give me a letter of reference when it's all over, it could really help with my new career."

"What's your new career? You have a new career already? What did I miss?" She laughs, but not at me, so I don't take offense.

"My new career as a freelancer." I try to smile, but I'm not sure I pull it off, because May is looking at me funny.

She pats me on the back. "That's the spirit, babe. You're going to be fine." She shifts her attention to Sammy. "Hey there, little man, are you ready to see some super cool stuff?"

Sammy's hand is reaching up toward a piece of gym equipment, his fingers hovering just inches away from it. His eyes are big and round. "Yeth, I'm ready."

"How about if we look at that gym equipment later? I have other things to show you first that are way cooler."

Sammy points at a stack of weights. "Cooler than that?"

"Yes." May is nodding. "Way cooler. Like ninja-stuff cooler."

My eyes pop open at that. "You'd better not let him touch . . . those things that are up there." I don't want to say *ninja swords*; that'll only pique his interest more.

May rolls her eyes. "Give me some credit, Jenny. You know I'm not going to let my nephew cut a finger off."

"I can cut a finger off?" Sammy's eyes are practically falling out of his head at this point.

May laughs. "No. Didn't you hear me? There will be no cutting off of any fingers today."

I feel the very strong urge to emphasize this point. "No cutting fingers off, Sammy. No fingers, no toes, no nothing. No cutting of *anything*."

Sammy nods vigorously. "Okay. I won't cut anything off."

I'm not nearly as excited about this job as I was ten minutes ago.

"Come on, guys," says May. "Let's go upstairs so that Mama can talk to Ozzie and the team and find out what they need her to do."

We walk up the stairs together, with May holding Sammy's hand. At the top of the staircase we're faced with another keypad. May enters in a code, there's a click, and she pushes the door open.

"Now, Sammy, you can't touch *anything* in this room. You can look at everything, but you can't touch it. No matter what."

"Okay."

Her voice goes stern. "You have to promise me, Sammy. You can't touch anything."

Sammy's a little breathless. "I promith. I won't touch anything. And I won't cut anything off."

"Okay, little man. I'm trusting you." Auntie May puts her hand on his back and pushes him toward the opening. "The light will come on as soon as you step inside."

Felix runs past all of us and disappears into the darkness. Seeing that tiny dog be so brave makes me realize how silly I'm being, acting nervous about entering the ninja room and then the meeting area or kitchen or whatever they call it in there. I made a bit of a fool of myself the last time I was here, and I don't relish facing the music, but damn . . . if that tiny excuse for a dog can walk around in here like it's no big deal, so can I. I'm as brave as a chihuahua, at least. I think.

The light goes on in the room as Sammy steps inside, and he stops so suddenly, I walk right into the back of him. I barely keep my laptop from swinging forward and knocking him unconscious.

"Sammy, what're you doing?"

"Whoa. Doeth a real ninja live here?"

That brings a smile to my face.

"Kind of," May and I both say at the same time.

She looks at me funny, probably because my cheeks are turning red as I imagine the man who owns these swords. I can't meet her eyes, so I focus on Sammy instead.

"You'll get to meet him later. His name is Dev, which is short for Devon."

"There'th a girl named Devon at my thchool."

"We don't have to tell Dev the ninja-man that, though, right?"

Sammy looks up at me. "Why not?"

"Because . . . sometimes men don't like to think that their name is a girl's name too."

Sammy thinks about it for a second or two and then nods. "Okay." His attention is back on the ninja swords in seconds. "I could cut a lot of thingth off with theethe thords in here."

I try really hard not to laugh. "Yes, you could. But you're not *going* to, because you promised Auntie May and Mama that you wouldn't cut anything. Remember, you are not allowed to touch *anything* in this room."

I start to wonder why on earth they would have a room full of such dangerous things lying around when Dev has a child; he must bring his son here from time to time, right? But then, it might make perfect sense to have the swords here rather than at his house. The more I think about it, the more it appears to be a very good parenting decision to have the swords here, yet a very bad parenting decision to have my kid here. That Mom of the Year award is definitely moving further and further from my grasp.

CHAPTER SEVENTEEN

May walks into the next room, holding the door open so we can pass through. Sammy starts heading off toward one of the swords instead, so I rush forward and take him by the shoulders, shifting him in the other direction. "Here we go, this way. Let's go see *Felix*. Won't that be fun?" I'm really trying to sell it, like hanging out with Felix is better than candy. Better than ninja swords, even.

Sammy remembers his buddy and shifts focus, moving to follow his Auntie May. "Where are we going?" he asks.

"We're going where they have cookies," says May.

I shake my head at her and whisper as he walks past. "He's already ingested an entire box of animal cracker cookies this morning for breakfast."

She gives me a sly grin. "Shooting for Mom of the Year, are we?"

"Judge not, lest you have children and be judged. God saves his most special mommy-curses for critical kid-judgers, you know."

"Hey, it's cool with me. You know whenever I'm in charge they eat lots of cookies."

I wave her off. "Shush, I don't want to know."

Goofing around with my sister about her Vegas rules is making this event easier to handle than I thought it would be. I could be fretting about what these people will think of me, but instead I'm thinking about kid-Vegas. What happens at Auntie May's house, stays at Auntie May's house. Vegas rules apply whenever she babysits, no matter where or when it is. It's the best way I know to allow my kids a little spoiling without making it a regular part of their lives.

"There she is," says a bright voice from inside the kitchen area. As I come around the corner I see the man who said it—Thibault, along with his Cajun accent and his friendly smile.

I smile back. "Hey, Thibault. How've you been?"

"Never better. Welcome."

"Thanks." I look around the room. Everyone but Dev is here, including a woman who I haven't met yet. But I don't need an introduction because I already know who she is: Little Miss Kickass. My sister's description of Toni couldn't have been more perfect. I would not want to get on this girl's bad side. Even though she's smaller than I am, she looks like she could definitely take me down.

The woman stands up and walks over, her high-heeled boots making sharp noises on the floor. When she's in front of me, she stops and holds out her hand forcefully, with almost military precision.

"Nice to meet you. I'm Toni." There's no smile there, but I'm not getting the vibe that she's unfriendly toward me; she's just all business. I can respect that. I'm a Wonder Woman fan.

I take her hand in mine and give her a firm shake. "Nice to meet you too. I've heard a lot about you."

Toni's right eyebrow goes up. "Do I want to know?"

My smile is suddenly warmer at what appears to be the tiniest hint of insecurity on her part. "It's all good, I promise. You really impressed my sister, so you must be somebody special."

I detect a very slight softening of Toni's features, or at least I think I do. "Good to know," she says, letting my hand go.

"This is my son, Sammy."

Toni looks down at him. The tiniest hint of a smile quirks up the side of her lips as she shakes his proffered hand. "Nice to meet you, Sammy."

"Nitht to meet you too, Mith Toni." His little hand falls to his side and he immediately starts scanning the space under the table, looking for Felix. I take hold of his shoulders to keep him from dropping onto all fours.

Toni turns, goes back to her chair, and resumes her seat.

May speaks up. "You've met Lucky and Ozzie, of course."

I nod. "Yep. Great to see all of you again." I finally allow my gaze to be drawn over to Ozzie. My face heats up once more as I wait for his judgment to be cast.

He nods at me, no signs of judgment anywhere. "Thanks for coming. You're really helping us out of a bind."

It always feels good to be needed. I wonder if Ozzie knows that well enough to use it to his advantage. He seems very cool and relaxed, but I think he's a hell of a lot wilier than he appears. I won't hold it against him if he's purposely buttering me up, though. I like butter.

"Well, I don't know for sure if I can help you, but I'm willing to give it a shot."

Lucky pulls out the empty chair next to him. "Why don't you have a seat here, and I'll show you what we're looking at."

I take Sammy by the hand and bring him around the table with me.

"But I want to go with Auntie May," he whines.

May follows behind us and I stop, waiting for her to catch up. I'm about to tell her she doesn't need to play babysitter, but she takes Sammy by the hand without hesitation and starts to lead him away. "How about we go meet Sahara?"

"Ith that the big doggie?" Sammy asks, sounding excited about the prospect.

I'm trying not to panic over the idea that Ozzie's dog could have Sammy as a snack between meals.

"Yes, that's right. You already met her once, didn't you?"

Sammy nods. "She'th big. Mommy thayth we can't have a big dog, 'cuth big dogth have big poopth and she doethn't wanna pick them up."

Everyone chuckles under their breath.

My face goes a little pink, but I know they're not laughing at my son. His little speech impediment makes him sound like he's cracking a joke when he's just saying whatever he needs to say. I don't hold it against people who find humor in it.

I've been told he'll grow out of it, but that if he hasn't by the time he starts school, he'll have speech therapy through the system. Regardless, I don't pressure him because it's part of who he is, and I think it makes him special.

May leads Sammy away into an area of the warehouse I've not yet seen, and I sit down at the table. Where I was working before, the environment was really casual. Meetings were held sometimes in a circle made of beanbag chairs. It feels nice to be sitting in a room full of grown-ups who actually act like grown-ups. With all the muscles around me, I can almost imagine I'm hanging out with the Super Friends, circa 1973.

Everyone takes a seat as Ozzie speaks. "First of all, I assume that May has spoken to you a little bit about the situation, but just to make sure we have all our bases covered, I'd like to start by having you sign an NDA." He nods at Lucky and one is presented to me.

"Absolutely." I scan it to be sure I'm not signing over a kidney or anything, then use the pen Lucky gives me to put my signature on the paper. It looks like nearly every other one I've seen. Confidentiality has been pretty much standard procedure in every job I've had since college.

"Good. Now that that's out of the way, we can talk about the case. This one concerns a marine accessories retail chain called Blue Marine. Maybe you've heard of it?"

I shrug. "I'm not really into fishing."

"It doesn't matter. You don't need to know about the marine business to know something's not kosher with this particular outfit. We've been hired by one of the owners of the business, who is also the major shareholder of the corporation. The other shareholders are not aware of our involvement."

I nod, letting him know I get it. So far, so good.

"There're some irregularities in the accounting, and Lucky, who is our financial expert, has been going through the books. He's also made a site visit to verify some of the things he found. I'm going to let him give you more detail on that, but the gist of the matter is, we suspect pretty substantial embezzlement is going on." His expression goes dark as he delivers that bad news. "We have no idea who is responsible; we don't know if it's a single actor or more than one person, and we don't know if the other owners are even aware there's a problem."

And the plot thickens. I hate to admit to myself that I'm actually getting excited about working in the middle of this mess.

"Because this is a closely held corporation, a family business, we want to be careful about not stepping on toes. This operation is entirely covert. If and when you make site visits, you will go as a customer, as an undercover employee of some sort, or maybe even a vendor. But under no circumstances will any of our team let anyone at Blue Marine know what we're up to. And that includes the person who hired us, Hal Jorgensen."

Ozzie pauses to let that sink in. It seems like everyone's on board by the way they're nodding, so I nod too.

"Hal will be aware if and when we put someone in place, but that person will not interact with him; and on the off chance that they *do* interact with him, it will be as a new employee or a new vendor would with a business owner who they've never met before."

Ozzie's waiting for something, and I notice that everyone around the table is nodding all over again, so I go ahead and nod more too, although I don't really know what the hell he's talking about. Who is he going to put in place over there?

"Lucky, why don't you give her a rundown of what you found. And anyone else who has something to add, feel free. We want to give Jenny as much information as she needs to get her job done."

I lift my finger, and everyone stares at me.

Ozzie lifts an eyebrow at me.

"Can I ask one question first?" I say, trying not to sound meek, but failing badly.

Ozzie gestures at me. "By all means. We don't stand on formality here. If you have something to say, just say it."

"Do we know exactly what my job is going to be? Or is it something I'm going to have to figure out later, once we get deeper into the financials?"

Ozzie looks at Lucky. "Lucky, why don't you answer her question."

I turn to face the man who will now be telling me whether this is a job I can handle or not. This is way more interesting than stringing together code for a company I kind of hate.

Lucky opens up a folder in front of him. It's very thick. After thumbing through a few papers, he pulls one out and places it on top.

"This is just a little report that I typed up for you. It needs to stay here in the file, but this will give you an idea." He slides the folder closer to me and points at the first paragraph as he reads aloud. "After going through the financial records of Blue Marine Incorporated, I discovered some irregularities, not only in the accounting used but in the numbers reported, particularly with respect to the charges being assessed by certain service providers. For example, recycling of waste oil, a service that must be utilized by Blue Marine by law, is costing 79% more than the industry average." He pauses to take a breath. "Similarly, janitorial services for the stores are running 159% higher than the average. However, during a site visit, I saw no evidence of any janitorial service being used that's worth the premium being paid. On the contrary, I found a store in need of these services."

I interrupt his recitation. "So, you suspect that someone is creating dummy companies and taking money for themselves, skimming off the top?"

"That's my theory. That's the one I'm running with, anyway, until I get more information."

I nod, encouraging him to continue.

"I have access to the server remotely, using Mr. Jorgensen's username and password; however, I don't know if that's enough."

I shrug. "It might not be."

"What do you mean?"

"They could be using the local drive of a single computer that isn't networked in or viewable via the server. I wouldn't know without getting onto or *into* the actual computers themselves."

"We could get you into the computers if you need that kind of access," Lucky says.

I nod. "Are you thinking of dropping a virus in there and making a clone over here, or actually going on-site?"

Lucky's eyes open a little wider. "You could do that? Do the virus thing?"

I shrug. "Sure. It's not the easiest thing in the world to engineer, but it's doable. You probably saw something like it in *The Girl with the Dragon Tattoo*."

Thibault speaks up. "I didn't think that was real. People can really do that?" He smiles as he looks at his coworkers. "That girl Lisbeth was badass."

I turn my attention to the whole table, trying not to take credit for Lisbeth's badassedness. She was way meaner than I could ever be. I liken myself more to Mr. Spock than anyone else. Passive and logical with pointy ears, pale skin, and a deadly cool hairdo.

"Sure," I say. "I could do that, and a lot worse. Believe me." I pause, worried that I've just painted myself as a computer psycho. "Not that I would, of course."

Toni speaks up, apparently unfazed. "Where can you get a virus? Do we have to buy it, like a program or something?"

I shrug. "Well, I could write a program fresh for you, or I could talk to some friends. One of them will probably already have one. It wouldn't cost anything." I don't want to elaborate and tell them that some people actually write horrible viruses for the joy of terrorizing people. That's not what we're doing here, and with Mr. Jorgensen's permission it's not illegal to clone a system.

"We'll talk about the logistics later," Ozzie says. "For right now let's just get an overview of what the problem is and how we think Jenny can help us."

Lucky nods and then looks at his paper again. "If we were to go on-site, I believe you'd find all the computers networked together. We could access data from any of the computers from a location at the company via the server."

"You might actually need to get on the individual computers physically first, though, before you can know for sure whether their local drives are clean," I say. Now I know why May asked me to come on board. Lucky is clearly not the guy for this part of the job.

Ozzie responds. "Do you have a recommendation as to how we should proceed?"

My heart goes a little faster, knowing that everybody is watching me and judging me by my response. Even so, I kind of get how May is excited about being on this team. It feels good to have people counting on me, people who are really dedicated and hardworking.

I take a deep breath and give him my response. "Well, if I were to have the perfect situation in front of me, and if we had all the time in the world to figure things out, I would say going on-site maybe after hours and getting into their computers would be the best way to go. As long as I have their passwords, and I don't need to try to crack into anything, we could get in there pretty quickly and take a look around." I pause, imagining myself in the dead of night searching through a stranger's files. I'm definitely going to need to build some sort of algorithm to search and compile data quicker than I could do on my own, but I could do that part at home after the systems are cloned. "How many employees are we talking about? Because that might change my answer."

Lucky answers without looking at his file. "There are eight employees in the main office, and another twenty to thirty employees at various stores."

I chew my lip as I think that through. "Hmmm . . . that could take a while working on-site. It might be better if we made clones of the individual computers, so I could work out of sight during the day. If we have to go in after hours, it's going to be very difficult for me." I cringe at that truth. "I'm sorry, but I have three kids, so my time isn't exactly all my own, if you know what I mean."

Thibault holds his hands up. "Hey, we're here to work with you, however it's good for you. If it's easier for you to make clones and work from home or work at the warehouse during the day, we'll do it that way. We want to accommodate you as much as possible."

Thibault has no idea that he's just put a crack in my heart. It's one of those happy cracks that appears when you realize that all your life you've been working for the wrong people and you really should have looked harder to find a job like this one in the first place.

I clear my throat so I can talk without that lump that just appeared messing me up. "I appreciate that. And trust me, my kids appreciate it. I think it would be better if I could work from home. I could come to the warehouse if you need me to, but any time I spend on the road is time I could be on the computer. This could get really tricky." I look at Ozzie, willing him not to be offended at my next statement. "Do you know how many hours you were expecting me to work?" It's going to take me at least ten hours to do this thing they've just described, but probably a lot more than that, and all I've been offered is five hundred bucks. It could easily turn out to be a less-than-minimum-wage situation, which I'd love to avoid, but I don't want to come right out and say that in front of all these people.

Luckily, Ozzie picks up on my meaning right away. "The fee we offered you was just for a consultation from you, to do what you're doing right now. You've already earned it. If you actually decide to do the work, we'll just pay you your hourly rate, whatever it is."

"Okay." My face is burning red again. Should I admit the truth? That I don't have any idea what my hourly rate is? When I look around at the people at the table and then hear my son giggling in the other room, I make my decision very quickly; the truth is always the best way to go, regardless of where you end up.

"I've actually never freelanced before, so I don't exactly have an hourly rate."

"You know what you're doing though, don't you?" This question comes from Toni, and there's a hint of a challenge to it. But this is her house, and I'm in no position to come back with attitude of my own, so I answer with as much humility as I can muster.

I nod. "Yes, I'm fully qualified as both a computer engineer and software engineer. But if you'd like to see my diplomas and some samples of my work, I'd be happy to provide them."

Ozzie sounds a little perturbed as he shoots Toni a hard look. "You don't need to do that. You've already been fully vetted by Thibault."

Fully vetted? What's that mean? I decide to hold my tongue on that for now.

It's possible there's a little spark of rebellion in Toni's eye, but then she looks away, and I can't see how she feels about the situation anymore. She just got put in her place, so she can't be very happy. May once described her as a little prickly, and now I know why. She's like a little Bahia hairy dwarf porcupine sitting over there, ready to challenge anybody about anything, stick a few well-placed quills in their faces.

I don't know if she means for this to be the result, but it makes me want to work even harder, so I can prove her wrong. So I can show her that I know what I'm doing. The stuff they want me to do is tough and more than a little time consuming, but I can do it. I haven't met a computer problem I can't tackle and wrestle to the ground. The world is lucky I use my powers for good and not evil. I could so be Lex Luthor if I wanted to be.

Thibault speaks up. "How about you just charge what you think is fair, maybe the industry average or whatever, and we'll take it from there?"

"Okay, I can do that." My heart is racing. If I do a really good job for them this time, maybe they'll call me again when they need computer or software expertise. I have to be extra fair with my pricing and work as hard as possible to get this done right. If I could have a freelance career working out of my home, it would be a dream come true. Miles has health insurance that covers the kids, so I'll never have to worry about them being sick again. I could hear "I have a tummy ache," and instead of falling into a panic, I could just smile and say, "Go lie on the couch," and not worry about having to call a boss who's going to threaten to fire me over it.

Thibault stands up. "Boss, we've got that other project we're working on with the chief of police, and I need May for that meeting." He shoots me an apologetic look.

"Right." Ozzie turns his attention to me. "I'm going to leave you in Lucky's capable hands. Feel free to let your son run around. There's nothing in here that could hurt him. You might want to keep him out of the other room, though."

I smile. "Yeah. Those knives are very tempting."

Ozzie, Thibault, and Toni stand. Ozzie walks over to the doorway and leans into the hallway that leads to the place were Sammy and May are. "May! Time to go!"

"Coming!" Felix starts to bark, as if he's answering Ozzie's call too. It makes me smile to think that May has her own little family here.

May appears, holding Sammy's hand. "Should I stay here?" she asks her boyfriend and boss.

"No. I told Jenny that Sammy can run around as much as he wants. Bring the dogs out here, and they can keep him busy for a little while. I don't think it's going to take much longer for her to finish up with Lucky."

"Okey-dokey." May bends down and looks Sammy in the eye. "I need you to do me a favor, Sammers. Can you look after Felix and Sahara for me? I have to go do something."

Sammy nods. "Yeth. I can do that."

"And can you promise me something else?"

"Maybe," he says with caution. "What ith it?"

"Can you promise me that you won't go in the other room where the dangerous swords are?"

"Becauthe you don't want me to cut anything off, like fingerth?"

Somebody snorts off to the side. I think it might have been Toni.

"Yes. Because I don't want you to cut anything off."

"Okay." He nods enthusiastically, "I promithe I won't cut Keep it on one line or break aaany-thing off."

He's being so dedicated with his assurances, my hackles go up. The little devil is thinking he's created some kind of loophole. I go back over his answer to her question, but May is faster than I am.

"Nice try," she says, "but what we need you to promise is that you won't even go *in* that room."

He gives her his very earnest look. "But I *could* go in there and not touch anything. Jutht *look*."

May shakes her head "Nope. You can't even go in. You want to know why?"

"Yeth. I alwayth want to know why."

She smiles. "I know. Because you have a great mind, Sammy. The reason why you can't go in there is because the man who owns all those swords is a real ninja. And real ninjas don't let anyone touch their weapons."

Sammy's eyes are very wide, and I'm almost afraid of what's going to come out of his or May's mouth next.

Sammy's voice is almost a whisper. "Why not? Do they kill them?"

May shakes her head. "No. But it brings them very bad luck, and next time they try to fight, they get injured. You don't want to injure a real ninja, do you?"

Sammy shakes his head. "No. But I *do* want to touch hith thordth."

She rubs his head affectionately. "I know you do. Maybe one day he'll let you touch one, but not today." She stands up and turns him toward the dogs who have just entered the room. They trot over to a large dog bed and curl up together. "Go play with the doggies. They're bored."

Sammy runs off to lie down in the bed with the dogs, and May looks over at me. "We good?"

My son is lying in a dog bed when he should be at daycare, and I'm working in a warehouse where I was formerly kept prisoner in a panic room. *I'm perfect.* I smile back at her. "Yep. All set."

"Call me later," she says, holding her hand up to her ear with two fingers extended, mimicking our future call.

"Oh, I will. Don't worry." I wink so she knows I'm not mad at her. But we do have a lot to talk about. And at some point, I'm going to have to try and slip into the conversation a question about why Dev wasn't at the meeting today. I'm just hoping it's not because he's regretting flirting with me and heard I was going to be here.

CHAPTER EIGHTEEN

After everyone's gone, it's just Lucky and me in the room together. He has a pen out and a blank piece of paper, and he's staring at me attentively.

"Do you know when you might be available to do a night visit to the job site?" he asks.

"I don't know. I guess it would depend on what you think we're going to be doing, and how long you think it'll take. Since it's at night, it's possible May could watch my kids for me, but it depends on her schedule."

"Okay. So, we need to talk to May."

"I could text her, if you want."

"That's a good idea. Why don't you go ahead and do that?"

Taking my phone from my purse, I quickly tap out a message to my sister, asking her when she might be free for a sleepover so that I can get down to business here with the Bourbon Street Boys.

"What's next?"

"I was thinking we could get over there to the administrative offices around eight p.m. and work until about four in the morning. Mr. Jorgensen tells me that the last person is usually out the door by six-thirty in the evening, and they come in around eight o'clock in the morning. I'm guessing it'll take us a few hours to go over all the computers, but just in case, we'll have more time than that before we can expect anyone to show up and spoil our fun. Does that sound right to you?"

I nod. "Yes, it sounds about right, but I wouldn't want to commit to anything until I actually got in there and started working. It's really difficult to say how long it'll take without having more details about the people who work there. Because we don't know the background of any of the employees and how sophisticated they might be with their computer use, we won't know for sure how deep the problem goes until we have our hands on their drives."

He nods. "Yeah, you're right." He pauses for a moment and smiles at me. "Did I mention how happy I am to have you working on this case with me?"

My heart warms at the sentiment. "Maybe? Yes? No?" I chuckle. "Everyone has made me feel very welcome."

"I think you're really going to like working here, despite your first impressions. I promise it's not normally like it was on Friday."

I try to focus on the positive and not the incident in the panic room. That was just a wrong place, wrong time kind of thing. Except for the part where I spent quality time with Dev. *Wrong place, right time?* "Well, my sister May loves it, so it must be a nice place."

"I realize that right now you only plan to be here temporarily, but if you decide at any point that you might like a more permanent gig, you should let me know. There've already been several cases we've worked on where we had to bring in outside talent, and we've had to turn down several more jobs because we just weren't sure we could bring in somebody qualified enough to help. From what your sister and Thibault both tell me, you can pretty much handle anything we've been approached about so far."

I'm flattered but also a little worried. "How does Thibault know anything about what I do?"

Lucky leans back in his chair a little bit. "He's in charge of background checks. Whenever we think about working with someone from outside the team, he does a thorough check. Law enforcement allows us to use their databases."

I get a little nervous over that. *Does that mean he did a credit check on me too?* I don't have the best credit in the world, which is kind of embarrassing. Bouncing child support checks never helps with that situation. "I guess I passed . . ."

"Yes, you passed. And it doesn't hurt that you had a very glowing recommendation from your sister. You're her hero, you know. And we respect the hell out of her, so what she thinks matters to us."

"You sure know how to make a girl blush, Lucky." I know I sound goofy saying that, but I can't think of how else to describe what I'm feeling. It's been a long time since somebody slathered my family and me with compliments like this. It's seriously flattering to be told on the day you're laid off from one job that you're respected so much by a new coworker, especially when it's someone on a team of people who are consulting for the New Orleans Police Department. But it doesn't change a lot of very important things for me.

"It's just the truth," he assures me.

"I did just get laid off from my job, but I'm not sure I'm up to the task of being a Bourbon Street Boy person."

He shrugs. "It's up to you. Thibault says you're good for the work, and what you've said so far on the Blue Marine case makes sense to me, so if you do well with this job, there's no reason why you couldn't at least consider doing more consulting for us. If you're worried about your kids, don't be. When you work behind the scenes like I do, the demands are a lot less."

"Are you saying you never go out into the field? Because I thought we were going out into the field on this job."

"Yeah, very occasionally I go out into the field, when there's really nobody there but me, or it's just an easy task like wandering

150

around a store kind of thing. But, like Dev, most of my work is done here in the warehouse."

I busy myself with my phone for a couple seconds, checking to see if my sister has responded and hiding any reaction I might be having to hearing Dev's name. My heart is fluttering the tiniest bit.

No luck on an answer from May. I turn my attention back to Lucky. "That must make your family happy, that you don't do the risky stuff." I smile at him, trying to cover the fact that I'm delving into his personal life now.

"The only family I have swims around a little bowl, so it doesn't matter either way. But I'm not much for hand-to-hand combat anyway. I like dealing with numbers, not bad guys." He grins again, completely fine with being a chicken poo pansy, just like I am.

My smile comes both from the general fact that I like talking to him and from the fact that what he says is completely ridiculous. "Your family swims around in a bowl?"

He shrugs and then goes to his paperwork, flipping open the folder again. He talks at the papers, like he's maybe a little bit embarrassed about his answer. "I have a goldfish."

I'm trying not to laugh. I can't tell if he's joking or not. I play along, anyway. "What's his name?"

Lucky is smiling shyly as he looks at his papers. "Sunny."

"Of course it's Sunny." I do laugh then, because he's a grown man, but inside him obviously lives a small boy. "We have a gerbil at our house."

Lucky turns his head to look at me. "What's his name?"

"Harold. We keep it casual, though, and call him Harry."

Lucky laughs. "Of course his name is Harry. What else would it be?"

"Oh, I don't know. I was gunning for T-Rex, but the kids lobbied hard for something softer."

Lucky chuckles, and encouraged by his response, I jump in with more details. "We inherited him from my son's preschool classroom."

He lifts his brows. "Adopting a classroom pet? That's a big commitment."

I roll my eyes. "Tell me about it. The sucker grew testicles one day, and the teacher said it was interfering in the learning process, so Harold had to go." I pause, realizing with a start that I've once again over-shared. I tense up, waiting for the awkward silence to take over.

But I needn't have worried. Lucky just keeps on rolling with the conversation. "And how exactly do testicles interfere in the learning process?"

It's difficult to keep a straight face at this point. "Well, apparently, testicles are very distracting. The kids liked to look and point and talk about them. A lot. And I don't know if you've ever spent any time around three-year-olds, but they tend to fixate on things like gerbil 'nads."

Lucky barks out a laugh and then leans back in his chair. "The only young boy I've been around is Dev's son, but I get what you mean. I've seen that curiosity in action many times. The kid's like a dog with a bone sometimes."

I'm completely curious right now about Dev's son and Dev's relationship with him, but now is not the time to delve into that. I can't interrogate Lucky about another man's child when that man isn't here. It just seems too sneaky. Too devious. My curiosity is just going to have to take a backseat to propriety. Seeking a distraction, I gesture at the file.

"Do you want me to look through that? Is there anything in there that applies to what I'll be doing?"

"Sure. Take a look." He slides the file down the table to me. "I'm not sure a lot of it will apply, but you're welcome to it."

I check my phone again—still no response from May—and open the file. I make an attempt at scanning the papers inside, but my mind really isn't on the task. I keep thinking about Dev and his son, and the fact that his child sounds a lot like mine. I wonder why, when I mentioned getting them together, Dev seemed so against the idea. I wonder if his son likes McDonald's as much as Sammy does. I've promised my boy a trip there, so I know what I'll be eating for lunch. I can plan on a stomachache after, too. I should probably stop by the drugstore and buy some Alka-Seltzer on my way home.

"I can make a copy of the file for you if you prefer."

I snap out of my trance at the sound of Lucky's voice. "Sorry? I'm a little distracted."

He smiles. "I got that. Don't worry about it."

"Is it that obvious? Dang. I'm going to have to work on my stealth mode, I guess." I shrug, feeling like I need to explain myself. "I'm really sorry. Seriously. I woke up today to my boss telling me I'd been laid off. It was a bit of a shock."

"Your sister mentioned something about that. She told us that you were really dedicated to your job there, and that she thinks your being let go had something to do with you having kids."

I shrug. "There's no way for me to know for sure, but I have called in sick several times. I don't ever do it for myself; whenever I'm ill, I just work through it and keep to myself so no one catches my cooties. When it's my kids, though, I don't have any other choice but to stay home. The daycare won't take them when they're sick, and I get that. Nobody wants someone's kid making their kid sick. That's not cool."

"Of course. And anybody who would fire a person for being a good parent to their kids doesn't deserve to be operating." His mood has gone a little dark. "When it comes to family, you don't need to worry about that garbage here. It would never happen. Dev has a son, I have Sunny. Everybody understands those commitments."

Because he seems serious, I can't laugh. But inside I'm chuckling. He talks about his fish like it's his child. I want to ask him how long goldfish live, because if he's this attached I'm worried for him. In my experience they don't last more than six months, and I'm afraid when those six months are up for Sunny, Lucky's not going to do very well with it. Is he crazy? I'm starting to think everybody here has at least one screw loose. The only one who seems completely sane is Thibault, but I'm not going to bet any money on that. I'm sure he has issues. We all do. I guess I fit in here more than I realized.

"Mommy, I'm bored."

I look over the table toward the dog bed. Sammy is leaning against Sahara with both of his arms extended over her back. His right hand is flipping one of her ears back and forth, and his left one is poking Felix in the forehead, over and over. Felix's eyes are half closed, and he's swaying a little in a half-seated position. It's possible Sammy has managed to hypnotize the poor dog with the finger poking.

I look at Lucky. "Do you need me for anything else? I mean, after we figure out what our schedule is for going to the site?" I check my phone one more time for May's answer, but there's no response yet. I'm going to give her a piece of my mind for ignoring me. *Another Sister Code violation.*

Lucky shakes his head. "No, I don't think so. I'll have a copy of the file delivered to you in the next few hours, so you can take a look at it this afternoon. Write down any concerns you have, and we can discuss them next time we're together. Be sure to keep track of your hours, because Ozzie will want to pay you for the work you're putting in."

I nodded. "Okay. Will do." I stand, gathering my purse and my phone. "I promised to take my son to McDonald's, so I should probably get going."

Just as Lucky is about to respond, the door to the kitchen opens and my heart starts hammering away in my chest. *Dev.*

Sahara gets on her feet, causing Sammy to fall back into her bed. He's left there staring up at the ceiling, laughing and moaning at the same time. "Whoaaa, Thahara. You bounthed my head on the floor."

Dev stands in the doorway looking at Lucky and me, smiling in what looks like confusion. "What's this?"

Lucky answers, which is a good thing because I have no idea what to say. "This is our computer specialist. She came to do some work for us, like we discussed."

Dev's responding grin leaves no doubt in my mind about how he feels. Relief flows through me.

"Great news. Welcome aboard." He looks to his left, catching Sammy's attention. "And who's this? Did we get another puppy?"

Sammy smiles and does his best canine imitation. "Woof! Woof!"

Dev nods. "Nice. Good puppy. *Stay.*" He points at Sammy and gives him a hard look as he walks around the table to where Lucky and I are sitting. Then he drops into a chair next to me like it's no big deal, like it doesn't make my heart go faster. "So what's the scoop? Are we going to start work right now, or do we have time for lunch?"

I open my mouth to answer, but Lucky beats me to it.

"Jenny was just saying that she has to take her son to McDonald's. And Sunny's waiting for me at home, so I was going to leave them to it."

Dev rubs his hands together. "I love McDonald's. Can I go?"

Sammy jumps up from the dog bed and then continues to hop with every word that comes out of his mouth. "Yeth! You can go. Right, Mama?" It's not unusual for him to make instant friends with someone he deems worthy, and treating my son like a dog gives you a leg up in this three-year-old's evaluation process.

I pause for a few seconds, trying to figure out what my answer should be. Do I want him to go? *Yes.* Should he go? *Debatable.* Would I enjoy having another grown-up to talk to at McDonald's? *Absolutely.*

"He can, if he really wants to."

Dev smiles. "It's settled, then. Off to McDonald's we go. I'll drive."

Everybody stands and moves toward the door, so I do the same. I probably shouldn't be this excited about my near future being spent at a fast-food joint, but I am. Luckily, I have Sammy to focus on as we make our way out the door, so I don't have time to act all goofy over Dev inviting himself along.

CHAPTER NINETEEN

It feels like there are two places between Dev and me, even though there's only one. I've never been in a vehicle that has a bench seat in the front. "How old is this car, anyway?" I look over into the backseat at my son strapped into his car seat. He's smiling while looking out the window, like he's having a really great day. McDonald's tends to have that effect on him, but I think Dev is part of the reason, too. When he held Sammy up above his seven-foot height on the way to the car, Sammy screamed with glee, like he was on a roller coaster.

"This gorgeous vehicle rolled off the manufacturing line in 1975."

"It's older than I am." I laugh.

"Yes, but she drives like she just rolled off the line last year." His car decides in that moment to let out a big, loud pop and a poof of black smoke billows from the tailpipe. I turn around and look out the rear windshield; the black haze is slowly dispersing over the street behind us.

Barely containing my mirth, I turn back to the front and press my hands together, lowering my head and half-closing my eyes. "I'm going to go ahead and pray for the environment, if you don't mind."

Dev reaches up and strokes the dashboard. "Don't listen to her, Bessie. She's just jealous because she drives around in a mom-mobile and not a well-oiled cruising machine."

I could tease him more, but I just smile. It's fun driving around the city with Dev at the wheel. I feel like we're in a tank, and nothing could hurt us, not even a pack of raging black rhinos. Even without this giant car around us, I'd probably feel that way just being with Dev. He's very intimidating to look at, but I know he's soft inside, like an ooey-gooey chocolate truffle candy.

"What are you smiling at?" Dev asks.

I just shake my head. I don't trust myself to open my mouth and let any words out. I'd probably start gushing about how cute he is and how much I like him and how much I want to go out on a date with him. And we've planned to do something later this week, but I'm not going to be the one to bring it up. I don't want to seem overanxious. It's not really a date, anyway. It's just a bet that he won and I lost. He'll probably just give me another one of those friendly, brotherly kisses on the cheek after it's all over. The mere idea of it makes me happy. *I can pretend it's not brotherly, right?*

"Oh, so we're going to play coy, are we?" He taps his thumbs on the steering wheel as he nods. "Okay. I see how you are. I can handle it."

I'm not going to read too much into that statement. He's just being flirty and cute. It's fun. I know we haven't known each other for very long, but the way he teases and jokes around so easily, I feel like I'm with an old friend, like I can be myself.

Sammy starts chanting from the back seat. "McDo*nald'th*, McDo*nald'th*, McDo*nald'th*."

Dev glances up in his rearview mirror at our backseat passenger. "You're not excited about eating at McDonald's, are you?"

Sammy stretches his arms really high in the air, straining his whole body with his enthusiastic answer. "Yeth, I am!"

Dev play-frowns. "Nah. Maybe we should go somewhere else. Maybe we should go to a really fancy restaurant for your mommy."

Sammy frowns, worried Dev is serious. "No! I don't like fanthy rethtauranth. Fanthy rethtauranth don't like kidth."

Dev smiles. "How could anybody not like you? You're awesome."

Sammy smiles absently. "I'm awethome. I'm totally awethome." He turns his head and looks out the window, swinging his legs so they bang into the seat. If it were in another car, I might worry about it, but this car is a piece of junk. I know Dev is in love with it, but the backseats have stuffing coming out of them, for God's sake.

"Okay," Dev says with a sigh of defeat, "I guess we'd better go to McDonald's, then."

Sammy doesn't seem to hear Dev. He just keeps staring out the window, his face falling little by little.

Dev sees him in the rearview mirror and glances over at me. He whispers. "What's up with that? Did I say something wrong?"

I shake my head, my concern for my son taking over my thoughts. "No, I don't think so. He's got something going on at daycare, I'm pretty sure. He had a 'stomachache' this morning." I use air-quotes to emphasize my point.

Dev nods, turning his attention back to the front windshield as the stoplight turns green. His voice remains low so Sammy won't pay attention to it. "You'll figure it out, eventually. You just have to ask the right questions and get him talking."

I shake my head as I stare at the traffic going by. "I wish I knew what the right questions were. But sometimes this kid is just a great big mystery to me. So different from my girls."

Dev pats my leg a few times before putting his hand back on the wheel. "Don't worry about it. We'll stuff him full of burgers and fries and he'll sing like a canary."

I smile. Dev apparently knows exactly how little boy brains work.

"Hey!" Dev says all of a sudden. "What's that over there?" He's pointing out the front window.

Sammy's attention snaps back to us. "Where?" He strains in his seat to see out the windshield.

Dev is still pointing. "Over there! What are those big yellow things? Looks like a big M or something."

Sammy grabs the edge of his car seat and squeals. "It'th McDonald'th! We're almotht there!"

"Hallelujah," says Dev. "I'm starving. I could eat eight hamburgers right now."

"I could eat *ten* hamburgerth," Sammy says, his face split in half with a giant grin.

"Oh yeah?" says Dev. "Well, I could eat fifty hamburgers right now."

"Well, I could eat twenty trillion billion gadillion hamburgerth right now," says Sammy.

Dev shakes his head. "Dude . . . you are seriously hungry."

"Yeah, I know." His voice switches to pitiful mode. "My mommy made me eat cookieth thith morning for breakfatht. It'th not really food."

I laugh in indignation and turn around to glare at my son. "You little traitor. You asked me for those cookies. You said it was the only thing your sore tummy could eat."

"Yeth, but you shouldn't give me everything I athk for becauth you'll thpoil me."

I turn around and don't say another thing. Those words are not Sammy's; they've come directly from Miles's mouth, and I will not be sharing my opinion on that today. Not with my sweet, innocent little boy there to hear it, anyway. *Bastard Miles.*

"Hmmm," Dev says under his breath. "Trouble in paradise?"

I shake my head and mumble back. "Don't even ask."

WRONG PLACE, RIGHT TIME

Dev pulls into the McDonald's parking lot and slides into a space that I could have sworn his car would not fit into if I hadn't seen it with my own eyes.

"You're pretty good at driving this tank."

"They call me the smooth operator," Dev says in his best corny-sexy voice.

I burst out laughing so hard, I start snorting.

Dev puts the car in park and turns off the engine, staring at me. "You think that's funny?"

I can't answer him; I'm still laughing too hard. I just wave my arm at him and accidentally hit his shoulder. He acts like he has to duck away, like I'm abusing him.

Time to go. I need to get some fresh air before I become hysterical; I'm already halfway there. I grab for the door handle and almost fall out of the car when it works too easily. I keep my hand out to steady myself as I walk around to the other side of the vehicle to get Sammy out of his car seat, just to be sure I won't fall. I'm weak in the knees from all the serotonin floating around in my brain. Whoever said laughter is the best medicine knew what she was talking about.

I'm so happy, it's like I'm on drugs, and that's quite an accomplishment, considering where I am; normally, McDonald's is a guaranteed headache for me, and the pounding in my skull starts before I even get in the door. But right now? I'm floating, my feet barely touching the ground.

When Dev gets out of the car and I see his giant frame standing there, I realize he's right; he *is* a smooth operator. It takes a lot of finesse for a guy that big, who stands out that much, to be so humble and kind and cool. In my entire life, I've never met a man like him.

McDonald's is the typical madhouse that it always is seven days a week at this hour of the day. Coming here on a weekday at lunchtime makes me think half of the city must be unemployed and trying to find a place for their kids to run free so they can just relax, take a breath, and have a cup of coffee. The tables are filled with parents, and the outdoor play area is overflowing with wild, screaming children.

We stand behind a long line of fellow patrons. Little kids—siblings, probably—wrestle and fight with each other amongst their parents, jostling the crowd of desperate-looking people staring at the menus above the employees' heads. *Ahhh, McDonald's . . .*

Dev rubs his hands together. "Who wants a Happy Meal?"

Sammy jumps up and down with his hand up. "Me, me, me!"

Dev looks down at me from his great height. "What would you like, Mama? Happy Meal? Fries and a shake? A sedative?"

I smile, charmed. "I think I'll have a fry and a sedative, please."

He frowns at me. "I didn't hear any protein in your answer."

"Protein schmoteen. A fry will fill me up just fine, thank you very much."

"Huh-uh. You gotta have some protein. You want chicken, fish, or red meat?"

I'm not in the mood to argue with him, so I shrug. "You pick."

He gives me a wry look. "Sorry, but I have yet to meet a woman who will allow me to select food for her and then be happy with the choice I make. Just tell me which one you hate the least."

"I hate beef the least."

He affects a Cajun accent. "An excellent choice, mademoiselle. I shall order you the smallest burger known to man."

I glance down and see my son about to blow a gasket, he's so happy and full of three-year-old, animal-cracker-cookie-fueled energy. "If you don't mind, I'll take Sammy out to the playground to help him work off some of the energy he's got bottled up."

We both watch Sammy spin circles and then fall to the floor onto his knees. I reach into my purse, pulling out my wallet.

Dev puts his hand on my wrist to stop me. "Lunch is on me."

His hand is so warm, I want him to keep it there. "I can't let you do that. You bought the pizzas."

"I don't keep score. Besides, I get to write this off. The company will pay for it if I turn in my receipts. If you pay for it, that doesn't happen."

"Should I feel bad about your boss paying for my lunch and my son's lunch?"

"No. He told me to, so we're good."

I want to mull that over for a little while, and decide whether I should take advantage of Ozzie's generosity, but unfortunately this is not the best place to do that. Sammy's going to make himself nauseous with all the spinning he's doing. "Okay. Thanks. We'll be outside. I'm going to find a table out there for all of us. I don't trust Sammy on his own, even though the air-conditioning would be nice."

Dev is looking at the menu, but he answers me. "Don't worry about the heat. I'm used to it."

I take Sammy by the hand, and together we walk out to the playground. I barely get his shoes off his little feet before he's running away, screaming like a wild animal suddenly let loose after years in captivity. He leaps onto the nearest net he can climb that will bring him into the tunnel system, which looks like a playground for giant hamsters.

By some miracle, a family gets up from a table just as I'm looking around for a spot to claim, and I snag it, happy to dust off the salt and the fries and the various bits of lettuce that have fallen from their lunch. I sit down and the sun hits me in the face. Normally this would be immediate cause for complaint from me, but today, not so much. I close my eyes and soak up the beautiful warmth and the energy. Yes, it's going to make me sweat, but I don't care. Right now, my life is exactly how I want it, and that feeling doesn't come to me very often. I'm going to enjoy it while it lasts and not question where it's coming from.

CHAPTER TWENTY

I probably shouldn't make a big deal about having a McDonald's baby burger and tiny order of fries delivered to me at a dirty plastic table out on a playground made for oversize hamsters, but when Dev arrives with that tray along with his dimpled smile, I can't help but feel like I just won the lottery.

Everyone stares at him as he walks by, even the children. It's like a superstar has entered our midst. People are whispering, and I can almost guess what they're saying; they're wondering which NBA team he plays for.

I pretend like I don't notice how amazing he is. And I pretend not to feel proud that this man is here with me. I don't really have the right; we're just coworkers and maybe friends. But being friends is pretty awesome when it's with a guy like Dev, so I allow myself to be happy.

"Here you go." He puts the tray down in the middle of our small table. "A little protein, some carbs, and a tiny bit of sugar to keep you sweet." He hands me a miniature shake and grins.

Taking it from him, I try to will my silly blush to go away. "I don't normally allow myself to have those things. It's like eating dessert in the middle of the day."

He sits down, somehow managing to fold himself nearly in half so he can fit onto the tiny chair. It looks really uncomfortable, but he's not complaining. "I try to avoid sweets for the most part, but when it's a special occasion I let myself indulge." He holds up a second shake and wiggles it at me. Between his two big fingers, it looks to be about the size of a thimble. I doubt the contents will even spike his blood sugar a single notch.

"You must not get out very often, if McDonald's is your special occasion." I giggle because I think I'm pretty funny, but when he answers, my laughter stops.

"I'm not just at McDonald's." He takes a sip of his mini-shake. "I'm at McDonald's with a very pretty lady and her cute son." Dev turns toward the playground, so he doesn't see my face turning red, thank goodness. "Where is the little bugger, anyway?"

I search the clear areas of the giant plastic tubes and see a shock of my son's hair going past one of them. "He's up there. It looks like he's either chasing someone or being chased."

Dev distributes the food on the table, leaving a small Happy Meal box for Sammy in front of the empty seat between us. "So what's the rule around here?" he asks, when he's done. "Does he get to eat after he plays, or does he have to come eat before?"

I'm charmed that he's thought to ask for my house rules. "Normally, I get him to eat two bites of each item and then he can go play for ten minutes, but then he has to come back for another two bites, and so on."

Dev nods. "Very reasonable. You're a very fair mom."

"Thank you." I'm not sure I can eat the food he's put in front of me. It isn't because I'm not hungry; it's that he's suddenly making me feel . . . strange. I want to run around the block a few times to work off my nervous energy. This emotion reminds me of how I felt in high school or college, whenever I had a crush on someone. Whenever I was . . . falling in love. *Oh boy.*

"You want me to go get him?" Dev asks.

"No, that's fine, I'll do it." I stand and walk over to the over-sized gerbil run, calling out to my son at my arrival. "Sammy?"

He doesn't answer, which isn't surprising. He knows what I'm there for, and he'll do anything to avoid having to eat when he'd rather play.

"Watch this," Dev says from behind me. He walks over to a part of the tubes where kids can look down into a hole covered in a net. Walking under it while bent in half, he slowly stands once he's directly below it. His head is soon covered in the net and then it's up inside the tunnel.

I don't know how many kids are in there exactly, but by the sounds of the delighted squeals, there are at least five.

"Sammy, paging Sammy," Dev says in a booming voice. "You are needed at the French fry table immediately. Please report to the French fry table."

The distinct sounds of my son giggling warm my heart. His little body comes shooting out of the tunnel and down a slide five seconds later, and he runs over to my side. "Where are my fryth, Mama? Dev thayth I gotta eat 'em."

I follow my son and Dev back to the table, and sit down. I expect Sammy to eat two bites and tear off again, but instead he digs in, eating like I've starved him for two days. I marvel at how Dev is able to completely remove any McDonald's headache from my brain, and at the same time, get my son to eat all of his lunch. *Is there anything this man can't do?*

CHAPTER TWENTY-ONE

After loading Sammy into the back of my car and strapping him into his car seat, I stand outside the running vehicle with Dev by the driver-side door. With the air-conditioning going full blast to remove both the heat and the stifling humidity from the interior, Sammy has already fallen asleep.

"Well, that was an adventure," Dev says, smiling.

"Life with Sammy is always an adventure."

"So what are you going to do now?" Dev asks, tapping the top of my door with the side of his forefinger.

"I'm going to go home and see what I can do to get my home office set up for this freelance work. I'll probably go online and check some other sites too, to see if I can find some more stuff to do."

"Dating sites?"

My face goes warm. "No, not dating sites. Freelance sites."

"You should maybe go on that dating site," he says, not looking at me. "You shouldn't stay in your house every night and just watch television alone."

My heart suddenly feels like it's made of lead. Here I was thinking he was worth taking a risk for, and now he's trying to get me to date other guys? *How could I possibly have read that so wrong?*

"What makes you think I do that?" I ask, offended at the vision he's created in my own head of me, sitting on my couch, alone in my family room being a grade-A lame-o.

"It was you who told me you do that. Besides, I saw you on that dating website. You were just at the beginning part of the process. You haven't even looked for a date yet, have you?"

I cross my arms over my chest. "Have you?"

He's looking at me finally, shrugging. "Not exactly."

"Well, if I should look for dates, then you should too."

This is a ridiculous conversation. I'd really like to go on a date with *him*, but I'm not going to say that now.

"I'll do it if you'll do it," he says.

"Fine." I can go out with another guy. Maybe I'll find one cuter than he is, even. Taller, too.

"How about if we do our dinner together," he pauses, "you know . . . the dinner that you're paying for, and we'll discuss our dating strategy going forward?"

Do I want to speed off in a huff, burning rubber and leaving behind the acrid stench of tires and hurt feelings? Of course I do. I'm only human, after all, and it's been a *really* long time since I've spent any time with a cool guy, *and* I don't own a dildo. *Yet.* And of course, I'm more than a tiny bit sad that Dev is asking me to help him find the woman of his dreams, especially after it seemed like he was sending me signals telling me he was interested in dating me himself.

Then it hits me: *Maybe he's a player.* Maybe I've completely misread every single thing about him because I have no idea how to play these games.

I lift my chin. "Okay. I think I could do that."

"When?" he asks.

"How about Friday? I might be able to convince May to come over and watch the kids for a couple hours."

"Okay. I'll ask my mom if she can watch my son. You ask May, and let me know what she says. If the babysitting is a go, I'll pick you up at six-thirty."

"Do you know where you want to go? I need to know what I should wear."

He winks. "I'll let you know." He leans down and gives me a quick kiss on the cheek, again before I even realize what's happening. The idea that he's a player comes once more. This definitely feels like a game of some kind, but at the same time it doesn't feel like he's doing it to mess with me in a mean way. Not after the way he was with Sammy. A real player wouldn't bother, right? I'm so confused. I watch him walk to the warehouse door and punch in the code to enter.

The door starts to open, and he looks back at me, waving. "See you soon."

I wave back. "Yep. See you soon." I climb into the car and put my seatbelt on. I should be exhausted; it's been a long day. But I feel as light as air.

CHAPTER TWENTY-TWO

Wednesday night is finally here—my big night working with Lucky at the Blue Marine offices after hours.

It's still light outside when May arrives to watch the kids for me. She walks in without ringing the bell, and I'm standing in the family room with my purse over my shoulder. She is focused on finding the kids and doesn't see me. "I'm here!" she shouts down the hallway toward the kitchen.

I clear my throat so she'll see me. She turns her head and smiles. "There you are! Wow, and don't you look snazzy."

"Oh my god, you sound just like Mom."

May comes into the room and gives me a hug and a kiss on the cheek. I return the affection, hoping she doesn't sense my nervousness in my embrace.

"Are you freaking out?" she asks, holding me out at arm's length, staring into my eyes as if she can act as a human lie-detector that way.

So much for hiding my emotions. "Yes. Does it show that much?"

"No. You look snazzy *and* confident."

I shake my head at her. "You are such a terrible liar." I turn my attention toward the staircase. "Kids! Auntie May is here to hang out with you!"

Something that sounds very much like a herd of very small wildebeests comes next, as the children charge down the staircase. The first one to the bottom is Sophie. Her feet barely hit the floor before she's running and throwing herself against her aunt. "Auntie May! You haven't been here in forever!"

May hugs Sophie, who's clinging to her waist, while rolling her eyes at me. "So dramatic. You know I was here just last week."

Sophie's voice is muffled as she speaks into May's shirt. "But you never do sleepovers anymore."

"I have a lot of work, now that I have a different job, so it's harder for me to do sleepovers. But I'm here tonight, right?"

"Yes!"

Melody is the next child to appear. She arrives at a more sedate pace, waiting for her sister to detach herself from Auntie May before she holds her arms up for a hug. "Hi, Auntie May. I'm so glad you're here." She smiles sweetly, like only my little Melody can. I'm so proud of her for not laying a guilt trip on her aunt.

May's face melts a little. "Oh, sweetie, I'm really glad to be here, too. I think it has been too long since I got my cuddle on."

Sammy arrives last, carrying an armload of toys. It's a miracle he didn't tumble down the stairs head over heels with the pile he's got. I glare at his sisters, because they should've helped him out. I wasn't there, but I know exactly what happened. They left their little brother up there to fend for himself so that they could be the first ones to hug their aunt. I have no idea why it's such a competitive sport with them.

"Do you need some help, Sammy?" I ask.

"No. I have my toyth. I'm very thtrong." He's a foot away from May when he opens his arms and drops everything in a giant pile.

Pieces of toys along with whole action figures scatter in all directions like shrapnel from a bomb. He walks over to his aunt and holds his hands up in expectation.

May puts Melody down and takes Sammy into an embrace. He clings to her like a baby monkey, wrapping his arms around her neck and his legs around her waist, burying his face in her chest.

Her arms wrap around him and squeeze. She closes her eyes and inhales the scent of his hair. "I missed you, Sammers. Nobody gives little boy hugs like you do."

"My hugth are the betht, aren't they?"

"They're not better than mine," says Melody, frowning at her brother.

May is too sly for their games. "Sammy, you give the best little *boy* hugs, and Melody, you give the best little *girl* hugs, and Sophie gives the best *big* girl hugs."

Sophie rolls her eyes. "I knew you were going to say that."

Attempting to head off an argument, I speak up. "Okay, kids, who's ready to go have some dinner?"

Sammy wriggles out of May's arms and drops to the floor, running over to grab his Spider-Man and Superman action figures. "I'm ready!" He holds them both out in flying position, Superman head first and Spider-Man butt first. Sammy has told me many times this is how Spider-Man prefers to get around, and I'm not one to argue; I really don't know him that well.

Melody raises her hand. "Me! I'm ready!"

Sophie rolls her eyes. "Whatever."

May reaches over and tickles Sophie's neck, making her giggle a little. I can tell my daughter would rather not be reacting like that, but May knows her sensitive spot.

"What's up with this *whatever* stuff?" May asks my oldest. "Since when are we saying *whatever* to each other?"

"Didn't you hear?" I ask. "It's the latest thing with all the big kids. And since Sophie is a big kid, she's decided it needs to be an integral part of her vocabulary."

"Well, if she says it when I'm here, she's going to get it." May gives her niece a fake stern look.

Sophie gets a sly little smile. "Whatever."

May lunges at her, and she runs off shrieking to the kitchen.

May looks at me, pausing between the family room and the hallway. "Are we all set? Is there anything special you need me to do?"

I shake my head. "No, I don't think so. Their dinner's there on the table, there's some sorbet for dessert, and you know where to find all their stuff. They've already had their baths, and Sophie's homework is done. All you have to do is have fun." I try to sell it with a big smile.

May's not buying it. Her expression softens. "Don't be nervous, sweetie. You've got this. You know what you're doing, and Lucky is a nice guy."

I nod. "He is a nice guy. I'm not worried about Lucky at all. Although, honestly, May, he's a little bit too good-looking, don't you think?"

"I know," she says, enthusiastically. "It's weird, right? It blew me away when I first met him, but I don't notice it so much anymore. The more you're around him the less you'll be distracted by it."

"I hope so."

"Hmmm, is there a little somethin'-somethin' going on there maybe?" she asks in a suggestive tone.

I shake my head vigorously. "No way. Seriously, don't even go there. I am *not* interested."

May uses her coy voice on me next. "That's good, because I think *some*body would be a little bit disappointed if he found out you were interested in Lucky."

174

My heart does a little double skip followed by a triple skip. "What are you talking about?" I'm trying so hard to be coy like she is, but I'm not sure it's working.

"Don't play. You know exactly who I'm talking about. Dev."

"Oh. Dev?" I shrug, playing it so cool. "He's pretty nice. He took me and Sammy to McDonald's the other day."

"Oh, believe me, I heard about it."

I'm seized by the sudden need to know every single detail. I walk over to my sister and grab her arm, breathing my hot breath right in her face. "Tell me!"

She starts to walk toward the kitchen, pulling her arm from my kung fu grip. "Sorry, Sis, but you have to get to work. We can talk about this later."

I whine at her. "But I want to know nowwww . . ."

She laughs. "Don't worry; I'll give you all the dirty details when you come home."

"But I might not be back until four o'clock in the morning."

Her teasing voice disappears in an instant. "Don't wake me up. I don't want to be up before six." She goes back to smiling. "But I will have breakfast with you, and we can talk all about it then. And you can tell me about your exciting night working with the handsome Lucky doing undercover ops."

A dark cloud instantly settles over me. "Don't say that."

"Don't say what?"

"Don't say *undercover ops*. This is just a job. I'm the person on the no-risk crew. Lucky and I don't get involved in all that commando bullshit."

"Okay, okay. Don't be so sensitive. I was just joking around." She tilts her head at me and narrows her eyes. "Are you worried about something in particular?"

I sigh out an annoyed breath. May is a really smart girl, but sometimes she can be really dense. "Of course I'm worried."

I gesture toward the kitchen. "I have three kids. I can't afford to do something risky that might put my life in jeopardy."

May looks at me like I'm off my rocker. "Calm down, Jenny. You're just going to be working on computers in an empty office."

"Exactly. But what if somebody comes in? What if the person who's doing this embezzlement or whatever decides to come work in the middle of the night? If they're taking as much money as Lucky thinks they are, they're going to be really pissed. Maybe they'll have a gun or maybe they'll throw some punches. I can't afford to have black eyes the next time Miles comes over here to get the kids. He'll take them away from me."

May walks over and puts her hands on my shoulders, staring deeply into my eyes. "First of all, you'll have Lucky there. Lucky will be carrying a firearm, just in case. Don't freak out about it! Second . . . nobody's going to come in there in the middle of the night to work. Who does that? And, last but not least, Miles is *not* going to take the kids from you. He doesn't want that responsibility, remember? He can't even take them for an entire weekend, for shit's sake."

A little voice speaks up from behind May. "What do you mean, my dad doesn't want the responsibility?"

My heart sinks when I realize it's Sophie uttering those horrible words. I step around May and squat down so that I can look into my daughter's eyes. "Darling, Auntie May is just trying to calm me down when I'm acting like a silly mama. She doesn't know what she's talking about. Of *course* your father would love to have you at his house more often. He's just really busy with work. But this Christmas, he's going to take you for *two whole weeks*! Won't that be exciting?"

Sophie shrugs. "Maybe. But if he has that stuck-up girlfriend with him, maybe not."

"Girlfriend?" May's curiosity is obviously piqued.

I stand and shake my head at her. "Don't even ask. Just let the kids have a nice, peaceful evening without talk about girlfriends or any of that stuff." I look at my daughter and point to the kitchen. "Go. Set the table, so Auntie May can serve you your delicious spaghetti dinner."

May pulls me into a hug. "You're going to be totally fine. Better than fine. You are gonna kick butt and take names, and bring all that crap back to Bourbon Street Boys so you can show them how amazing you are."

I pull out of her embrace because it's way too tempting to stay there and chicken out. "Thanks. I'll call you when I'm headed home."

She winks at me. "Excellent. I can't wait to hear about your adventure."

She leaves me standing in the front hallway, shouting out to the kids as she goes. "Whoever wants to be my favorite niece or nephew . . . Auntie May is really thirsty! Whoever gets her a big glass of water will be her favorite for the next two minutes!"

I hear them scrambling as I walk out the door, and it makes me smile. I may be nervous about this job I'm about to do tonight, but I would never be nervous with my sister as a substitute mom to my children.

I push away the dark thoughts that want to intrude, the ones that say if anything ever happened to me she would become that person permanently.

CHAPTER TWENTY-THREE

After I meet Lucky at the warehouse, we get into his SUV and ride over to the Blue Marine headquarters. It's nine-thirty at night, and although we're arriving later than we originally planned, I feel much better about being here at this time. Lucky pulls around to the back of the building and parks the vehicle in a space in the corner, far from the door we will go through.

"You ready?" He has a laptop in a bag strapped over his shoulder, and a briefcase full of files. He pauses with his hand on the door, waiting for my response.

I nod, trying to look more confident than I feel. "As ready as I'll ever be."

"That's the spirit. Come on. Let's bang this thing out and go have a drink."

I don't know about the drink part, but I'm definitely on board for getting this thing banged out. I just want to get it over with and leave. I feel weird slinking around in the dark, sneaking into someone's business, even though I have permission to be there from one of the owners. I keep worrying that one of the other owners or an employee is going to show up and yell at me. Or worse. I stop myself from imagining what that *worse* thing could be.

We get out of the car and walk quietly over to the back door. The gravel in the parking lot crunches under our feet, and it sounds to me like we're announcing to the entire neighborhood that we're here and up to no good.

"Are you nervous?" Lucky asks. He's talking in a regular tone of voice instead of whispering like I think he should be doing.

"Very. Does it show?" I try to giggle, to show how cool I am, but it comes out more like a cackle. It reminds me that I still need another piece of my witch costume for Halloween. I have less than a month left to prepare, and I have nothing for my get-up other than a few parts that are left over from years past.

"No, it doesn't show. But I think it would be kind of weird if you weren't nervous on your first night of work."

"I think even if this were my *fiftieth* night of work, I'd still be nervous about sneaking into someone's building at night."

"Sneaking? This isn't sneaking. We have permission to be here. See?" He holds up a set of keys and jingles them at me.

I reach up and grab them to stop them from making so much noise. "I guess I'm just worried that some random employee or one of the other owners will come by while we're in here. What if they call the police?" I let the keys go so he can use them to open the door.

"Already got that covered." He uses two different keys to do the unlocking.

"What do you mean you've got it covered?"

"Ozzie contacted the police and let them know what we're going to be up to tonight, so the cops are going to swing by later to make sure everything's cool."

I breathe out a huge sigh of relief. "You have no idea how much better that makes me feel." Most of the phantoms that were haunting me disappear into the night air. I have nothing to worry about. The cops are in on it with us. *Phew!*

He pauses in the process of turning the door handle to give me one of his big Hollywood smiles. "I thought that might make you feel better."

He pushes the door in and holds it open for me, but I stand there and give him an awkward look.

"I know you're being a gentleman holding the door for me, but would you mind going in first?"

"Absolutely." He doesn't hesitate for a second. He walks right in and turns on a light. Two seconds later he faces me again. "All secure. You are free to enter."

Feeling like a total weenie, I come in behind him. I'm careful to shut the door and lock it. I wish I could put a bar across it too.

Time to face the music. I turn around and examine the space around me. We're in a back hall with a bathroom on one side and a janitorial closet on the other.

"Come this way," Lucky says. "The offices we're looking for are down the hall on the right and the left."

I follow behind him, my eyes scanning side to side. The coward inside me is expecting someone to jump out and attack us at any second. My blood pressure is through the roof, and my heart is beating like crazy. The only good news in this scenario is that I'm probably losing a lot of weight with all the sweat that's started to roll off my body.

Lucky turns on some more lights. "Do you want to work together in the same room, or do you want to split up?" He turns around and looks at me as he waits for my answer.

I give him my best mom-look. "Are you kidding me?"

He smiles again and hitches his computer up higher on his shoulder. "Same room it is." He points to the right. "Let's start in here."

I stay in his shadow and take the seat next to his. We're sitting at two computers used by administrative personnel, but there's no way for me to know who they are or what they do yet.

Lucky sets his laptop down along with his briefcase. I put my purse next to his things. I'm very tempted to take my can of pepper spray out of my purse and set it on the desk next to me, but I don't. May said that Lucky has a firearm, and I know he's been trained by Dev and Ozzie on how to use it. I don't have anything to worry about. The cops are going to be here soon, I'm sure.

Lucky pulls something out of his briefcase and unfolds it. It's larger than a regular-sized piece of paper. "This is a little schematic of the office and all of the computers in it," he says. "I thought we could start at the individual stations, and then we could move to the server after."

I take a look at the diagram and place myself on it. I point to the desk on the schematic where I'm sitting. "This is me here, and that's you there."

He nods. "Yes, exactly. So you're sitting at one of the accounting spots, and so am I. Perfect." After he puts a mark on the paper over the two computers we're working on, he turns to his computer. "Let's fire these babies up and see what we can find."

I wiggle the mouse at my station, and the monitor goes on. It's asking me for a username and password. Because I read the file Lucky had sent over, I know that we have access to this information. Before I can even think to say something about it, Lucky is pulling two papers out of a file folder and handing one of them to me. "Here are all the usernames and passwords. A copy for you and a copy for me."

I nod and start entering the data immediately. The faster I can get this done, the sooner we'll get out of here.

Lucky starts to whistle, but it doesn't bother me. It's better than working with somebody who wants to chat. With this type of work, it's better for me to either hear some kind of random noise or nothing at all. I need to keep all of my attention on what I'm doing. It's monotonous, but when I get in the zone, I'm a machine. Nobody can work faster than I can.

I easily maneuver myself into the computer. From there it's a simple thing to call up the different parts of the different drives and examine their contents to see if anything funny is going on. We were given a full view of their system's architecture before we got here, and I studied it at length from home while the kids were sleeping last night, so I know what I should be looking at. Anything that's not supposed to be here will jump out at me.

Other than the fact that this particular employee spends a lot of time doing her online shopping at work, I don't see any cause for alarm on her computer; but just to be sure, I take the thumb drive that I brought from my purse, plug it into her tower, and upload the virus. When it's finished doing its thing, I look over at Lucky. "I'm cloning this machine. Are you cool with doing that one too?"

Lucky looks over at me. "What do you think? Should I?"

I shrug. "I don't see anything going on with this station, but just to be sure, I'm going to go ahead and clone it anyway. It can't hurt, right? It's just going to take a little bit of extra time." I want to get out of here as soon as possible, but that doesn't mean I want to shortchange the operation. Having clones will make it possible for us to monitor what's going on later and dig deeper off-site. And if we don't need them, we can just delete them."

"If you think we should do it, then I'll do it," Lucky says. "Do you have another one of those thumb drives?"

I nod, reaching down to dig in my purse. I pull out the second thumb drive and hand it to him. "Here you go. Just double-click on that executable file, and it'll do the rest."

"And there will be no evidence that they can see that this has been done?"

I go back to my computer and ensure that the process is finished before shutting things down. "No, there shouldn't be. It's a pretty decent program. I checked it at home before I left."

"Do I want to know where you got it?" He's smiling, so I know he doesn't mean anything bad by it.

"Let's just say I got it from a trusted source."

In fact, I got it from one of my former coworkers. There are a few kids barely out of high school working for my old employer who spend way too much of their free time wreaking havoc on the Internet. They aren't bad kids, per se; they just lack the maturity needed to restrain themselves from causing trouble out of pure boredom. Lucky for me, they looked up to me as a kind of mother figure when we worked together, so it wasn't too difficult to convince them I needed their help.

They actually thought it was funny when I asked for the program. I told them that I was making a clone of my daughter's computer so I could watch what she was doing in chat rooms and such. Because they know very well the kind of garbage that's out there on the Internet, they were more than happy to act as big brothers and step in with a solution to my "problem."

"Okay, I won't ask any more questions." Lucky puts his thumb drive into the tower he's working on and starts the virus running.

I look down at the schematic. "Where to next?"

Lucky's attention is on the computer when he answers. "Wherever you want to go is fine with me."

I pick the next logical spot, trying to move around the room in an orderly fashion, taking my purse with me. This is already going faster than I thought it would. We might even be out of here by midnight. I hope it'll be early enough to catch May while she's still awake so I can talk to her about whatever Dev said.

CHAPTER TWENTY-FOUR

I'm in one of the back offices finishing up cloning the last drive when a strange sound comes from the end of the hall near the back door. My hand freezes on the mouse.

Holy crap. What was that?

Lucky is in a different part of the office working on another computer. After three hours of working together, I calmed down enough to agree to work separately, but now I'm definitely regretting that decision.

All of my attention is focused on that hallway. *Did I hear something or am I just imagining it because I'm so tired?* I want to call out to Lucky, but I'm afraid if somebody is coming in, they'll hear me.

I grab my cell phone from the desk next to me. Thank God I brought it with me. Unfortunately, I left my purse and everything else in the first office that we started in.

I quickly type out a text message to May, cursing myself for not getting Lucky's number. I turn off the sound on my phone and send the message. It's one in the morning, so May is probably sound asleep, but maybe I'll get lucky and this message will wake her up.

Me: *At Blue Marine. Someone coming in. Don't have Lucky's number. He's in the other room.*

More sounds come from the hallway. Someone is definitely breaking in. There are two voices, and they're speaking in hushed tones. My palms start sweating and my heart races. My worst nightmare has come true. *We're busted!*

I reach over and turn off the computer monitor, pick up the paper with passwords on it, and drop down below the level of the desk. I'm tempted to hide completely underneath the thing, but I want to verify whether I'm just imagining things, and I need to be able to see over the desk to do that. I wonder what Lucky's doing. *Is he panicking like I am? Is he sending a text to Ozzie? Is he calling the police?*

The voices become clearer as they get closer, so now I can tell that at least one of them is a girl.

"Are you sure?" she asks.

A guy answers. "Yes, I'm sure. Would you stop freaking out? You're making me freak out."

They could be teenagers or maybe college students. Their voices are too youthful to be older than that. I'm not sure whether this reassures me or makes me more panicked. Kids are prone to making rash decisions. Kids do stupid things when under pressure. *Do they have a gun?*

"You guys leave lights on in here?" the girl says. "That's very wasteful, you know." *Apparently, we have a future environmentalist in the building. Nice.* I roll my eyes. Doesn't she realize what she's doing is more serious than leaving a few lights on? She's breaking and entering! Where are her parents when she's off breaking the law?

"How am I supposed to know?" the guy says. "I don't work here."

Interesting. The guy doesn't work here, but he seems to be the one initiating this little visit. *Is he here to steal something? Is he related to somebody who works here?* I feel like a total spy right now. I strain to hear as much as I can. Who knows? I might be asked to be a witness at some future date.

I duck down even farther. Only the top of my head and my eyeballs are over the top of the desk now. Shadows appear outside the glass windows of the office I'm in. I thank my lucky stars that I didn't bother turning a light on when I came in. The glow of the computer screen is enough to illuminate the whole room, especially with the lights from the office across the hall shining in. Lucky will be in full view if they go into that office more than a few feet. He's too big to hide anywhere.

"Come on," the guy says. "It's in here."

Now I can see the two figures clearly. They're young, but the guy is big. Really big. Like football-player big.

I've seen enough. I duck down all the way below the desk, and climb into the knee-hole very carefully and quietly. I pray they can't hear me breathing. I nearly have a heart attack when the light to the office goes on.

What will I do? What will I say? Will the big guy beat me up? Will he call the police? How will I explain my presence here? Will they believe I'm part of the cleaning crew? That I have permission to be here?

I knew I shouldn't have come. I knew this was a bad idea. Why did I do this? This is like breaking and entering. Why did I think this had no risk? A thousand other thoughts are running through my brain, and my ears are on fire as I try to imagine the many different scenarios that could possibly roll out in the next five seconds.

I hear footsteps on the carpeted floor. Closer and closer they come . . .

Here it comes . . . The moment of truth . . .

A loud crash rings out from another office.

"What was that?" the girl asks, sounding almost as panicked as I feel.

"Wait here. I'm going to go check."

"I'm not waiting here by myself! Don't leave me alone! No way!"

When I hear them leave the office, I let out a long sigh of relief. Lucky caused a distraction to take the heat off me, but now he's in trouble. *What should I do? We're a team!* I can't abandon him, much as I might want to.

I grab my cell phone and text the first person I think of who can save me. *Dev.* I don't stop to question why it's him who comes to mind and not the actual police, who are supposed to be acting as our backup.

Me: *Help! We're busted! Someone's here!*

His answer comes immediately.

Dev: *Can you get out without being seen? Do they have weapons?*
Me: *I don't know!*
Dev: *Call 911. Give them as much detail as you can. Hide. I'm on my way.*

I dial 911, holding the phone to my ear and covering my mouth so that I can muffle my voice as much as possible. I hear nothing in the office from Lucky, and I have no idea where the couple has gone, but they can't be far.

The dispatcher at the police department picks up my call. "Nine-one-one, what's your emergency?"

I whisper as softly as I can and still be heard. "Hi. I'm with Bourbon Street Boys Security, and we're at the Blue Marine administrative offices doing some night work, and there's been a break-in. Can you send someone?"

"Ma'am, we have already received a call from your location, and officers are just outside the rear door. Can you tell us if there are any weapons involved?"

Relief flows through me. Of course Lucky called them. It's probably what I should've done in the first place.

"I'm not sure. There are two people who look to be in their early twenties, maybe, or late teens. One of them is not familiar with this office, but the other one is; however, he doesn't work here."

"Do you recognize them? How do you know this information?"

"I overheard their conversation. I don't know what they're here for, but the male said something about showing the girl something. He's very big. I didn't see any weapons, but that doesn't mean there aren't any."

"Thank you. Are you in a secure location?"

"Yes. I'm hiding under a desk in the office on the left, farthest from the back door." I'm actually very proud of myself that I remembered my location and was able to pinpoint it so accurately. I feel kind of secret-agent-ish. Now that the police are right outside, my fears have taken a backseat to my involvement in this little scenario. It's not nearly as awful as it was two minutes ago. Adrenaline is making me tremble all over, though. I'm sweating too. *Fun on a Wednesday night!*

"Copy that," the dispatcher says. "Please hold the line."

My ear and cheek are sweating where the phone is pressed up against my face. I can smell my breath, and it ain't pretty. But I'm not moving, no matter what. I'll stay here until I cramp up and keel over. The only way I'm crawling out is if Lucky comes and tells me it's all clear.

"Ma'am are you still on the line?" asks the operator.

"Yes. I'm here."

"The officers are going to enter the location. Stay where you are. Do not get involved."

"Don't worry, I won't."

The next thing I hear is a banging on the door and someone shouting. I've watched enough *Criminal Minds* episodes to know that they're doing their knock and announce before entering. I hope they don't break the door in. I don't remember hearing those two people locking the door behind them.

The back door bangs open and a voice comes to my ears much clearer.

"This is the New Orleans Police Department! We are entering the building! If you are in this building, you are trespassing. Please come out with your hands up. Do not draw any weapons." I hear little footsteps running and then the girl screaming.

A male voice comes next; I think it's the tall intruder. "Hey! We're not trespassers! My dad owns this place."

I roll my eyes. *Holy shit.* What are the chances that the one night we decide to come work here, an owner's son also decides to come out to the office to cop a feel with his girlfriend?

The lights go on and shine brightly into the office. I squeeze my knees against my chest. I don't think Ozzie would want Lucky or me to show our presence here to these two kids. The file says that there are four owners of this business, and I have to believe that this kid is related to one of the owners who is *not* in the know about our operation. Mr. Jorgensen would've made sure to keep an eye on his kid on the night he knew we'd be coming here.

A police officer is in the middle of the hallway, speaking to the two intruders. I can't see anything, but I can tell from the sound of his voice that he's not by the office I'm in. I stay put anyway.

"Turn around and put your hands behind your back."

"I told you, man, this is my father's office. I'm not intruding, so you can't arrest me."

"Son, I am not going to debate this with you. I don't know who you are, and I'm not in the habit of taking the word of people who break and enter a business at one o'clock in the morning. So turn around and put your hands behind your back. We'll work this out after I have you secured."

"Jerry, just do what he's saying."

"Shut up, Heather. He can't tell me what to do. This is my property."

I hear a boom and a struggle and then some swearwords. "Get off me, man!"

There's more grunting, followed by sounds of clicking. "You have the right to remain silent . . ." The voices get fainter as the intruder is hauled off down the hallway. When I finally get brave enough to pop my head up above the desk, there's a man standing in the hallway looking right at me. My eyes go wide. Thank God he's wearing a police uniform, or I probably would have passed out with fear.

He winks at me, gives me a little salute, and walks away, headed for the back door. I sink back down onto the carpet, feeling like I'm going to vomit. My head is spinning and I'm covered in cold sweat.

I cannot believe that just happened. Sounds of the girl whining and her boyfriend grumbling disappear as the delinquents and the arresting officers leave the building. There are locking noises and then silence.

I wait there in that office sitting on my butt listening to my heartbeat in my ears for the longest time, surprised I'm not having a heart attack. I didn't know my heart could even go this fast. I hold my hands out in front of me and marvel at how much they're trembling. I look like a drug addict in bad need of a fix.

Soon enough, there's a sound coming from the doorway. Then Lucky is there standing next to my desk, looking down at me as he holds his hands out. "Can I help you up?"

I grab his hands and use them to leverage myself onto my feet. I brush my pants off and straighten myself up as best I can.

I waste a little more time smoothing my hair back into its ponytail. It's probably hopeless, but I need these few extra seconds to calm myself down. It isn't Lucky's fault that this happened, but I am very tempted to take my anger out on him anyway.

"So, that was unexpected." He gives me a half grin.

"It most certainly was." I don't share his sense of humor over it.

He gestures at my computer. "Are you finished here?"

I grab the seat and pull it over, sitting down on it. "Almost." Work will calm me down and take my mind off the craziness I just suffered. Turning the monitor on, I verify that the upload of the virus is complete. "Yes. All finished." I eject the thumb drive from the computer and pull it from the tower. Standing, I move the chair back into the spot where it was when I first arrived. "Are *you* finished?" I'm really proud of myself. Inside, I feel like I want to tear some doll heads off or Hulk-out on this guy, but outside I'm as cool as a cucumber. Lucky would never know from looking at my calm expression that I want to maim him.

"The only thing we have left is the actual server. How about if we go do that one together?"

I nod. "I'm just going to make a quick phone call and I'll join you."

Lucky nods and walks off. I step into the hallway and call Dev. He answers on the first ring.

"Are you okay?" The sounds of traffic are in the background. He's still on his way to rescue me, I think.

I sigh heavily, so relieved to hear his voice on the other end of the line. It somehow magically makes all the crap I just went through seem like not such a big deal anymore. "I'm fine. The police showed up and hauled two kids out of here. I can't believe I panicked like that over teenagers. You don't need to come out here. Really, we're fine. I overreacted."

"Hey, don't say that. You had every right to freak out. And you handled it perfectly."

"Perfectly? I don't think so. I called you, and I'm pretty sure I should've called the cops."

"I'm your trainer, in charge of your personal security. I'm glad you called me. But next time, yeah. Maybe call the cops first."

We both chuckle.

"What are you doing now?" he asks.

"Just finishing up with the server." I peek around the corner, but Lucky is out of sight. "I probably need to go help Lucky out."

"Okay. I'll let you go. Thanks."

"For what? Making you panic?"

"No," he says, his voice going softer. "For calling me when you were scared."

I snort. "Scared? Who was scared?"

He laughs. "That's my girl."

I hang up feeling like my brain is filled with helium. I could float, I'm so high with a combination of post-panic adrenaline, boy-crush hormones, and the idea that when things got too hot to handle, I still did almost everything right. I didn't panic too much, and I walked away without a scratch. I am the honey badger, and I don't take no shit from nobody.

CHAPTER TWENTY-FIVE

O n my way to join Lucky, I take my cell phone, which still has that one unanswered text to my sister floating on the screen, and send May another message telling her it was a false alarm and to ignore it. *Lie.*

I enter a large storage closet that houses all of the office supplies and the server for the Blue Marine administrative offices. Lucky is there and he's just finished hooking his laptop up to the computer.

"Ready?" he asks.

I nod. "Yep."

He goes to work, following the instructions I gave him before we got here. I watch over his shoulder to make sure he doesn't miss any steps, correcting him and pointing things out when he makes minor errors.

"I'm so glad you're here with me," he says, waiting for a command to run its course.

I don't know what to say to that. *He's glad that I was here when intruders came? He's glad that my life was at stake? Is he crazy?*

"When stuff like that happens, you just have to fly by the seat of your pants. You're obviously a quick thinker and good on your feet."

I'm trying not to warm at his compliment, but it's difficult. Who doesn't like to be called a quick thinker?

"Well, I sent a text to my sister, and I called Dev before I called nine-one-one, so I don't know how cool I actually was."

He looks up at me for a moment. "Really? That's awesome. You're even better than I thought you were."

I refuse to smile, even though I definitely feel complimented now. It doesn't feel like that big a deal to make a couple calls. Anyone would have done what I did. "Why? I don't get it."

"You didn't freeze up. You didn't panic. You just saw the situation, and you handled it. You did exactly the right thing."

"I felt like I was completely out of my element, and that I was doing everything wrong."

He stops working to focus on me. "No, absolutely not. I know you haven't had any training in this kind of thing, in security work of any kind, but I think you're a lot like your sister. I think you're a natural."

"I don't get why you think my sister is a natural. I mean, she's a great photographer, nobody's debating that, but she's not a ball buster."

He points to the computer screen. "Am I done here?"

I type in a new command and then nod when it finishes five seconds later. "Yep. We're done."

Lucky powers down and closes his laptop. As he disconnects it from the server and packs it into his case, he responds. "Being a ball buster only comes in handy once in a great while. What we need on our team, what we consider an asset, is somebody who can think on her feet, who has quick reflexes and a sharp mind. Somebody who's observant, who can evaluate a situation, and on-the-fly make the right decision on how to deal with it. Your sister, from the moment she walked through our doors, was able to do that. You really can't train that stuff. You're either that kind of person or you're not." He focuses on me with a very serious expression. "We can work from a certain base and improve on it, but if you don't have the base to begin with, there's not much we can do. Your sister was born with that, and now I know you were too." He shrugs as he throws his computer case's strap over his shoulder.

"Lucky, I don't mean to be rude, but I have to tell you . . . I was scared shitless when those people were in here. I'm not so sure I have this fly-by-the-seat-of-my-pants base you're talking about."

"So? So was I. That's a totally natural reaction. If you had reacted any other way, I'd worry about you."

"Do you mean to tell me that every time you guys are faced with a conflict, you're scared?"

Lucky puts his heavy hand on my shoulder and stares me down. "Never underestimate the power of fear, Jenny. Fear keeps you alive. And if you're special, fear helps you focus. Fear helps you zero in on the solution that you need to execute immediately. May has that instinct. I think you do too. But we're gonna let Dev and Ozzie decide if I'm right." He lets me out of his grip and moves to leave the server room.

I rush to fall in behind him. Just the sound of that man's name makes me feel calmer. "Why does Dev decide?"

"Dev is our trainer, but not just with physical training. It also includes mental training. Dev can usually tell pretty early on whether somebody has the mental strength to handle the entire training package."

Now I have a bunch of questions, but I'm afraid that every single one of them is going to sound like me seeking compliments. So instead of asking anything, I just mull over what he said. We collect all of our things from the first desks where we started, turn out the lights, and head down the hall together.

"Are you sure it's safe to go out there?" I ask.

"I'm going to double-check before we open the door." Lucky takes out his phone and sends a text. A few seconds later there's a response and he nods. "We're good to go. Stay behind me."

I sigh loudly.

He pauses. "What? What's wrong?"

"Why do you tell me to stay behind you if everything is okay?"

He grins at me. "Wouldn't want you to get lazy on me."

I give him a glare. "You're so lucky I don't believe in hitting."

He dips his head back and laughs. "That's why they call me Lucky. Because I am."

We walk out into the sultry night together to an empty parking lot. After locking the door behind us, Lucky makes his way over to his vehicle. I wait for him to unlock the doors and get inside.

"Do you think those two were wondering what this car was doing here?" I ask.

"I doubt it. People leave their cars in this industrial area all the time for different reasons. And if they were, so what? Right now they have bigger problems to focus on."

"Do you think they'll get charged with breaking and entering?"

"I doubt it. But they are going to have some explaining to do. I'm going to let Mr. Jorgensen know what happened from the inside, and he can just deal with it however he feels is best. I don't think those kids are going to be worrying about a random car in the parking lot when they have to explain to their parents what they were doing inside their offices in the middle of the night."

The trip back to the warehouse is a mostly silent one. I'm lost in thought about what we've done tonight and about the work we have ahead of us. As we're pulling into the industrial park near the port, Lucky speaks. "Are you available tomorrow to start working on this? Or are you going to need a day to go over what you found?"

"I think I'm going to need a day to do that." And recover. I can just imagine trying to work on four hours of sleep. "Can we get started on Friday?"

I need to go retrieve my things from my old job along with my last paycheck. That severance had better be there, and it better be good, or heads are going to roll. I'll be ready to start fresh with the Bourbon Street Boys on Friday. I get a little thrill knowing that I have a job waiting for me, and it's the kind of place that allows me the flexibility to work my own schedule. I don't have to be jealous of May anymore.

"Friday is great," Lucky says. "I'm going to take Sunny to the vet tomorrow. He's not looking so hot right now."

I chew my lip, wondering if I should delve any deeper into this issue. But after what we went through together tonight, I decide it's fine. "Can I ask you a question about your fish?" I've never met an adult with a goldfish, let alone an adult who's attached enough to a goldfish to take it to a doctor. It's just too cheesy not to ask about.

"Sure."

"What is a grown man like you doing with a goldfish who he worries about so much that he takes it to the vet?"

Lucky pulls up to the warehouse door and puts the car in park. Turning off the ignition, he lets out a deep breath. Then he just stares at the steering wheel.

I've probably overstepped my bounds again, but in fairness, I *did* verify with him first that I could ask the question. He had to know this was coming. He must've been asked this question before. I mean, I can't be the only person in the world who thinks being a dedicated goldfish owner is weird.

"Sunny originally belonged to my little sister."

He doesn't say anything after that, so of course I'm compelled to gather more information. At this point, it would be rude not to ask. "Did she not take care of it?" I can see him as the avenging older brother, there to teach her a lesson. *If you can't take care of your fish properly, I'll do it!*

Lucky shakes his head. I take that as a simple no, but then he elaborates. "It's not that she didn't want to; it's that she couldn't."

There's obviously a story here, and I'm pretty sure it's not one I should ask about. But then I feel like it would be really insensitive to drop it. I struggle with how to continue.

"How old is your sister?" That's the safest question I can come up with.

"My sister, when she had Sunny, was fifteen."

The next obvious question dangles in the air between us. He used the past tense, but he used it in reference to the fish. What am I supposed to do with that? Keep going? Stall out? Why did I ask him the question in the first place? I should have just kept my damn mouth shut. *When will I learn to stop prying?*

Because honesty is always the best policy, I decide to stop the charade and come right out with it. "Lucky, is everything okay with your sister? I get the impression you're really sad right now, and I'm sorry if I brought up a subject that makes you unhappy."

He shakes his head. When he speaks, his voice is rough. "It's okay. People don't ask me about her because they're afraid they're going to upset me, or they're afraid to bring up bad history; but it's almost worse when they do that, you know?" He turns to look at me, and the lights outside the warehouse show me that his eyes are bright with unshed tears.

I nod. "I get it. When somebody isn't around anymore, sometimes the only thing you can do to feel better is to talk about them." I had a friend in college who lost her sister. The only thing that made her smile was telling me stories about the things they did as kids.

He nods, chewing the inside of his cheek.

I reach out and put my hand on top of his. "Did your sister pass away?"

He nods.

"Was it recently?"

He shakes his head no. "She passed away eighteen months ago."

"How old was she?"

"She was sixteen."

My heart clenches up and starts to ache. I want to cry with him, but I think he needs somebody to be calm right now. And I can be that person when I have to be. "What happened? Was she sick?"

"No. She wasn't sick. Not really. She was sad. Depressed."

I squeeze his hand and swallow several times, trying to keep myself from losing my shit. I've asked as much as I can. To go any further, to delve into the details of what happened, will serve no good purpose now. "You must've been close, even though there's a big age difference."

His voice is devoid of any emotion that I can hear. "I thought we were close. But it turns out we weren't close enough."

I squeeze his hand harder and lean in, forcing him to look at me. "Lucky, if you're even suggesting that you are to blame for what happened, you need to not go there."

"I don't think she blamed me for anything. But I blame myself. If I had just paid more attention . . ."

I shake my head. "No. Sometimes these things are battles that are fought completely inside. Nobody sees it. It happens all the time. Most people who are depressed are also very loving. They don't want others to suffer with them. They feel very isolated, but not because other people aren't trying to be with them or aren't trying to understand. They just can't connect. There is a huge disconnect when you're depressed, and it often takes a professional to recognize it." I sigh with frustration, wanting him to understand, but knowing he probably isn't going to take my word for it. "You can't blame yourself. There's no end to that kind of torture. It'll ruin the rest of your life, and I guarantee you, your sister would not want that for you."

Lucky pulls his hand out from under mine and takes the keys out of the ignition. I think he's just going to get out of the car and not say another word, but he stops staring out the window and turns to look at me. "Thanks."

"Thanks for what? Digging into your private life? Lecturing you about something that makes you sadder than anything in the entire world? I can think of lots of better ways to spend an evening. I'm sorry that I overstepped my bounds. It's a problem I have."

He shakes his head and tries to smile. "No, you didn't do that. You're a nice person, and you saw that there was something going on, and you asked about it. I'm glad you did. It's been a long time since I've talked about her."

"How come? I'm just curious. You don't have to answer me if you don't want to."

"Like I said . . . it's difficult for other people. Ozzie and the rest of them know what happened. They were here. They were the ones picking up the pieces when I fell apart. I think they worry that if they talk about it, I'm going to lose it again. I haven't been good for a long time."

"You look really good to me. Maybe too much." I laugh.

His smile is sad. "My sister always said I was too handsome. She told me I should grow a big old beard to ugly myself up a little." He grabs his stuff and opens his door.

I take that as my signal that the conversation is over and get out too. I'm relieved to know that Lucky feels like he can talk to me, but I'm also a little dizzy over the fact that the conversation went so deep. Here I thought we were just going to work an assignment together and that would be that. And then I thought that a break-in in the middle of our operation was the most stressful event I was going to be dealing with.

It's amazing the things I've been through in such a short span of time. Just a few days ago I was living my normal life with nothing going on. Now I'm going out to dinner with a totally handsome, seven-foot-tall bald guy who may or may not just want to be friends, I have a new job as a freelancer, I'm hiding under a desk calling 911, and I'm counseling a guy about what I assume is the suicide of his younger sister. I have never had such an odd and interesting week.

CHAPTER TWENTY-SIX

Waking up at six-thirty to get the kids ready for school is even harder than I thought it was going to be. I'm exhausted from the previous night's work, and four hours of sleep was not enough to erase that. But at the same time I feel very gratified. I can safely say that in all the years I've been working, I've never had a shift quite like I did last night with Lucky.

I had hoped that I'd be able to discuss all the fine details with May over breakfast, along with the other things that have been weighing heavily on my mind, but she got called away shortly after waking up.

Before parting ways at the front door with a hug and a kiss on the cheek, she and I promised we'd make time for each other this evening.

The extra time I would have used gossiping with my sister, I spend on a quick phone call to an old friend from college. I have a feeling I'm going to need her legal advice for my meeting with my old boss today, and thankfully she's able to tell me exactly what I want to hear in less than ten minutes. Today is not going to totally suck. *I hope.*

After dropping the girls off at before-school care and Sammy at daycare—I refused to buy in to the stomachache excuse again—I'm headed over to my former job to pick up my last paycheck and the things I left there at my desk. If it weren't for my new temporary job with the Bourbon Street Boys, I'm pretty sure this trip would be one of the most humiliating experiences of my life, but instead, I'm walking in the front door with my head held high. I only went one day without a job offer, and I didn't even try to get it.

So what if it's my sister who technically got me the job? Last night I was able to use my skills to impress a guy who I know is very intelligent and can hold his own behind a keyboard, and that's not nothing.

Now I see what my sister meant when she talked about being part of a team that feels almost like a family. The Bourbon Street Boys are something special. I shouldn't get ahead of myself, though. It's not like I've been offered a permanent job; and even if I were, I don't know that I would accept it. There's still that whole danger aspect, which everyone kept trying to convince me wouldn't be there but ended up being there anyway. I think we got pretty lucky with the people who broke in being just kids. They could've been career criminals with guns.

"Hey, there! Long time no see." It's Eddie, the kid I got the virus program from, and one of my favorite people in this place. I run my security badge through the machine and then wait as it turns red and the guy at the desk looks me up.

"I'm just coming to get my things," I say to him.

He nods, recognizing me as the lady who often brought him coffee and doughnuts. "Go ahead. I was told you were coming."

I turn to my former coworker. "Hey, Eddie. What's up?"

He leans and mumbles in my ear as we continue on through some glass doors and toward my old supervisor's office on the far side of the cubicle farm. "Did you hear the latest?"

"Nope. I don't work here anymore, remember?" I weave in between desks, waving at people as I walk past. I don't feel like hanging around and chatting. Being here is embarrassing enough; I don't need to prolong the experience.

"Well, apparently, we're getting some new funding. And they've got new investors coming in who're gonna be taking a really close look at our operations. We're all supposed to be on our best behavior." He snorts after that.

I know exactly what that sound means. Eddie has a prank planned. This silly boy could never be completely well-behaved, but when he's warned he has to toe the line, forget it. That's the surest way to get him acting up. He's worse than my son. My guess is management will send him on vacation just before the investors show up.

I try not to let my anger at the news show. "It's funny you say that, because I heard that times were tough and they were letting people go because of their dire money situation."

Eddie backs off the happy-mania a little. "Hey, I'm just telling you what I heard going around the rumor mill. But I think it's true; they have dates on the group calendar where everything's blacked out, and they're not saying what we're going to be working on during that time or who's going to be taking lead or whatever. They just told us to get our shit straight. We had to get rid of all our squeaky toys—can you believe that? How am I supposed to code without Lionel?" Eddie has a little rubber man he squeezes, making the eyeballs pop out over and over. It helps him focus.

"You should apply for an exception for Lionel."

"I know, right? I mean, what's the big deal? Who's going to come in here and care if Lionel's sitting at my desk with me?"

There are so many things going through my head right now, and none of them are good. Did they get rid of me because I was going to make a bad impression for the company, like a stress ball named Lionel? Were they showing off, proving that they could be ruthless and cut anybody who might not be the most economical employee? Did I do something wrong?

The wise part of my personality is telling me that I should just get my box of belongings, collect my last paycheck, and go. But the other part of me, maybe the reckless part of me, wants to know what the hell happened. I worked so many hours for these people and sacrificed so much. Why don't they appreciate that? They seemed to appreciate it well enough at the time. I was always told what a great employee I was. My performance reports were impeccable.

"You come in for your stuff?" Eddie asks.

"Yep. And my paycheck."

"There's a box of your things on your desk. They haven't replaced you with anybody yet."

I roll my eyes. "That's surprising."

"I don't want the old man to catch me slackin', so I'll leave you to it. Good luck. Let me know if you need anything else." Eddie pats me on the back.

I stop to give him a little hug, which I think surprises him. "Don't get yourself into too much trouble, Eddie. I like you. You're one of the good ones."

When I release him, he pulls back and looks at me with a surprised expression. "You think so?"

"Yes, of course." I grin at his disbelief. "Would I pull your leg?"

He shrugs. "Maybe not. But I gotta tell you, there aren't many people who would agree with your assessment of me."

"Screw them. What do they know?" I wink at him.

He points at me as he walks backward toward his cubicle. "I got your back, Jenny. Any time, day or night. You got my number." He puts his fingers up to his ear and mouth, miming the words *Call me* while giving me an exaggerated nod.

I turn around, shaking my head at his silliness. I doubt very highly I'll ever take him up on that offer, but it's nice to know that a kid with a super-charged brain like his is on my side. A person can never have enough smart friends, as far as I'm concerned.

I've reached Frank's office, a glassed-in space that looks out over the maze of cubicles where I used to toil away along with all the other worker bees. He's on the telephone, but when he sees me approaching he hunches down, talks fast, and then hangs up, trying to pretend like he was just sitting there casually with nothing going on.

I narrow my eyes at him. He's up to something, and while I shouldn't really care what it is because I don't work here anymore, I have a sneaking suspicion it involves me. Operation Do Not Mess With Me is in full swing.

"Hello, Frank."

He stands. "Jenny! So nice to see you." His voice is saccharine sweet. *Yuck.*

I know Frank well enough to know when he's hiding something. You don't spend six years working more than full time with someone, often stuck in meetings that go on for hours, without becoming fluent in their body language. He's worried about something; I can tell by the way he's wringing his hands before he reaches out to give me a handshake. And when his palm touches mine, I know for sure he's got something on his mind. *Sweaty palms. Ew.*

"Just here to get my stuff and my last paycheck." I keep it light and breezy so he won't see my sneak attack coming. I'm so glad I ran into Eddie before I got in here. I have ammunition now, and I plan to use it. Frank flat-out lied to me to get rid of me. He thought I'd be so upset and scared about being unemployed that I'd just go running out to find another job and not question anything he said. I hate it when people in positions of power take advantage of those weaker than they are. I think that's why I enjoy reading superhero comics with Sammy so much. The good guys always win *and* they get to wear capes.

Unfortunately for Frank, I know how the world of venture capitalism works. I'm not one of these young whippersnappers running around in this office, living on ramen noodles and wondering when I'm going to get laid next. I've been around the block a few times, so I know that when new investors come in, a company will do anything it can to make its balance sheet look crisp and clean. Management gets rid of anything that the money men might consider deadwood, and older employees who cost them more in salary and who have kids that get sick from time to time are considered deadwood.

It was probably an easy decision for Frank to get rid of me and replace me with one or two young kids right out of school. He's not going to be around for the long haul; he's like all the rest of them, ready to pump and dump, get his share of the pie and fly away. Hardly anyone cares about the long term anymore. All they care about is mo' money, mo' money. *Jerks.*

Frank opens up his desk drawer. "Here you go, just like we discussed. Two months' severance." He holds out a white envelope at me.

I shake my head, never taking my eyes off him. "Sorry, Frank. But that's not gonna work for me."

His hand pauses in midair, the envelope flopping down from his fingers. He cocks his head, playing stupid. "I'm sorry . . . We discussed this on the telephone, right?" He tosses the envelope across the desk, and it lands in front of me. "Like I said, we can't keep you on at this time. We're having some trouble with the company, and we need to streamline operations. It's nothing personal—I hope you know that."

I don't move a muscle, other than to blink. "I heard otherwise."

His eyes open a little wider. "What did you hear?"

"I heard that you have new money coming in." I wait for his reaction, and I'm not disappointed. His mouth opens and closes a few times and he frowns, squinting his eyes up into two little tiny slits. He couldn't look guiltier if he tried.

"I don't know where you heard that, but that's false." He puts his hands out, palms up. "We're status quo here. Nothing has changed. The only thing we're doing, like I said, is streamlining a little bit. Cutting the fat."

Oh, wrong move, buster. Calling me fat.

"I believe you, Frank. As we both know, whenever a software company—like *this* one, for example—wants to bring in money from new investors, that's the first thing it does. Cuts the *fat*. That's stage one. The next stage is to give the money men a little tour. Romance them. Maybe you'll even be tacky enough to take them to a strip club. But that's really not my problem. The only one who has a problem here is you."

A storm cloud moves over Frank's expression. "What exactly are you saying?"

"You know what I'm saying. Tell me you're not that naïve."

"Spell it out for me." He's no longer playing stupid. Now he's daring me to continue. But he must have mistaken me for some brainless cow if he thought I wasn't going to rise to that challenge.

"See, there's another part of this process that I'm fully aware of, having been a part of it before, and I'm sure you're well aware of it too, which would explain why you're trying to play dumb with me right now."

He tries to interrupt, but I keep going. "When these new investors conduct their due diligence on this company, they're going to ask you if you've entered into any lawsuits with anyone. And they're also going to ask you if there are any *threatened* lawsuits." I pause a few seconds to let that sink in.

Frank gives me a sly smile. "If that were the case, and I'm not saying that it is, there wouldn't be any problem for us. Because, as everyone knows, our balance sheet is clean. We have no lawsuits, nor any threatened lawsuits. All of our patents are up to date, and we haven't used anybody else's intellectual property in our work.

You of all people should know that, since you headed our committee for purity of IP."

I never liked that stupid title. Purity of IP? What does that even mean? He acts like this company was always coming up with fresh ideas, but Frank wouldn't know a fresh idea if it was attached to a two-by-four that bapped him over the head. It's time he got a little wake-up call, and he has no idea who he's messing with. I'm the girl who just handled a midnight break-in without peeing her pants. Last night, I was super-spy. Today, I'm an avenging angel, making sure I get a fair shake from this turdbasket.

CHAPTER TWENTY-SEVEN

You're forgetting one little thing, Frank," I say, my nostrils flaring as I try to hold in my anger. I didn't want to have to go here with him, but I don't like how he handled things with me. And I really don't like the way he's talking to me as if I'm stupid. And I really, *really* don't like how he let me hang out in the wind, high and dry, after promising me a promotion less than a month ago. He must think I was born yesterday.

"Remember the promotion you promised me? Remember how you asked me to work all those extra hours, and told me I was going to get paid for it in the end with my promotion? How you told me I was management material?"

He gives me a pitying smile. "Jenny, this is all water under the bridge now. It's over. You just need to let it go."

"Don't you *dare* look at me with that cocky expression on your face and act like you feel sorry for me. The only one you should be feeling sorry for right now is *you*, because you underestimated me. You took advantage of me like you take advantage of all of your employees, and you thought you were going to keep getting away with it. Maybe you have for a really long time, but that's done. I'm not going to put up with it. Everybody knows that I was the one selected to be fired because I have children and because I am a single mother. There is no other reason. I have a better work record than anyone else on this floor."

"Who told you that?"

I can't keep my volume from rising. I didn't want to think he was going to try to paint me as a slacker and a person who deserved to lose her job, but I suspect that's what's about to happen, and it makes me livid just to imagine it. "Nobody had to tell me that! Everyone knows it. It's obvious. And this may be an at-will employment situation, and I may not have a contract with you for my job, but that does *not* mean that you can fire me just because I have children. There are *some* laws that you have to follow in this state. And you know what? Maybe what you did skirts the edge of legal, but it also skirts the edge of illegal. It's definitely not right, I know that. This is *not* how you treat people."

I take a deep breath and let it out before continuing. "Let me tell you how this is going to work." I sit down in the chair opposite his desk and motion for him to do the same. In this moment, as I see the flicker of surprise in his eye, I come to realize that I can take care of myself. Last night's fiasco proved that. Frank the Snake can try to take advantage of me, but I will eat him alive. I am the King Snake in this room, not him.

He stands there for a few seconds, being obstinate, but when he realizes it makes him look like an angry child he sits down and rests his hands on the arms of his chair. "Go ahead. Say what you have to say, but it's not going to change anything."

"Here's what's going to happen, Frank. You're going to take the check that you have in that envelope there, and you're going to tear it up into little pieces. Then you're going to call accounting, and you're going to tell them to cut me a new check for double the amount that you had on that first check." I manage a small smile. "I think that's fair. Six months would be even more fair, seeing as how you gave that waste-of-space Nick nine months' worth when he left—even though he wasn't nearly as good as I am, and even though he didn't work nearly as many hours for you as I did. But we know the glass ceiling is fully intact here, and I don't have the energy to fight that battle, so I'm just going to go ahead and let you get rid of me and my big mouth for the bargain price of four months' severance."

He looks like he's about to speak, but I shush him with a raised finger. "Now . . . if you want to stick to your two-month offer, go ahead. That's your right, of course. But then you'll force my hand and we'll just see what happens next."

He shrugs. "I'm not hearing anything from you that tells me I should do anything with this check other than hand it to you and say good luck with your future." He laughs. "But you know what? Don't even *think* about asking me for a reference now." He leans forward and stabs a finger into his desktop, dropping his voice to a near growl. "You think you can come in here and threaten me, and then get a good reference?" He shakes his head in disbelief as he leans back in his squeaky chair. "I don't care how many years you worked here, and I don't care *how* good your work was. You're done now. You're not going to work in this town ever again if I have anything to say about it."

I smile at him very patiently. Because he's a man who's never dealt with a glass ceiling, and because he's used to railroading people and getting his way, he doesn't understand what's happening right now. So I'm going to spell it out for him real easy and real slow so that he can keep up.

"Frank, listen closely. I'm done playing, so you need to pay attention. You have investors on the line who are poised to hand over probably several million dollars to you because you've told them that you have this revolutionary program that's going to change the world. You and I both know that it's not going to do that, and that you're very likely going to get the lawdogs of Vedas Incorporated after you, because it could be argued that you're using pieces of their patented code to make yours work properly. Remember? I was in charge of *IP Purity*." I say the words with extreme distaste. "I warned you, in writing, of the problems you were going to have with that code, but you chose to ignore me. However, that's not my problem anymore. Regardless of whether your investors find that little nugget of information during their due diligence, you still have the issue of outstanding lawsuits."

His eyes narrow, telling me he might finally be catching on, but I keep going.

"If you refuse to pay me what you owe me—four months' severance—I will sue you. It's that simple. What you've done is illegal and morally wrong. You are *not* allowed to use people and then throw them to the curb so you can make your bottom line look prettier and lie to investors about your balance sheet. You can't do that to investors, you can't do that to employees, and you can't do it to all the people who are going to get hurt down the road as a result of your terrible decisions."

He laughs, but it doesn't cover up the concern in his tone. "You're nuts. You'll never win a case against me. I can fire you whenever I want, however I want. You can't put handcuffs on me."

I shrug. "You may be right. I don't think you are, but regardless, how long will it be before a judge makes that decision? Will your investors wait? When they see that lawsuit on file in the public record, will they ask you questions about it, do you think? Will they worry some of their investment funds will actually be going toward the defense of that suit or to an eventual settlement with me? Because I'm pretty sure investors want their funds going toward the development of the IP portfolio."

I sit there patiently and wait for him to put it all together, to do the addition and subtraction and realize that the end result is that he needs to do the right thing.

"You're blackmailing me." He's sputtering and probably a little incredulous. I'm sure he never saw this coming from sweet little Jenny, the den mother for the entire software development crew, the girl he trusted with making sure all of his products left the building totally aboveboard. If it weren't for me, he'd already be out of business, and we both know that. He needs to honor that. I'm proud of myself, sitting up straighter with the stronger backbone I have in me now.

"Sorry," I say, "but I checked before I came over here to make sure I wouldn't do anything stupid that could get me in trouble. This isn't blackmail; this is a business negotiation. I have the legal right and standing to file a suit. This is not frivolous. I'm doing you a favor by letting you know what the law is, how the world of venture capital works, and what my intentions are. Did I mention my former college roommate is a lawyer at Hancock and Finley?"

He opens his mouth to answer, but I cut him off.

"I talked to her about what happened here, and she says I have a case. She says Louisiana's civil code supports my argument. So this isn't going to go away, Frank. Sorry to rain on your parade, but that's what happens when you try to screw me over. If I file a lawsuit, it's going to be on the books for at least the next couple of years."

I put my hands on the arms of my chair and lean in, staring him down, angry that he's put me in this position and made me feel dirty. I don't like business negotiations, even when they are legal. I prefer that people just treat me fairly of their own accord. But if he wants to get down and get into it, I'll play. This is the new Jenny. Jenny, the girl who goes on nighttime special ops and drops viruses on people's computers while they're lying in bed dreaming of

WRONG PLACE, RIGHT TIME

sugarplum fairies. "So . . . ," I say, using my most threatening voice, "do you want to dance with me, Frank? Because I'll dance. I can do the salsa, the tango, I can do the cha-cha, the can-can, the . . ."

"Enough!" he shouts, standing and leaning over his desk to blast me in the face with his terrible coffee breath. "I've heard enough from you. You think your little threats mean anything to me? They don't, Jenny. You know what you are? You're just a sad, overweight, desperate loser, who's got nothing better to do than work sixty hours a week and neglect her kids in the process. I feel sorry for you. That's all. Just pity, nothing more, nothing less." He tries to laugh, but it comes out kind of shrill, even for him. "So I'll tell you what . . . I'll go ahead and pay you your four months' severance, and I'm going to laugh all the way to the bank. You want to know why? Because I would've paid you more than that, if you hadn't been such a bitch about it. But you made the offer and I'm accepting it. You can call your little friend at that law office and ask her about oral contracts if you think you're going to get another fucking cent out of me."

I shrug. "Fine. That's all I wanted." His words are stinging badly, but I'm not going to give him the satisfaction of crying over it. I'll bawl later, out in my car when I'm alone, though. *Overweight? That was low.* Dev's comment to me, that he could whip my butt into shape in six months, has me wishing he were here to punch this guy in the face for me. He'd do it, too. He'd be like Hellboy, not caring about proper office etiquette. Boom! Everything in splinters around us. My avenging angel, there for me just like he was on the phone last night.

Frank glances up and scowls, then he gestures wildly at some-body behind me. I turn around and catch no fewer than four people staring through the glass at us. They probably heard every single word we said. I don't care, though. They know it's true. They'll probably throw a party in my honor at the local bar after work.

I turn around to face Frank, smiling. "Go ahead and write that check so I can get out of here."

Frank picks up the telephone and calls accounting, making the arrangements for me to pick up my severance. Part of me feels like the champion of the world, and the other part of me feels dirty. I hate having to threaten people to make them do the right thing. Miles is the only one I've had to do that with before, and it always makes me feel like the one who should be apologizing.

Frank hangs up the phone and starts pushing papers around on his desk. "The check is waiting for you in accounting. Go get it and take your things. And make sure you leave your security card at the front desk when you go."

I stand. "Frank . . . I just want to say one more thing." I wait until he's looking at me before I finish. "If you ever say anything untrue about my service here in this office, you'll be very, very sorry."

His eyebrow goes up. "You're threatening me again? Seriously?"

I shake my head. "No, I'm not threatening you. I'm just telling you that by law, you have to tell the truth about my work here. And the whole time that I was here, not once did you ever say anything negative about me or my work product. Not to me or to anyone else that I'm aware of. All of my evaluations have received top marks. You can't change history; it is what it is. So, if somebody calls you and asks you about my performance here, you'd better tell the truth. That's all I'm saying."

He doesn't say anything in response; he just acts busy. I could force him to acknowledge what I've said, but I'm not going to push it. I think I made out really well here, and I don't want to tempt fate into reminding me I'm just a mere mortal.

I start to leave, but hesitate in the doorway. I don't want to walk away with this dark cloud hanging over my head. My life is changing in fundamental ways right now, and that means I need to design this new life of mine intelligently, with light and not shadows.

I turn around to look at my old boss. "Frank, thank you for giving me the opportunity to work here with you and your team. I learned a lot. I met a lot of cool people, and I enjoyed working for you."

He doesn't say anything. He completely ignores me, as if I'm not even standing there. I shrug and walk away with a heavy heart.

Nobody ever said doing the right thing was going to be easy.

CHAPTER TWENTY-EIGHT

I pick Sammy up from daycare on the way home from my meeting with Frank. Normally the little punk doesn't want to come with me when I arrive because he's having too much fun with his friends, but this time when I get there, I find him sitting in a chair in the director's office waiting for me. My heart sinks when I notice that his eyes are red-rimmed; he's been crying hard. *I guess it's time to clean this closet out, too.*

"Hello, Sharon," I say, trying not to sound as stressed as I feel. "What's going on? Why is Sammy in here with you?"

Sharon, the director, stands and motions for me to shut the door. "Sorry, I tried to call you, but I wasn't able to get through."

I fish my phone out of my purse and see that I have several missed calls. "Oh, gosh, I'm sorry. I was so distracted taking care of some things, I didn't even notice my phone was buzzing." *Mom of the Year strikes again!*

I drop my purse to the floor and crouch down with my arms open, looking at my son with pity in my eyes. "Come see Mama, baby."

Sammy jumps off the chair and runs over, throwing himself into my embrace. He doesn't say anything; he simply cries.

I stand on unsteady feet and practically collapse into the chair in front of Sharon's desk, my purse somehow getting tangled in my feet. Sammy is clinging to me like a monkey, and all I can do is look over his shoulder at her with questions in my eyes.

Sharon sits down in her seat with her hands folded, placing them in front of her on the desktop. "We've been having a little bit of trouble recently, and Sammy was in my office so that we could discuss it. After talking to him, I decided it was probably a good idea that you and I have a little conference."

Oh, boy. Here it comes. If she tells me that Sammy can't come to the daycare anymore, I'm going to lose my mind. It's one thing to freelance from home, but it's a whole other thing to try to work and watch Sammy at the same time. It just can't happen. I'm only one person, not three.

"I knew something was going on here, because Sammy has been telling me he has stomachaches before school every day. And you know how much he loves it here . . . or used to love it here. I don't think he's very happy anymore." I try to detach Sammy from my neck so I can look into his face, but the harder I try, the more he clings to me. He's obviously not ready to talk about it, so I let him wallow in his misery as I continue with the director.

She nods. "Sammy has been having some difficulties with a couple of other children. These are kids who he used to get along with, but for some reason, there's a conflict now. I don't know that anyone is at fault, per se, but certainly there's some behavior on both sides that I don't condone. It's not something we can have here at Sunnyside Daycare."

I'm trying not to get defensive, but it's hard. She's giving me the distinct impression that she believes Sammy to be a troublemaker. And while I know he's very high-energy and he likes to tease, my baby doesn't have a mean bone in his body. He's usually the one at the bottom of the heap when there's a pile-on.

"Do you know what's going on?" I ask. "Do you have details?"

"We're still investigating. But what I *can* tell you is that there was some shoving, and there were some children who were injured."

I force Sammy's head back a little so I can take a closer look at his face. He couldn't be more pitiful, but I don't see any bruises or cuts anywhere. "Sammy, tell me what happened. I'm not blaming you for anything; I just want to know."

Sammy shakes his head and tries to dive back into my chest. I think he feels guilty, but that's not all that's going on here. If he were the bully, or if he were the one causing all the trouble, he wouldn't have a stomachache; he'd still want to go to school. It's going to take some finesse to get to the bottom of it, and it's not going to happen here in this office. Not this close to the scene of the crime.

I sigh heavily. "I have to work tomorrow, but then I can take a few days off and talk to Sammy and figure out what's going on from his end."

Sharon gives me a funny look. She seems decidedly uncomfortable when she responds. "You see, though, the problem is, I'm not sure we can take Sammy tomorrow."

It takes my brain several long seconds to process that little nugget of awful. "Why not?" I'm actually pretty proud of myself, how I'm maintaining a hold on my temper, because this woman is seriously asking for me to lose my mind and Hulk-out right here in her office.

She's a daycare director. She knows better. You don't tell a working single mother in the late afternoon on a Thursday that her kid can't come in the next day without any kind of prior warning. And you sure as crap don't say it in front of her kid!

"The parents of the other children involved are not happy with the fact that their children were physically abused."

I stand and hold my hand out awkwardly; Sammy is still think-ing he wants to crawl into my blouse. "Stop right there. Just stop. You've known my son for over a year. You know as well as I do that he is *not* a mean person. He would never just hurt somebody out of the blue for no reason. That's not who he is."

Sharon nods and closes her eyes. "I realize that. I also know that he has some things going on, and some issues that you need to address at home. These are things that we can't do anything about here at the school."

I frown at her. *What in the hell is she talking about?* "I don't understand what you're trying to say." My arms are about to fall off. Sammy is so heavy, he feels like a bag of bricks. "Can you just stop running around in circles and tell me what you really mean?"

Sharon takes her time answering. When she finally does, she's cringing as she speaks. "You do realize that Sammy has a speech impediment, right?"

My jaw drops open. All I can do is stare at her. I'm trying to figure out if she's joking with me, because I can't imagine what her purpose would be in saying this other than to be cruel and ridicu-lous. *Is she seriously making this about my son's lisp?*

I guess she's tired of waiting for me to respond, so she con-tinues. "You know, when children are young, it might seem cute, but as they get older it's really not cute anymore. And it's up to the parents to do something about it."

I shake my head, stopping her from crossing any further over the line than she already has. "Do not . . . no. Do *not* go there." I stand and walk to the door, reaching down to grab my purse on the way. Unfortunately, the strap is tangled around the chair leg, and in my struggle to get it free, I flip the chair over. It makes a loud crashing sound that causes Sammy to start crying again as he climbs up higher into my arms, practically strangling me with his efforts.

"You don't have to worry about Sammy tomorrow or ever again." I throw my purse over my shoulder and turn around to glare at a woman who has a lot of nerve calling herself a director of a daycare. She should go be the director of a damn prison. "I have never been so appalled at someone's behavior as I am right now with yours. And you call yourself a daycare provider? How dare you."

I don't want to hear what she has to say in defense of her horribly cruel words spoken in front of my son . . . words that should have been kept private between adults . . . because I can't trust that I won't slap her across the face after hearing what she says.

I leave her office as quickly and as gracefully as I can, while my son clings to me like we're stuck together with Spider-Man's web glue. It's only when we're at the car, standing at the back door with his car seat waiting to take him, that Sammy finally lets go of me and speaks.

"Mommy, I don't want to come back here ever again."

I use the cheeriest voice I'm capable of when I answer. "Well, guess what . . . you don't ever have to come back here again. I don't like this place anymore."

Sammy sounds happier already. "I don't like that plathe at *all*. Thothe people are mean and they're thcary too."

I talk aimlessly, not sure how to handle this situation, but pretty sure that keeping him talking is a good thing. "You know, I never knew that before. I always thought they were so nice. But apparently they're mean. And stupid."

I'm strapping Sammy into his car seat when he looks at me with a serious expression. "Mommy, that'th not nithe to call people thtupid."

Tears rush to my eyes, but I blink them away. "You're right, baby. It's not nice to call people stupid even when they're stupid."

Sammy smiles. "You're funny, Mama."

I reach in and squeeze his cheeks together, kissing his pudgy little lips. "You're funny too. You make me laugh all the time. You're my best baby boy."

"Thophie thayth I'm your only boy, tho if you thay I'm your betht boy it doethn't really mean anything."

I'm going to have to have a talk with Sophie, obviously. She needs to understand how much her brother actually listens to her.

"I'll tell you what, Sammy. How about if I tell you right now that you are my favorite littlest child."

Sammy gives me a huge grin. "I like that. That'th awethome. I'm your favorite."

I wink at him and don't bother to correct him. "Just don't tell your sisters I said so."

Sammy puts his fingers around his mouth and then throws his hand up.

I look at him in confusion. "What are you doing?"

"I'm locking my mouth and throwing the key in the garbage."

"I gotcha." I pat him on the head. "You ready to go see your sisters?"

"No." He frowns, losing all of his happy glow in an instant.

"Why don't you want to see your sisters? Your sisters love you."

"Maybe they'll make fun of me." He says it with such a pitiful voice, it makes my heart break.

"They would *never* make fun of you for real, Sammy. Only mean people do that, and your sisters are not mean. They might tease you once in a while, but that's not the same. Do you understand that?"

He nods, but doesn't appear to be very convinced. I stand there for a few seconds and sigh. I'm not going to be able to fix this in the parking lot of the daycare from hell.

I shut his door and get into the front seat, checking my boy in the rearview mirror. "Are we ready to rock 'n' roll?"

223

He nods. "I'm ready to rock 'n' roll. Ith Dev gonna come to our houthe?"

I stare at him for a few seconds. "Why would you ask that?"

He's looking out the window when he answers. "Becauthe I like him. Maybe he wanth to come over and play with my Thpider-Man. He could borrow it."

"Well, as a matter of fact, I'm going to see Dev for dinner tomorrow. So maybe he'll come inside before we go out to dinner and play with Spider-Man for a little while. Not a long time, just a little while."

Sammy is already looking happy at the prospect. "Like an hour. An hour will be good."

I shake my head. "No, more like ten minutes."

"Okay, I'll tell him almotht an hour, 'kay?"

Rather than argue the finer points of timekeeping with my three-year-old, I start the car and begin our trip home. "We'll see, Sammy, we'll see."

My poor baby with the swollen, bloodshot eyes is sound asleep by the time we arrive home at five o'clock. The school bus pulls up to the stop just down the street as I'm unloading his sleeping form from the car, so I stand in the driveway and wait for my girls. A feeling of joy washes over me as they come running around the corner and across the grass to join us.

"Who wants pizza?" I ask. I should probably do a better job of cooking for them tonight, but I'm exhausted. Pizza every couple weeks isn't going to kill them. My Mom of the Year award is going to have to wait. Again.

The chorus of happy answers is loud enough to wake Sammy up, but when he finds out why they're so excited, he starts screaming in happiness too. They all tumble into the family room and immediately start playing superhero action figures together. I watch for a little while, letting their joy soothe me. I may not be perfect, but I'm an okay mom most of the time.

The doorbell rings, startling me from my thoughts, and I walk over to look through the peephole. May is standing there with Ozzie at her side.

I open the door with a big smile. "What are you guys doing here?"

May grins back at me. "We thought we'd come over and have dinner with you. Surprise! You have enough for two extra plates?"

I hold the door open wide, sighing with relief over having adult company for the evening. I love my kids, but I think tonight I could use a nice conversation with my sister. Hopefully Ozzie won't mind us girl-talking in his presence. "I was just going to order pizza, so there's always enough for two more."

"Excellent." May walks in and goes immediately into the family room with the kids.

"Auntie May!" They jump on her all at once and pull her down to the floor. She falls into a pile, collapsing in giggles right along with them.

I stand in the entrance to the room with Ozzie next to me, watching the love-fest. My heart grows two sizes bigger, stuffing my chest full.

"She adores those kids," he says.

"Can you blame her? They are pretty damn cute, if I do say so myself." Sammy is clinging to her back while the two girls struggle to get away from the tickle monster who has them pinned to the floor. May uses her best evil laugh to make it that much more exciting for them.

"They are. She's going to make a great mom someday herself."

I look up at him and narrow my eyes. "Are you trying to tell me something?"

He looks down at me and stares. Before he can respond, though, the doorbell rings again.

I look at the door. "What the heck? What's going on?"

Ozzie shrugs, being the man of few words that he is.

I point up at his face. "Don't think you're getting out of that conversation we were just about to have."

It's possible his mouth quirks up in a shadow of a smile, but I don't have time to verify; the doorbell is ringing again.

I check the peephole and panic.

Dev's here.

CHAPTER TWENTY-NINE

I am not prepared for this. *Dev? At my house? With my sister and the kids here? And Ozzie? God, no!* Not after the day I've had. Part of me wants to turn him away, to tell him that we're going to be together tomorrow anyway, and I really need to work on the things that Lucky and I collected yesterday at Blue Marine.

But of course I'm not going to do that. I've been thinking about him almost constantly since the last time I saw him, and I'm dying to know if he's been doing anything like that about me. He probably hasn't. He's probably already been on that dating website and found somebody to go out with on Saturday. Just the thought of that allows me to be more subdued than I probably would've been when I open the door to let him in.

"Hey, there . . ." At first my eyes go to Dev, but then they drop to the figure next to him. Time stands still for a few seconds. I know what I'm seeing, but it's not quite computing.

A small boy in a wheelchair. And he has Dev's eyes.

I look up at the tall man, my smile even brighter. "And you brought your son with you! How exciting!" I look down at his son and lean over with my hand extended. "I'm so happy to meet you! Hi, my name is Jenny. You must be Jacob."

"Yes. That's me." He smiles.

I have no idea why Dev's son is in a wheelchair, but I can see that it would probably be very difficult if not impossible for him to walk. His body is very small and twisted to the side. He looks like he has a severely curved spine.

I look up at Dev, hoping that my expression is not as crazy as it feels on my face. I'm sure I must look like the Joker, trying so hard not to look weird and unnatural when of course I look weird and unnatural, with a smile that stretches way too far. How could I not? I'm getting a cramp in my left cheek.

"Hey," Dev says, almost shyly. "Ozzie and May mentioned they were stopping by, and they said I should come by with Jacob for a few minutes. I told them it was maybe not a great idea, since you had no warning we were coming . . . I tried to text you but didn't get an answer. I probably should have waited to hear from you . . ."

I step back quickly and open the door wide. "No, don't be silly! Of course you should stop by! I'm so glad you came. We were just about to order some pizza. You should join us!" I look down at Dev's son as he uses a joystick to maneuver his wheelchair over my threshold. "Do you like pizza, Jacob?"

I hate to admit this even to myself, but I don't even know if he can eat pizza. I may have just committed a major faux pas by asking. I wasn't prepared for this. If I'd known he was coming, and that he's disabled, I could have researched his condition online or talked to someone or something, so I'd know what to do or say without sticking my foot in my mouth. *Gah, I hate that I'm this ignorant!*

"Sure, I love pizza," he says, acting like I'm a totally normal person asking a completely acceptable question.

Phew. Disaster averted.

As Dev walks by, I look up and pat him on the shoulder, hoping like hell that all my internal thoughts have not been put on display by my traitor face. "Thanks for coming by."

I can see from his expression that he's nervous or uncomfortable, and I'd hate for him to feel that way because of me and my stupid reaction. He's probably wondering if he did the right thing by coming here, and I don't want him to have any doubts about that.

I used to feel nervous about walking into a room full of strangers with Sammy, knowing they were going to laugh as soon as they heard him speak, but I got used to it. Sammy's little issue is nothing compared to what Dev and Jacob must deal with, so I want them both to know that in this house they have nothing to worry about. They can be themselves.

No sooner are those thoughts floating through my mind than I hear Sammy's voice rise above all the others as the giggles die down. "Who ith that?" he asks.

I slam the door shut, probably too loudly, and rush to join the others in the family room. I nearly shove Dev out of the way in my effort to get there before Sammy can say anything that will end up hurting somebody's feelings.

Before I can say anything, though, the young boy in the wheelchair responds. "I'm Jacob. I'm Dev's son."

I get there in time to see Sammy walking over and standing in front of his chair. "I went to McDonald'th with Dev. He'th cool."

Jacob smiles. "Yeah. He is. He takes me to McDonald's sometimes too."

May grabs the two girls and pulls them into her lap so they can sit down and act like they're not staring at Jacob. She tickles them, but they mostly ignore it, more interested in their brother's activities. They know he's going to ferret out the story before anything else happens in this room, unless I can get in there and stop him. I just need to do it without being obvious about it.

I take a deep breath and send up a prayer to the universe that the powers-that-be will guide my son toward doing the right thing.

If I had time to prepare, I probably would've sat him down and explained why Jacob was in the wheelchair, and how we should discuss it when he was not around and how we should keep certain things to ourselves. But I didn't have a chance, so I have to count on his childish innocence and my former attempts at mothering to win the day.

"How come you're in that chair?" Sammy asks.

"I have cerebral palsy." Jacob says it like it's no big deal, but of course Sammy is completely confused by that explanation.

Sammy narrows his eyes and looks at Jacob suspiciously. "Can you walk?"

Okay. So much for asking the universe to lend a helping hand. I take a step into the family room, thinking I'm just going to throw up a big distraction and stop this conversation in its tracks. But Dev takes me gently by the hand, effectively stopping my progress and giving me a heart attack in the process. *He's holding my hand again!*

When I look up at him, he nods at me and gives me a signal that I should just wait.

I look first at him and then his son, trying to decide if that's the right thing to do. But eventually I figure that he must know these situations much better than I do, and having spent part of an afternoon with my son, he certainly knows what Sammy is capable of. *Please God, do not let my son hurt anyone's feelings.* Dev lets my hand drop, and I work like hell to get a grip on my emotions. One minute I'm sailing on air, and the next I feel like I've plunged to the earth like Icarus, ready to go splat.

Jacob answers matter-of-factly. "Yes, I can walk, but I don't like doing it. I'm really slow, and it's not comfortable, but my dad makes me."

Sammy nods. "How fatht can you go?" He points at the wheelchair.

Jacob nods sagely. "Pretty fast, actually. Probably faster than you can run."

Sammy's eyes get wide. "Wow, that'th really fatht." He holds up one of his feet with two hands, so Jacob can see his Spider-Man shoes. "My thneakth are pretty fatht."

Jacob nods. "I like Spider-Man."

Sammy's eyes brighten. "Me too! You want to play action figureth with me?"

Jacob shrugs, Mr. Cool all the way. "Sure. But I didn't bring any of my guys with me."

Sammy runs off to the corner of the room and drags a bucket full of toys over. "No problem. I have a whole bunch. You can share them." Sammy picks up the bucket and leans in toward Jacob, giving him a full view of its colorful interior. "You can have any that you want. You can even uthe my favorite oneth." He points to the most scarred and well-loved figures of the bunch: Spider-Man, of course, and Superman too.

It's all too much for me. I turn my back and walk toward the kitchen. Tears fill my eyes and I can't blink them away this time.

I get to the kitchen without drawing the kids' attention, but I'm not alone. Dev is behind me.

"What's the matter?" he asks.

I wave over my shoulder to tell him to go away and shake my head. "Nothing. I'm fine."

His hand is there on my shoulder, turning me around. I try to keep my head down so he can't see my face, but he puts his finger under my chin and forces my face up. "Are you upset with me because I came here without calling you first?"

I grab his forearms and squeeze, shaking my head vigorously while looking at him. "No, please don't think that. Never think that. I'm really, really glad you came, and I'm especially glad that you brought your son. It's just that I was having a really shitty day until you guys got here, and when I saw my son being so cool, I realized that as crappy as my day was, at least I've got one thing going for me."

Dev nods. "You've got great kids."

I can't say anything because his words make me cry even more. I nod my head.

Dev pulls me into a hug and holds me close. My face barely comes above his belly button, but it doesn't matter. Even this awkward hug is enough to fill me with more happiness than I can stand. I hardly even know this guy or his son *or* his boss, but here they are in my home, making all this craziness I'm going through seem worthwhile.

"I should've called you," he says. "This was a shock. I know it was."

I pull away and look up at him. "Please don't say that. I swear to you, it's not a shock. I was maybe a little bit surprised, but it wasn't a bad thing at all. I just . . ." I step away from Dev and wave the air around my face trying to cool myself down. "If I could explain to you about my day, you would totally understand why I acted like an idiot when I opened the door."

He leans down to look me in the eye. "Tell me about it."

"Not right now." I sniff really loud, trying to keep my dripping nose from becoming too disgusting. "I need to order pizza." Reaching into my back pocket, I pull my cell phone out.

Before I can locate the telephone number of our favorite pizza place in my contacts, Dev takes my cell away from me and sets it down on the counter. He jabs his thumb over his shoulder. "Do you hear that?"

Now that he's pointed it out, I can hear the laughter and the happy squeals coming from the other room again. Jacob's voice is part of it this time.

"Those are the sounds of people who do not give a crap whether there's going to be pizza here in the next half hour or not. So you can take five minutes to tell me what's going on."

I let out a long hiss of aggravation and frustration as I realize he's right and I do want to get this stuff off my chest. "Well, let's see . . . I went back to my old workplace to get my last paycheck and my stuff, and I ended up going head-to-head with my boss about my severance."

"I hope he gave you something."

"Oh yeah, he did. He gave me what I wanted, actually, but I had to be a world-class superbitch to get it. I don't like acting like that, and I don't like feeling like I'm threatening somebody just to get them to do the right thing. I want people to do what they're supposed to do without me having to force them, you know?"

"I do. I'm glad you stuck up for yourself."

"Yes, well I thought that was going to be the worst part of my day, but unfortunately it wasn't. When I went to pick Sammy up from daycare, I found out that he's been having a problem with some other kids."

"A problem? What kind of problem?"

I throw my hands up. "I would love to know! But all I heard from the director is that there was some shoving and some pushing, and some kids got hurt. And now, Sammy's no longer allowed there." I drop my voice to make sure no one in the other room will hear me. "And apparently I am a horrible parent, because my son has a speech impediment and I haven't done anything to fix it."

Dev's face screws up. "Say what?"

"I know, right? I don't get it. I mean, he's not even in kindergarten yet, and this woman is telling me that I need to get him into speech therapy or I need to stop thinking it's cute or whatever . . ." I look off into the distance, because if I look into Dev's eyes right now, I'm going to start crying all over again. "People suck."

Dev takes a step closer to me and puts his hands on my upper arms, shaking me gently so that I'll look at him. I comply, craning my neck to see his face.

"Not *all* people suck. Apparently, the person at that daycare does, but most people who run daycares are nice and they understand that not every kid is born exactly like another. Differences make them unique and special, not deficient."

"Thank you. I agree with you one hundred percent. And it's not like I'm this neglectful parent, okay? I realize that my son has a lisp. It would be impossible to miss. But I don't think putting pressure on him at this age is a good idea. Am I crazy for believing that?"

Dev squeezes my arms again. "No, of course not. I'm sure that you've listened to your pediatrician and you're following whatever orders your doctor has given you. Besides, if there were something really wrong, your maternal instincts would kick in and you'd do whatever needs to be done. So you don't need to worry about whatever that person said to you. You're a good mom, and you're doing the right thing, whatever it is."

I have to smile at that. "You don't even know what I'm doing, so how could you possibly say I'm doing the right thing?"

He shrugs and smiles a little, making his dimple cave in just a bit. "Because. I know what kind of person you are. You're not going to do anything that's going to hurt your kids, and you're not lazy. I can tell by the way your kids act and by the way they treat people. They're kind and gentle and fun. You don't get a kid like that by being an asshole."

I can't stop grinning. "There are at least two people who I know for a fact would disagree with you, based on my behavior today."

Dev pulls me back into another hug and squeezes me hard. "I promise I will let you know if you're ever being an asshole in my presence."

I pat him on the back. "Me too. Same goes."

"You want me to order the pizzas?" he asks.

I shrug, taking a step back to break up our embrace. A sustained hug-fest in the kitchen is probably a little too heavy for a pizza party. I don't want my kids to catch us, since I'm not even sure what this thing between us is yet. "Go for it. I think you have the number already."

Dev pulls his phone out of his pocket and holds it up at me. "Sure do. I'm going to go get everybody's order." He turns around and leaves the kitchen for the family room without another word.

I open the refrigerator and pull out a bottle of wine for the grown-ups and a bottle of apple juice for the kids. As I take glasses out of the cabinet and line them up on the counter, I can't stop myself from humming. Here I thought I was going to be crying in my wine and lying in bed wondering where I went wrong, but instead I'm surrounded by people I love and who love me back, looking forward to an impromptu pizza party. And tomorrow I'm going out to dinner with the hottest, most understanding man I have ever met.

Obviously I've done something right somewhere; I just hope I don't screw it up. I definitely need to talk to my sister one-on-one, as soon as possible. Before I forget, I send her a text. Even though she's in the other room, I need to keep this on the down-low. I don't want Dev knowing I'm analyzing or planning anything that has to do with him.

Me: *We need to talk, asap.*

Ten seconds later, her reply beeps on my phone.

May: *Now??*
Me: *No. Tomorrow morning. Coffee here. 8. Don't b late.*
May: *Wouldn't miss it for the world.*

CHAPTER THIRTY

I throw the door open and welcome my sister in before she even has a chance to touch the handle. After a hug and a kiss, she hands me an envelope.

"What's this?" I ask, taking it from her and turning it over. It's plain, nothing written on it.

"It's your gift certificate and your first paycheck." She's grinning from ear to ear.

"Are you sure about the gift certificate?"

"Don't be silly. It's not a gift. You earned it. And now we have an excuse to go shopping together."

I love shopping with my sister, and it's been ages since we've done it. "Fine. I'll take it." Ushering her into the kitchen, I gesture toward the table. "Have a seat. I'm just getting these muffins out of the oven."

May follows my orders, sitting down in her chair and wrapping her hands around the freshly poured mug of coffee in front of her. "It smells like heaven in here."

I nudge the oven door closed with my elbow and set the hot muffin tray down on the counter. "I got up really early this morning and mixed these up before the kids were even awake." I don't mention to her that I couldn't sleep at all last night because I was so worried about Sammy, or that I had to make last-minute plans to bring him to the emergency daycare, the one I hate because it always smells like dirty diapers but the one place that will take him with no notice when necessary. Finding him a new daycare is my top priority after I turn in my report to the Bourbon Street Boys team, but I don't need to stress my sister out over things she can't control.

May lifts a brow at me. "Wow, somebody's seriously motivated. Did you buy that dildo after all?"

"No, I did not buy a dildo. Shut up." I hold up a muffin. "You want one of these, right?"

"Do bears poop in the woods?"

"Yes, they do." I wrangle the last confection onto a plate, feeling like a superhero because not one of them caved in during the process. "Fun fact . . . did you know that bears plant oak trees with their poop? All those seeds they eat . . ."

"Has anyone ever told you that you watch too much Animal Planet?"

I snort as I answer. "I tell myself that all the time, actually. You have no idea . . . I am constantly comparing people to animals in the wild kingdom. It's ridiculous. I really need to get a life."

I sit down with two plates and several muffins between us.

May takes a look at my offerings. "I'm not sure I can eat more than one of these things."

"Don't worry about it. I'll probably eat whatever you don't finish. I'm seriously stress-eating right now."

May unwraps a muffin from its paper holder. "I came over here this morning to chat with you, and I have two hours, so lay it on me. Tell me what's going on."

I take a sip of my coffee before beginning. "Before we get into my junk, tell me about you and Ozzie. What's going on with you two?" His little comment about May being a good mom someday has been weighing on my mind.

She's chewing her muffin and smiling at me. "What do you mean what's going on? We're fine."

I give her my big sister don't-piss-me-off look. "When he was over here last night he said something about you and kids. I got the feeling he was trying to tell me something, but then everything got so crazy with the little buttheads making all that noise, I never got a chance to ask him about it. Is there something you want to tell me?"

If she tells me she's pregnant, I am going to throw my plate across the room, I swear to God. My outburst will be fueled by two emotions: happiness and frustration. Of course my sister will make the best mother of all time, but with Ozzie? Is she ready for this? Am I ready for this?

May is frowning at me. "No. What are you talking about?"

Obviously Ozzie can't know my sister is pregnant without her knowing it, but that doesn't mean she isn't playing hard to get with me. She's gotten a lot wilier since hooking up with Ozzie. "Just tell me. Are you pregnant?"

May's jaw drops open. "What? No. Where would you get that idea?" She looks down at her stomach. "Am I getting fat?"

I whack her on the arm. "Of course you're not getting fat. My god, you've never been so thin. Is he even feeding you over there?" I'm afraid my jealousy is coming out in my tone. Luckily, my sister doesn't take offense.

"No. I eat like a pig, I swear. Ozzie cooks the most amazing food. It's just that Dev has me doing so many workouts, I burn all the calories and then some." A cute smile pops up on her face. "I actually think I look pretty good."

I nod like crazy. "You do. You look fantastic. I am totally jealous of you right now. You're one of those thin bitches we used to mock."

May winks at me over her coffee mug. "Dev cannot wait to get his hands on you. It's going to be so exciting." She wiggles her eyebrows, making me think there's a second meaning to her words.

I can't believe she just said that. *How can she be so casual about my love life?*

"Why are you looking at me like that?" she asks, lowering her mug. "Do you have a piece of muffin stuck in your throat? Do you need a Heimlich?" She puts her hands up onto her neck. "This is the sign for choking. Give me the sign if you're choking."

I shake my head at her; she is so ridiculous. "I'm not choking, dummy, I'm just trying to figure out how you can say what you said so casually."

May tilts her head like a confused canine. "What did I say?"

I bug my eyes out at her, waiting for her to figure it out. I can almost see her pressing the rewind button in her brain.

Her face relaxes and she smiles. "Oh, I get it. That sounded kind of funny didn't it?"

"Maybe a little."

"What I meant was that Dev is really excited about getting you on a *workout program*. Lucky told me that you were maybe thinking about coming to work with us; so if you do, you'll start working out with Dev just like I did, and you'll see the same results. I promise."

She has touched on so many things, I don't know where to start. *Dev? Job? Working out? Lucky?* I let my brain go on autopilot and pick for itself.

"How do you know what Dev wants?"

She shrugs, trying to act cool, but she doesn't fool me for a second. "Oh, I don't know. We chat sometimes, when we're working out."

"About me?"

She wiggles her eyebrows. "Wouldn't you like to know."

I grab her arm and squeeze it. "Yes! That's why I'm asking you these questions! Please don't make me beg. It's embarrassing." I pick up a muffin and pull the wrapper off very carefully. It allows me to focus on something other than my sister looking at me with what I assume will be pity in her eyes.

"It's so cute. You both like each other, but neither one of you wants to be the one to say it first."

I disregard my muffin and stare my sister down. "How do you know that, though? Did he say it?"

"He doesn't need to. I can tell."

I shake my head, disappointed. My sister is pretty smart, but that doesn't mean she can see what's going on in a guy's mind. In my experience, men are too closed off to get an accurate read. "Well, I think he's pretty cool, but I'm not sure he really likes me seriously. I think he's attracted to me, sure, but not into me for a relationship. Not a serious one. He could be a player."

"Why would you say that?"

"Because we were on the computer together looking at a dating site, and he was telling me how I should go find a guy and set up a date with him. It was the perfect situation for him to suggest himself, but he told me to go date someone else. I mean, that doesn't sound like a guy who's interested in me."

May is frowning. "That is weird. He asked me lots of questions about you, even when we were talking about other things. He just brought it up randomly, several times. Why would he tell you to go out with other guys if he's so interested in you, though?"

"Exactly." I'm so sad right now. God, this sucks. I'm going to be single for the rest of my life.

"Maybe I read him wrong. Maybe I got the signals crossed or something."

I nod. "He's probably just being really friendly, asking you about me because you guys are coworkers and he likes you."

May doesn't look very convinced. "I don't know. He seems to be interested in more than just a friendly way. But you never know with Dev. He plays it pretty close to the vest, I guess."

"Why do you say that?"

"Well, his son, for one thing . . ."

"Jacob? What do you mean?" I take a big bite of my muffin to keep myself from talking for a while. I want to hear everything May has to say on this subject.

"I didn't find out about Jacob until recently. I mean, I knew that Dev had a child, but I didn't realize that he had a child with special needs, or that he was a single dad doing everything himself."

"How could you not know everything about the situation? You're dating his boss, and you see Dev every day." Obviously my sister needs some training in how to be a proper busybody. I thought I'd taught her better than this . . .

She shrugs. "Ozzie isn't somebody who'd share people's personal details with me. If I ask about something specific, he'll usually tell me, but he doesn't elaborate and he doesn't just volunteer stuff." She shrugs. "I guess I never thought to ask about Dev's family life."

I shake my head. "Sometimes I'm not even sure we're related."

She pokes a finger at me and then herself. "You were always the psychoanalyst. I was always the patient, remember?"

"I guess so. I'm starting to think I should've let you be the doctor more often."

May reaches over and puts her hand on mine, squeezing it gently. "I'm sorry that I haven't been more concerned about your life. I should have asked you more questions about what was going on with Miles and the kids."

I put my free hand on top of hers, making a tower of sisterly support. "Don't say that. You haven't done anything wrong. You're the best sister in the world. Seriously. I didn't want to talk to you today to make you feel guilty about anything, because you have nothing to feel guilty about."

She sits back, apparently mollified. "So, what are you going to do about Dev?"

"Well, we're going out to dinner tonight, so we'll see. I guess I'll just play it by ear."

May's expression brightens. "You're going out for dinner? That's awesome!" She takes a giant bite of her muffin, causing a pile of crumbs to fall and land in her lap. She brushes them onto the floor and then freezes when she realizes what she's doing. "Oh cwab. Feev not here."

I ignore her muffin-talk about her dog not being here to clean up her mess. I'll vacuum it up later. I have bigger problems to fix right now.

"It's not a date," I say. "We had a bet and I lost it, so the loser had to buy dinner. And on this dinner event or whatever it's supposed to be, we have plans to discuss our dating strategy moving forward."

May's mouth is still too stuffed with muffin to answer, but she tries anyway. "Vo vabing vabbevy?" More crumbs fly.

"Yeah. Dating strategy." I shake my head, disappointed in myself. *Why can't I just get up the guts to tell him how I feel?* "It's so stupid."

May finally manages to swallow her chunk of muffin and speaks in a strained voice. "Whose brilliant idea was this?"

"I don't remember. Most of the time when I'm with him, I feel really comfortable, like I'm hanging out with someone I've known for a long time—a real, solid friend, you know? And then he'll do something or say something that makes me notice how cute he is or how nice he is or how fun he is, and all those good friend-type feelings go away and I go gaga over him and start acting like I have only half a brain." My voice rises as my inability to manage a single-adult life becomes clearer with my explanation. "And then the next thing I know we're talking about going out on dates with other people. It's really frigging frustrating, if you want to know the truth. I'm totally out of practice with this being-single shit. I've barely started doing it, and I already want to quit. And I hate that Miles is so much better at it than I am."

May shakes her head. "It's not you that's the problem here. And don't even *begin* to compare yourself to that turdbasket, Miles. *Ugh.* He's such a dick and you are so not a dick, okay?"

We both smile. She always had a way with words, my sister.

"This stuff with Dev . . . don't let it get you down. I think he's just a complicated guy. In fact, I think all the people at Bourbon Street Boys are particularly complicated people. They had rough lives growing up here in New Orleans. We thought we had it tough, but it was nothing compared to what they went through, believe me. Ozzie has told me some stories . . ." She waves her hand around, dismissing that thought before she can elaborate. "Anyway, they went through a lot of tragedies together that brought them close. They're a special breed for sure, and it takes longer to get to know them, but when you do get there . . . when you're accepted into their group . . . it's totally worth it."

I yearn for the kind of acceptance she's describing. If only I could woman-up and stop worrying about everything all the time. "I'm really happy for you, that you found Ozzie and his team. It's difficult for me, but clearly good for you." It feels nice to finally admit that out loud. All the risks she takes fade a little in my mind when I see the happy expression on her face and hear the confidence coming out in her voice. She's found her place in the world, and that's something to hang on to. Hell, I'm thirty-two and I still haven't gotten there; I'm starting to doubt I ever will.

"Thank you," she says. "I was worried you didn't approve."

"Actually, I didn't. I've been freaked out about what you've been doing, to be honest. I know Ozzie's a good guy, but your life has really changed since you met him, and I worry about the risks that you run going out and taking pictures of criminals."

"But you know that I'm being trained, and I have the whole team around me. I'm never alone doing the work. And most of what we do is behind the scenes."

I nod. "I know that. But still, my first day there? Remember? There was that big . . . incident or whatever. Do you even know what it was all about?"

May nods, getting serious all of a sudden. "We have an idea."

I raise my eyebrows at her. "Is it top-secret, need-to-know stuff, or am I allowed to hear about it?"

She doesn't answer me right away, which only makes me more curious. I up the ante by handing her another muffin and then settle down deeper into my chair. This promises to be really good, if the expression on my sister's face is any indication.

CHAPTER THIRTY-ONE

My sister looks a little uncomfortable. "I'm not really sure, actually," she says. "You're not technically an employee of the Bourbon Street Boys, or at least not as far as I know. Did they officially offer you a job yet?"

"No. Lucky hinted around that there could be a job for me, but I don't get the impression that he's the one who would do the offering."

May shakes her head. "No, it would officially come from Thibault or Ozzie. But I know there's a job opening. I guess you just need to let them know you're interested. Everybody has kind of gotten the impression that you're on the fence about it, and nobody wants to push you."

I nod. "That's a fair assessment. I am on the fence about it. I can see all the benefits, and I really do need a job right now, but there's still that element of risk there . . . So, I've decided to think about it a little bit longer." I pause for a few seconds and then try to act casual. "So, you know where that big dent in the door came from? Who did it?"

May nods. "I guess I can tell you that much. You've signed an NDA and you were kind of involved." She sighs. "We think we know. We had surveillance set up around the building, and we caught some images on tape. Ozzie and Thibault are looking into it right now . . . along with Toni."

The way she mentions Toni's involvement makes me pay extra attention. "Does it have something to do with her? Toni, I mean?"

"I think so. Ozzie's not positive, but based on some of the things that we've seen, and some of the things that Toni has said, I think it has something to do with her past. With her ex."

"Ooh, gossip. Tell me." I have to believe that anything having to do with Toni's ex will be an interesting story. In fact, I can't imagine anything about Toni's life being boring. I'd bet even her daily routines would make mine look positively stodgy in comparison. She probably brushes her teeth while twirling nunchucks and puts on mascara while throwing Chinese stars into targets across the room. I wait anxiously for May to spill the beans.

Normally, my sister would jump all over the opportunity to gossip with me about interesting people, but she's chewing her lip, acting like she's not sure that she wants to.

"What's up? What are you thinking? 'Fess up, sister, or I will be forced to withhold muffins." I snatch one up and hold it by my shoulder.

"Ozzie has told me some things about Toni's past, but I'm pretty sure it's not something he'd want me to discuss."

Of all the things that May has said or done since she met Ozzie, this one makes the biggest impression on me. She has never kept a secret from me in our entire lives as far as I know. Until now. It makes me both sad and happy.

May throws a big muffin crumb at me. "Why are you looking at me like that? You look like I just slapped you across the face or something."

I pick the crumb off my shirt and throw it back at her. "No, I'm just thinking how much it sucks when your baby sister grows up and leaves the nest."

"Oh, that's so sweet," she says in a mocking tone, right before going totally serious. "What the hell are you talking about?"

I unwrap the muffin slowly as I respond to her command. "Dev and I were talking, and he was sharing his opinion about you with me, and it really got me thinking about a lot of things."

"Like . . . ?"

"Like, how I've always looked at you as my baby sister, as somebody who I needed to protect. But how, now that we're older and we have our own lives, that's not an accurate picture of who you are or who I need to be."

"Uh-huh . . ."

I sigh in frustration. "I don't know if Dev is some sort of guru or whatever, but every time I talk to him, I feel like I get a clearer picture of who I am and what my life is all about."

I feel sad about the next part. Admitting it out loud is harder than just thinking it inside my own head. "And I don't necessarily like everything that I'm seeing. I feel like I've been afraid of way too many things for way too long, and I've basically become a turtle hiding in a shell, letting an adventurous life pass me by. I guess that's why I feel so conflicted right now about Bourbon Street Boys, about the kids, about the whole dating thing . . ."

"It sounds like you're having a midlife crisis."

I shake my head. "No, I don't think it's that. I don't have the urge to go out and buy a Corvette or date an eighteen-year-old or anything. But am I ready to jump into being a freelancer with a security firm? I don't know. This job has really changed you, May, and I have to believe you see that."

She nods. "I do. But I think they're all good changes. And what do my changes have to do with you? We'd be doing different jobs. You could work from home most of the time. It's not the same thing."

"I agree they're good changes in you. Now I do, anyway. I didn't agree last week, but after getting to know the team a little bit better, and seeing them in action, I realize the big attraction. I see why you're excited about going to work in the morning, and I also see why you find Ozzie so attractive. He's confident, he's smart, and he's very loyal."

"And he's awesome in bed. Don't forget that part." She can't stop grinning.

"You and I both know that's not the reason you're with him. But it is a nice side benefit."

May gets a far-off, misty look in her eye that I'm almost jealous of. I quickly move the conversation forward to keep from dwelling on anything negative. I'm thrilled she's so happy.

"Anyway, it's been nice having Dev to talk to, and I think I could really have fun with him as a friend, so even if that's all that's going on between us, I'm happy."

"I'm happy for you too." May smiles. "You guys could make a cute couple, though."

I shake my head. "Let's not get ahead of ourselves. We just met each other last week."

"So? Love at first sight is a real thing. Trust me, I know."

I laugh. "You told me, when you met Ozzie, you thought he was a hideous beast-man with that beard of his. You said he was completely and totally ugly. That was no love-at-first-sight situation, no way."

May frowns at me. "That impression lasted only about ten minutes. Once he shaved, and I saw how amazing he was, I was done. I fell for him like a rock."

I roll my eyes. "Whatever."

May crumples up her muffin paper. "So, did you find anything good on those computer files or whatever you went after the other night?"

"Well, I should probably save this for the briefing later today, but I did find some stuff on the clone drives last night after the kids fell asleep."

May sits up really straight in her chair. "Really? Tell me."

I lean in, excited about what I found after working into the wee hours of the morning. "There's somebody there at Blue Marine who sits at station number three, named Anita, who's been messing around with the accounts. I haven't shared everything with Lucky yet about it."

"So? Tell me anyway."

I'm too excited about my results to wait. "I think I can prove the existence of at least two fake companies that this woman has set up to divert funds into an account she owns."

May's jaw drops open, and it takes visible effort for her to start talking. "Oh . . . my god. That is . . . incredible. How did you find it?"

I shrug. "Well, she had some pretty high-level computer skills going for her, I'll give her that much."

"But not as much as my sister does," May says, squeezing my arm.

I smile. "You know it." I use this opportunity with my sister to explain what I did in a way that a non-geek could understand, knowing she'll cross her eyes if I say anything too technical. "She was using file-hiding software that had a pretty difficult AES 256 encryption matrix . . ."

May's eyes cross almost on cue with my description. "Oh my god, you are such a nerd."

"I'm a geek, not a nerd. Big difference." I try again to explain. "Let's just say she had a super-hard password on the system, but I figured it out. And I might have accessed some legal documents online that I wasn't supposed to see that allowed me to track the companies back to her. I think she paid a lot of money to some lawyer to keep that all secret, but she should have budgeted for a computer engineer too." I grin like the Cheshire Cat.

May leans over for a spontaneous hug. "You are so awesome. I knew you could do it. But do me a favor. Don't tell them like you told me. Use all the fancy words."

I laugh. "Why?"

She suddenly sounds desperate. "Because! I want them to offer you the job! If you act like it's no big deal, they'll think they can just hire some doofus off the street to do it."

I'm a little surprised by that. "Do they want to hire some doofus off the street?"

May shakes her head. "No, of course not. They want to hire you. But Toni tends to be very negative about people coming on board, so I'm afraid she's going to make the team worry that you don't really want to be there. But if you can show them that what you do is very special and that not any doofus off the street can do it, I think they'll be more inclined to ignore her."

"Wow. I didn't realize she disliked me so much."

May shakes her head vigorously. "It's not that she doesn't like you. I promise. She's just really prickly, like, *all* the time. Even when she's being nice to me, I'm suspicious she's just messing around. So don't take it personally." She looks like she's about to say something else, but she stops herself.

I'm instantly suspicious. "What were you going to say?"

"What? What do you mean? I wasn't going to say anything." She's way too bright and cheerful now to be telling the truth.

I give her my best annoyed-mother look. "Don't play, May. You were about to say something about Toni. What was it?"

May fiddles with a wrapper from one of the muffins for a little while before she answers me. "I really shouldn't say."

I steal the paper from her to get her attention. "No, you really *should* say."

May is opening her mouth to answer my question when her phone rings. She picks it up to look at the screen, and holds up her finger at me. "I have to take this. It's Ozzie."

I try not to be annoyed when she pulls his call up. Instead, I clean up our mess as she exchanges a short conversation with her boyfriend. I really want to know what she was going to spill about Toni. If I knew the woman better, maybe I could fix whatever I've done wrong. I wouldn't want to work at Bourbon Street Boys if Toni hates me; it would be way too uncomfortable.

I'm rinsing the coffee mugs in the sink when May stands.

"Are you leaving?" I ask.

"Yes. Ozzie has something he needs me to do right away."

How convenient. "Are you going to finish telling me about Toni before you go?"

"Maybe another time." She throws her purse strap over her shoulder and shoves her phone inside the bag. "You're going to be at the warehouse today at eleven-thirty, right?"

"Yes. I'm going to finish typing up a report about what I found this morning, get dressed, and drive over."

May gives me a hug and a kiss on the cheek. "Great. I'll see you then. Thanks for the muffins." She grabs another one off the plate on the counter and heads down the hallway toward the front door. "I'm going to give one to Ozzie. Don't be surprised if he asks you for the recipe!"

I shake my head as I walk over to the hallway and watch my sister go out the front door. I can almost imagine myself doing something as inane as exchanging a recipe with that giant hulk of a man—the man she fell in love with after meeting him one time. Our lives are totally crazy right now, but for the first time ever I'm starting to like crazy.

CHAPTER THIRTY-TWO

I should probably be more responsible and finish typing up my report for the team first, but I'm anxious. All this talk about Dev and a potential relationship with him has made me realize how badly I need to get out into the world and stop pretending like I'm eighty-five years old and done with dating. I'm only thirty-two. I still have a lot of life to live. I still have a lot of sex to have. And if it's not going to be with Dev, it needs to be with someone else. I can't count on the fact that my sister's vibes about him and me are right.

After I'm sure my sister has gone, I go into my home office and start up my computer. I'm still in my sweatsuit, sporting a pretty righteous case of bedhead, but it doesn't matter. My future date will never see me looking like this. If the stories that I've read online are true, I'll probably pick the worst guy in the whole town to go out on a first date with, and I'll have a really funny story to tell my friends later.

I go to the dating website and stare at the home screen. I'm still logged on from when Dev and I were on there together. *What should I do now?* Should I start a new search, or should I use the one I already conducted when I was looking for Dev?

Since I can't decide, I decide to fill in my own profile. That takes me all of ten minutes, and then I'm stuck back at the beginning again. *How do I find a date?*

My search results to find Dev are still there: a list of almost thirty names with one-liners from their ads. I try to imagine what my potential date might look like, and what he'd like to do in his free time, but the only thing that comes to mind is a man who looks like Dev and enjoys his hobbies too. I should just go ahead and admit I'm more than a little infatuated with him.

I click on the search results to refresh them. There are twenty-nine names now. "Oh, what the hell. Might as well start with these guys and see where it gets me."

I scan through the offerings and find myself narrowing them down to the same three that I had chosen before. I know the one that says he's still looking for his favorite person is Dev, so obviously I avoid that one. How desperate would that be, to purposely pick him and then pretend like I forgot? *Ugh, how embarrassing.*

Instead, I click on the one that says *Take my hand and we'll wander off together somewhere.* When I click the Read More link and absorb his more detailed profile, I am struck once again by how much he reminds me of Dev. New Orleans is a pretty big place, though, so I guess it shouldn't be surprising that there's more than one guy who meets my criteria and seems similar to another. Rather than second-guess what I'm doing, I go ahead and click the Send Message button and type out a quick note.

Saw your message on the site here. Would you like to meet for a drink? The message is automatically signed with my username: *nola4evr.*

I pause only a few moments before clicking the Send button. I have nothing to lose, right? Maybe just a little bit of my pride, but

I don't have a whole hell of a lot of that left over. Apparently I don't need much of it to survive.

I sit there for a little while wondering what I should do next, and then catch a whiff of my stink-breath. "Whoa." My next step becomes very clear. Time to get ready for work. A little thrill runs through me as I realize that I actually have a job to go to. Not bad for a girl who was laid off on Monday.

Just as I'm about to log off the website, I hear a beep, and a little window pops up. Inside the little window is a heart that looks like it's beating. My pulse jumps when I realize that someone has responded to my message. I read the response as my anxiety builds.

Sounds great! Where?

I respond without thinking.

Not sure exactly where you live, but how about Harry's Harborside Tavern?

I'm not sure what to do next. What is the protocol for a first date generated on a website? Do I thank him? Do I ask him what he's going to wear? I feel like a complete dweeb.

Saturday? 7 PM? he asks.

That's fine, I say back, assuming my sister will babysit for me when she hears I have a real, live date.

Perfect. See you then. I'll be the guy in the blue shirt.

Should I say something about what I'll be wearing? I have no idea what that'll be yet. Will that make me seem flaky? Oh well. I might as well stick with honesty as my best policy at this point. In the event I do hit the lottery and pick a great guy right off the bat, I don't want him to fall for somebody I'm not. I'm not one of those cool girls who always knows what to say at exactly the right time. I'm better off keeping it short and sweet.

Ok. See you then.

Satisfied that I have now fulfilled the terms of my deal with Dev, I head upstairs to my bathroom to undo the mess that last night's attempted sleeping had on my hair and face. With enough makeup, I might be able to hide the ravages suffered by this worried mom.

CHAPTER THIRTY-THREE

I shouldn't be nervous. I know these people I'm about to have a meeting with, at least a little bit. I worked overnight with Lucky. Hell, I'm going out to dinner with Dev tonight after cruising a dating site with him. But I'm sitting here in the parking lot, palms sweating, with my cute little briefcase next to me and my laptop all packed up and ready to go.

What if my report is too amateurish? What if I haven't given them enough detail? What if I've given them too much detail? There's no way for me to know if I've put this thing together correctly, because I've never done anything like it in my entire life. Sure, I've attended plenty of meetings with some pretty high-ranking executives present, but I was always having conversations with people who speak the same language as I do.

I worry about being too technical with these non-geek coworkers, but also about not being technical enough. I don't want them to think I've oversimplified my report just so they can understand it. My goal is to strike the right balance between completely geeking out and dumbing it down.

A vehicle pulls up next to me and the main door to the warehouse begins to open, telling me whoever is in the car has a remote.

The driver's-side window of the dark SUV opens and Toni is there. She nods at me first and then at the door. I'm not sure what she means, though. Is this a cool-girl greeting? Does she want me to get out of my car? Is she daring me to drive in first? I don't want to look completely stupid and guess the wrong thing.

She rolls her eyes at my lack of action and gestures for me to roll down my window.

Once my window is down, her words come in loud and clear. "You should follow me in. Park inside."

"How come?" Being in there behind a locked door I don't know the combination to will make it much harder for me to leave when I'm ready. They're probably going to want to discuss my report after I've gone, and it will be a hassle for someone to come and enter the code to let me out.

"Because," she says, annoyed, "we like to stay incognito here. Parking outside tells people who's here."

"Oh. Okay." I have nothing left to say to her about that, but the specter of that risk has risen again, niggling at my conscience. Am I doing the right thing by being here? By thinking about working with them on a more permanent basis?

I don't have time to figure it out right now. Toni has pulled in and is expecting me to follow her. As I drive forward and find myself drawn into the darkness of the warehouse, I realize that we're not the first ones here; there are several cars parked inside, including May's and Dev's. As I park and shut off my engine, I hear barking. Sahara and Felix are bounding down the stairs to greet us.

I don't know what it is about that silly little canine couple, but they instantly calm me down. I don't need to worry about where I'm parking or what that means right now. I can get my puppy cuddles on, give the team my report, and then go to the mall. That's my kind of Friday. No need to freak out.

May comes down the stairs after the dogs at a more sedate pace, meaning she doesn't fall into a pile of legs and fur at the bottom of the staircase, unlike the pups. Felix goes ballistic, trying to untangle himself from his girlfriend. Sahara stands there looking dazed as he bounces around her ankles, barking like he's being shocked by a Taser or something.

"You made it!" my sister exclaims.

"Is he okay?" I ask, gesturing at Felix.

"Oh, he's fine. He hates it when Sahara bowls him over. He's scolding her right now."

Hilarious. Is that what I look like when I yell at the kids? I shut my car door and walk around to the passenger side so I can grab my things. "I made it on time. It's a miracle."

She looks inside the car. "Is Sammy okay?"

"Yes, for now. I still have to find him a permanent spot somewhere, but he's fine for today." I make a mental note to place a few phone calls after I leave here.

"Hey, Toni," May says to her coworker.

"Hello. Everything good?"

"Yep, couldn't be better. Excited to hear what Jenny has to say about what she and Lucky found."

Toni apparently has nothing to say to that. She climbs the stairs in front of us, not looking back.

She's a tough nut to crack, but if my sister is to be believed, worrying about whether she likes me is a wasted effort. The only thing I can hope for, probably, is mutual respect. Hopefully after she sees my report, we'll be halfway there.

May lowers her voice to keep our conversation private as we look up the stairs. "Are you nervous?"

"Do bears poop in the woods?"

"Yes. Because bears are busy being farmers—haven't you heard?"

"What?"

May is grinning up at me as I ascend the stairs sideways. "You know, how they plant acorns and seed stuff with their butts?"

I roll my eyes. "Oh, ha, ha." I lean down and whisper at her with as much threat in my voice as possible. "Don't you dare tell anybody about my Animal Planet obsession."

"I can be bribed."

"Want to come to the mall with me? I have a gift certificate to spend." I wiggle my eyebrows at her.

"Animal Planet? Who watches that dumb show? Not my sister." She grins. "I'm there. Lunch hour?"

I nod. We're at the top of the stairs now, and Toni is pressing in the code that will give us entry to the sword room. She pushes the door in hard enough to let it swing open for all of us, but she doesn't bother holding it.

In any other circumstance I might consider this person rude, but being forewarned by May makes me a more charitable person today. Plus, I can't afford to make any of these people into bad guys in my mind. What if they offer me a job? What will I say? Will I chicken out because I'm worried there's a mean girl in our midst? I hope I'm not that person, so easily frightened away.

The dogs run past me, almost knocking me over in their enthusiasm to get back into the meeting area. "Damn," I shout, trying to catch myself before I fall, grabbing the door handle for all I'm worth. My briefcase swings around and whacks me in the stomach. "Holy hell, someone's in a hurry." I stand there in a hunched-over position catching my breath, praying no one saw me. When I look up, I notice Toni looking at me strangely. *Great.*

"Somebody needs to train those dogs," May says grumpily.

I bug my eyes out at her. "Yeah, somebody needs to."

"Oh look! Swords!" May says. Clearly this is a distraction designed to keep me off the dog-training subject, but I go ahead and look at the swords anyway. They are impressive, even though

259

I've already seen them a couple times. And Dev owns them. What I wouldn't give to watch him swinging one of those around . . .

Voices from the other room stop me from commenting or going any further on that train of thought. May's silliness had helped me to relax a little, but now that I hear the men, I'm back to being nervous again. *Will I ever feel comfortable here?*

CHAPTER THIRTY-FOUR

May gives me a gentle shove on the back. "Hurry up. I don't want to be late."

I walk in and nod at Lucky from across the room. He gestures at the empty seat next to him. There's also an extra seat next to Dev, whose back is to us, but I'm not brave enough to take that one. I head over to the other side of the table to sit next to my partner in crime, fellow computer-cloner Lucky. As I take my seat, Dev looks up at me and smiles, his warm gaze soothing my nerves in an instant.

Ozzie speaks and all the voices quiet down to listen. "Looks like everybody's here now, so we can get started."

I surreptitiously check my watch, making sure I'm not late. I'm relieved to see that it's exactly eleven-thirty.

"I'd like to begin with Blue Marine." Ozzie looks at Lucky and me.

Thankfully, Lucky takes the lead. "As you all know, Jenny and I headed over to Blue Marine Wednesday night and cloned all their computers and got access to their server. I've analyzed some of the data that we found, but I'm pretty sure Jenny has more detail for you." He swivels his chair to face mine.

I try to sound normal when I respond, but I have to clear my throat twice to get my voice to work properly, my first two attempts at speaking sounding more frog than human.

"Yes, so, as Lucky said, we did some work on Wednesday night. We had a schematic of the office and the various computer systems that were in place, and cloned everything. I spent quite a bit of time on the cloned systems to see what I could find, and there was one station in particular that caught my attention."

I reach into my file folder and pull out the report that I typed up, embarrassed that I only have three copies. I hand one to Lucky and the other to Ozzie, using the third one as a reference for myself. "I'm sorry I didn't make copies for everyone."

"Don't worry about it," Thibault says. "Just give us the highlights. We can look over a more detailed report later if we need to."

Thank God for Thibault. He has a special knack for making me feel more relaxed. I can't even look at Dev right now, though; I'll probably forget how to speak English if I see that dimple.

"Okay. So, like I said, there was one station that caught my attention. I detailed it in the first paragraph there." I glance at Ozzie and Lucky, verifying that they're looking very intently at what I wrote for them in the report. So far I don't see any funny expressions, so I think I'm good with the first paragraph. *Yay for me.*

"The employee who works at this spot is named Anita."

Lucky looks up at that moment with a sharp hiss of breath.

Thibault is shaking his head. "Tsk tsk," he says, leading me to believe this is a very bad sign. *Did I do something wrong?*

Ozzie ends the mystery for me. "Anita? Isn't that the wife of one of the owners?"

Thibault answers. "Yes. I believe she is. Right, Lucky?"

Lucky is nodding. "That's my understanding." He looks at me. "Keep going."

I nod before picking up again. "Okay . . . where was I . . . ?" I use my finger to find my place and then flip to the back of the report to remind myself what's there. I take a couple of moments to decide how technical I want to be with them. I don't want to short-change my work, like May said, but I also don't want to act like I'm showing off. It's easy for me to geek out and for people to get the wrong impression.

I stare at the paper as I continue. "Right. Okay. So, you can take a look at the more detailed screenshots that I provided at the end, and the more technical details, but in essence she had hidden some files using special software with a pretty heavy-duty encryption tool on her local drive, and in these files and via some other sources online, I found documentation that seems to suggest that she has created several entities, which I verified through the Department of State do exist. Each of them shows her as the sole owner. I cross-referenced this with the payments that Lucky tagged in the system as suspicious, and they're all linked. Every one. She's been paying herself for services that appear as if they were rendered but were more than likely not rendered at all or were rendered for significantly less money than she paid herself."

I pause, giving them a few seconds to absorb the information, before continuing. "She did try to hide her identity, and she might have gotten away with it, but . . . she didn't."

"I don't get it," says Toni. "What do you mean by that?"

"What I mean is, she probably had help. Either she or someone she knows is a pretty sophisticated computer user, and there was some degree of legal work done too to hide the various entities and the ownership of them. The info I needed to find was not available as a matter of public record. But I found it. She just got unlucky, I guess. Most people would have missed it or wouldn't have been able to access it." *Yes, I am a computer badass, and I'm not afraid to admit it.* Frank should have never let me go.

"Did you hack into someone's computer?" Toni asks, as if she doesn't believe it.

"It might be better if I don't share all the details with everyone." I shrug. "For deniability reasons. You understand." Not that anyone will be able to trace what I did, but still. It doesn't hurt to keep the circle of people-in-the-know very small, and I'm pretty sure she's not a decision maker around here.

Toni scowls, but Thibault smiles, and I take that as a good sign. Ozzie's expression is as unreadable as ever. Dev and Lucky are nodding. May looks like she just watched her baby take her first step. I think she's having a hard time not clapping. My chest is ready to explode, my heart is so full right now.

"How much money are we talking here?" Thibault asks.

I turn to Lucky for that. I found all the connections and did the tally, but I don't want to step on his toes. He's the financial guy, not me. I know how to be a team player.

"Nearly a million dollars over five years."

Dev whistles in appreciation of the awfulness, forcing me to look up at him. We catch each other's eyes and my face starts to burn. I have to look away. I cannot believe how silly I feel, with my stomach doing flips and my heart going nuts, just looking at him. *He's like the cuttlefish, hypnotizing me with his powers of adorableness.*

Ozzie's focus is back on me. "I know this is more of a legal question, but what do you know about prosecuting for embezzlement? Do you know if we have enough evidence here?"

Now my heart is stopping for a whole other reason. "Uhh . . . I have no idea. Sorry." *Oops. Was I supposed to research that?*

Lucky picks up the conversation. "No worries. It's not your area of expertise. This report is really nice. Very thorough. It must have taken you hours to put it together." He pages through it for effect, holding up a screenshot for Thibault to see.

"It did, but I had a lot of coffee and the kids were asleep, so . . ." I shrug, appreciating Lucky's efforts at making me feel better but still sad that I didn't think to look up the legal aspects. Sure, it's not my area of expertise, but I knew what we were doing the work for.

"I told you she's good." My sister is still beaming.

When Ozzie is done paging through the report, he hands it over to Thibault. Then Thibault takes his turn with it, nodding with every turn of a new page. Dev nods his head and winks at me before shifting his focus to studying Thibault's expression.

"You're right, Lucky. This is nice. Very nice work product. I don't even understand most of it."

Dev speaks, his voice making me flush all over again. "So what's the plan? What's our next move?" I can't look at him, afraid everyone will see in my expression how over the moon I am.

Lucky answers. "Well, I need to sit down with Jenny and have her show me all this on the computer, and then we need to invite Mr. Jorgensen to come in and show him what we've found. And at that point, I assume he'll want to get the police department involved." Lucky looks over at me. "Are you cool with that? Do you mind sitting with the client and explaining what you found? I think you're the only one who can really explain the details."

I'm anxious to keep the good vibes flowing. "Absolutely. I want to help however I can. You guys hired me to do this job, so I'll do anything you need to finish it up."

"That brings us to our next order of business," Ozzie says. The room goes silent and Thibault puts the report down on the table, turning his attention to me.

I look around at everyone, but the only one giving me any hint as to what's going on is Dev. He's smiling at me and then he winks.

I have to look away because my face is turning beet red. I feel like I just caught fire.

"I think, based on this report that we're looking at here, and the feedback that I've gotten from Lucky out in the field and from Dev as well, not to mention the information that Thibault was able to find, and of course May's recommendation"—Ozzie pauses to glance at his girlfriend, making her blush—"I'd like to move forward with our earlier conversation if that's okay with the group."

Everybody at the table with the exception of Toni nods in agreement. She doesn't say anything; she just stares straight ahead into space.

Ozzie turns his attention to me. "I know we had a bit of a rough start with you last week, but we've all been really impressed with your work product and your performance in general. Thibault, Lucky, and I have conducted an analysis of our business, and we've come to the conclusion that we've been turning down a lot of work because we're lacking some particular skillsets in our current roster. It appears as if you could pick up some of the slack on that."

He pauses to let that sink in and maybe to gauge my reaction. I remain as cool as possible under the circumstances. Having Dev across the table helps to remind me that I can handle myself well under pressure. I just have to remember that night in the office and how I didn't run out the door screaming in a blind panic. I dealt with that, I dealt with Frank's sorry ass, and I can certainly deal with this too.

"So, if you'd be willing, we'd love to have you join the team. We'd start you out on a ninety-day trial basis, to see if it's something that's a good fit for you and for us, but if it all works out the way we think it will, you could be a full-time employee and entitled to all the benefits that come along with that."

I swallow a couple times trying to get my voice to work. *Should I do it? Should I take the risk?* Should I stop worrying about all the things that *might* happen and instead focus on all the things that *could* happen?

I look across the table at Dev and he's staring me down with a serious expression on his face. He nods, like he has all the confidence in the world in me, like I actually could be a member of the Super Friends team. My heart soars and my courage hops up to ride shotgun.

I nod. "I'd like that. The trial basis sounds like a good idea." That's my out. If I hate it, no harm, no foul; I'll back out and there'll be no commitment to anyone that I have to blow off, and May will be safe from her team's ire. I refuse to consider where Dev falls in this scenario.

Ozzie nods. "Great." He looks around the table. "Does anybody else have any other business to discuss right now?"

I'm pretty sure they continue on and talk about another client at this point, but I don't hear any of it. I sit at the table in a daze, unable to believe my good fortune. Or is it my misfortune? I have no way of knowing right now. All I do know is that I'm sitting at a table with my sister—arguably the best friend I've ever had—and a man with a killer dimple who's giving me the most adorable look I could ever imagine, and I've just been offered a full-time job. It feels like this trial version is not just a trial for my job but also a trial for my heart.

Will I survive is the question. And if I don't, where will I be then? What if this turns out like my last job, where I work really hard and then get destroyed and left out in the cold?

It doesn't even bear thinking about right now. Always looking in my rearview mirror isn't the way for me to move forward. *Up, up, and away!* as Superman says. I'm going to focus on my future and not the mistakes of my past.

CHAPTER THIRTY-FIVE

Well, it's here; the moment I've been thinking about for the past several days. I drop the curtain in the front window back into place. Dev is in the driveway getting out of his car. He looks nice, wearing khakis and a cotton, button-down shirt.

I look down at myself, glad that I splurged at the mall today and bought this dress when I went shopping with May. I've spent so many years in comfy, boring clothes, going to work in sneakers and jeans, I almost forgot what it feels like to dress up.

The kids are happily installed at Auntie May's townhouse. It's a rare treat for them to have a sleepover there. Usually, May prefers to watch my kids here, but when she offered to take them to her place, I'm pretty sure she did it because she was thinking that this date might go really well. But it can't go *that* well; it's not like I'm going to sleep with my coworker on a first date. Besides . . . it's not a date. I lost a bet, that's all.

The doorbell rings, sending my heart rate soaring. I check my eye makeup and teeth in the front hall mirror really quickly before I go to the door and open it. I try to affect an air of casualness that I don't feel as I lean on the doorframe.

"Hey there, Dev."

"Hello." He stands on my porch towering above me, and if I'm not mistaken, he seems a little nervous. "You ready to go? Or did you want to stay here for a drink first?"

I do have a bottle of wine in the fridge, but I'm worried the conversation will stall out if we're left in this empty, quiet house together for too long. "We can go. It's fine. Unless you have later reservations . . ."

He shakes his head. "Nope. We're all set."

I grab my purse off the front hall table, double- and triple-checking that I have both my phone and my wallet. Since tonight's dinner is on me, I made sure to stop off at the ATM to get some extra cash earlier. Every once in a great while my debit card doesn't work, and I don't want to suffer that kind of embarrassment tonight. Actually, I don't want to suffer that embarrassment ever in my life, but because Miles gives me bouncy checks sometimes, it's unavoidable. The bank doesn't like fronting me money for some strange reason.

After I lock the front door behind me, we walk down the front steps together. "Where are we going?" I ask.

He accompanies me over to the passenger side of the car and opens the door for me. I'm charmed. I know it's old-fashioned, but I can't help it. Miles never did that for me, even when we were dating.

"You'll see. Don't worry, you'll like it. I promise."

I get into the car and smooth my dress down as he closes the door. I have a few moments to admire his amazing body as he makes his way around the front of the car and over to the driver's side. I feel really lucky to be with him tonight, even if this is just a friendly date. I'm also feeling especially fortunate that we work together, because if we run out of things to talk about at dinner, we could always discuss business. I'm super curious about his friends' backstories, so if nothing else, this dinner is an opportunity to get to know my own coworkers a little bit better.

Dev starts up his beast of a car and reverses out of the driveway, using the heel of one hand on the steering wheel to spin it around and around. We leave the neighborhood heading north, and soon we're out on the main road that I know will take us to an area of town I don't frequent very often. But I'm not going to worry about it, because I trust this man. I know he would never put me in danger.

"Great job at work today," he says.

"Thanks. It was no big deal." I was never very good at accepting compliments about my work. Performance evaluations are something I can deal with, because they're mostly on paper, but when people compliment me to my face, it always makes me feel like I need to squirm around in my seat. I stare out the side window, waiting for that sensation to pass.

"Well, Ozzie thought it was a big deal. And so did I."

"Toni didn't." I try not to sound bitter about that.

Dev shakes his head a little. "Don't worry about Toni. She'll come around. She's just stubborn and protective."

I look at Dev. "Does she actually think I would do something to harm you guys?"

"I don't think so. I don't think she believes you'd do anything purposely, anyway. But she does worry that having people on the team who lack training could be a liability. And she's not wrong about that."

I want to defend myself, but she's probably right. This isn't a regular job that you walk into and work for eight hours and leave. It's a security company that deals with really sensitive information, and I'm about as far from security material as a person can be.

"But don't worry about it," he says. "We'll get you whipped into shape in no time."

"Do you mean that literally or figuratively?" I laugh a little, but he doesn't join in.

"Both. I'm in charge of your training, so you have nothing to worry about." He looks over and flashes me a big, cheesy grin.

"Sounds exciting." I say this with a complete lack of enthusiasm.

He reaches over and pokes me on the leg. "Be careful. I'm your trainer now, so you don't want to piss me off."

"Oh my, that sounds like a threat. Let me check my pulse." I make a big show of resting my fingers at my wrist. "Hmmm, nope. Sorry. Not scared."

"You will be. I promise."

I know he's joking, but it sends a special thrill up my spine to hear him say that. I like it when he goes from joking to serious. It makes him seem almost a little dangerous, and although I'm kind of allergic to real danger, the sexy danger is something I could get used to.

We travel along in companionable silence, listening to the radio and enjoying the cooling temperature that allows us to drive with the windows open for a change. When *Boys Don't Cry*, one of my favorite songs from the eighties, blares from the speakers, Dev and I start singing together. At the chorus, we raise our voices louder and louder. By the time we pull into the restaurant parking lot, we're practically yelling the last lines of the song. Happy brain hormone-drugs are pumping through my veins as he glides into a parking spot near the front doors and shuts off the engine.

"You ready to get your catfish on?" he asks.

I look up at the sign above us. "The sign says Chicken Licken. I think I'm supposed to be getting my chicken on." I am definitely overdressed for this eatery, but I don't care, because so is he. It's like I'm on an adventure right now, and anything could happen. Fun stuff. Sexy stuff, maybe. *Woo hoo! Bring on the catfish!*

"Stay right there." He opens his door and gets out, shuts it, and then jogs around to my side. My door opens and he's standing there with his hand out. I slide my palm into his and use the contact to lever myself out of the car. I feel like a princess. A princess standing outside of Chicken Licken, the fried food capital of New Orleans, if the smell is any indicator.

"Trust me," he says, "this'll be the best fried catfish you've ever eaten." He leads me up to the front door. The odor of grease gets more pungent.

"What if I don't like catfish?" I ask, looking at him sideways.

He grabs the door and pulls it open, looking down at me with a very serious expression. "If you don't like catfish, I'm afraid we can't be friends anymore."

I poke him in the belly as I walk by. "Good thing I like catfish."

Okay, so I'm flirting, even though he called us friends. Sue me. He's too damn cute with that dimple of his. I'm pretty sure he knows it's killing me every time he uses it.

Several people greet Dev by name as we walk into the restaurant. A rotund lady easily in her sixties leads us to a booth in the back corner.

"The usual?" she asks.

"Of course. Bring me a double order so I can share it with this lovely lady here."

The woman looks at me and winks. "I was wondering when you were going to bring somebody special by."

Does that mean I'm the first? My face goes warm with the compliment.

"This here is Jenny. She's my friend from work." Dev's voice has taken on a distinct Cajun flair. I like it. A lot.

The lady nods. "Jenny, it's very nice to make your acquaintance. I'm Melba, and you are welcome here anytime, even if you don't bring this tall drink of water with you." She gestures at my date who's not really a date.

"I hear you have the best catfish in town." I smile at her, caught up in the mood of the place.

"You heard right. But I'll let you judge for yourself." She looks at Dev. "Sweet tea?"

He winks at her. "Bring us two."

I'm not going to complain about all the calories in that tea that's probably just as sweet as an actual Coke. Tonight, I'm going to splurge. I'm going to eat catfish and drink sweet tea until my stomach begs for mercy.

We're alone at the table now, the sounds of satisfied diners surrounding us with a happy buzz. The smell of greasy, fried food hangs in the air, probably coating my hair and clothing, but I don't care. This is already one of the best non-dates I've ever been on.

"So, did you enjoy working with Lucky?"

I nod. "Yep. We had a little bit of a scare with those people breaking in when we were working, but besides that, it was fun." I realize as I'm telling him this that I actually did enjoy myself. I have a sneaking suspicion that this job is going to be a lot like pregnancy; at the time, it seems really awful and hard and scary, but looking back all you can remember are the good parts. The fear kind of fades out to a mere wisp of a memory, the details fuzzy and hard to recall.

"Lucky tells me you did just fine. And you don't need to worry about that kind of stuff in the future. Going on-site is very rare for Lucky, and it'll be the same for you."

"He told me that he works at the warehouse most of the time and sometimes from home."

"Yep. That's pretty much it. Lucky tends to be a homebody."

I play with my fork, wanting to talk more about Lucky and his life, but not wanting to seem like a busybody. It's just that he's such an interesting person, a genuine mystery, and I do looove me a puzzle. It's why I'm so good at what I do, maybe. And why this job with the Bourbon Street Boys is really starting to excite me. I could be solving puzzles every day working with them.

"Have you met his goldfish Sunny?" I ask, trying to sound casual, which isn't easy, considering I'm bringing up a goldfish as a conversation starter.

Dev shakes his head. "Nope. Lucky moved to a new place a while back, and I don't know if anybody's been there yet. Maybe Thibault has. Sunny moved in with him sometime after he changed apartments."

"How come you haven't been there? Doesn't he like visitors?"

Dev looks off in the distance. "Lucky is . . . private, I guess you could say."

I stare at the table, drawing imaginary lines on the surface with my fingertip. "He told me about his sister." I glance up at Dev to gauge his reaction, and catch him looking very surprised.

"Really? That's . . . unexpected."

"Why? I mean, I know it's really personal stuff, but it just kind of came up in conversation." I don't want Dev to think I pry deep secrets out of people the first day I work with them.

"He doesn't talk about it with anybody. I mean, it happened, and of course we talked about it back then, but nobody talks about it now."

"He said it's because it makes people uncomfortable that he doesn't talk about it. It's not that he doesn't want to."

Dev shrugs. "Well, it is uncomfortable, but that doesn't mean nobody should be talking about it. I guess I just don't bring it up because I don't want to make him feel bad. I figured he'd want to move on from it."

I nod. "Yeah, I get it."

"Did he say something to you about that? About us not talking about it?"

I shrug, not wanting to get into the middle of their relationship and cause problems; I'm the newcomer here. But if I can help Lucky out, I'd like to do that. I decide to tread lightly and feel my way as

I go. If Dev starts to sound mad or uncomfortable, I'll change the subject. I'll talk about pink fairy armadillos. That'll take his mind off his coworker like nobody's business. Personally, I find them fascinating, and they're a favorite of my girls.

I continue, watching Dev as I speak to make sure I'm not making him uncomfortable. "He did mention that nobody seems to want to talk about it, but he writes that off as everybody feeling bad for him and not wanting him to dwell on it, like you said. It's not like he's mad at anybody over it."

"Are you saying he *wants* to talk about his sister and what happened?"

"I am. I think he does, anyway. I think he's still in mourning, and it might help him to remember her in a positive way. Like, to have people there to listen to him talk about her, about his memories of her. He blames himself, you know."

"That much I do know. He's always taken the blame for everything that happens in his family. Whether he should or not is immaterial. It's just how he is."

"There's a big age difference between Lucky and his sister. Or there was." I hate talking in the past tense after somebody's died. It almost feels disrespectful to the life they had. It doesn't make any difference that I never knew this particular person, either.

"Yeah, they have a split family. His father remarried and got together with somebody much younger, and they started a second family that included his sister. Lucky is close with all of them, but he was especially close with her. But, still, he had to work, you know? We all have to work."

I reach over and put my hand on his. I know exactly what he's thinking right now; he's torturing himself over being a parent and a working man.

"It's not easy, working and being responsible for family members at the same time. You always feel like you're neglecting something."

275

He hisses and shakes his head in disappointment, staring at our hands on the table, my tiny one in comparison to his huge one. "Tell me about it."

"How's Jacob?" I ask, forcing a change in the conversation. We need to turn this mess around or we're both going to end up so depressed by the end of the dinner, we'll never want to go out together again. And I really do like hanging out with Dev, so I don't want that to happen.

"He's awesome." Dev is smiling, the sadness over Lucky and his situation pushed to the side for the moment. "He had a great time at your place with your kids. He thinks Sammy is hilarious."

I roll my eyes. "Sammy is hilarious. The kid constantly has me in stitches. The problem is, it makes it hard to discipline him."

Dev turns my hand over and touches my palm with his thumb. He does it so casually it should be no big deal, but it's sending thrills up my arm and into my chest. Every tiny touch from him gives me a shock of pleasure now. Things feel different between us.

"He doesn't seem to need much discipline," Dev says. "He's very polite, and he's obviously worried about how other people feel. He's compassionate. That's a big deal for a kid his age. Most little boys are complete sociopaths."

I laugh. "You say all that, but every once in a while I wonder about him. His favorite hobby is ripping the heads off his sisters' dolls."

"If Jacob had any sisters, I'll bet he'd do the same thing."

"Nooo, not Jacob. He's too sweet."

"Trust me. When he rolls his wheelchair down the sidewalk, he specifically steers it so he can run over ants. Tell me that's not sociopathic behavior."

"Okay, so he's not going to win any Upstanding Citizen of the Year awards right now, but he's barely five. Give him some time."

We look into each other's eyes, smiling at how silly we're being. Two parents, complimenting each other's kids . . . Does it get any cheesier than this? Probably not. Luckily, we're interrupted from going too much further down that road by the delivery of our sweet teas. I pull my hand away from Dev's, gripping my glass and taking a sip. It's as sweet as I was expecting, with a little twist of lemon. *Perfect.*

Dev takes a long drink, swallows, and then sighs with satisfaction. His eyes are closed in bliss. "Best sweet tea in Louisiana."

Melba has already left our table, but she hears him and laughs. I can see why he comes here a lot. They treat him like he's somebody special, and he is. I'm glad I'm not the only one who sees it. Guys like Dev deserve to be treated well. I have to look down in my glass to keep from smiling like a goofy fool at him.

CHAPTER THIRTY-SIX

So, what are you and Jacob doing for Halloween?" I ask.

Dev opens his eyes and leans forward a little. "Halloween is a really big event at the Lake household."

"It is, huh?"

"Yes. I have to get very creative with the costuming. Every year, the bar is set a little bit higher. By the time my kid is in his last years of trick-or-treating, I'm going to be recruiting people from Hollywood for these costumes of his."

I lean in, intrigued. "Really? What did he go as last year?"

"Shark."

I blink a few times, trying to picture it. "Shark?"

"Yep. Shark. Bull shark to be exact. Toughest, baddest-ass shark in the world."

"Second only to the great white," I say, repeating facts I've heard on my favorite TV channel.

"I beg to differ," Dev says. "The bite force of the great white is not nearly as strong, being that their diet is mostly soft-fleshed animals like seals, whereas the bull shark regularly has to crunch through sea turtle shells."

I sense a fellow Animal Planet fan and lean in, ready to go head-to-head. "Maybe, but if you really want to go as a badass animal, I suggest you look no further than the saltwater crocodile."

"Agreed." Dev leans in and winks at me. "I think you just solved my costume problem."

"How will you build a croc costume?"

"I have no idea." He picks up his glass and takes a sip. "All input is welcome." He crunches on some ice as he waits for me to respond.

I chew my lip and think about it for a few seconds. "Maybe you should do something easier, since you don't have much time. Like Batman and Robin."

"Did it already. Two years ago."

"How about . . . traditional stuff, like a ghost or a witch or a vampire?"

"Amateur hour. We did that when Jacob was two years old."

"I was going to be a witch, but okay . . ."

"You can do better than that." Dev gives me the eye. "I bet you've got all kinds of creative ideas floating around in that brainy head of yours."

"I might have some creativity, *maybe*, but I don't have time to do anything with it. That's my biggest problem. I always cop out and get some cheap costume at the drugstore."

"Well, now that you're working with us, you'll have more free time on your hands, right?"

I shrug. "I guess we'll see."

Dev gets serious. "Are you happy? Are you glad you got the job?" He seems to really want to know my answer, leaning in and staring at me.

I want to see that smile light up his face and that dimple cave in on his cheek, but I also know that I need to be honest with him.

Just like I need to be honest with myself. I take a breath before answering.

"I am happy. I'm also a little bit worried."

"What are you worried about?" The concern in his voice makes it easier for me to think about my answer and make sure it comes out right.

"I'm just . . . worried that I won't be able to do the job. And I guess I'm also worried about the danger involved."

"The danger is very minimal, I promise. I wouldn't want you working there if I thought it was something to worry about."

The way he says it makes me curious, as if he has some sort of personal responsibility toward me. "What do you mean?"

He shrugs and leans back against his seat, suddenly acting casual again. "You're a single mom. You can't afford to take risks that other people could, so I wouldn't want you to work somewhere that wasn't right for you."

I love that he gets me. It's like he's validated my feelings or something. "And you think Bourbon Street Boys is right for me?"

He nods. "I do."

We could probably talk about this subject all night, but our fried catfish shows up along with some hushpuppies and a pile of coleslaw, and the next twenty minutes are spent diving in and enjoying every last morsel of food that Dev was absolutely right about.

Truth be told, I am not the biggest catfish fan in the world, but the serving of it I'm indulging in here could easily change my mind on that. The batter is crunchy yet flaky, and the catfish itself, tender and fresh. It doesn't even taste like fish.

Dev takes a long pull from his sweet tea, and then sits back in his chair, letting out a long sigh as he rubs his belly. "Did I tell you this was great or what?"

I wipe the grease from my lips with my paper napkin and put it on the table next to my empty fish basket, leaning back in my seat too. I hope he doesn't expect me to eat dessert, because I don't have any room left.

"Yes, this was really great. Thank you so much for bringing me here." I look around the restaurant and see a lot of happy faces. "How did you find this place?"

"I've been coming here since I was a kid. Everyone on the team has. They treat us well here, and we like to support them as much as we can."

Melba comes over and takes our baskets away, interrupting the conversation. Once she's gone, my eyes drop to the table. *Holy crap.* The only things left are two placemats, mine and Dev's. His looks brand new, but mine, on the other hand, is covered in a sample of every bit of food that passed through my lips. Fish? Yes. Fish coating? Yes. Hushpuppy guts? Yes. Coleslaw? Of course. It's like a Chicken Licken bomb went off at our table, but only left shrapnel in front of me. *How embarrassing! Now he knows I eat like a total warthog!*

Dev doesn't say a word. Instead, he lifts his placemat up, reaches over and slides my placemat to his side of the table, and then places his down in front of me. Now he's the warthog, and I'm the princess who wouldn't dare drop a speck of hushpuppy anywhere but on her napkin.

I know it's crazy, but tears well up in my eyes. This has to be the single most chivalrous, charming thing a man has ever done for me. Forget opening doors and throwing jackets over puddles. When a man covers for me, taking the heat for my horrible table manners, he wins my loyalty for life.

When Melba returns with sweet tea refills, she looks down at the table and smiles. She doesn't need to say anything; she just looks at me and winks. My heart feels like it's filling up so full with happiness that it's going to explode.

"You got a costume yet?" she asks Dev.

"Maybe. I might have found my inspiration tonight." He gives me a look. I almost have a heart attack from it. *Gah, that dimple!*

"Have you seen the pictures?" she asks me.

I shake my head no.

She points at Dev. "You need to show her. You need to work harder at impressing this girl. I like her."

She walks away without saying anything else, and I look down at the table, embarrassed that I've been given such a high compliment.

"Do you have ideas for your kids' costumes yet?" Dev asks me.

"No, I still need to go to the store. My life is a mess." I sigh, imagining myself once again shopping for crappy costumes my kids will whine about. "I'm always scrambling around at the last minute trying to pull it all together."

"If you need any help, just let me know."

I'm not sure how that would work out, but I like the idea of him being involved in my Halloween celebration. "Okay. Thanks."

"Do you usually trick-or-treat around your neighborhood?"

I nod. "Yeah, it's pretty good. We hardly have any apple-givers."

He smiles briefly before continuing. "Mine's not the greatest. Jacob is always complaining that so many of the lights are turned out, it eats up all his battery in his wheelchair trying to get around the neighborhood and get enough candy."

I feel shy saying it, but it seems like the perfect solution to me. "You guys could come and trick-or-treat with us if you want. Almost all the lights are on every year. Jacob could clean up with an awesome crocodile costume."

Dev nods like he's considering it. "I'll talk to Jacob and see what he thinks."

His casual acceptance of my offer sends a thrill through me. It's almost like a commitment in a way. Trick-or-treating together. *Do friends do that, or just couples?*

"So, did you pick out a date from that website?" he asks, throwing a giant virtual bucket of ice-cold water over the situation.

Here I am thinking about us being a couple, and he's thinking about how he wants to date other people. *Ugh.* I completely suck at reading men. I suppose I can't be too depressed that he's bringing up the dating thing. I did look on that website, and I did set up a date.

Is it possible we're both terrible at this flirting thing and neither of us has the guts to just come right out and tell the other how we really feel? I want to believe that could be true, but in reality it's probably more that he's just keeping his options open. I can hardly blame him. I comfort myself with the thought that the last thing I should be looking for is a committed relationship. I have hardly any free time as it is.

I clear my throat to get the lump out of it. "Actually, yes I have. Have you? "

"Yep. Got something set up for tomorrow, in fact."

"Really. What's she look like?"

"I have no idea."

I frown. "Why not?"

"Because. I searched without photos. I want to be attracted to a person for who she is, not what she looks like."

"That's very . . . un-guy-like." I say and then snort accidentally. *Oops. The warthog is back. But damn . . . is he for real?*

He shrugs. "Meh . . . I figure it'll just cut down on the B.S. People aren't honest about their looks anyway. Half the photos on there are Photoshopped, and the others are pictures taken ten years ago. What's the point? It's the person inside you fall for in the end, not the outside wrapper."

"Your explanation makes complete sense . . . but only if you're a woman. Guys don't think that way, do they? Who told you to search without photos?" I know it wasn't anyone on the team. No way could I picture Lucky or Thibault advising Dev to search for a girl based on her personality.

His grin comes off so guilty, he might as well shout from the rooftops that he's busted. "My mother," he finally admits.

I can't stop laughing.

"What about you?"

My laughter peters out. "I must admit, I'm shallow. I looked at his picture."

"Easy way out," he says, teasing me.

This feels like a challenge now. "Where're you going on your hot date with your mystery woman?"

"Wouldn't you like to know?" He leans in and gives me a sexy little wink.

I act super cool, like a cucumber that's been sitting in the chiller drawer of my refrigerator for a solid week. *Ice. Cold.* "No, not really. I'm sure it's not nearly as interesting as the place I'm going."

He laughs. "What time are you meeting him?"

His question throws me off. "Why? What does that matter?"

"Because, the time of the meeting says everything about the person's intentions."

I sit up straighter, suddenly worried about my so-called date or meeting or whatever the hell it is. "Really? Like how?"

"Well, let's see . . . Is it a lunchtime thing? A late afternoon thing? An evening thing? Dinner? A movie? A drink? It all means something, you know."

I stare at him, trying to figure out if he's joking. At first there's nothing to clue me in, and then that little dimple appears. "Oh, be quiet. I know you're just teasing me." I pick up my tea and have a sip of it to keep my hands busy. I feel like such a doofus. I have no idea what I'm doing with this online dating stuff.

He shrugs, trying to act all cool. "If you say so."

"I guess you're some kind of ninja dating master, but this is my first time, so I'm just figuring it out as I go. I can't imagine it's all that complicated, though." I don't recall seeing a rulebook on the website. *How do people know these rules? Are they written somewhere?* I'm going to have to Google that when I get home.

"Ninja dating . . . what?" he laughs. "I haven't done this either. Not lately, anyway. This is my first time in years. I'm just hoping it won't be a complete disaster."

"I'll bet we'll have some really good stories after tomorrow," I say, trying to look on the bright side.

"I'll give you a call Sunday, and we can trade notes."

I hate that the idea makes me so happy. He's suggesting a simple phone call, not another date with me. This whole thing is so confusing. It's sad to think that I'm not any better at figuring men out now than I was at twenty. I shrug, because I'm cool like that. Like that cucumber in my fridge. *So ice cold.* "Sure. I don't have any plans except to hang out with the kids."

He looks over at Melba. She's standing behind the counter near a cash register. "Do you want dessert?" he asks.

"My god, no. I have no room left in my stomach. Not even for a bite."

He signals to Melba and makes some gesture with his finger, swirling it around and poking the air with it—some kind of restaurant sign language I do not understand at all. When he finishes, he shifts his attention back to me.

"What was that all about?" I ask.

"I told her to wrap me up a dessert and bring the check."

I nod, a little sad that our date is almost over. Not that it was a date. We're just two friends going out for a catfish dinner. That's it. I'm going to keep saying that to myself over and over until I actually believe it.

"Jacob is going to be psyched about Halloween."

I'm back to smiling again. Who cares what this is? It's fun, and that's all I need to know. "My kids, too. They really liked hanging out with Jacob. Sammy is having a little bit of a hero worship issue, I think. Jacob's an older kid and his wheelchair is really fast, so . . ."

Dev smiles. "That'll make Jacob happy. I won't tell him, of course, but he doesn't get to interact with other kids very often, so it's good that they started off on the right foot."

I tilt my head at him. "Doesn't he go to daycare or school?"

"Sometimes, for a couple hours at a time, he goes to daycare. He was too young to start kindergarten last year. It's really hard to find a place that can take care of his needs, so he spends a lot of time with my mother and me. It's also why you don't see me full-time at the warehouse. I work there as many hours as I can, but I have to be there for my son a lot, too."

I nod. "I get it. Do you do his therapy for him?"

"Most of it. I get training from his physical therapist, and then I continue the work at home. He doesn't like it, so it's a bit of a battle, but it needs to be done."

"He told Sammy that he has cerebral palsy. I'm not really familiar with that disability. What does it mean for him and for you?" I pray that I haven't stepped over the bounds of social decency by asking him these very personal questions, especially because I'm doing it almost out of selfish reasons. I don't want to make assumptions and say or do something stupid the next time we're together.

Dev doesn't hesitate. "There are a few different kinds of cerebral palsy. He was diagnosed with spastic CP, which means essentially that his muscles spasm a lot and get really tight. It was caused by a lack of oxygen at birth. His joints are painful, too. It's really tough for him. I have to keep him stretched out, and we do a lot of massage to try to keep his muscles from pulling his skeleton into bad positions and wearing down the cartilage in his joints. Because his muscles and tendons are always pulling in directions that aren't good for his bones, they don't always grow properly. That's why he probably looks a little crooked to you."

My heart aches for Jacob. "It sounds very painful."

"It is, but he's a real trouper. He's tough. He has been since the day he was born. You could see it in his eyes when he was just a day old. Even when he's in pain, he's determined to push through. He's my hero."

"Geez, he's my hero, too. To be so young and to have such a heavy burden? I couldn't even imagine . . ." I don't finish my thought, but inside my head all I can think is how stupid and shallow I've been, whining about how tough my life is. How much time have I wasted fretting about my son's lisp? A lisp is nothing compared to Jacob's challenges.

"Everybody is given his own burden to carry, and we're never given anything we can't handle. When I look at my son, I see a superhero. I see a human being who is handling something so tough, most of us would be crushed under the weight of it. But he doesn't get crushed. He rises above it all. I admire his courage, and at the same time I'm there to whup his butt when he starts to forget how amazing he is."

I want to cry, I'm so in love with this man right now.

My heart lurches as that thought crosses my mind. Is it possible that I'm in *love*-love with him, like not just right here in this moment but in general? *Gah, how lame is that?* He's relegated me to the friend zone and I'm looking at him with goo-goo eyes, hoping he'll decide one day to be my boyfriend.

I could spend days, weeks, or even months beating myself up about this, but I'm not going to do that. Any girl would feel the same way, and I don't think any woman in the world would blame me for being so mixed up and full of hope. He's not only a great guy, but he's also a great dad. Why didn't I marry a guy like him instead of a turd like Miles? What a waste of ten years that was. I console myself with the fact that I have three great kids . . . and the thought that Dev is probably horrible in bed. He has to be, right? No man can be everything—great dad, great coworker, great friend, great in the sack . . .

"I'd really love to know what's going on in your head right now," he says.

My eyes widen. "Why?" Was it written all over my face that I was falling in love with him? That I was imagining him naked and on top of me?

He gives me an almost evil-looking grin. "Because. It looks like sexy stuff."

"Oh, be quiet." I'm completely and totally busted. My face burns bright red. Thankfully, the lighting is bad in here. Perhaps I'll get lucky and he won't notice. "You don't know what you're talking about." I look anywhere but at him.

"Okay. If you say so." Clearly, he doesn't believe me. So much for being sneaky and incognito about my feelings. I'm about as incognito as a peacock in heat. *Look at me! Over here! Ready to get it on like Donkey Kong and bear your children too!*

Melba comes over with the check and a big box wrapped up inside a plastic bag with the handles tied together. "Here you go. One hot fudge brownie with all the toppings and extra cherries on top."

Dev reaches into his back pocket, but I stop him with my hand out. "No, no, this is my treat. I lost the bet, so I'm paying."

Dev shakes his head at me as he pulls his wallet from his back pocket. "Sorry, but I have a personal policy of never letting a woman pay for meals. My mother would never forgive me if I made an exception just because you lost a bet with me."

I frown at him. "That's not fair. These were your rules."

He shrugs. "You can get the next one."

I want to argue that this violates his so-called rules, and that by his reasoning he'd always end up paying, but I don't want to talk him out of a second non-date that could maybe by some chance turn into a real date. I'm not that stupid. "Fine. But don't think you can invoke this personal policy on our next . . . meal together."

Dev gives Melba a pile of cash and tells her to keep the change. She walks away happy.

"Ready?" he asks.

I nod, not sure where we go from here. Will he just drop me off, or will he come into my place for a drink? I have no idea what I'm doing. I'm a complete newbie at this non-dating, maybe-dating thing. The last time I went out with anybody, I was practically a teenager. I'm tempted to text my sister for advice, but I don't want him to see how clueless I am. I fight the urge to take my phone out and instead busy myself with gathering my things and smoothing imagined wrinkles out of my dress.

Following him out to the car, I decide on my way that I just need to keep doing what I'm doing, namely following his lead and seeing where it takes us. Knowing him as I do now, I trust that he won't lead me astray. He's too good a man for that.

CHAPTER THIRTY-SEVEN

I don't know if Dev is as nervous as I am on our ride to my house, but it seems like he might be. We share maybe five minutes of small talk all the way back, and then we're pulling up into my driveway.

Will he keep the car running? Will he assume I'm going to invite him in? Will he ask if he can come inside and take my clothes off? These are the thoughts that are traveling through my crazy, confused, and sexually starved brain as he parks in the driveway. He pauses as the motor idles, staring out the windshield. I wish I could get inside that brain of his and read it.

He puts his hand on the ignition and turns to look at me, his expression unreadable. "I'm going to walk you to the door if that's okay."

I nod. "Of course. I appreciate it." I'll pretend I live in a scary neighborhood and that I need a big, strong man to walk me to my door. *Save me, Spider-Man!*

It's not the sexy invitation I was fantasizing I might get from him, but maybe I'll be able to steal a kiss good night. I'm feeling a little bold for some reason. Maybe it's a side effect of eating fried catfish.

He shuts off the ignition and comes around to open my door for me once more. It's just as charming the third time as it was the first. As we walk up to the front door side by side, the schoolgirl in me is sweating it, big-time. *I want him to hold my hand and ask me if I'll be his girlfriend! I'm fifteen years old again! Wheee!*

I wish I could walk up the porch in slow motion and make the moment last longer, but his strides are those of a seven-foot-tall man. We're at the front door in no time.

I fish around in my purse for the keys and then, when I find them, hold my purse against my chest as I look up at him. "I really enjoyed our evening, even though you cheated."

His grin comes slowly. "Cheated? Who cheated? I played fair."

"The deal was that I was supposed to pay. You changed the rules to suit your purposes."

"And what purposes would those be?"

This doesn't feel like a conversation between just friends, but I don't want to ruin it by pushing for something that I can't have. But will that stop me from flirting? No. Not tonight. Not when he's using that dimple to make my heart go pitter-patter.

"I have no idea," I say, grinning. "You should just tell me instead of making me guess."

Oh my god! I forgot how fun flirting can be. He's still smiling down at me as he tries to come up with the perfect response.

I jingle my keys in my hand, letting him know that if he doesn't come up with something quick, I'm going to open that door and disappear. Does he want me to do that? Or does he want me to remain out here on the front stoop with him in this sticky heat, with the cicadas singing all around us. I swear, I could stay out here all night. All he'd have to do is ask.

"You in a hurry?" he says.

I shrug. "Not really. Are you?"

"I wouldn't say no to a glass of wine."

My heart hammers loudly in my chest. I hope he can't hear it. "Come on in. I have a bottle in the fridge."

My hands are shaking so badly I can't put the damn key in the lock. How embarrassing! So much for being a cool cucumber; my cucumber is warm and limp, left out on the counter for days and days . . .

He doesn't say a word; he just takes the keys from me and gently slides the one we need into the lock. "Are you cold?" he asks close to my ear.

I laugh self-consciously. "It's like eighty degrees out right now."

"I guess that means you're shaking for another reason." He pushes the door open and gestures for me to precede him.

I sigh at him, annoyed that he won't let me be a dork in secret. "I'm just nervous, okay?" I hate admitting that. For a moment there, I was living in an illusion where I knew what I was all about and was making him sweat.

He's smiling again. I swear he looks like the devil himself, and very pleased about it too. "What are you nervous about?" he asks. "You're not worried about being alone in the house with me, are you?"

I frown at him, feeling bad that he might actually believe that. "You're crazy. I actually feel safer with you here in the house with me than I would by myself."

"Hmm, that's very interesting," he says, following me into the front hall. "So if you're not nervous about me being in the house with you alone, then what is it?"

I look up at him and bat my eyelashes. "Don't make me say it."

He tips his head back and laughs really loud. "Say what?"

I shove him out of my way and walk down the hall. "You cannot possibly be that dense."

He follows me into the kitchen, still chuckling. I expect him to continue teasing me, which is why I squeak with surprise when his arms come around me from behind.

He leans down and puts his mouth near my neck. "Don't be scared. I won't hurt you."

Shivers move over my entire body, making goosebumps stand up on my skin. I can barely speak, my voice coming out a mere whisper. "I know you won't." Suddenly I'm jelly inside. I can barely stand on my own.

I'm staring at the inside of my refrigerator, but I don't see anything there. Not the wine or the other things I bought to have for dinner over the next couple days. My vision has gone blurry with all of my body focused on the sensations he's creating with his hands. They're so huge!

His right hand is open and resting on my stomach; it covers the entire thing, creating the sensation that I'm this tiny person in his big, strong arms. I love it! His other hand is on my hip, his fingers pressing into that small space just in front of my hipbone. So intimate. *God, I want him so badly!*

"If you don't like this, you need to tell me," he says in a deeply gruff voice.

I shake my head vigorously but say nothing. I don't trust myself to speak. I'm liable to blurt out the first thing that comes to mind, which will no doubt be way too heavy for this occasion. We're just having fun. We're two single parents without their kids for a change, goofing around in an empty house. It's almost like we're teenagers again, and our parents have gone away for the weekend. Dev has managed to turn back time for me. It's a gift on several levels.

He uses the pressure from his hands to turn me around. I'm afraid to look up at him, but I do it anyway. He's impossibly tall and impossibly handsome. I can't believe he's here with me.

"You are so beautiful," he says.

I smile, charmed by the almost innocent look on his face. "I think that sweet tea went right to your head."

I expect him to smile, but he doesn't. He looks as serious as a man can be. "Oh, no. I have all my faculties and perfect vision. I feel very lucky tonight."

Who feels like a million bucks? *Me. I do.*

"Me too." I put my hands on his upper arms as he draws me closer. I slide my fingers around his biceps, secretly enjoying the bulges underneath his shirt. I would so love to see this guy naked. Is that wrong of me? We haven't even been on a *real* date yet.

He leans down, and I tip my head back to try to make it easier on him. The foot-and-a-half difference in height between us is not conducive to a sexy, romantic moment; he's bent nearly in half to kiss me.

When our mouths meet, I'm surprised; his lips are softer than I expected them to be. He pushes them against mine, first gently and then with more pressure. I'm also thrilled. This doesn't feel like a friends-only kiss. This feels like a he's-interested-in-being-more-than-friends kiss. I'm not going to question why he's asking me about dating other guys when he's ready to say goodbye like this; I'm just going to try and enjoy the moment.

When our tongues join the game, I start to panic, though. I realize that I have no idea what I'm doing. I haven't kissed a man in almost a year, and before that, the only man I ever kissed for ten years was Miles. The awkwardness has me backing my head up and breaking off contact. It feels so strange to be here with him. Good, but strange. Like I've done something I shouldn't have. My head is going crazy with questions, the foremost being *Are you going to break my heart playing games with me?*

"Is something wrong?" he asks.

"No. I'm just . . ." I shake my head and look down. I'm so embarrassed and disappointed in myself. I have the hottest guy in town standing right here in my kitchen and I can't even kiss him without turning it into a soap opera? What am I? Brain dead?

His finger lifts my chin, forcing me to look at him. "Am I going too fast?"

I laugh bitterly. "Jesus, I hope not."

He smiles. "That's good news. I think."

I shake my head. "I'm sorry I'm being such a freak. It's just that . . . I've been alone for a year, and I suddenly realized that I am really out of practice. I think I forgot how to kiss."

He leans down again, talking gently as he comes closer. "Don't worry, it's like riding a bike. You just need to get on and start pedaling."

I lift my mouth toward his as he gets closer. "Start riding?"

"Yeah," he says with a smile in his whispering voice. "Get on and do your thing."

Oh, what the hell. Why not? Why not just throw all caution to the wind and take a leap of faith? My heart races as I realize what I'm doing. I'm going to give this a shot. I'm going to kiss this man and see where it takes us.

Our lips come together much more confidently this time. Both of us give in to the passion that's been building between us. Screw being just friends. This feels too good to keep it on a mere friend-ship level.

His hands are all over me. One is grabbing my ass and squeez-ing, the other is at my back, pulling me into him. Our bodies are touching everywhere. My arms are almost straight up in the air, wrapped around his neck and pulling him down to deepen our kiss. *I guess I haven't forgotten how to kiss . . .*

When he moans against my mouth, it ramps up the heat another couple notches. I didn't think I was capable of experiencing this kind of passion in such a short period of time. Two minutes ago I was talking myself into being his friend; now I'm trying to figure out how long we have to mess around before I can get him into my bedroom.

One of his hands slides around and grabs my breast, and all I can think is, *Go under my shirt! Take off my bra! Let's make this happen!*

He's grinding into me, but we're in a terrible position for it. If he were a guy of normal height, it might have worked, but with him, it feels like somebody's pressing a hammer into my stomach.

I speak between kisses, my words coming out in gasps of breath. "Do you want to go to my room?"

He stops all of a sudden and pulls away from me, leaning back so he can look me in the eye. "Do you?"

I panic. Why is he asking me that? Does he not want to go that far? Did I read too much into his passionate embrace?

I shrug. "Only if you do. We don't have to. It's fine if you want to stay here in the kitchen." I look to my left. "In front of the refrigerator."

Next thing I know, my world is turning upside down. I let out a quick scream before I realize what's happening. He's holding me in his arms, and with his long strides we're already halfway down the hallway.

I start laughing like a maniac. "What are you doing?" My hair dangles in the air, hanging over his arm, and my legs are flopping around as I try to get upright.

"You're making me crazy. You think I don't want to go to your bedroom? You're nuts." He swings me around the bottom of the stairs and accidentally clunks my head on the corner banister. Luckily it was more my hair hitting it than anything else, but the sound it makes is terrible.

"Oh, shit! I'm so sorry!" He drops my legs and cradles my upper body in his arms while he looks down at me. "Are you okay? I can't believe I just cracked your head. What an asshole." He reaches around and rubs it enough to make my hair go into knots.

I start laughing again, letting my head drop back. "Well, that's one way to woo a woman—knock her unconscious and carry her up to her bedroom caveman style."

He swoops me up in his arms again, holding me like a baby but tighter this time. Now we're both laughing as he runs up the stairs diagonally to keep from checking my cranium against the banister again.

He stops at the top. "Which way?"

"Left." I've stopped laughing, and started whispering. I can't believe we're doing this. My heart is totally into it, but my head is worried. *Am I making a mistake? Am I going to ruin everything by doing this?*

My bedroom doors fly open, and Dev plows through without hesitation. Three feet from the bed he launches me from his arms, and I go flying through the air. I scream and laugh the entire way. I've barely made contact with the mattress when he's jumping onto the bed next to me.

For two seconds, he looks like a real superhero—Superman, arms out and flying toward me. Unfortunately, I don't have the nicest bed frame in the world, having purchased it at a bargain basement sale before I was married to Miles. When his giant body flops down on the left side of it, the entire thing cracks and collapses under his weight. The mattress shifts, rolling me sideways right into him.

I scream in fright and surprise, and he yells right along with me. He's falling too. We're a tangle of arms and legs, and we're headed right for the floor.

"Oof!" he grunts out as he lands on the carpet on his back.

I land on top of him, causing him to cough out a groan.

I heard a crack as we were headed south. Looking up from my position on his chest, I catch him rubbing his head.

"That's gonna leave a mark." Apparently, he hit his head pretty hard on my side table.

"Oh my god. I can't believe you just broke my bed."

He looks at me, and I look at him, and we both start laughing. Within seconds I'm hysterical. I have to roll off him and cross my legs to keep from peeing on my floor.

I lie on my back, staring up at my ceiling with my legs crossed and my hands holding my crotch. A few latent snorts and giggles keep popping out so I don't trust myself to let go yet. I cannot remember the last time I got this silly. Maybe never.

Dev turns his head to look at me, and I do the same. We stare at each other for the longest time as our laughter dies down.

"This has got to be the sexiest date you've ever had. Am I right?" He wiggles his eyebrows at me.

I start laughing all over again. I can't help it. He called it a date! And he's wacky, just like me.

He props himself up on his side and looks at me for a little while. Then he opens his mouth to say something, but a buzzing sound cuts him off, and he loses the happy expression on his face.

"What's that?" I ask, my remaining laughter suffering a quick death.

"It's my phone." Reaching down, he pulls his cell out of his pocket. Reading a text there, he immediately sits up.

Dread fills me. "Is there something wrong?"

He sighs heavily, his shoulders slumping down. "It's my mom. I have to go."

It flashes through my mind that we're once again a teen couple, stealing moments that we really don't deserve to have. "Is everything okay with Jacob?"

"I don't think so. I think he's cramping up. She wouldn't ask me to come home otherwise." He looks at me, his expression sad. "I'm really sorry."

I stand up suddenly and put my hand out for his. "Please don't apologize. I completely get it. If my sitter called and told me there was something wrong with my kids, I'd be out of here like The Flash."

Dev takes my hands in his and stands. "This happens pretty often, though. It's probably not an everyday thing for you." He drops our contact and checks his phone again.

I shake my head at him. "It doesn't matter. We're parents. We do what we have to do, right?" I pat his arm and then take his hand, not worrying about what he'll think of me taking liberties. "Come on. I'll walk you out."

He tugs on my hand, stopping me from leaving the room. I let him pull me up against him. We wrap our arms around each other, and he looks down at me. "I was seriously going to sex you up. So, you either just got really lucky, or really unlucky."

I can't help but smile. "Maybe we'll find out one day."

"Maybe." He gives me a kiss that feels more like a goodbye kiss in its sterility, but I'm going to go ahead and hope it's a we'll-try-again-later kiss. We walk down the stairs together to the front door, and I open it for him. The only thing I can think right now is that tomorrow I have a date with a stranger that I really don't want to go on.

Dev detaches himself from me and walks out the front door. When he gets to his car he opens it up and says his last words to me. "You need to call me on Sunday."

"Okay. Why?" I want to hear him say that he can't stand to be away from me, that he looks forward to hearing my voice, that he wants to be more than friends.

"Because. You have a date on Saturday, and I want to hear all about it."

And just like that, my heart sinks like a stone all the way down to my toes. I try to keep my cheer going on, though, because I'm not a teenage girl anymore, and he's a dad with stuff he has to do that doesn't involve me. I've had my heart ripped to shreds before, and I know how this stuff goes. I can be brave. I can hang. I might even be able to have casual dates and casual sex with this guy, because he still wants me to date other people.

I'm getting the message loud and clear now. We went out on a date, but we're not in a relationship. A non-dating date of sorts. I guess we're supposed to date other people and then talk about it together. This type of arrangement must be something new going on in the singles' world that I missed out on while being married for ten years. I'm just going to have to adapt, if I want to have Dev in my life. And I do want that.

"Okay!" I yell, sounding like a cheerleader on speed. "No problem! I want to hear all about your date too!"

He gives me a thumbs-up and gets into his car.

I shut the door and lean against it, willing the tears to go away. But of course, they don't listen. I slowly walk up the stairs and indulge in my hurt feelings. Tonight, I will cry myself to sleep one more time.

CHAPTER THIRTY-EIGHT

Getting ready for this evening is a bittersweet moment for me. It's the real deal, not a non-dating date like I had with Dev, but I'm not exactly excited about going on it. I look at myself in the mirror, trying to lift my mood for the big event.

"It's only a drink," I say out loud. "It doesn't even need to be alcoholic. Coffee, if you want. You just need to get out there and pop your dating cherry."

Thinking about the cherry that I gave up to Miles long ago, and the fact that I was thinking for a little while last night that I was on my first real date in years, makes me get sad all over again.

I frown at my reflection. "Stop that. You are *not* going to pine for a guy you had a fabulous time with! That's ridiculous! Dev will be a great friend for you. Hell, he might even end up being a friend with benefits if you play your cards right." I take in a deep breath and let it out slowly. "Just relax. You're a single woman, free to enjoy your life. You've had two nights in a row to go out without the kids. This is a special moment, and you're not allowed to ruin it by worrying about every last stupid little thing."

Properly chastised, I force a smile and point at myself in the mirror. "That's better. Remember: you da woman, Jenny. You da woman. Wonder Woman."

I'm wearing the same dress that I had on last night with Dev. I probably shouldn't, because it still smells faintly of fried food, and it reminds me of his hands on me and us rolling around on my bedroom floor, but my budget wouldn't allow for two new outfits, and my old clothes are too fugly to be worn on a real date. I bought May a pretty little sweater and myself this dress yesterday, along with a cheap pair of shoes that caught my eye and a sexy bra and panty set. The rest went into my savings account. I'm only on a trial basis with this new job, and still a little unsettled about whether I'll be keeping it, so I need to watch my pennies. Besides, a little spritz of perfume will cover up that fried catfish scent in a jiffy. I double my usual dose, spraying enough perfume to gag a maggot and forcing myself to leave the confines of my bathroom.

I check my watch. I have thirty minutes before this date is officially supposed to start. There were no new messages from my date, so I have to assume we're still on. Is he feeling nervous like I am? Is he wondering where this will go? Or is he one of those guys who's just looking for a quick roll in the hay?

There was a place on the profile to say what you're looking for, and I sure as heck didn't put that I was looking for a one-night stand. Of course, I'm not silly enough to think that a guy wouldn't go for that option if it were presented to him. But I'm not presenting that. The thing with Dev last night? When I brought him up to my bedroom? That was an anomaly. It won't happen again. I'm not that kind of girl. Unless Dev wants it to happen. I might make an exception for him.

I force my brain away from that line of thinking, refusing to let myself go down that path again. I need to focus, put my game face on. I'm going out on a real date with a perfect stranger who reminds me so much of Dev it's uncanny. I reread his profile and it only solidified that feeling for me.

I don't want to show up early, but standing around my house, berating myself in the mirror, and dreaming of what can't be with Dev isn't getting me anywhere. It's tempting to cancel this thing altogether, so I know I have to leave. Besides, it's better if I'm gone by the time May gets back from the playground with the kids. They'll whine about me leaving and then I'll have a guilt trip to battle on top of my other worries.

I get into my car and head toward the tavern. I'll be there in twenty minutes, traffic willing. On the way there I let my mind wander, replaying the events of the night before. I wonder if Dev and I would've actually done the deed if his mom hadn't called and he hadn't destroyed my bed doing his superhero dive. I had to sleep on my mattress on the floor last night. I have no idea what I'm going to tell the kids when they ask me about it.

Dev must weigh 250 pounds, maybe even 275, of pure muscle. He probably has to have a special bed at his house: extra long and extra strong. I get all hot and bothered just thinking about that. *Long and strong. Big bed. Hmmm . . .*

"Stop that!" I look around me, almost hoping I'll see a neon sign flashing on a nearby business saying, *Get your dildos here! Special sale! Total anonymity guaranteed!* Obviously I've gone way too long without sex, but what the hell, man . . . I'm a healthy woman. I'm practically at my peak, medically speaking. I should be having sex daily! This kind of frustration is to be expected.

The lightbulb goes on above my head. *That's what my problem is! That's why I'm falling in love with a guy I barely know! I need more sex!* I have coitus on the brain. An affliction, almost. I'll call it coitus-wantus-way-too-muchus. And it's getting in the way of my normal cognitive processes. It would explain everything.

Maybe this guy I meet tonight will be cute. That picture he put up on his profile was pretty nice. Dev says that everybody Photoshops their photos or uses old ones from when they were younger, but even if this guy is older than he appeared, he's probably the kind of guy who gets better with age. Maybe we'll hit just the right vibe together, and he'll proposition me, and I'll be like, *Sure, I'd love to have sex with you tonight. I'm free, I'm open to new things. I'm a risk-taking, adventurous type, living purely for the moment.* Ha! My palms are sweating just imagining it. No way am I going to pull this off.

As I drive into the tavern's parking lot I'm feeling pretty good, all things considered. I look down at my dress, enjoying the way it hugs my waist and flares out at my hips. My hair is cooperating, its natural waves framing my face, and my makeup is perfect—not too much and not too little, with a slightly smoky lid. Dev seemed to find me pretty irresistible in this getup. Maybe I have more options than I thought. I get out of the car with a big grin on my face. Denial can be awesomely powerful when used in moderation.

I check my phone just to be sure there are no texts from May. She'll be getting a very special reward for being my babysitter two nights in a row, because I know my kids are driving her crazy. They drive *me* crazy after two nights in a row, and I gave birth to the little buttheads.

I send her a quick text, just to let her know how much I appreciate her efforts.

Me: *Thank u so much. Ur my hero.*

She answers right away.

May: *Have fun! Don't do anything I wouldn't do!*

I smile but don't reply. Her statement leaves the field wide open. I've heard the stories about her and Ozzie and their escapades.

Time to get your sexy on, girl. I walk up to the entrance of the tavern, swinging my hips a little more than usual. I feel amazing. I am going to own this place.

The front door is scarred and slightly warped wood, welcoming me to a place that I've enjoyed hanging out in before. This used to be where Miles and I would come, before we had kids, to enjoy a beer and a game on the television above the bar. This place is where my good memories are kept, so I have a special sense of confidence glowing inside my heart when I grab the handle and pull it toward me.

Cool air and the smell of stale beer hit me first. I might be a little overdressed tonight, but my complexion is flawless for once, and for the first time in a long while I'm actually wearing nail polish and a bra-and-panty set that match. I hope this guy appreciates all my efforts, because tomorrow it's all coming off and I'm going back to being a geek mom in jeans and sneakers, with cotton polka-dot underwear and a racer-back sports bra. Tonight, though? Watch out. *I'm a vixen with all the fixin's.*

As a special treat, I decide right then and there to take the kids for a picnic in the park tomorrow. They've been really patient with me, and they haven't complained one bit about not having me with them two nights in a row. That's a big change for them, and with Miles and his new girlfriend on the scene I should keep my children's lives as consistent as possible. This has been my selfish weekend, but tomorrow it will be all about them.

My mind is now clear of any guilt, and I am ready to par*tay.* I scan the backs of the people sitting on stools around the bartop, hoping that the man with the blue shirt will be there so I won't have to stand here looking all alone for too long.

At first, I don't see him. But then, in the shadows of the tavern's back corner, I catch a hint of blue. I think he's there, with a mug of beer in his hand. He's staring at me like he knows me. And he's really tall. Freakishly so.

My heart skips one beat, and then another. I begin to tremble as my eyes take in the details of the man in the blue shirt. I whisper to myself when it becomes apparent that my night is about to go right in the terlet. *Oh my god. This can't be happening to me right now!* It's Dev, and he's here to witness my shame.

And then an even more awful thought: Is *he* my date?

He can't be. He was sitting right there next to me at the computer when I clicked on his profile. I saw his picture, and I saw the picture of the man I'm here to meet, and it was most definitely not Dev's.

I take a moment to let the awful sink in. We're going to have our first dates in the same place, with each other as witnesses. What a disaster! When he asked me where I was going I should've just told him! *Why did I decide that flirting and playing hard to get were a good idea?*

Destiny must really have it in for me. It's the only explanation for what's happening here. There're over a thousand bars in this town, and he could've chosen any one of them, but he's here! In my bar! *Dammit!*

I recognize the expression on his face as the one that's probably reflected on mine. He's confused, but then it's as if he's seeing something funny.

I'm so embarrassed. He's laughing at me! He's probably noticed that I'm wearing the same dress that I wore last night. What does that say about me? Probably nothing good. He's wearing a different shirt. Maybe he has on the same pants, but this shirt is definitely blue and the one he wore last night was yellow.

My eyes scan the crowd again. There's another guy wearing a blue shirt here, but he's got to be in his seventies. I don't think it's legal to Photoshop your picture that much.

Dev makes his way around the bar. I meet him halfway. He speaks first, saving me the trouble of having to come up with something charming and witty, a feat I'm completely incapable of accomplishing at this point.

"I guess I know where you're meeting your date now."

My smile probably looks more like a grimace than anything else. *Humiliation level: Eight out of ten.* "I guess you do. Seems like we have the same taste in bars."

He nods and looks around, over my shoulder and then out to the sides.

I check my watch. I'm exactly on time. "So, your date's not here yet either?" I ask.

"I don't think so. It's hard to say for sure, because I never saw her picture."

I shake my head at him. "Why didn't you look? How are you going to find her if you don't know what she looks like?"

He shrugs. "I just figured she'd find me."

I nod, feeling awkward but glad for the conversation. Silence would be worse. "I guess that's a good strategy. You're kind of hard to miss."

"Plus, it takes all the pressure off. She can look at me and decide without confronting me whether she actually wants to talk to me or not."

"That's very considerate of you." I look more closely at him, narrowing my eyes a little bit. He doesn't seem at all worried about being stood up. "How long are you planning on hanging around here to see if she shows up?"

He shrugs. "I don't know. A half hour?"

I nod because I can't think of anything else to do, and scan the crowd again. Just then, the door opens, and a man with a blue shirt walks in. He's definitely heavier than I expected him to be based on his profile, but he does have brown hair like the man in the picture. I wait to see what will happen. He appears to be searching for someone.

Dev gestures with his chin. "Maybe that's your guy. I should probably go, give you your space."

"Okay," I say, not really paying attention to Dev anymore. I'm focused on this new guy, trying to figure out if he's the one I saw in the picture. I don't think he is, though. His nose is totally different. Would somebody Photoshop a different nose onto his face like that? I should've looked at that picture more closely. I should've printed it out. Dev warned me that people play games on those sites. Imagining this guy being my date, I could just picture myself holding the printout up at his face, pointing at it in anger, and yelling, "Explain yourself, sir!" Photoshopping dating site pictures should be outlawed and violators pelted with rotten eggs. I hate this. What am I even doing here?

"I'm going to go back over to the corner," he says. "You give me a signal if you have any problems."

Dev has all of my attention now. "What? Are you like my bodyguard?"

He seems confused. "No. Not unless you want me to be."

Maybe I'm still hurting over the fact that he wanted us to go out with other people after breaking my bed. My response comes out crankier than I mean for it to. "I'm fine. I can handle myself. I have pepper spray." I pat the side of my purse confidently.

"You should get a Taser, like your sister. I've learned from first-hand experience that it's very effective."

Before I can ask him for more details, he leaves me standing there. I'm alone next to the bar now, and the man with a fake nose who I thought might be my date walks over to join a group of friends and grabs a beer from one of them. They all laugh at something he says.

If he *is* my date, he can forget it. I didn't sign up for a fake nose *or* a group gathering. My righteous indignation disappears a few moments later when a girl comes in the front door, walks over to the man, and gives him a hug and a kiss. *Game over.*

CHAPTER THIRTY-NINE

I check my phone again; another fifteen minutes have gone by. I realize as I'm looking at the time that I'm not really interested in dating a guy who shows up fifteen minutes late to our first meeting. I respect other people's time, so it's only fair that they do the same for me.

Dev is busy looking at his own phone, so I don't bother signaling him to let him know what I'm doing. I'm going to head over to the ladies' room before leaving. My night is an official bust. I'll just pee first, and then I'll go home. I probably still have time to pop some popcorn and find a good chick flick to lose myself in. The night is still young, and so am I. *Kind of.*

I look in the bathroom mirror at myself and frown. What a shame that I got all dressed up for no reason. This dating thing sucks. I think when I was younger it was different. Times have changed and not for the better. These days, men blow girls off and Photoshop their faces, pretending to be someone they're not. *Jerks.*

I leave the bathroom and come out into the tavern, scanning the crowd once more so I can at least locate Dev and say goodbye. But he's not there. He's gone. My heart gets a crack in it, and it's not the good kind. *He left without saying goodbye?* And I thought my night couldn't get any worse. *Wrong again!*

The sadness that I'm feeling right now is completely out of proportion to what's happened. Dev is his own man and he was here to meet his own date. His leaving has nothing to do with me. I should be happy for him. Hell, maybe his girl showed up and they're out in the parking lot making out in his car. Or maybe they really hit it off and they're doing more than that.

I know I'm being ridiculous, but I can't help it. I was only in the bathroom for five minutes, and I'm sad that he would take off without saying goodbye. It was actually kind of awesome seeing him here. It seems that I can't get enough of this man.

I walk outside to my car, but when I get ten feet away from it I stop short. There's somebody waiting for me. I have a momentary heart attack until I realize it's a very tall man in a blue shirt. *Dev.* My heart soars like it has wings, like it has rocket boosters attached to the bottom of it and somebody has lit the fuse. I want to sing like Maria in *The Sound of Music. The hills are aliiiive!*

I try to bust out my sexy walk on my way over, but end up twisting my ankle in my stupid new shoes. Dev's arms go out like he's going to try to help me, but he's still five feet away. I recover without actually busting my ass, thank all that is holy, and limp the rest of the way over. I pull my keys out of my purse to distract him from commenting on my very ungraceful entrance.

"I thought you left." Dev says.

"I thought you left, too."

We stare at each other as the sounds of the cicadas ring out around us, setting a rhythm to the night that is so uniquely New Orleans. "Are you here waiting for me?" I ask.

He shrugs. "When I thought you'd left, I figured I'd just go home. But then I got out here and saw your car, so I got concerned.

I figured I'd wait for you a little while, and if you didn't show up, I was going to launch a manhunt."

I can't help but smile. "A manhunt? That sounds serious."

He nods slowly. "It is."

I want to believe that there's a lot more to his answer than just those two simple words he gave me, but before I can wonder about it too much longer, he pulls me away from my train of thought.

"Did your guy show up?"

I shake my head. "Nope. I guess that's just the way it goes sometimes." Now that I'm standing here with Dev, it really doesn't seem like such a bad deal after all.

"Are you sure he wasn't in there? There were a lot of guys who looked like they might be single."

I shrug. "He told me he'd be wearing a blue shirt, and the only ones in there with blue shirts were you, a senior citizen, and one other guy, but he had a girl with him."

Dev's eyes go a little wide. "A blue shirt?"

I nod. "Yes, a blue shirt. That's how I was supposed to identify him. And I put my picture on my profile, so he should've been able to find me easily. I didn't Photoshop it, and I didn't use one that's ten years old, either."

Dev smiles. Then he puts his fist on his forehead and tips his head back, laughing like he's at a comedy show. "Oh, God!" he moans, standing up straight again.

"What? Is this funny? Is me getting stood up that hilarious?"

"Oh my god," he says, looking at me again, "no. It's not that. I can't believe this."

I'm starting to get miffed, because I have no idea what he's talking about. It feels like he's laughing at me, though. I fold my arms across my chest. "What? What don't you believe?"

His fist comes off his forehead and he grabs the front of his shirt and pulls it out at me. "I'm wearing a blue shirt."

I shrug. "Yeah. So?"

He shakes his head. "I'm your date."

I look at him like he's crazy. I think all this dating stuff has caused him to drop a few marbles along the way. "What? No. You're not my date. My date's name is Brian something-or-other." The site only gives first names, but that seemed like enough at the time.

"You picked the guy you said was my twin, didn't you?"

Now I'm embarrassed all over again. *He knows! He knows I'm crushing on him!* I need to try to play this off. "What are you talking about?" Yes, this is my plan. I'm going to play stupid and see how far it gets me.

"You picked the guy, who you said was my twin, to go out with. That was me." He points at his chest.

The picture he's trying to paint for me is beginning to come in clearer. "What are you saying? Do you have *two* profiles on that website?"

Now it's Dev's turn to look embarrassed. "Yes," he says reluctantly.

Now I'm not just confused, I'm also annoyed. "Why? Why would you do that?" I'm trying to figure out if he set this up as some elaborate trap to catch me looking like a fool. But as soon as that thought enters my mind, it leaves. No one is that clever, first of all, and second of all, he's not mean like that.

He looks up at the night sky and then down at his feet. He's rocking back and forth from his heels to his toes when he finally answers. "I might have been a little bit concerned that nobody would want to date a guy with no hair who's so tall he looks like he should be in the circus."

If he'd given me any other excuse, or maybe if I were a different person with fewer scars on my soul, I might be mad at him for the trickery; but my heart goes out to him. He always seems so confident and sure of himself, it never crossed my mind that he might be self-conscious about his condition.

I look him in the eye so he'll see that I mean what I say. "That's ridiculous. Why would anybody care about that?"

He lifts a non-brow at me. "Are you serious? Have you been out in the world lately?"

I let out a long sigh. He's right. People are completely material-istic and focused on looks in our world. Hell, I looked at the photos on the website, and I picked a guy based not just on his personality but on how handsome his picture was.

"Where did you get that picture you put on the profile?" I ask.

"It's a picture of my cousin. I got his permission, though, so I wasn't being a total creep. I mean, I didn't steal anyone's identity." He looks up at the stars in contemplation. "I may still actually be a creep, though, now that I think about it." He turns his attention to me. "I'm really sorry I did that and that you got involved." He tries to look cheery, but doesn't quite pull it off. "You're the first person who asked for a date, though, so there's only one victim of my stupidity."

"I don't get it. Why the mystery? Why not just be yourself?"

He looks at the ground. "Call it a lack of self-confidence. That's probably the most accurate way to describe my thought process."

"How could a guy like you lack self-confidence? You're tall, good-looking, charming, smart, a great dad . . . the whole package."

His smile is so adorable it makes it hard for me to breathe.

"Did you forget to put in your contacts today?" he asks.

I shove him gently. "Stop. And you have a great sense of humor, too."

He shrugs. "You see what you see, but believe me, most women don't get the same impression when they look at me."

I sigh. "Well, let me apologize on behalf of all women for those few dopes who are deaf, dumb, and blind. Believe me, they do not represent the majority."

"That's nice to hear."

He kicks at the gravel, moving it around with his toe, and for the first time I can really see the vulnerability. It only makes him more attractive to me, knowing that he's not full of himself, that he's a humble, self-effacing person. I much prefer that type of man over a guy who thinks he's God's gift to women.

I stand there digesting everything that he's told me. Here we are, two single people, both looking for love. We made a pact to find it with other people, but destiny brought us back together again. That can only mean one thing, and I'm not so dense that I'm going to ignore it this time.

"So where does this leave us?" I bite my lip after I ask the question to keep from blurting anything out that shouldn't yet be said.

He reaches down and takes me by the hands. My purse drops to the ground at my feet, but I ignore it.

"I think this means that we should go out on a real date and see what happens."

I try not to be too excited that he's thinking the same thing I am. "It's a risk, though. Hearts can be broken."

He shrugs. "No guts, no glory. I'm up for it if you are."

I bite my lip again. He's so beautiful. So good inside. I don't care that he put a false profile on a dating website. I *get* it. I mean, I really, really get it. I get feeling lonely, I get lacking confidence, I get being paranoid and worried that people won't like you for who you are. After Miles left me, I had no hope that I would ever find somebody who would want to be with me again. How stupid would I be to walk away from this opportunity?

"Okay, I'm in." I feel like I'm going to vomit, I'm so scared and happy at the same time.

Dev smiles and then that look comes over his face again. That beautiful, gorgeous dimple that I love so much caves in and turns him from a warrior into a teddy bear. A bald one. A big, bald, teddy bear of a man who makes me feel safe and happy and ready to take on the world.

"Well . . . we've already had dinner," he says. "What would you do on a real date after dinner?"

I'm feeling sexy, so I risk the answer that's in my heart. "I'd ask you if you want to go have a drink at my place."

"Are your kids home?" he asks, getting a devilish look in his eye.

I pout. "I'm going to be a terrible mother and say, unfortunately, yes. They are. On a real date I probably would have made sure they'd be elsewhere. Sorry. I'm seriously out of practice."

He scowls. "My son is home too." He squeezes my hands and looks at me forlornly. "Too bad you're such a classy lady."

I raise my eyebrows at him. "Why is that bad?"

"Because . . . if you were a little more on the wild side, I would tell you about how big my backseat is."

I can't help giggling.

"Why are you laughing?" He moves in closer and pulls me up against him, his hard body sending a shock of pleasure through me. The giggling stops immediately.

I look up at him, my eyes full of the heat building inside me. "Because. I'm really not all that classy."

CHAPTER FORTY

I can't stop giggling. My dress is bunched up around my waist, and we're crammed into his backseat, trying to use it as our launching pad into this new thing we have going on, whatever it is. I'm not going to label it or wonder how long it's going to last. I want to enjoy it while I can.

"I'm too damn tall," he says, frustrated as he bangs his head on the back passenger window.

I pull him down to kiss me again. My lips are swollen from all the making out we've been doing. "You're not too tall; you're perfect."

He grins and dives in. Our tongues tangle together and our mingled breath heats up our faces as we move to deepen the connection.

His hand is between my legs, his fingers stroking me over my panties, making me squirm with anticipation. Sweat drips off his forehead and lands on my neck as he looks down at the space between us. "What I wouldn't give for a bed right now," he growls.

"We could do this sitting up," I suggest.

He stops everything he's doing and stares down at me. "Really?"

I nod, biting my lip to keep from laughing. It's not that this is funny; it's just so much fun I want to laugh and get buck wild naked at the same time. I've never experienced anything like it. I'm in a parking lot, screwing a near stranger in a Pontiac, for God's sake! Then it hits me: How poetic is my sex life right now? It's literally being *resurrected* from the *ashes* inside a *Phoenix*. I can't stop giggling.

Dev tries to get up, managing to not only give himself a few new bruises in the process but also to yank his headrest right off the top of his seat.

"Oh my god!" I squeal as he growls and throws it onto the floor in the front of the car.

"Get over here," he says, as he sits down in the backseat, stretching his legs as best he can under the seat in front of him. His knees are against the back of it, and a bulge is standing up at his crotch, straining his zipper.

I'm on my knees next to him, staring at it. "Wow," I say. I felt his package before when he was kind of on top of me, but I don't think I fully appreciated how big it was then.

He looks down at it too, and then up at me. "I'm at your mercy."

Smiling all evil-like, I reach down and undo his belt, button, and zipper, freeing him from the top of his boxers with careful maneuvering. "Holy shit," I whisper. "You're proportional."

He leans his head back on the seat and sighs. "Are you trying to make me lose it before you even touch me?"

I reach up and slide a piece of hair out of my face, tucking it behind my ear. He turns his head to watch.

"What?" I ask, feeling shy.

"Don't look at me like that," he says. "You know what you're doing to me."

I feel like the champion of sex, a goddess he must worship. I temporarily forget that I haven't done anything like this in a really long time. Taking his hard length in my hand, I begin to stroke it up and down. He closes his eyes and sighs. He begins frowning and moaning as I find my rhythm.

I lick my lips. I'm so turned on from him touching me earlier and from watching him now. I'm not sure what to do next, but I feel like I'm going to explode with wanting and anticipation.

He opens his eyes. "Are you going to climb on or what?"

I don't waste any time. After removing my sexy new panties, I gather my dress up around my hips, and do my best to climb over him without kicking any sensitive parts. Leaving my shoes behind on the floor makes it easier.

I kneel over him, one leg on either side of his legs. His erection is between us, standing up almost an entire foot toward the roof of the car. He slides what must be a special-order condom over it and we both stare down at this thing I know will never work. *It's the size of a damn nightstick! What am I supposed to do with that?!*

"What if it doesn't fit?" I say in a breathless whisper.

"We'll go slow," he says, reaching under my dress and touching me between my legs.

I close my eyes and enjoy the sensations for a few seconds before making my move. Enough of this playing-around stuff. I have a challenge before me. I just wish I'd taken more gymnastics classes when I was younger.

I lift up on my knees and realize very quickly that this is not going to cut it. I put my left foot up on the seat next to Dev and lift my body even higher. Finally, I'm able to position myself over him, and his hard tip is resting just at my entrance. I look like a crazy person, but I totally do. not. care. The cops could come at this point and I wouldn't stop.

His thumb comes up and rubs at my most sensitive spot. "Easy," he says, watching my expression.

I stare down at him as I slowly lower myself over him. I've never hated condoms more in my life than I do in this moment. Thankfully, all of Dev's attentions have made it easier for us to move against each other without too much friction. He slides into me with little resistance.

"Oh, God," I say in a half-whisper, half-moan.

He puts his free hand on my hip, helping me, guiding me down. I'm finally able to go back to both knees, but I have to stop before he's fully buried inside me. It's too much.

I close my eyes and wait.

"You okay?" he asks.

I nod. "It's . . . awesome." I smile, feeling a warmth come over me as his finger moves in small circles. I lift up experimentally and then go down again, enjoying the feeling of our bodies so close, this big beast of a man inside me. The windows are completely steamed up, impossible to see into or out of, and I've convinced myself we're a million miles from anyone else.

"You feel so good," he says, his breath ragged.

I put my hands on his shoulders, holding on for dear life. I'm afraid I'm going to break something inside me if I ride him like I want to. He said to take it slow and that's what I'm going to do. *Dammit! I want to go faster!*

My breath comes out choppy, as I try to control myself.

"Let it go," he whispers, like he's reading my mind. "Let it happen. Do what you need to do."

My hips roll in small circles as I move up and then down again. "Fast, yes, that's better," I say mostly to myself. My eyes are closed now. The darkness swirls around me, and I let myself get taken over by the sensations.

With every second that passes, the need to find my release pulls at me, drawing me in deeper. I relax and take more of him into me.

"Yes, that's it, babe. That's it," he says, pushing his hips up to meet me.

The seat starts squeaking in rhythm with our movements, and I'm sure the car is rocking too, but I don't care! Let the world know what I'm doing! *I'm having sex in a Phoenix with a giant who's proportional, and it's awesome! Woo hoo!*

Noises start coming out of my mouth that I have no control over. I only halfway hear them anyway. I'm close . . . so close. Just a few more strokes, a few more . . .

"Oh my god!" I yell, laughing and crying at the same time as I cling to Dev. It came out of nowhere! Fireworks! Explosions! Fans cheering! I hear it all in my head when the end finally comes and the orgasm takes over my whole body. I yell like a banshee as my body pulses with the release, and Dev roars like a sexy and very pleased lion. I cling to him, a drowning woman with him as my lifejacket. I feel him throbbing inside me as he finds his own release.

A few seconds later, coming down from my sexy high, I realize how sweaty I am. My face literally slides off his as I pull back. I stare into his pale face as drops of salty water pour down his temples.

"Wow," I say, wondering how I'm going to extricate myself from this mess I've made. Sex in his car? Out in the parking lot? I must be high. Did I even have one alcoholic drink? I don't think so. There's no excuse for my behavior except that being with Dev makes me lose my mind. In a good way, though. I'm not going to let myself have any regrets over this.

He leans in and gives me a kiss right on the lips. It's chaste, but slow. Sweet. Kind. My heart folds in on itself and then explodes. *Oh, crap. I am in so much trouble.*

"You make me happy," he says. Then he spanks me on the side of my butt. "Ready to get out of here?"

I nod and then execute the nearly acrobatic moves it takes to un-impale myself from his still semi-hard erection, so I can fall onto the seat next to him and put my panties back on.

I'm not sure whether I should be embarrassed or proud at this point. Thank goodness he's not staring at me, because I'd probably burst into tears. Not that I'm sad. Just confused. Floating in the ether. Wondering what in the H-E-double hockey sticks is going on with my life. It's like I've entered the twilight zone or something. *Maybe I am having a midlife crisis. Maybe I should shop for a Corvette tomorrow.*

"I'd like to stay out later with you," he says, "but I'm afraid my mother wasn't really prepared for that."

I look over at him. "You were just going to have a drink with your date?"

He takes his time answering. "Yeah. I just . . . It seemed like the right thing to do."

I pause in the process of sliding my shoes back on and look up at him. "The right thing to do?" *What does he mean?*

He looks out the window for a few seconds before turning back to me. "I had a really nice time with you last night. It didn't seem right to take another woman out for a regular date after that."

I have to bite the insides of my cheeks really hard to keep from smiling like a loon. I nod. "Sure. I get it." My voice gives me away. I wanted to sound cool, but I don't. Not at all.

"I don't mean to put pressure on you," he says.

I shake my head. "No, I'm happy." I try to grin, but it wavers.

"What's wrong?" he asks, looking at me so seriously, so earnestly, it makes tears come to my eyes.

"Nothing. I'm just being an idiot is all. Status quo."

He takes my hand and squeezes it. "I've done something wrong."

"No." I place my other hand over his. "You've done everything right. I really like you. I just worry that we're rushing into this and it seems so amazing . . . I'm worried I'm going to ruin it."

He gives me a sad smile. "You too, huh?"

I nod. "I'm not normal."

He reaches up and strokes my cheek tenderly with a finger. "I hate normal. So boring. So predictable."

I look down, trying to control my emotions. Nothing can take the smile off my face, though. "Good thing."

It seems like a couple minutes go by before either of us speaks again.

"We still on for Halloween?" he asks.

I look up and nod. This is safe ground. Our kids in costumes. This I can handle. "Yep."

"Great. So, I'll see you next week? Your place?"

I nod, wondering if this means I won't see him at work. "Sure."

"I'll come around five o'clock so we can be sure we don't have any wardrobe malfunctions."

"Yes. Good idea." I casually push my dress down to where it belongs and make sure my buttons are all done up and nothing's hanging out where it shouldn't.

Dev places his hand on my leg as I'm about to open the back door. "Promise me something."

I look down at his hand and then up at his face. His expression is unreadable.

"What?"

"Promise you'll always be honest with me. You'll always tell me exactly what you're feeling when I ask."

I nod, happy to make that promise. I don't want any more lies or games in my life, especially not from a guy like Dev. I can't afford to be emotionally devastated right now. I have kids, barely a job, and a mortgage, not to mention a bruised heart. "I will if you will."

"Deal." He leans in and gives me a very thorough kiss before leaning back. "Stay there," he says, opening his door and launching himself out of the backseat. He's surprisingly agile considering his size and the fact that his pants are still half undone.

He comes around the back of the car and opens my door, offering me his hand. He's all put together, with his pants zipped up and his shirt tucked in, and except for the sweating, you'd never know he just had hot sex in the backseat. I take his extended hand in mine and step out like I'm a princess about to be presented to her subjects. *A princess who just got it on like Donkey Kong in the back of a Phoenix, yo!*

Standing in front of him properly dressed again and smelling like hot slippery bodies, I look up and smile. "Thank you for the sex."

He smiles slowly, devastating me all over again with that dimple. "You're welcome. And thank *you* for the sex, too."

"You're welcome. See you at work?" I walk off slowly, leaving my awkward farewell on the table. I don't know how to be cool when I'm falling in love, and I'm a little afraid of what this might mean for my life and my children, but I'm still willing to take the risk. Nothing ventured, nothing gained, and there's so much to gain with this gorgeous man who just had awesome sex with me in the back of his Pontiac.

"Yeah. See you real soon."

I wonder if he's going to reach out and pull me back, but he doesn't. He lets me go, and that's okay. I'm happy, content, still coming down off my sexy high. I walk over to my car, my head up, my body appreciating the fresh evening air, even though it's muggy and warm, and my thoughts floating lazily around my brain. I feel enveloped in something nice. Maybe real, true, rock-my-entire-world love. Whatever it is, I like it, and I'm not going to ruin it by over-analyzing it right now.

CHAPTER FORTY-ONE

I can't believe Halloween has arrived. I just got the last bits of our costumes together yesterday, and here we are, waiting for Dev and Jacob to arrive at our house.

"When are they gonna be here?" Sammy whines. His little finger starts lifting toward his face.

I grab his hand, stopping him before he can smear his makeup. He didn't want to wear his mask, so I had to improvise a Spider-Man face with lots of eyeliner and dark eyeshadow. We'll be lucky if he makes it out the door without destroying it.

"They'll be here soon. Just relax. I still have to put my costume on." I stood in front of the Halloween section of the local craft store yesterday for a half an hour, trying to decide if I was going to go with the standard witch look, or kick it up a notch. There was a French maid's costume that was particularly tempting, but in the end, I decided it was probably better to be a little more subtle. Sophie's already suspicious enough of my motives toward Dev. I think her father getting a girlfriend has been a real problem for her. Another issue for me to deal with.

Thankfully, even though Sophie is poised for a breakdown, I found Sammy a permanent daycare that I think we're going to like better than the last one, so at least I have that off my plate. One crisis at a time, I can handle.

The doorbell rings, and then the stampede begins. Sammy disappears in a flash.

"I'll get it!" yells Sophie as she runs pell-mell down the stairs. I imagine she's at the head of the pack, with Melody and Sammy hot on her heels.

"No! I'll get it. You still have to put your cape on!" Yep, that's Melody, the first one dressed for Halloween as usual. She's the last one down the stairs any other day of the year, but not today. She's a princess, for the third year in a row. I can always count on my middle child to make my life easier.

I hear voices at the front door, but I'm not quite ready to come down. "I'll be right there!" I yell.

I lean in closer to the mirror, putting on another layer of mascara. Just because I'm not a sexy French maid doesn't mean I can't do a little somethin'-somethin' with this witch costume.

The black nylon dress that was included in the kit fits me surprisingly well, considering I bought it at the craft store. I smooth it over my hips and stand up straight, admiring my reflection. Ever since that night in Dev's car, I've felt better about how I look. Not that I was overly paranoid or down on myself before, but I'm not so worried about my mom-bod now. *Because this mom-bod can do it in the backseat of a car and make a man sing!*

I think Dev worked some serious sexual healing on me or something. Crazy, I know, but why fight it? I've spent most of my life doubting myself, so it's nice being able to feel confident and relaxed for a change. I think my week at Bourbon Street Boys has also helped. They're a great team of people to work with professionally, and fun to hang out with, too. I've stopped in every day this week, although most of my work has been done at home. Between stolen moments in the warehouse with Dev and late-night phone

calls after the kids were in bed, I've found this space of content-
ment with him. Every night we've spent hours laughing over shared
jokes and the idea of future dates, planned for when we can both
wrangle babysitters. It's kept our budding relationship exciting and
fresh, something to look forward to. We have to take things slowly
because of our situations with the kids and work, but sometimes
slower is better. It builds the anticipation.

The Blue Marine job being over doesn't mean my work is done,
thankfully. I already have another case ready to start on Monday.
This one should be interesting; it involves an identity theft that was
brought to the company by the local police department.

"Are you coming down, or am I coming up?" Dev is at the bottom of the stairs. His voice makes me tingle all over. I've only seen
him a few times at work because he's been busy with Jacob, but
when I have, the looks between us have been practically smoldering.
I can't keep from smiling and nearly giggling every time he's within
ten feet of me. I'm sure everyone on the team has noticed. May says
that Dev is acting different too. She's never seen him smile so much.
I do a little cha-cha move in front of the mirror in celebration of
my awesome life.

"I'm coming down. Just putting on the finishing touches." I'm
still a little nervous about one thing, though. Our kids are together
again for the second time, and I worry that one of my little monsters
will say something insensitive to Jacob. We've talked extensively this
week about him and his medical condition, but the natural curiosity
of children will eventually win out, I'm sure. It's just a matter of
when and how they do it that has me on edge. The last thing in the
world I would want is for Jacob to feel bad when he's with my kids.

I turn from my reflection. It's not going to get any better than
this. I need to face the music, go downstairs, and see the guy that
I'm seriously crushing on.

I go down the stairs and arrive at an empty foyer. The voices are coming from the kitchen now. I follow the sounds and stop in the entrance. The kids are gathered around the giant bowl of candy I have on the table, picking through it, arguing over which kind is the best. Jacob is at the head of the table, looking like he's in charge of the group.

Dev looks up and catches me watching them. He smiles at me. "There she is. *Finally.*" He exaggerates his impatience so the kids will pick up on it, and they don't disappoint.

"Finally," Sammy says, rolling his eyes. "You took forever."

"That's the longest you ever took to get ready for Halloween," Sophie says.

Busted.

"You look pretty, Mommy," Melody says.

"Thank you, baby." I blow her a kiss and then stick my tongue out at Dev.

Dev winks at me. I shake my head. There is absolutely no way a mom can be cool when her kids are there to tell all her secrets.

"Who's ready to go trick-or-treating?" I ask.

A chorus of voices rises up so loud, it makes my ears ring.

My kids are all costumed up, but when I look at Jacob, all I see is a pair of green pajamas with black magic marker scribbles all over them. There's also a single stuffed green sock dangling from each of the four corners of his wheelchair.

I smile at the little guy, hoping my expression is encouraging. "Wow, look at you."

"I'm a crocodile," he says.

I nod. "Crocodiles are awesome. A crocodile can defeat a bull shark. Did you know that?"

He nods. "Yes. My dad told me, and then we looked at a video on the computer."

"The rest of his costume is out on the porch," Dev explains. "It was too big to wear in the house."

"Oh. How exciting. Too big? Let's go get it on, shall we?"

Sophie runs out of the room, yelling as she goes. "I want to see it first!"

"No, me!" Melody is the next one gone.

I look down at Sammy, expecting him to tear out of here while yelling like a wild man. Surprisingly, he doesn't move. He puts his hand on Jacob's wheelchair and looks at his new friend. "You can go before me." He points out to the hallway. "It'th that way."

I have to turn my head for a moment to collect myself. My sweet little angel. I love him so much. Seeing him be so kind and gentle makes me want to call up that old daycare director and give her a piece of my mind. There is *no* way he was causing trouble with other kids over there. He was being bullied, I know he was. One of these days when I can trust myself to be civil, I'll call her and ask her what she thinks happened. But I'm not in that place yet.

Dev walks up and puts his hand on my back, pulling me up against his side as we walk down the hallway behind the boys. I hold the bowl of candy under my opposite arm. "You ready to have some fun? Get your sugar rush on?"

I look up him, still impressed by how impossibly tall he is. "I was born ready. Are you?"

He reaches down and grabs my butt. "I already have enough sugar right here."

I whack him on the stomach with the back of my hand, acting like he's a troll for doing that, but we both know better. Of course there's been no time this week for more sex, what with the kids at home at night and strict bedtimes for everyone, but that doesn't mean I haven't been thinking about it eighteen hours of every day. Forget buying a dildo; I'm only settling for the real thing.

I still can't believe we did what we did in the back of his car. It's awakened something inside me that I didn't even know was there. I feel young, wild, and free. Even more so than I did when I was just out of college. And that's a pretty big deal for a single mom with three kids. I'm going to relish it for as long as it lasts.

The kids are gathered in the foyer waiting for us slowpokes.

"Sophie, can you open the door?" Dev asks.

She nods very seriously, as if she's been given a critical task. She stands there, holding it open so we can all go out before her. I kiss her delicate little cheek on the way past. I'm so proud of her.

Out on the porch are two giant lumps; they look like cone-shaped piñatas designed to resemble . . . pickles.

"Cool," Sophie says. I'm pretty sure she has no idea what she's looking at. I lock the door behind her, setting the bowl of candy we're giving away on a chair on the porch next to the sign Sophie made instructing people to serve themselves.

"What're those?" Melody asks.

Sammy runs over to the nearest piece. "That'th a crocodile! A big one! Awethome!" He looks up at me. "Mama, I want to be a crocodile!"

I envy my son's creative vision. No way would I have pegged these two papier-mâché monstrosities as crocodile parts. "Not this year. You're Spider-Man, remember?" I couldn't believe my luck when he told me he wanted to be old Spidey again, and his costume still mostly fits. *Yay for Spandex!*

Jacob speaks up. "I can be Spider-Man's pet crocodile. We can be a team."

Sammy thinks about that for a few seconds and then nods. "Okay. I think Thpider-Man could have a crocodile for a pet."

Dev leans down and whispers in my ear. "Crisis averted."

"You're telling me," I mumble back.

Dev lowers Jacob and his chair together down the stairs to the front walk, and then spends a few minutes attaching the crocodile tail and head onto the wheelchair. When he's done, we have a five-foot-long reptilian beast rolling down the sidewalk, surrounded by Spider-Man, a fairy princess, and a tiny, beautiful vampire, complete with cape.

I look up at Dev. "What are you supposed to be?" He's dressed all in green. Now that I have time to focus on him, I realize how thoroughly he's covered himself in one color. I can't stop laughing.

He pauses and holds his arms out. "Isn't it obvious? I'm a green bean."

I shake my head, grinning until I get a cheek cramp. "You're too much."

He doesn't say anything; he just reaches out and takes my hand. We walk down the street together, the witch and the green bean, letting the kids go up to the neighbors' front doors on their own. It's a pretty big deal, because normally I insist on accompanying them all the way in.

Within two houses, a routine is established. The girls are in the lead, but they look back as they're going up to each door, making sure the boys are close behind. Sammy walks next to Jacob, in the grass if necessary. He has taken his ownership of a pet crocodile very seriously; he's not letting him out of his sight.

"Trick or treat!" Their voices ring out around the neighborhood along with the hundred or so other kids busy hauling in their sugary treasures. Several of the parents walking by stop to say hello. These are people who would normally just pass me by with a wave, but when they see Dev, they're compelled to be more sociable. They probably think an NBA player has moved onto the block.

I feel like I'm the most popular girl on the street, something I never experienced when married to Miles. And Dev is a serious charmer. Even though he's dressed as a giant green bean, he manages to engage everyone in intelligent conversations that have them laughing and inviting him over for a beer sometime. By the time the kids are done with their trick-or-treating, I've fallen even harder for him. It almost makes me worry.

"Why do you look so sad all of a sudden?" Dev asks as we're walking on the sidewalk in front of my house.

I manage a smile. "I'm not. I was just thinking how much fun I'm having."

"And that makes you frown?"

I shake my head. "No. I just have these melancholy moments sometimes, worrying how long the good stuff is going to last. Just ignore me."

He grabs me and pulls me in close. "Don't worry about that stuff. We're having fun, right?"

I nod into his chest, my cheek rubbing on his green beanery. "Yes, we are."

My next thought is cut off by the vision of my front door opening as my girls climb up the front steps.

Who's in my house? "Stop!" I yell at the kids. They all pause and turn to look at me. Jacob and Sammy turn more slowly, Sammy leaping out of the way of the moving wheelchair before it knocks him over.

"Looks like someone's home," Dev says, standing straighter and walking over the grass.

For a moment there, I thought there was an intruder in my house, but now I know better. With the light on behind him, I can see the silhouette of my ex-husband in the doorway. And he's not alone. *What in the hell . . . ?*

CHAPTER FORTY-TWO

Dev goes a few more steps before he realizes I'm not with him anymore. He turns around and looks at me questioningly.

"I cannot believe him," I say quietly so my voice won't carry.

Dev looks at the front door and then back at me. "Is there a problem?"

"That's my ex-husband." I grind my teeth together before finishing. "And I'm going to guess that's his new girlfriend."

Dev looks once more at the house before he turns to me. "Why are they in your house?"

I start walking, taking long strides. "That is an *excellent* question that I am going to go find the answer to."

As I move to pass by Dev, he reaches out and takes my hand.

I hesitate and look up at him.

"I know you want to go in there and rip some heads off. Believe me, I get it. But don't forget, you have an audience."

I squeeze his hand. "You're right. Don't worry. I would never kill my ex with this many witnesses around."

He chuckles. "That's my girl."

His words have a very soothing effect on me. *He called me his girl!* So my ex-husband is a dick. Big deal. My new boyfriend is awesome. I'm so much better off in my new life with Dev by my side and the Bourbon Street Boys as my employer than I was with Miles and that whole mess of an existence we had together. There was too much sadness there. Too much disrespect. Dev would never treat me the way Miles did, and I'm proud to know that at this point in my life, I'd never let a man treat me like Miles did again. I'm stronger now. Smarter. Less naïve and seeing more clearly what I want in life and who I want to live it with.

As I get closer, I get a better view of the woman my kids have been talking about. The one that has Sophie so upset. She can't be more than twenty years old. Hell, I wouldn't be surprised if she were still a teenager. Jesus, I'd love to know what my ex is thinking he's doing. Talk about a midlife crisis.

"Hey, kids!" Miles is all teeth and fake charm.

"Daddy!" Sophie is the first one there, of course, throwing herself at his waist, hugging him hard. Jacob stops at the bottom of the steps, waiting for his father to bring him up. I vow to myself that I will use my next paycheck to put in a ramp so that he doesn't have to do that anymore.

Miles's attention moves from his children to the other people in the group. "Who's this?" He detaches the girls from his body and walks toward us. At the bottom of the steps, he stops next to Jacob and holds his hand out. "Nice to meet you. My name is Miles."

At least he's not being a total jerk. We arrive just as Jacob is giving him his tiny hand. "My name is Jacob. I'm Spider-Man's pet crocodile."

"Really? Cool."

"Hello, Miles," I say, trying to sound friendly but not really pulling it off. "What are you doing here?"

"I can't see my kids on Halloween?"

I shrug. "Of course you can. But a call or a text might've been nice." I look up at his girlfriend for a second before addressing him again. "But maybe that would've interfered with your plans to go into my house when I wasn't home."

His expression darkens. "Don't start, Jenny."

Dev holds his hand out for a handshake, inserting himself into the conversation. "Hey, bud. I'm Dev. Nice to meet you."

Miles tips his head back to look Dev in the eye. He shakes his hand, maybe a little star-struck, if I'm reading his expression accurately. "Miles. Nice to meet you too." He narrows his eyes. "Don't think I've heard you mentioned before."

Dev releases his hand and smiles. "Nope. Probably not. I'm the new guy on the block."

"What are you supposed to be tonight?" Miles asks, looking Dev up and down. "The Jolly Green Giant?" He laughs at his own lame joke.

Dev laughs good-naturedly. "Close. I'm a green bean, actually."

Miles shakes his head, but wisely says nothing. He's lucky, because I'm seriously considering slapping him right now. I just need one more reason. *Just give me one more, Miles. Just one.*

Miles turns halfway and looks up the stairs at his girlfriend. "Chastity, why don't you come on down here and say hello?"

The girl, who's still learning her social manners, apparently, walks down, teetering on very high heels. I have to grit my teeth to keep from mumbling anything unkind. She's young. She'll learn eventually how to act, I hope. As long as she doesn't stay with Miles for too long, anyway.

"Hi," she says, "nice to meet you." She gives me her hand, but only manages to get her fingers into my grasp. They're as limp as a pile of worms.

"Nice to meet you." I want to say that I've heard a lot about her, that my kids don't like her, and that I think she's too young to be dating an old man like Miles, but of course I don't. I just smile and smile and smile. It's easier to do with Dev at my side.

"I'm going to take Jacob inside if it's okay with you," Dev says to me.

"Of course. Go ahead. I'll be right in."

Dev gets on with the business of lifting his son and his chair up to the porch, walking backward. I admire the way his muscles strain under the weight, smiling to myself as I picture him under me in the backseat of that stupid Pontiac. He is *such* a good man. Seeing him here next to Miles makes it that much more obvious. I can't believe I was so blind. I spent ten years with that turdbasket.

I shift my focus to him, speaking quietly so only he will hear me. "So, why are you really here, Miles? Because I know it's not to visit the kids." They're in the house now, digging into their candy, so I can afford to be honest.

He hisses out a sigh of annoyance. "I don't want to have another fight with you."

I shrug casually. "I don't either. I just want you to be honest. You can do that, can't you?" I glance at his girlfriend, who's staring at the ground. *Good.* She's uncomfortable. She should be. "Oh wait, that's not really your forte, is it? Being honest . . ."

"Just shut it, Jenny. I'm here for the watch."

I frown at him. This is coming out of left field. "The watch? What watch?"

"The watch that I gave you. It's mine. I want it back."

My jaw drops open. "Are you serious?"

"Yes, I'm serious." He has the grace to look uncomfortable, at least.

I'm whisper-yelling now. "Did you seriously break into my house so that you could steal the watch you gave me for my birthday two years ago?!"

His jaw tenses up. "I didn't break into the house, Jenny. I used to live here. I still have a key."

I shake my head. "Well, you shouldn't. I'm changing the locks. Don't ever come in here again without my permission."

I walk away, because I don't trust myself not to get physical with this man. He's obviously got a screw loose, and he doesn't realize he's about to tangle with a Bengal tiger on her front lawn. In *her* territory. I will use my *claws* on his sorry ass.

His tone changes. Now he's trying to sound pitiful. "I'm a little short on cash, Jenny. I need that watch."

I laugh bitterly. "Why don't you get a real job, Miles? Then you won't have to worry about stealing jewelry from your ex-wife." In typical fashion, he probably decided that his one week of commissioned sales should be enough to last him for the month and he's slacked off and spent every last dime he made that week. *God, I'm so glad I'm not married to that sloth anymore.*

The kids are all inside, but the door is still partway open. I walk up to the porch and shut it before turning around to face the couple below me. They're both looking up at me. "Chastity, I don't know you, but let me give you a little piece of advice: If you're as smart as you are pretty, you shouldn't settle for a guy like Miles. Trust me. You're better off without him."

"Fuck you, Jenny," Miles spits out.

I smile and nod at him. "Nice. Classy. Just what I would expect from a guy like you." I walk into the house and shut the door behind me, locking it for good measure. I pull my phone out of my back pocket and send myself an email.

Dear self: Change locks immediately.

Not that I could forget anything like that. This incident will be swimming around in my head for at least the next month. I cannot believe he actually broke into my house to steal my watch! Wait until I tell May. She's going to go ballistic.

Dev is standing in the entrance hall waiting for me. "You okay?"

I nod but don't trust myself to speak. It's so embarrassing that he witnessed that. Will he judge me a loser because I married one?

He takes me into his arms and hugs me, somehow knowing exactly what I need. His kindness, gentleness, and understanding, his knowing that I just need the space to handle my own problems . . . it blows me away.

"How did I get so lucky?" I ask.

"Lucky?"

"Yes. Lucky to have you in my life."

He kisses the top of my head. "We both got lucky. And I think we can thank your sister for that."

My sister and fate. Fate is what locked me up in that panic room with Dev two weeks ago. I thought I was in the wrong place at the right time, but I was wrong. It was definitely the right place to be and the right time to be there.

The kids are in the kitchen, no doubt with their candy poured out all over the table. I can hear them commenting and exclaiming over the awesome things they collected in the neighborhood.

I pull back from Dev and look up at him. "Thank you for being so cool."

He smiles, pointing to his body. "Yo, lady. I'm a green bean. It doesn't get any cooler than this."

Even with that stupid green outfit on, I can see his muscles underneath. I'm inspired. "I think I'm ready to start my training now."

His non-eyebrows rise as his face lights up. "Really? That's awesome. We can start Monday."

I walk down the hall with him toward the kitchen to join our children. "Should I be scared?" I ask.

"Yes. Be very scared."

I stand at the entrance to the room admiring the kids and the happy camaraderie they share. When I first got divorced from Miles, I yearned for the simplicity of a child's life. I didn't want stress, I didn't want worry, I didn't want all these responsibilities. But now that I'm with Dev I have a different outlook. I like the complications. I like the excitement. I like steamed-up windows and random sex in the parking lot. I like being with a guy who's seven feet tall and bold enough to go out on Halloween dressed as a green bean.

Dev steps up behind me and leans his chest on the back of my head. "Happy?" he asks.

I nod. "Yes. Very."

CHAPTER FORTY-THREE

L ife could not possibly be better. I'm headed into my second week of work at Bourbon Street Boys, I have a new boyfriend who's way better than any I've ever had before in my entire life, and my kids are happy. What else do I need?

Before when I drove into the port, I felt uncomfortable. I felt like I didn't belong there. But this time, right now, bright and early Monday morning, it's completely different. I'm ready to kick ass in this new job, and I'm ready to begin a new case as an official part of the team. I'm ready to shed the fear that has been ruling my life for way too long.

I came early today on purpose. Before-school daycare had spots for my kids, and Ozzie is always here, so I figured he could let me in and I could sit down at one of the cubicles and go over the preliminary file that Lucky sent me via email over the weekend. I want to be ready to knock their socks off in the meeting, to show them how serious and dedicated to the job I am. I have a little less than ninety days to show them my stuff, and I'm ready to prove that no one can do this job better than I can.

I pull up to the front of the warehouse and let the car idle for a few seconds. Should I feel bad about ringing Ozzie's doorbell at seven o'clock in the morning? He doesn't seem like the type to sleep in, but if he's had another wild night with my sister, I guess it's possible.

I chew on my lower lip as I consider my next step. Maybe I should wait just a little while longer. I could always open up my laptop and do some work in the car. I'll buzz him at seven-thirty. Or maybe . . .

My next thought is yanked right out of my head when a sound off to my left distracts me. My window is halfway open, letting the cool morning air in. I hear footsteps.

I turn to look just as something flashes in my peripheral vision.

"Don't move," says a man's deep voice.

My eyes bug out as my brain computes what they're seeing. In my near vision is the barrel of a gun. It looks so much bigger up close like this than I would have expected after seeing them on television.

Then it hits me. *This gun is real. This isn't TV. You are being held up by a criminal with a weapon that could kill you in less than one second!* I have never seen this man before in my life. He's heavy, sloppy, in need of a shave, and not attractive. *Surprise, surprise: real-life criminals do not look like Colin Farrell.*

My jaw drops open, but I can't seem to make my voice work.

"Where's Toni?" he asks.

I blink a few times, hoping my heart is going to start working again real soon. I'm on the verge of passing out from sheer terror and also a severe lack of oxygen.

He wiggles the gun at me. "Are you deaf? I asked you a question. Where's Toni?"

"Uhhh, in bed?"

The guy leans in closer, giving me a better look at his scraggly face and a heavy dose of his morning coffee breath. *Damn.* My hand goes up on its own and slowly waves the space in front of my nose, trying to clear the air a little.

"You think this is funny, huh? You know what this is?" He pushes the gun in through the window, stopping the end of it just by my left eye.

I blink a few times. My eyelashes literally brush up against the metal. "That's a gun. I'm pretty sure that's a gun. It's kind of hard to see when it's resting on my eyeball, though." My breath is coming out in little gasps. I look up at him, pleading with my eyes. "Please tell me there aren't any bullets in it."

His southern accent is thick. "Now, why in the hell would I pull a gun on you and not put bullets in it?"

"Because you don't want to go to jail for shooting me?" *A girl can dream.*

"Unlock your doors." He pulls the gun away from my eye and points it at the corner of my door.

"You want my car?" My fingers move very slowly over to the unlock button of my door, like they have no choice but to obey.

In the back of my mind, I'm thinking that if I were watching this happen to someone on a television show, I would know the right thing to do. I would probably be yelling at the girl in the car, telling her, "Don't open the door, dumbass! He's going to kill you!"

But I'm not watching television. I'm sitting right here, the star of the show, and it's a really bad scene. I find that there's a certain amount of paralysis involved in being terrified. My body does not want to listen to my brain right now. Maybe it's the gun. Maybe that's the real problem here. When there's a gun pointed in my face, I find I'm very motivated to do exactly what I'm being ordered to do. It's so much easier to ignore an armed criminal from the comfort of my family room. *How very inconvenient.*

The locks go up. I expect him to tell me to get out, but he walks around the front of the car, pointing the gun at me the entire way. Next thing I know, he's climbing into the passenger seat.

He shoves my computer onto the floor to make room for his fat ass.

I find this very offensive. So offensive, in fact, that I momentarily forget to be terrified. "Could you not break my computer, *please*?"

He settles himself in the seat, turning partway to look at me, his girth making it difficult for him to do so comfortably.

"You don't seem to understand what's happening here, girly. You don't need to be worried about your laptop; what you need to be worried about is not getting shot."

Tears well up in my eyes. All I can think right now is how sad my babies would be if I never came home again. "Please don't shoot me. I have three kids. And my ex is a total asshole, so if I die, they're going to grow up with him as their only parent, and they're going to be seriously messed up from it, I can promise you that. He tried to steal a watch from me. A gift he gave me for my birthday. What kind of guy does that?"

"Cry me a river. I don't give a shit about your kids or your ex."

The man is obviously a criminal and is either already a murderer or is possibly about to become one. His answer is not surprising at all, but I find it unacceptable. It pisses me off. Do I expect him to have party manners? Apparently, yes. I do. Clearly, I'm nuts. Being threatened at gunpoint does not bring out the hero in me. It brings out the crazy. I can't seem to let his bad manners slide. They eat away at me until I can't stay quiet any longer.

"Don't say that about my children."

His mouth falls open a little. "Lady . . . are you nuts?"

I squeeze the steering wheel with both hands and stare out the windshield. My brain is buzzing. I can hardly think straight. All I can remember is that this guy does not give a shit about anything, and he's threatening my life and thereby threatening to leave my kids mom-less.

"Yeah, I might be nuts. Just keep saying mean things about my kids and see what happens."

I have no idea where this foolish courage or recklessness is coming from. I realize that it's highly possible I will piss this guy off so much that he'll shoot me just to shut me up. But I can't seem to stop myself. It's like this weird adrenaline is coursing through my veins, controlling my brain, controlling my mouth, controlling everything that's happening around me. And the only way to get rid of this nervous energy seems to be through talking. So talking is what I do.

"I've had enough of people shitting on my kids, okay? My son got kicked out of daycare because the stupid director has a problem with kids who have speech impediments. I mean, how fucked up is that?"

I look at the guy, but he's just staring at me, so I keep going. "That's wrong. You should never be rude to a child just because he has a disability. You should try to understand where he's coming from, put yourself in his shoes. And if you have something to say about it, you don't say it to the kid. You can scar him for life doing that. You say it to the parent. Alone. Handicaps are not a choice. You should never make a kid feel bad about being who he was born to be."

The man has nothing to say to that. His mouth hangs open like he's been hypnotized. I shake my head, disgusted. I'm getting nowhere with this guy, and now instead of scared, I'm pissed. This reaction of mine must be some kind of survival mechanism or something, because it makes no sense. I know that, and yet I can't change how I feel.

"So what's next? Am I supposed to drive you somewhere? I'd really rather not, if I have any say in the matter. But I'll tell you what . . . I don't mind letting you use my car. You'll have to come over here and get into the driver's seat, though." I reach over to the door handle, hoping he'll just let me leave. I'll jump out and run faster than I've ever run before. He won't even see me, I'll be such a blur. Like The Flash. *Fyoo! Gone-ski! See ya later, suckah!*

"I want you to take me to Toni," he growls.

I put my hands back on the steering wheel and sigh in annoyance. Looking at him, I glare. "Did you *do* your research?"

"Do my research? What the hell you talking about?" He sounds even more frustrated than he did before.

I hiss out a sigh of annoyance. Like I have time for criminals who fail to do the simplest Google search before perpetrating their crimes.

"Research. It's basic stuff. Before you go somewhere and point a gun at somebody, and, oh yeah, take a *hostage* in a vehicle, don't you think it might make sense to find out if I actually *know* anything at all about this so-called Toni person? Or hey! Here's an idea! Maybe you could have just waited for him to show up!"

"You work with *her*. Don't pretend like you don't know her. And she's never here. I've waited before. I've only seen her one time, and she pulled inside that place. It's locked up like a goddamned fortress. I figure with you here, she'll have to come out and deal with me. Face up to what she has coming."

"Listen, I know *of* her. But I do I know her? No. She's not a very open person, in case you didn't already know that. She keeps to herself. She doesn't share personal details." My voice rises with my frustration. "I have no idea where she lives, I have no idea what days she comes to work, and I have no idea what her hours are!"

"You expect me to believe you work with her and you don't know anything about her schedule?"

I shrug. "Believe it or not, I don't care. It's the truth." I gesture out the front window. "Do you see anybody here? You see me opening the big door? No, you don't. Because I don't have the combination to their front door. I am not an employee of this place."

I don't know where I'm getting this stuff. I'm just letting it flow. I'm praying the universe is in charge and my guardian angel has the wheel, because if it's only me driving this bus, I'm in trouble. Big trouble. This man is losing his patience with me.

He punches my dashboard to emphasize his point. "What are you doing here if you're not an employee? I've seen your car here before, you know. You're lying, that's what you're doing."

I take an extra-deep breath to try to cool myself down. I can't afford to piss this guy off any more than I already have. "I'm not lying. I was just doing a little freelancing for them, that's it. But you know what? After this bullshit, I'm not doing it anymore. It's not worth it. I'm so tired of being falsely imprisoned . . ."

"You ain't falsely imprisoned here."

I look at him, wanting so badly to slap him. "Oh really? What do you call this?" I gesture around us. "Do I want to be here? No! Do I have a sign on my forehead that says *Kidnap me*? I don't think so. Why does this keep happening? What does all this say about me?"

He shrugs, confused. "I don't know. That you're in the wrong place at the right time?"

I slap the steering wheel, glaring at him and the evil force that seems to delight in allowing me to feel joy for approximately twenty-four hours before ripping it away from me. "Exactly. Wrong place, right time." I pause, thinking about that for a moment. "Or maybe it's the wrong place at the wrong time."

He jabs the gun in my direction. "As far as I'm concerned, it's the right time. Call Toni. Tell her to come outside or to get her ass over here. Tell her you have something important you have to show her right away. Don't tell her it's me, though, or you'll be sorry." He pokes me in the shoulder with the gun.

"Call her? With what?" Thank goodness I shoved my phone in my back pocket when I left the house. I look around the car and act stupid.

"On your cell phone." His eyes scan the interior of the vehicle, and he notices my purse on the backseat. He reaches around to grab it, dumping its contents into his lap. "It's got to be in here somewhere."

My eyes land on the can of pepper spray sitting on his leg. If I could just distract him with something . . .

He picks up the can of pepper spray and turns it over, reading the label. He snorts. "Guess you won't be needing this." He pushes the window button down and tosses the can outside into the parking lot. He looks up at me. "You really don't have a phone?"

"I think I said that already." I look out the window so he won't be able to see my eyes as I craft the story I hope will get me out of this mess. "I have problems with my text messages. The autocorrect kills me. Turns all my sentences into cuss words. So it's in the shop. They're fixing it." *Yeah. The autocorrect anti-cussword task force tech support team is on it.* Hopefully he's dumb enough to believe my story. If I get locked in my trunk or kept prisoner somewhere, like always happens in the movies, I'll be able to call for help. Dev would be so proud.

He laughs. "Good. That'll make this easier." He turns around. "Drive."

My heart stops beating in my chest for several painful seconds. I gulp in some air, trying to force my system to reboot. How does my not having a phone make his plan easier? I'm supposed to drive? Am I going to die? Is he going to force me to chauffeur myself to a remote body-dumping location? This seems incredibly unfair, especially considering the fact that I just discovered the best sex of my life. *I can't let my sex life end here!*

"Drive where?" I ask, hoping someone from the team will drive up and save the day as I stall for time.

"Out of here. I'll give you directions once you leave the port. We can give your friends a call from another location. Make Toni come to us where we can be alone and none of those jerks will have the upper hand, hiding behind their steel doors." He looks over at the warehouse and sneers.

It takes me all of three seconds to decide what I have to do. This guy is a complete idiot. He has no plan. He's functioning off pure hatred, maybe with a little dose of revenge on top of it, changing his mind about what he wants to do as the wind blows. And I somehow got caught in the middle of it. I'm no commando. I've had zero training for anything. I can't negotiate with a kidnapper or judo chop him into submission. Today was supposed to be my first day training with Dev. If I'd had just one day of training—one single, solitary day—I might have been in a better position to make a good decision about how to handle this situation. But I didn't. I have just my mother-instincts telling me that I need to take a small risk to avoid a bigger one. I can't leave my kids without a mom.

"Drive!" he says more forcefully, jabbing me in the shoulder with the gun hard enough to leave a bruise.

"Fine! I'll drive!" I'm shaking. Terrified. Pissed beyond words. If I could get my hand on that gun, I'd shoot him in the dick with it.

I put the car in reverse and grip the steering wheel, staring at the door thirty feet in front of me.

"What you waiting for? Let's go." He looks behind us. He's expecting me to back up and drive away. To go somewhere where he can shoot me and bury me in a shallow grave, probably. Too bad I'm not on board with that plan.

No. I do not accept this. I will not die today. I have three amazing kids and a boyfriend who also has an amazing kid. I have more left on this earth to do before I bite the big one: more Halloweens, more cases with the Bourbon Street Boys, and more sex with Dev.

It's time. *Time to Hulk-out.*

I slam the car into first gear, drop my foot like a brick onto the accelerator, and lift the clutch.

A roar worthy of the most awesome *Incredible Hulk* episode rips from my mouth, filling the interior of the car with echoes of my rage.

The warehouse door comes flying at me so fast, it's like it has left its spot on the building to join me in my mission of destroying my car to gain my freedom.

"What the . . . ?!" my captor yells, just as we're making impact.

The last thing I remember is a big, loud *BOOM!* . . . and then darkness.

CHAPTER FORTY-FOUR

D ev?" I wait. Nothing happens. "Dev, where are you?" I have the strangest sensation moving through me. I can't feel my body exactly, but there are tingles. And wherever I am, it's dark. I think Dev is here, or he should be, but I don't see him. I don't see anyone. *Where am I? Why is it so dark? Ack! Please don't let this be hell!*

Something squeezes my hand, bringing me instant relief. I don't need to panic. I'm not dead and I'm not about to meet Beelzebub himself. Dev is here. Nobody else has hands that damn big.

I feel myself smiling. It's not without pain, though. My nose and head are killing me. "There you are," I whisper. It's the best I can do.

Something tickles my ear, and then his voice is there delivering warm puffs of air onto my neck. "I'm right here. I won't leave you."

"Why is it so dark in here?" I struggle to open my eyes. When I manage to crack them open just a bit, the light is so bright, I slam my lids shut again. "What the . . . ?"

"Take your time," says a softer, female voice.

I tilt my head in her direction. "May?"

Somebody squeezes my left hand. "Yes, sweetie. It's me. I'm right here with Dev."

I attempt to open my eyes again. This time I have a little more luck with it. I manage to catch a glimpse of my very worried sister, before I have to give up again. This time I don't give in to the darkness because of the bright light; I do it because opening my eyes takes too much effort, and I'm exhausted for some reason.

"Where am I?" I ask.

Dev answers. "You're in the hospital."

"My kids?"

"They're fine."

My brain drifts off for a little while; I'm not sure for how long. But then I remember something Dev said to me, and it makes me worry.

"Did you say hospital?" I force my eyes open.

Dev is leaning over me, concern marring his features.

I look at him and then at May. She's been crying; her eyes are red-rimmed and puffy. "Are you okay?" I ask her.

She laughs with what looks like relief. "You're asking me if I'm okay? You're crazy." She leans down and kisses me on the cheek. Then she tries to hug me, but I wince at the pain it causes. I hurt all over, but especially on my face.

"Ow." I reach up and touch my forehead. There's cloth there where there should be skin. I roll my eyes up to try to see my own face, catching a glimpse of something white. "What's on my head?"

May takes my hand and pulls it away so that I'll stop trying to touch my injuries. I notice out of the corner of my eye that there's an IV stuck in the back of my hand.

"You were in a car accident. You hit your head on the steering wheel. The airbag failed to deploy."

I frown. "Well. That sucks. Not part of my plan."

Dev smiles. "You got lucky. You escaped with just a concussion, some bruised ribs, and a broken nose. Your passenger didn't do so well."

I search my memory for a passenger, but I'm coming up blank. I almost ask if my kids were passengers, but I know that's not right. I wasn't with my kids in the car when this happened. *So, who was I with?*

"Passenger?"

Dev and May exchange glances. The silence between us stretches.

Then a flash of memory hits me. This has something to do with Little Miss Kickass. "Is Toni okay?"

"Why do you ask?" May says.

My memory is full of holes, but I remember a few things. I frown, trying to bring the details in stronger. "There was a man . . . he was asking about Toni."

My sister looks at Dev. "I think she deserves to know what happened."

"I agree," he says, shrugging. "Do you want to tell her or should I?"

May looks down at me with her most tender expression. "Do you remember coming to work on Monday?"

"Monday? Yeah, sure. Today is Monday, isn't it?"

"No," she shakes her head, "it's Wednesday. You've been kind of out of it for a couple of days."

"Coma?" I say with hushed awe. *I am so in a movie right now.*

She smiles. "No. *Drugs.*"

I don't know why that disappoints me. Maybe because telling a story about falling into a coma is a lot more interesting than telling a story about being so drugged up on pharmaceuticals you can't remember anything for two whole days. I went from hero to zero, just like that. *Boo.*

"What happened?" I ask, not even sure I want to hear the story now.

"You came to work early on Monday, and there was a not-very-nice guy waiting there for Toni. But when he saw you, I guess he decided he was going to try to get some information out of you to help him find her."

"Why was he waiting for Toni?"

May's mouth twists up for a couple seconds before she finally answers. "He's the brother of a man she killed. In self-defense. Mostly self-defense, anyway. He was out for revenge."

My eyes nearly fall out of my head. "Killed? Seriously?" I look at Dev for confirmation. He nods and then leans in.

"He's the same person who put a big dent in the door on your first day. Do you remember that?"

I look at him and smile. "How could I forget? You falsely imprisoned me in your lame-ass, Hotel California panic room for, like, hours and hours."

He glances up at May. "I don't think she's remembering things correctly. I think that head injury has done some permanent damage."

I try to reach up to poke him, but my vision isn't the greatest right now. His beautiful face blurs and dances away.

He takes my hand and kisses my fingers, bringing his face back into focus. "No hitting," he says. "There'll be no more violence in your life. I'm putting an end to it today."

I pull my hand away. "What does that mean?"

May steps into the conversation. "We can talk about it later."

Dev shakes his head. "No. It's already decided. She's not coming back."

I glare at him. "Are you trying to tell me I'm not working at Bourbon Street Boys anymore?" I look over at my sister. "Can he do that? Can he fire me?" Panic starts to grow. *Fired? Again? But what about the team? And Ozzie? And Little Miss Kickass who needs to tell me the story about how she killed someone? And Thibault and Lucky and his goldfish, Sunny?* I feel like I'm losing my whole family in one fell swoop.

She shakes her head. "No, he can't fire you, and I don't think that's what he's trying to do anyway." She glares at Dev and then raises her eyebrows and nods. She's encouraging him to do something, but I don't know what.

I turn my attention to Dev. "What's going on?"

He sighs and looks down at the bed. Then he lifts his head and locks eyes with me. "You were worried about working with us because of the risks involved. On your first day, you got locked in the panic room. In your second week, you were taken hostage outside the front door. It seems like you're always in the wrong place at just the right time. I don't think I can handle the stress. I've been seriously worried about you."

I can't help but smile. He is so sweet. And so adorable, thinking he can boss me around like that. I reach up and stroke his cheek. "You are so cute. But you have a lot to learn about women."

My sister points at me. "This woman in particular." She drops her voice to a whisper, but she's still really loud. "*Stubborn.*"

I ignore her. "I know that I've had some seriously bad luck coming to the warehouse, but that doesn't mean that I don't want to work with you guys anymore. I used to be afraid, but I'm not anymore. It just means maybe that I should do my work from home. I think being at the warehouse brings a certain element of risk to it, which I'd like to avoid. So if you guys want to meet with me, I can use Skype." I take Dev's hand and hold it firmly, so he'll know how determined I am about this. "It's simple. I love the work, I love being a part of the team, and I'm not going anywhere." I look at my sister. "Unless Ozzie doesn't want me to work there anymore. I know I can't force anyone to hire me."

May pats my leg. "Don't you worry about Ozzie. He thinks you're amazing. He wants you to stay, but of course he'll understand no matter what your decision is."

I look at Dev. He seems angry, and I really want him to understand, so that he won't be mad at me anymore. I crook my finger at him. "Come closer."

He leans in.

"I'm getting tired, so before I fall sleep, I just want you to know that when I got locked in that panic room with you, I was mad. But that anger only lasted for about two minutes. Because after that, I started to get to know you. And I realized how much fun you are, and how smart you are, and how much I like spending time with you. Please don't be mad that I want to spend as much time with you as I can."

"Are you trying to tell me that you enjoyed your false imprisonment?" Some of the worry lines have left his face and his dimple is starting to make an appearance.

"Yes. I am saying that now. However . . . I am high on drugs, and therefore, you cannot use these words against me in the future."

He leans in and kisses me very tenderly on the lips. I try not to wince too much when he accidentally bumps my nose.

"You get better, and then we'll talk."

"Yes, we will." I look up at my sister. "How awful is my nose?"

"Wellll . . . you know that bump that you never liked?" She's referring to the bridge of my nose, the one thing about my face that I could never appreciate no matter how many times May told me it gave my face character.

"Yes?"

"It's gone. When the plastic surgeon went in there to fix you up, he couldn't save it."

I can't stop smiling. "Talk about being in the wrong place at the right time." I look over at Dev. "Look at me. I'm beautiful now."

"You were always beautiful to me, from the first time I laid eyes on you. You're the prettiest girl I've ever known."

"I'm going to give you guys some alone time," my sister says. She walks out of the room and her footsteps fade in the distance.

I look at the man hovering over me and smile. "Thanks for visiting me. How are my kids? How's Jacob?"

"Everybody's fine. Miles has your kids, and he's being very cool about it. We've reached an understanding."

My eyebrows go up at that. "You have? Do tell."

Dev shrugs. "I just gave him the straight scoop. He has my phone number. Anytime he has a problem, he knows he can call me, day or night. Your kids were at my house last night. They had a sleepover with Jacob."

I grab Dev's hand. "Did it go okay?" I'm so sad I missed that event. I'm also worried that I wasn't there to referee. My kids need that more often than I'd like to admit.

He pats my hand. "It went perfect. It was Jacob's first sleepover, and he could not stop talking about it after your kids left. Everything's going to be fine. Everything."

When he says *everything* like that, I know exactly what he means. He's not just talking about my concussion or my broken nose, or this weird situation with the Bourbon Street Boys, or with us or our kids. He means everything. Our world. The one we're creating together. It's going to be just fine. There's just one more thing I need to clear up.

"I need to talk to Miles," I say, attempting to sit up.

Dev gently pushes on my shoulder. "Just relax. There's plenty of time."

"No, I need to do it now." I hold out my hand. "Can I borrow your phone?"

Dev hands me his cell without another word.

I dial Miles's number and start speaking as soon as he answers. "Hi, it's me."

"Jenny? Hey. How are you feeling?"

355

"Fine. Thanks for asking. Listen, we need to talk."

"About what?"

"Just . . . listen. Okay?" I take a big breath and let it out slowly before continuing. "About the other night, when you broke in to the house . . ."

"Yeah, I . . ."

"You can't do that anymore. Ever. It's my house and the things inside it are mine, and that's the end of the story."

"I know. I get it. I was just . . . acting stupid." He sounds ashamed, which makes me happy.

"Good. I'm glad you're admitting that. Anyway, I also wanted to say that I think you need to do a better job of being a father to our kids."

He doesn't respond, so I keep on going. I'm on a roll and I can't chicken out. These things need to be said, for our children if not for my sanity. "All these weekends you either skip or cut short—it has to stop. You're hurting the kids and you're going to ruin your relationship with them. They need their father."

"You have a new boyfriend." He sounds surly now. Hurt, maybe. That's good. I can work with that.

"So what? He's not their father and you shouldn't expect him to be."

"No, I don't. I didn't mean that. I'm just . . ." He hisses out a sigh of frustration. "I'm just a little messed up right now. I'm not happy." He lowers his voice. "I'm regretting some of the decisions I made."

I want to stand up and cheer. "I'm not surprised. You've made some pretty terrible ones." *Like breaking my heart, for one.* But now I'm kind of glad he did that, because if he hadn't, I wouldn't have this tall, beautiful man and his adorable son in my life. I reach out and put my hand on Dev's arm. He covers my fingers with his.

"Can I ask you a crazy question?" Miles says.

"Sure."

"Do you think you'd ever want to get back together with me? Hypothetically speaking, that is."

"No." I say this with a firmness in my heart, mind, and soul. "Never. We were a bad match, Miles. We make beautiful babies together, but we create way too much misery when we stay in the same room for too long. I like how things are right now, with the caveat that you are going to step up to the plate."

"Step up to the plate, huh?"

"Yes. Attend birthday parties. Take the kids on alternate holidays. Keep them for the full weekend. Feed them like a parent, not a teenager. Candy is not one of the four food groups."

He laughs softly. "I was getting kind of tired of the stomachaches." He pauses. "But . . ." He doesn't finish.

"But what?" I ask.

"It's stupid. Never mind."

"No, nothing is stupid when it concerns our kids. What? Tell me."

"What if they don't like me? What if I tell them no more candy and no more trips to the pizza place, and they tell me they don't want to hang out with me anymore?"

"Miles, you have to stop trying to be their friend and start being their father. They have enough friends, but only one dad. They love you. They want to just be with you. You don't have to be a Disneyland dad. Just be yourself." He may be a prick for a husband, but he's a decent person when he makes the effort. I never would have married him otherwise.

There's a long silence before he speaks again. "Thanks for calling. I'm glad you're okay. You had me worried. I visited, but you were completely out of it. It made me think about . . . well, let's just say it wasn't anything good and leave it at that."

"You're welcome." I glance at Dev and he nods. "But don't worry, I'm fine. When are you coming to get the kids?"

"This weekend. I'll be keeping them through Sunday at eight."

"Great. Thanks. See you."

"Yeah. See you. And for the record, I'm glad you're happy. Dev seems like a nice guy."

I can't stop smiling. "Yeah. He's pretty great."

Dev points to himself and I nod, shutting the call down.

We stare at each other for a long while. I'm beyond thrilled to know this man is an official part of my life, but a little piece of me can't help but worry at all this happiness. Is it just a passing phase? Will he turn out to be a jerk, like Miles did?

"Who knows how long this will last?" I say in a whisper.

Dev shrugs. "There's no way for either of us to see into the future. There are no guarantees. But if we don't take this chance and the risk that goes along with it, we'll never find out how good it could be between us."

"I'm glad you locked me in the panic room and couldn't let me out. I consider it a blessing that you stink at remembering the door combination. That you forgot to use the right code."

He leans in really close, kisses me lightly on the lips, and says, "Who says I forgot anything?" He smiles and his dimple sinks in as he relishes his win over me.

It's then that everything comes into very clear focus for me, even though I have enough morphine in my system to fell a smallish rhino. I know in my heart that Dev is the guy for me. That day that I met him? I was in the wrong place, maybe . . . but it was definitely at the right time.